SINISTER TIDE

By the same author

THIS UNITED STATE
THE SISTERHOOD
THE CAULDRON
PRECIPICE
FURY
THE POWER
BY STEALTH
CROSS OF FIRE
WHIRLPOOL
SHOCKWAVE
THE GREEK KEY
DEADLOCK
THE JANUS MAN
COVER STORY
TERMINAL
THE LEADER AND THE DAMNED
DOUBLE JEOPARDY
THE STOCKHOLM SYNDICATE
AVALANCHE EXPRESS
THE STONE LEOPARD
YEAR OF THE GOLDEN APE
TARGET FIVE
THE PALERMO AMBUSH
THE HEIGHTS OF ZERVOS
TRAMP IN ARMOUR

COLIN FORBES

SINISTER TIDE

MACMILLAN

First published 1999 by Macmillan
an imprint of Macmillan Publishers Ltd
25 Eccleston Place, London SW1W 9NF
Basingstoke and Oxford
Associated companies throughout the world
www.macmillan.co.uk

ISBN 0 333 77956 8

1 3 5 7 9 8 6 4 2

A CIP catalogue record for this book is available from
the British Library.

Typeset by SetSystems Ltd, Saffron Walden, Essex
Printed and bound in Great Britain by
Mackays of Chatham plc, Chatham, Kent

For my Editor,
SUZANNE

Author's Note

All the characters portrayed are creatures of the author's imagination and bear no relationship to any living person.

The same principle of pure invention applies to all residences whether located in Britain or Europe. And equally, certain small villages in Britain are imagined and non-existent.

Prologue

The dark wave, a motionless fisherman on its crest, rolled across the estuary north of Dartmoor towards them in the chill night. A new moon cast a pallid light on the sea-sodden body.

'That man is dead,' Paula Grey said, her tone sombre. 'Look for yourself.'

She handed the night-vision binoculars to Tweed, standing beside her. They were leaning against the stone sea wall at Appledore, an old town located where the rivers Torridge and Taw met to form the wide estuary. On the opposite shore small houses, their walls white-washed, glowed in the moonlight. Instow.

'Yes, he is dead,' Tweed agreed. 'With the tide still coming in he'll soon be washed up on the beach below us.'

'Must have fallen overboard from a fishing smack out at sea,' commented Superintendent Roy Buchanan from Scotland Yard. 'I'm still wondering why you summoned me here so urgently.'

'I told you, Roy,' Tweed snapped. 'Because of the message that came into SIS headquarters in London. From that evil genius, Dr Goslar.'

'Probably a hoax . . .'

Buchanan, tall, lean, in his forties, stood speaking as Bob Newman, international foreign correspondent, came running up the steps from the beach. He addressed Tweed, the Deputy Director of SIS and a man he had worked with for years.

'Something very weird going on. Shoals of dead fish are floating in. They're spread all over the beach. Rock salmon, sea bass and mackerel if I'm not mistaken. Poisoned by the sea is my best guess.'

'You must be wrong,' Buchanan told him. He glued his own pair of binoculars to his eyes, scanned the beach below. 'Damned peculiar,' he went on. 'You're right. Whole beach is covered with them.'

'And there's an odd-looking chap nearer the sea using a video camera to record what's happening,' Newman added. 'Can't imagine why.'

'What's odd about him?' Inspector Crake enquired.

A short stocky man in a shabby overcoat, Crake stood next to Buchanan. Like Tweed, he was quiet and stood with both hands in his pockets.

'The way he's dressed,' Newman replied. 'He's sporting a deerstalker hat and a long check jacket. Quite tall and thin with a bony face. Jumps about a lot.'

'That will be our local reporter, Sam Sneed,' Crake informed them. 'Very ambitious to get a big story in the national press. He's mad keen to get out of here into the big wide world.'

'You're local?' Tweed enquired. 'You are. Any idea where this Sneed lives?'

'Yes. At 4 Pendel's Walk. Situated in the maze of cobbled streets behind us in Appledore.'

'Now there's a dead seal coming in,' Paula burst out, binoculars back in her hands, pressed against her eyes. 'I'm sure it's a seal. Where on earth could that come from?'

'There are seals on Lundy Island,' Crake informed her. 'You know, Miss Grey, I think you're right. That thing just cresting a wave does look like a seal. I don't understand any of this.'

'It's horrible,' Paula replied. 'Look now at the beach. It is *littered* with dead fish, as Bob said.'

'Something very deadly is happening,' Tweed said grimly. 'I sense the presence of Dr Goslar. We need samples of that sea water.'

Buchanan turned to a tall wooden-faced man behind him, his assistant, Sergeant Warden. His instructions were terse, brisk.

'Warden, we have airtight canisters in the car. Get them and take samples of the sea water. Wear rubber gloves. I'll come with you to the car, see if I can get paramedics here. That fisherman's body is about to reach the beach. He might just still be alive . . .'

'We need specimens of the dead fish,' Tweed called out. 'The seal should be collected too.'

'It's a sea of death,' Paula whispered.

'That's my impression,' Tweed agreed. 'And a few minutes ago I thought I heard the engine of a large powerboat vanishing out to sea.'

'I heard it too,' Paula confirmed.

There was a brief silence, heavy and disturbing, the only sound the breaking of the waves on the shore. Tweed glanced to his left where he could just make out the open sea. Not all that rough, so how could a fisherman fall overboard, then make no attempt to swim for the shore?

The fisherman's body slid up the beach. Shortly afterwards the seal flopped ashore a few yards away. Neither victim moved. A minute later a lean agile man ran up the steps Newman had mounted earlier. He clutched a large bulky object to his chest, ran over the promenade without a glance in their direction, vanished into Appledore.

'Sam Sneed, in one hell of a hurry,' Newman commented. 'Why the rush to get away?'

'As soon as we can, I think we'll visit Pendel's Walk,'

Tweed decided. 'Any idea how we get there?' he asked Crake.

'This should help you.'

Crake pulled out from a pocket a folded sheet of paper. He handed it to Tweed, after marking it with a pen.

'A crude map of Appledore. Get one at any news-agent's. You'll see I've marked with a cross where Sneed lives. An old house. Lives there with his sister, Agnes.'

'Thank you.'

'And now we have reinforcements,' Crake commented, 'I'll have this section of the promenade taped off. Scene of the crime, and all that.'

'You think there has been a crime?' Paula pressed.

'No idea. There's been a mystery. Lights are coming on in the houses behind us. I don't want the front crowded with ghouls. I'll go and instruct them now . . .'

A police car had arrived from their right. Four uniformed men got out fast. Within minutes police tape had been erected at either end of a section of the promenade, across the area behind them. Newman had volunteered to help Warden collect samples. Tweed had warned him to use the rubber gloves the correspondent always carried. Both men were now down on the beach. Warden was scooping up samples of the sea into large canisters. He had brought large transparent envelopes and Newman was using a scoop Warden had given him to collect dead fish. Buchanan returned from his car, where he had used his mobile phone.

'I got lucky,' he told Tweed. 'A couple of ambulances with paramedics had been summoned earlier. Turned out to be a hoax call at a place on the edge of Appledore. They'll be here any moment.'

'Hoax call?' Tweed said sharply. 'Get any details of who made it?'

4

'No. Some reference to a bad connection, the caller's voice distorted.'

'It would be,' Tweed said, offering no explanation for his remark.

'A big car's approaching from our left,' Paula reported.

They all looked in that direction. A Daimler with tinted windows cruised slowly along the front. It didn't stop when it reached the tape. Simply drove on, breaking the tape. Buchanan rushed after it as it broke through the second tape. They saw him hammering on the windows. It stopped, the engine still running. Buchanan was talking to the driver. Then the car drove on, disappeared as Buchanan returned, a livid expression on his face.

'What do you think about that?' he asked Tweed.

'Why did you let it get away?'

'It had diplomatic plates. The chauffeur said her passenger had to return for an urgent conference. You can't force the passenger in a diplomatic car to get out.'

'You saw the passenger?'

'Yes and no. I had the impression he was Middle Eastern. But the tinted glass separating passenger from chauffeur was shut. I only got a blurred view of him. Then the chauffeur said her passenger had an urgent appointment. I had to let them go.'

Buchanan's frustration registered in his voice. It irked him that there were so many people moving around he couldn't touch – all with diplomatic immunity.

'Her?' Tweed repeated. 'The chauffeur was a woman?'

'Yes. Quite a looker, from the little I could see of her. Which wasn't much. She wore dark wrap-round glasses. She had jet-black hair, I'd say.'

'A chauffeuse?' Tweed's tone was sharp. 'Are you sure?'

'Pretty much so. She wore a large peaked cap and I think she'd tucked most of her hair under the cap. But some of it projected at the back – saw it by the glow of a street lamp. What makes her important?'

'How old?'

'Late thirties, early forties would be my guess.'

'Interesting. Dr Goslar worked with a young woman assistant back in the old days.'

'Oh, come. You're not suggesting Goslar was the passenger? So what does he look like?'

'We never had any idea. Not a clue. I see two ambulances have arrived. Paramedics are on the beach. They'll take away the fisherman's body – if he's dead. I also want them to transport that seal in the second ambulance.'

'You must be joking,' Buchanan protested. 'Seals are heavy – and slippery.'

'The police may have a piece of canvas they could wrap it up in. There are enough of them to carry the seal . . .' He paused as a paramedic ran up the steps from the beach, reported that the fisherman was dead. 'Everything must be transported straight to Charles Saafeld,' Tweed went on. 'As you know, he's the cleverest pathologist in the country, probably in the world. He's also a brilliant biophysicist and a professor of bacteriology. The man's a walking brainbox.'

'There's a large roll of canvas in the police car,' Crake interjected. 'Perfectly clean. Never been used so far. It will be tricky but we can shift the seal into an ambulance.'

'Please do it, then,' Tweed requested. 'The canisters with water samples must also go to Saafeld.'

Paula nudged Tweed. 'The tide has turned, has

started to go out again. The waves aren't coming so high up the beach.'

'Then we need more samples of the sea,' Tweed decided.

'What for?' demanded Buchanan.

'Because there's something strange and sinister about this whole business.'

'We can manage that,' said Warden, who had just returned with Newman after depositing samples in the ambulance nearest to them. 'There were plenty of spare canisters. I'll go and organize that.'

'Don't bother to consult me,' Buchanan said ironically. 'After all, I'm only your superior. Now, go and do it.' He looked at Tweed. 'I haven't a clue what you're after.'

'Neither have I. The key to all this is what Saafeld finds. If anything.'

Buchanan raised his eyebrows, then strolled off with Crake to help supervise the operation. Tweed was left alone with Paula and Newman, who had removed his rubber gloves carefully and slipped them inside a samples bag. For a few minutes they stood in silence.

It was late March. The night air was chilly. Paula glanced to her right where the two rivers were surging into the estuary. There had been a lot of rain recently. Looking behind her she saw houses of dark grey stone huddled together, a small hotel. A bleak prospect in the dark. It was more cheerful to look across the estuary to tiny Instow. The distant group of modest houses was far more cheerful – due to their whitewashed walls, standing like a toy village in the moonlight.

'What next?' asked Paula, zipping up her windcheater to the collar.

A cold breeze had started to blow in. She looked to her left and caught a glimpse of the sea. It had a swell on as the water surged out of the estuary. Newman had run back to the beach to make sure the new specimens of sea water Tweed wanted were collected. He returned at that moment, reporting the men down there were doing a good job.

'Then I think we'll go and have a word with Mr Sam Sneed, ambitious reporter, at 4 Pendel's Walk. If we can ever find the place.'

Before leaving, Tweed had asked Inspector Crake whether they could drive there. He had advised them to walk, pointing to a side street leading off the front. Tweed soon realized that Crake had been right. The side street was narrow. Emerging at the other end they entered a maze of even narrower ancient cobbled streets. By the light of a street lamp he studied the map Crake had provided.

'We turn left here,' he said to Paula and Newman, 'then the first on the right for starters.'

'This is creepy,' Paula said.

The labyrinth of streets, little more than wide alleys, was another world. She felt completely cut off from the front they had left. The streets were lined with ancient terraced houses built ages ago of granite, Dartmoor granite. There were no lights in any of the thin, blocklike houses. No sign of a human being. The only sounds were their footfalls on the cobbles.

Paula kept glancing back over her shoulder. Inside her shoulder bag her hand gripped the hidden Browning. It was a secret world with some streets running into the distance, then vanishing behind a corner. Hampton Court Maze has nothing on this, she thought. Leading the way, Tweed turned again, into a street curving uphill. A wall lamp suspended from a bracket faintly illuminated a name. *Pendel's Walk.*

No. 4 was, of course, more than halfway up the hill. Here there were lights behind shabby black curtains closed over the narrow windows. Tweed gestured and Paula and Newman stood on either side of the door. A motorcycle was perched against the wall. Newman felt the engine. It was warm. Tweed pressed the bell, had to wait a couple of minutes before a lock turned, the door opened on a chain. A plump middle-aged woman in a print dress peered at him.

'Mrs Sneed?'

'Miss, if you please. Who are you?'

She had been drinking. The alcoholic fumes came out to meet him. Tweed had the Special Branch identity in his hand, forged by boffins back at Park Crescent. As good as the real article.

'Sorry to call on you so late. My name is Tweed. You must be Agnes. I need to have a word with Mr Sneed.'

'He's busy.'

'Miss Sneed, I have authority to ask him to help me. It will only take a few minutes.'

'Better let him in, Agnes. Special Branch can get in anywhere.'

A gnomelike face had appeared at Agnes's shoulder. He was still wearing the deerstalker hat, the heavy check jacket. He gave Tweed a smirk. His expression changed when Paula and Newman followed Tweed inside.

'Hey! How many of you are there?'

'My assistants, Miss Grey and Mr Newman,' Tweed introduced.

They had walked straight into a cramped sitting room. Arranged at random were sofas and armchairs, covered with well-worn chintz. Sneed, still looking disturbed, ushered them to sit down. Agnes had rushed ahead, shoved a gin bottle behind some cushions, sat down with her back to them.

'I'm just finishing some work,' Sneed said nasally. 'Give me a minute and I'll be with you.'

He disappeared through a half-open door, closed it. Tweed sat carefully in an armchair, feeling broken springs under him. He smiled at Agnes to put her at her ease.

'Your brother is a reporter, I understand. So I suppose he works all hours,' Tweed suggested.

'No. He's on the daytime roster. Another rep works nights.'

'I sympathize – he's on a local paper so he can't make a lot of money.'

'He's doing all right just now. Sometimes you get lucky—'

Agnes broke off. Her face was flushed as though she realized she had said too much. Her right hand reached out for the half-full glass on a small table, then she withdrew it into her lap. Without the glass.

'You've lived here for long?' Tweed went on genially.

'All my born days. When Mother died my brother and I decided it seemed sensible for us to stay on here.'

'Familiar surroundings,' Tweed chattered on. 'Your brother is busy in his workroom tonight . . .'

'Making copies of the the video—'

Again she broke off. Again her expression suggested she had said too much. She kept clasping and unclasping her plump hands. She glanced down at her watch. Tweed turned in his chair as though to make himself more comfortable. He stared briefly at Newman, who got the message.

'Excuse me,' Newman said.

He stood up swiftly, went across to the workroom door, opened it before Agnes could protest. He walked into a dark room with tables piled with photographic equipment. A dim red light was the only illumination. No sign of Sneed. He went over to a door in the side

10

wall, opened it, found himself in an alley. He heard Agnes calling out.

'You can't go in there . . .'

Newman ran the few paces down the alley, found himself back in Pendel's Walk. At the bottom of the hill he heard a motorbike starting up, saw a thin figure wearing a crash helmet astride the saddle. The machine disappeared round a corner. Newman pressed the bell of No. 4 three times and Tweed opened it.

'Sneed's motorbike has gone – with Sneed on it,' Newman reported to Tweed. 'There's another exit from that room he disappeared into.'

'I thought he was there a long time.'

Tweed had stepped into the street. Paula stood behind him in the entrance. She suddenly felt a plump hand push her into the street. She nearly stumbled on the cobbles but Newman grabbed her by the arm. Agnes shouted behind them.

'Now you can all shove off.'

She slammed the door and they heard a key turn in the lock. Paula shrugged and smiled.

'For a plump lady she's got some strength.'

'I'm popping back up the alley to take another look at Mr Sneed's workroom,' Newman decided.

He began running and his companions followed. As Newman re-entered the alley they heard a door slam shut. They reached it just in time to hear bolts being thrust home. Paula shrugged again as they looked at the closed wooden door.

'We're not welcome,' Paula commented. 'Not wanted on the voyage. And dear Agnes can really move when she wants to. So it was a waste of time.'

'We'll get back to our car on the promenade,' Tweed announced. 'And it wasn't a waste of time. We did learn quite a bit . . .'

When they eventually found their way back they

were just in time to see the two ambulances driving away. The policeman on duty lifted the tape so they could walk to where Buchanan stood with Crake.

'Any joy?' enquired Crake.

'Not really,' Tweed told him. 'So the ambulances are on their way to Saafeld?' he continued, addressing Buchanan. 'The drivers know his place in town?'

'Of course,' Buchanan replied tersely. 'And I phoned Saafeld to warn him what was coming – that it was at your suggestion. That one of the specimens on the way to him was a dead seal. I was relieved to get him on the phone at this late hour.'

'Saafeld is an owl. He likes working through the night. How did he react to the news of the seal?'

'As though it was a normal delivery. Thanked me for warning him. Said he'd now be able to contact someone else. It was a very brief conversation. He's remarkable. I made another phone call.'

'That's right. Keep me in suspense.'

'I got that Daimler's registration number, of course. While you've been away, seeing Sneed, I checked the number. Wait for it. The Daimler belongs to an Arab embassy in London. An Arab state on the Gulf which is hostile, the one which discovered it was sitting on vast oil reserves six months ago. We're talking billions and billions of dollars.'

'Didn't the girl who was driving give you any reason why they were in this part of the world?'

'Yes. She quickly volunteered the information that her important passenger was looking for a large house he could buy in the West Country.'

'You believed that?'

'No. I hadn't asked her what they were doing. Any idea what is happening here?'

'Too early to say. It could be something sinister, dangerous, even catastrophic.'

12

1

They were driving away from Appledore. Newman was behind the wheel of his Mercedes SL with Tweed beside him. Paula sat behind them. She thought Tweed's mind was miles away when he suddenly gave an order to Newman.

'Drive slowly. Put your headlights on full beam.'

'Will do. Mind telling me why?'

'So I can see the road surface more clearly. I noticed that where Buchanan had stopped the Daimler there was a small patch on the promenade. The Daimler has a slow leak when it stops.'

'That tells us exactly what you mean,' Paula said ironically.

Tweed didn't reply. He was leaning forward against his seat belt, peering through the windscreen. After a short time they left Appledore behind, were driving through hedge-lined open countryside. Tweed sat still as a Buddha, motionless as he continued his vigil of staring through the windscreen.

'Stop!' he said suddenly.

Newman glanced again at his rear-view mirror, steered the car on to a grass verge, put on his hazard lights. Tweed was out of the car before anyone could say a word. Paula followed him. Tweed was examining something on the road with the aid of the left headlight. He was stooping when Paula reached him.

'What is it?'

'Another oil patch. The Daimler stopped here for a short time.'

'Why?'

'To take a delivery.'

'Delivery? What kind? Who from?'

'How long do you reckon it would be between the time we saw Sam Sneed rushing up the steps from the beach and our arriving at 4 Pendel's Walk?'

'I'd say at least an hour, probably longer. I happened to look at my watch when Sneed appeared at the top of the steps and it was 10.30 p.m. It's now 12.30 a.m.'

'The timing is right, then.'

'What timing? Don't go cryptic on me,' she said in exasperation.

'Time for Sneed to get back to his house, make copies of the video, then deliver the original to the mysterious passenger in that Daimler. He'd use his motorbike to get here, make his delivery, then get back to his house before we arrived. And don't forget his sister, Agnes, let slip he had made copies of the video.'

'So what is going on?' Paula demanded as they walked back to the car.

'We witnessed a demonstration. I know, to my cost long ago, that Dr Goslar is a brilliant planner. Back to Gidleigh Park Hotel on Dartmoor,' he instructed Newman as they climbed back into the car. 'You can drive as fast as you like now, safety permitting. I think we might get a drink at the hotel, even considering the late hour. We are guests.'

Eventually Newman drove slowly through Chagford, an ancient Dartmoor village of grey stone houses and closed shops. The final approach to the magnificent-looking old hotel led up a narrow drive over a mile

14

long where only one car could hold the road. The hotel was a blaze of lights as Newman parked the car close to the entrance. The moment they walked into the comfortable and luxurious hall a waiter greeted them.

'Any chance of the odd drink?' Tweed enquired. 'I know it's late – or should I say early?'

'Certainly, sir,' replied the waiter with a smile. 'I'm only temporary staff, but the manager has gone to bed. So I won't ask him. What would you like?'

'Double Scotch for me,' Newman said promptly. 'No water.'

Tweed and Paula each ordered a glass of Chardonnay, then they all went into a large empty lounge. After taking off their coats and piling them them neatly on a chair, Tweed and Paula sank into a comfortable sofa while Newman hauled an armchair close to them.

'I like this place,' said Paula. 'And don't they keep it warm?'

'Everything is perfect,' Tweed agreed. 'The food is excellent, the service impeccable. I've a mind to come here for a break one day.'

'You're always saying that,' Paula chaffed him. 'But you never actually do it.'

A chambermaid, on her way to bed, paused at the entrance to study the new guests. Paula, five feet six tall, was slim and very attractive. In her thirties, she had glossy dark hair falling to her shoulders. She had good bone structure with a well-shaped nose, a firm mouth with lips which hinted at concealed affections and a determined chin.

Tweed, a couple of inches taller, was well built, of uncertain age, clean-shaven, with penetrating eyes behind his horn-rimmed glasses. He was the sort of man you pass in the street without seeing him, a characteristic he had found invaluable on certain occasions as Deputy Director of the SIS.

15

The chambermaid thought they looked nice people, but her gaze lingered on foreign correspondent Bob Newman. Five foot ten in height, he was well built without a sign of fatness. He too was clean-shaven and had fairish hair. In his forties, he was a man many women looked at twice. They liked his buoyant smile.

'We are being observed,' Tweed whispered. 'It's all right, she has gone now. And here are the drinks.'

Tweed looked hard at the young waiter as he served their drinks. He decided he was intelligent and probably a trainee. He spoke to him just before the waiter was leaving.

'Are you by any chance local?'

'Yes, sir. Born in Chagford and I love this part of the world. Between us, I've turned down offers from London. I love the peace of Dartmoor.'

'Has anyone new moved into a large house recently anywhere near here? Someone mentioned this had happened.'

'You're probably thinking of Mr Charterhouse. He leased Gargoyle Towers about three months ago. They gossip about him down in Chagford.'

'Sounds interesting. Why the gossip?'

'They call him the Mystery Man. No one has ever seen him. He arrives late at night in a chauffeur-driven limousine. He has dark curtains closed over the windows and you never even get a glimpse of him. A poacher on his land at night had the closest look.'

'So you can describe him?'

'I'm afraid not. The poacher saw the limo draw up at the entrance and the passenger get out on the far side. The main door was open for him but there were no lights in the hall, which the poacher thought was strange. Jim, that's the poacher, gives the place a wide berth now. If you get close at night searchlights come

16

on and you're blinded. I shouldn't really be talking about him, I suppose.'

'Mr Charterhouse.' Tweed reflected. 'Sounds like an old friend of mine. Is this Gargoyle Towers far away?'

'No, sir. It's almost next door to us, in a Dartmoor manner of speaking.'

'How do you get there?'

'It's a very long and devious drive by car. But in daylight you can walk there. You start by going through the Water Gardens you pass driving up on your left just before you reach the hotel.'

'We're all fresh. After we've had our drinks we might feel like paying him a visit. I know he stays up half the night. How would we get there after leaving the Water Gardens?'

'There is a forest. I could show you on this map I have in my pocket. A lot of our visitors like to walk. But I'd advise you to borrow a pair of gumboots – there are plenty for visitors by the front door.'

'I should be all right in my boots,' Paula suggested.

'Perfect footwear for climbing, madam,' the waiter assured her. 'I will be at your service if anything more is required. Is the map clear, sir?' he asked after Tweed had scanned it.

'If will be an excellent guide, I'm sure. Thank you.'

Paula waited until they were alone before she spoke.

'Now, what is all this about?' Paula asked, turning to Tweed at her side. 'I'm confused. First we have a dead fisherman washed ashore. Then the beach is littered with dead fish. And, on top of that, a dead seal is beached. While all this is going on Sam Sneed, local reporter—'

'Ambitious reporter,' Tweed reminded her.

'All right, ambitious local reporter, uses his video camera to record the whole scene. Then he rushes off to

17

his little house. Meantime, a mysterious limo with tinted glass appears, breaks through the police tapes, is stopped by Buchanan, who can't do anything as the limo has diplomatic plates. The chauffeur is a dark-haired girl. We visit Sneed's place, Bob detects Sneed has just come back from somewhere – his motorcycle engine is warm. Agnes, his sister, lets slip her brother has made copies of the video. Sneed sneaks out of a back door, rides off somewhere on his motorcycle.' She paused. 'Funny, we didn't hear him start up his engine.'

'That's simple,' Newman broke in. 'He slipped out, wheeled his machine far enough away before he starts the engine so we won't hear him.'

'Later,' Paula continued, 'Tweed spots an oil patch outside Appledore. Then, when we get back, we hear about the invisible man, Mr Charterhouse. I'm confused,' she repeated.

'Cheers!' Tweed lifted his glass of wine. 'Paula, you have just given an excellent summary of events so far. The pieces of a jigsaw which don't link up. We need more pieces to begin to see the whole picture. And don't forget Buchanan found out whoever was in that limo belongs to a hostile Arab state sitting on a newly discovered treasure of oil. Billions and billions of dollars, Roy said.'

'I'm more confused than ever,' said Paula. 'Tweed, aren't you going to give us a reaction?'

'I'm very worried – almost frightened. I fear we are facing a danger the world has never before experienced. Truly global. Remember it all started with this strange communication from Dr Goslar – the message inside an envelope pushed through the letter box at Park Crescent early this morning. You'd both better look at it again, refresh your memory.'

18

He extracted an envelope from his breast pocket, took out the folded sheet inside, handed it first to Paula.

My dear Tweed, is it not time we crossed swords again? Years ago you were a formidable opponent – but I eluded you. Tonight, say about ten o'clock, be on the front at Appledore, north of Dartmoor. That is where the inevitable fate of this planet will start. Do not expect to win. H. Goslar.

'It's weird handwriting,' Paula commented. 'Almost old-fashioned copperplate. But the writing jerks up and down like the lines you see on a seismograph. I suppose it isn't a joke?'

'What we saw at Appledore wasn't a joke,' Newman commented.

'No,' Tweed told her, 'it isn't a joke. It's Goslar. I have a short specimen of his handwriting I obtained years ago. To me it looked genuine. I took the precaution of showing it to Pete Nield. Among his other talents he's an expert graphologist. He confirmed without a doubt it is Goslar.'

'When did you last encounter this Goslar?' Paula asked.

'Over ten years ago – before you joined us. He was very active during the Cold War, before the Berlin Wall came down. He cooperated with the Soviets and sold them data on American secret weapons. Formulae for producing certain poison gases. But he also cooperated with Washington, selling them data on Soviet secret weapons for large sums of money.'

'Can you describe him?'

'I have no idea what he – or she – looks like. We didn't even know whether it was a man or a woman. I have one picture of him – or her.'

19

Tweed took out his wallet, gave her a small photograph. It was dog-eared, as though it had been examined many times before being secreted in his wallet. The photo had been taken at night, and showed a tiny figure – its back – in the distance. The odd factor which struck Paula was both arms were held out at the side, away from the blurred body, dangling awkwardly. It wore some kind of headgear. She handed the picture to Newman.

'I think I might recognize that figure if I ever saw it standing with its back to me,' she reflected.

'Then you're cleverer than I am,' Newman told her.

'When was it taken?' she asked.

'Bob took it,' Tweed explained. 'That was the night we nearly caught him. It was taken at the very edge of the Iron Curtain. East of Lübeck on the Baltic coast. But by the time we got there Goslar had crossed over, threading his way through the minefield of the Iron Curtain. He obviously knew the safe path.'

'Maybe if it was enlarged,' she suggested.

'Paula,' said Tweed, 'we have blown it up, examined it under a high-powered microscope. The image gets worse, more blurred.'

'What is it wearing on its head?'

'Some kind of woolly cap. It was very cold that night.'

'Surely,' Paula protested, 'if he did business with the Americans someone in the States could describe him?'

'No go,' said Newman. 'I flew over there to see Cord Dillon, just appointed Deputy Director of the CIA. After the Berlin Wall came down Goslar moved to America. They welcomed him with open arms when he told them he could create a new gas which would destroy any enemy before they knew what had hit them. He bought a chemical plant, kept his word. They paid him ten million dollars – but he had expected twenty million. One morning, when all the workers were present, a huge bomb destroyed the entire plant. Over a hundred workers were killed. Goslar then disappeared. Maybe down to Mexico, or across the border into Canada. No one knew how.'

'But I don't understand why they have no description.'

'He always communicated by phone – from a street call box. The voice was recorded, of course, but it was just a screech although every word was audible. My theory is he feels he was tricked over the amount of money paid, so now he hates America.'

'But the Russians must have known who he was, could have described him,' Paula persisted.

'They never did,' Tweed replied. 'Goslar used the same technique. Always phoning his top contact in the Kremlin. Demanded once more that a certain huge sum be deposited in a Swiss bank account. Once he knew it had arrived, he told them where to find the formula – in some remote place outside Leningrad, as it was then, or Kiev, or wherever.'

'I'm surprised both the Americans and the Russians went along and dealt with the invisible Goslar.'

'They did it because what he supplied was pure gold. Moscow thought Goslar was a woman, Washington thought he was a man. Take your choice.'

'Goslar sounds ruthless. That bomb which killed all those workers at the plant in the States.'

'Goslar, man or woman, is the most evil person I've ever encountered. But I gradually built up a dossier on some of his habits and methods. They were so successful the same techniques will be used again. That just might give Goslar to me. Eventually.'

*

Paula asked to see the photograph taken at the edge of the Iron Curtain years before again. She sighed, then shuddered.

'What kind of methods?' she asked.

'He always has a secret base fairly close to his theatre of operations. He delights in leaving false clues. Bob and I followed up a number of them – they all led to dead ends. Except for the last one, which was when we almost caught him near Lübeck.'

'What was the clue?'

'Bob caught a glimpse of a red-headed woman entering a building in Lübeck. We'd found out he worked with a red-head. We waited for her to come out. We could see the entrance and the fire escape. What we didn't realize was there was a second fire escape. We heard a motor-cycle start up. We pursued it in a car. The figure crouched over the machine reached the Iron Curtain just ahead of us. It escaped, as I've explained.'

'What did the red-head look like, Bob?'

'I only caught a glimpse of her. In her late twenties, I'd say.'

'Over ten years ago,' Paula mused. 'So now she'd be in her late thirties – if she's still alive.'

'We went back to the building afterwards, broke into it. Place was empty. In a room at the back where the second fire escape led down we found a wig – red-haired, a woman's.'

'So Goslar is probably a man?' Paula speculated.

'Unless it was another false clue,' Tweed warned. 'I said earlier that Goslar always had a base not too far from an operation. So now you know why I asked the waiter if anyone new had moved into the area . . .'

'And he told us about this mysterious Mr Charter-house,' Paula interjected. 'Described him as someone no one in Chagford had ever seen. That he is driven in a limo with tinted glass to Gargoyle Towers.'

'Exactly,' Tweed agreed. 'It does sound like the behaviour pattern of Goslar. He leased the place three months ago. He would need that sort of time span to organize what we witnessed up at Appledore.'

'So we'd better check out Gargoyle Towers as soon as it's daylight,' she suggested.

'That might be too late. Goslar keeps on the move. It's a pity we didn't bring Harry Butler and Pete Nield with us – to say nothing of Marler. But I think we have to check out the place now, even though there are only three of us. At least both of you are carrying weapons. And we all have flashlights. We'll need them, I'm sure.' He looked at Paula. 'Unless you're tired. In that case we'll wait until morning.'

'Fresh as the proverbial daisy,' she assured him. 'Let's get on with it now.'

Tweed led the way out of the front door. Like Newman, he had equipped himself with gumboots. They walked back down the drive, aided by the light of the moon. Tweed found the entrance to the Water Gardens, just before the bridge which crossed the rushing stream. He switched on his torch, hurried along a tricky path hemmed in by shrubs and trees.

Paula followed Newman, who walked with a torch in his left hand, his Smith & Wesson in his right. It was an eerie experience, the only sound the surging torrent, the moon blotted out, threading their way along the uneven path, isolated from the outside world. They passed a house on the far side of the stream which had lights on in several windows. Then Tweed was climbing a flight of stone steps. Some distance beyond, he opened a small gate and they could no longer hear the water. The gate creaked as he opened it and started along a pathway. He paused to call over his shoulder.

23

'I think we've left behind the property belonging to Gidleigh Park. Here is the forest that waiter mentioned.'

He used his flashlight to check the map. They began to climb rapidly through a dense forest of evergreens which towered above them. They came to a narrow path which led steeply upwards. Tweed decided there should be a more negotiable path and continued past it.

'I'm going up this way,' Paula called out. 'Bet I beat you both to the top.'

'Stay with us,' Newman called back.

When he looked back she had disappeared. He shrugged and went on after Tweed. Within minutes Tweed found a gap in the forest and beyond it a wide drive climbing steeply. Switching off his torch, he mounted the drive, his legs moving like pistons. Newman, who had doused his own torch, saw him pause. When he caught up with him Tweed pointed.

'Gargoyle Towers. What a horror.'

The mansion's ancient and immense bulk loomed above them at the end of the drive. It was built of Dartmoor granite, three storeys high, with numerous turrets, clearly visible in the moonlight. Leering down from each turret was a grim gargoyle, as though watching them approach. No lights in any window.

'This is just the sort of place Goslar would choose as a base,' Tweed commented. 'I almost sense his presence. Let's hurry – and where's Paula?'

'She insisted on making her own way up along a path through the forest. Said she'd get there first.'

'So she's probably coming up by a devious route before she gets out of the forest.'

Tweed had started walking again, soon reached the entrance at the side of the grim bulk. A heavy studded wooden door stood partly open. Newman pushed ahead of Tweed, eased the door wider. It creaked ominously. Newman reached inside, felt round the wall,

24

found a battery of switches, pressed them. Lights came on everywhere. He stood quite still, his revolver gripped in both hands, staring. Tweed came alongside him, blinked.

The vast hall was empty. Doors leading off the hall were wide open with lights on inside the rooms. Tweed had the impression the place was empty. His impression was confirmed when they began exploring. Not a stick of furniture anywhere. No carpets on the woodblock floors. What struck Tweed as they moved from one large room to another was the clinical cleanliness. Not a speck of dust. As though the mansion had never been occupied.

On a window ledge he found a pair of leather gloves. Picking them up, he slipped them into his coat pocket. They found the same clinical emptiness on the first and second floors. They were returning quietly down the massive staircase leading to the hall when Tweed turned to Newman.

'Where is Paula? She should have got here long before now.'

'I told you. She went off on her own up—'

'I remember what you said.' Tweed came as close to sounding agitated as Newman had ever known him. 'Show me the damned path. And don't hang about. We go back the way we came . . .'

Newman walked ahead of him, back down the drive, into the forest again. Using his torch, he eventually found the path. Tweed pushed past him, moved slowly up the path. He walked with his head down, shining his torch. Here and there he could trace where her footsteps had trodden down bracken. Continuing his slow search, his head was bowed. Suddenly he bent down and picked up something. He swung round to Newman.

'I heard the distant sound of a helicopter taking off.'

'So did I . . .'

'Look at this.'

He opened his hand. He was holding a silver ring. His expression was a mixture of fury and anxiety. He held the ring out to Newman.

'This is Paula's. She always wore it. Her father gave it to her on her twenty-first birthday. She slid it off her finger to warn us when she was attacked. They've got her. Goslar has.'

'So what next?'

'Back to Gidleigh Park. I want to use a phone. My God, she's in Goslar's hands.'

2

The pathway Paula had taken between the fir trees was narrow and steeply twisting. Last year's bracken, dead and brown, brushed her feet on either side. It was eerily quiet. The night darkness made the heavy silence even more unsettling. Once she thought she'd heard faint heavy footsteps coming up behind her.

She paused, turned, listened. Nothing. Imagination. She plodded on up the incline. She would have liked to use her torch, but Tweed's orders had been explicit. *No lights.* Here and there moss-covered boulders leaned over the path, but her eyes were now accustomed to the intense blackness. She eased her way past them.

She was relieved she was wearing boots. The ground was damp and slippery. The fronds of a fir brushed her face. Like ghostly hands touching her face. She nearly jumped, then she realized what it was. The gradient of the path was increasing. She took careful longer strides. She wanted to get out of this clinging wood.

Hearing no sound, seeing no sign, of her companions, she guessed they had found another path up to the summit. Then she saw a gap in the trees ahead. Beyond, a strange house perched on a ridge. She paused to study it. Built of granite, it was a mansion with turrets at each corner silhouetted against the starlit night sky. No lights in the windows, it had an abandoned look. Vaguely she made out a wide terrace running its full length, a wide flight of steps leading up to it. A twig cracked behind her. She began to spin round.

A large hand clasped her mouth. She had managed to spin half way round, to catch a glimpse of her attacker. A *huge* man, over six feet tall, heavily built. An apelike figure, the impression emphasized by hair trimmed very short over the massive skull. A small moustache. His other hand and arm pinioned her arms to her body in a vicelike grip. Another smaller figure came beside her, grasped her right arm, pulled up the sleeve of her windcheater. The moonlight penetrating from the gap in the wood showed her he held a hypodermic.

She lifted her right leg, felt a leg of the ape, ground her boot down the shin. No reaction. It was like scraping down the side of a tree trunk. The needle plunged into her exposed arm. She used the fingers of her right hand to push the ring off her finger. Her head was swimming. She gritted her teeth, tried to fight the drug they'd injected into her. The world went hazy. She lost consciousness.

Paula had brief bouts of coming awake. She was lying on a stretcher, flat on her back. A rug or a blanket covered her. The sound of jet engines vibrated in her ears. A sensation of climbing fast. She was aboard a plane. Oh, God – where was she being transported?

Under cover of the blanket she flexed her hands,

27

realized her wrists were tied to the stretcher. Same thing with her ankles. She opened her eyes slowly, ready to close them quickly. Near, and in front of her, she saw the back of a huge man standing up. One large hand, covered with hair, grasped the back of a seat. The Ape. Her vision blurred, cleared again. A small man dressed in whites, like a hospital attendant, was coming down the aisle towards the Ape. She closed her eyes.

Again she gritted her teeth, struggling to stay conscious. The plane went on climbing as she heard voices.

'Time to give her another shot? Don't want her waking during the flight – not till we get her off and delivered.'

A growly voice. The Ape would have that kind of voice. The voice which answered was different, lighter in tone, more educated. Had to be the hospital attendant.

'We could wait a little longer.'

'Any risk in doing her again?' Growly voice.

'Not with the amount I'd give her, but still . . .'

'Then do her.'

As in a dream Paula felt the blanket lifted. A careful hand rolled up the sleeve of her windcheater. She braced herself, felt another prick in her arm. Her head was swimming again. She was aware the plane was flying level now. It would be a more moderate dose of the drug. Inwardly, motionless, she swore, then started counting. Anything to stay conscious. She loathed the feeling of helplessness. A wave rolled over her – reminded her of the wave carrying in the body of the dead fisherman at . . . What was the name of the place? She sank deep into the wave, deeper, deeeeper, deeper. Everything went. She was again completely unconscious.

*

The world stood still. No longer the sound of jet engines. No longer the gentle swaying motion of an aircraft in flight. She surfaced suddenly, quickly. She had a pounding headache. She felt muzzy. Apart from these discomforts she felt the situation was better. Or was it far worse?

Paula was still on her back, still tied to the stretcher. The blanket, or rug, whatever the damned thing was, still covered her. She was careful not to stir noticeably until she had found out what was going on.

The palms of her hands were wet. Slowly she slid them under the cover, drying them off. She had a strong bladder but now she desperately wanted the loo. She became aware her leggings had been pulled well down below her thighs, that her backside was perched on some kind of rubber-like receptacle. They had given her the facilities to relieve herself. She heard a heavy footstep some distance away. She performed very carefully so they would not hear her. Afterwards she felt better, but would have given a fortune for a shower. Then she heard lighter, more deliberate footsteps. Someone had entered the room.

The man, who called himself Dr Goslar, stood, profile sideways to their captive. When he spoke to the other man his voice was light, unpleasant. A small man, thin, he had a high forehead, was clean-shaven, his face long and pale. He wore an expensive blue two-piece suit, white shirt and black polka-dot bow tie, and rimless glasses, which gave him a sinister look, were perched on the bridge of his long nose. He spoke to the other man.

Paula saw all this as she risked half-opening her eyes. The man he spoke to was the Ape, clad in a thick grey pullover which clasped his bull-like neck tightly. She now saw that the cropped hair was brown, like stubble.

'It's time the drug wore off,' the thin man said in precise English. 'You know what you have to do with her, the questions to ask. We are in a hurry.'

'What's the rush?' demanded the Ape throatily. 'We're OK here.'

'You think so? I have a feeling this building is no longer secure.'

'Don't get nervous, Goslar . . .'

'Don't talk to me like that. You're being paid a lot of money for your services,' the thin man hissed.

Paula noticed he spoke with a slight lisp. While they argued she concentrated on strengthening her body. Slowly she eased her ankles up from the ropes as far as she could. She gently revolved her legs. She kept stretching her fingers. The circulation was present. She clenched her hands, unclenched them, repeated the process.

'Get on with it,' the thin man ordered. 'At least you've opened the window.'

Paula froze at this latest item of information. What the hell were the bastards going to do to her now? She had her eyes shut when the Ape swung round, came over to the bed where she lay. He began slapping her roughly across each side of her face. She let her head jerk but kept her eyes closed. He began slapping her very roughly and she let out a low moan. Opening her eyes she blinked in the overhead light, closed them again.

'Come on, you whore,' the Ape snarled. 'We haven't got all night. Time for you to take your exercise. Next thing you get is a bucket of ice-cold water. It isn't all that warm outside.'

You bloody swine. Give me just one chance and I'll kill you, she said to herself.

She opened her eyes, glared at him with hate. He had small eyes under bushy brows. The eyes were like

30

marbles, entirely without feeling. He hauled the cover off her, removed the receptacle by lifting her with one meaty arm. Shoving it under the bed, he padded to the end, removed the ropes binding her ankles, then bound them up again, leaving a strand of rope between them so she could hobble. He performed the same action with the ropes round her wrists, hauled up her leggings.

'You remember the sequence of the questions, Abel? The sequence is important.'

The thin man stood with his back to her. Again Paula noticed the lisp when he had spoken.

'I know what I'm doing, Dr Goslar,' the Ape growled irritably.

'Then hurry. We must leave soon. This building is no longer secure.' The thin man repeated what he had said earlier.

The Ape suddenly jerked her upright. She had a brief moment to check her surroundings. A large bleak room with the only furniture the bed she had been laid on. One door on an inner wall, closed. A large window, wide open. Which accounted for the chilly atmosphere she now experienced. She was suddenly lifted over his massive shoulder, upside down, her face and chest against his back, her thighs and legs hanging in front of him. He began ambling towards the open window. She used her pinioned hands to hammer his back, hoping to hit his kidneys. It was like hammering a punchbag.

He ambled towards the open window and she was really frightened now. He spoke as he paused by the window, his tone grim.

'Just one shriek. Only one – and I drop you. Got it?'

'You'll pay for this, you animal.'

'Lady, I've already been paid. Out you go . . .'

He swung round, grasped her legs in both hands, lowered her out of the window. She forced herself not to scream as the nightmare developed. She was suspended outside the window and for the first time realized how high up she was. Below at least thirty storeys of the building's wall plunged down. It was night. Street lamps cast an eerie glow over the empty street so far below. No sign of anyone. Facing her was another modern building soaring vertically above her. God knew how many storeys high these buildings were. She was in New York.

'This is the first question,' the Ape called out. 'Who is your boss?'

'Jackson.'

It was the first name which jumped into her head. When the Ape had lowered her over the edge of the window his coarse hands had thrust up her leggings, grasping her round the knees. Now she felt his hands sliding back, her legs easing through his hands. This is it, she told herself, gazing down into the abyss.

'One more chance, then you drop.'

'Tweed,' she called out urgently.

The hands reached her just above the ankles, tightened their grip. She twisted her neck, looked up briefly. The Ape had his head turned, presumably giving her answer to the thin man inside the room. She was poised next to the top of a window in the floor below. No light inside. Clenching both hands into fists she beat them against the glass, which broke. She didn't think he could see what she was doing. A small round section of the broken window perched on top of the glass still in place. Careful not to cut herself, she grasped it with her right hand, concealed it inside her closed fist.

'Why did Tweed go to Dartmoor – to Appledore?'

'He had a message to go there.'

'From who? Answer more quickly . . .'

'From Dr Goslar.'

Her head began swimming again. Was it the remains of the drug or vertigo? It seemed such a helluva a long way down. She'd end up squashed to mush. *Stop thinking like that.*

'What did Tweed think of what happened at Appledore? What did he see?'

'Dead fisherman floating in on a wave. Dead fish on the beach.'

'Damn you! What did he think about it?'

'That there must be poison in the water. He didn't know what to think . . .'

Hanging upside down had one advantage. The blood rushed to her head. She was thinking more clearly. She put her hands together, moved the small piece of round glass more comfortably inside her right fist, closed it again.

'Did he think Dr Goslar had something to do with what he saw?'

'He did once. Only once. He was puzzled. We couldn't grasp what was happening. It was dark . . .'

She stopped speaking. Way below her she saw the first sign of life. A car driving slowly round a corner, blue light flashing on its roof. For a second she thought of screaming, dismissed the idea at once. He'd drop her. She heard his voice calling out louder, speaking to the thin man somewhere inside the room.

'Police car's arrived . . .'

She didn't hear the thin man's reaction but felt the grip on her ankles tighten. The Ape was hauling her up fast. Her windcheater protected her against contact with the wall but her legs were being grazed. She took a deep breath as he heaved her inside the window, threw her over his shoulder. She had a brief glimpse of Goslar turned three-quarters away from her, saw he held an automatic in his right hand. No chance of cutting the beast's throat. She might manage that but Goslar would shoot her to ribbons.

'What do we do with her?' rasped the Ape.

'Throw her back on the bed.'

'I could shoot her—'

'You've got a silencer?'

'No . . .'

'The police will hear the shot. Do as I said – throw her on the bed. We've got to get out of here fast.'

She was thrown down on her back onto the bed. The Ape ran back to the window. He peered down, swung round, moving swiftly for such large man. Turning back, his thick lips opened, then closed. The thin man, standing by the internal door now open, hissed at him.

'What is it now?'

'The police car was just cruising. It's disappeared round the corner of another building.'

'We're going now. It may come back. The police play tricks like that. They may have seen her when you were hauling her up again. *Move!*'

During the brief moment when she was slung back over the Ape's shoulder Paula had seen through the open door. Had seen a wide empty space, dimly lit – and a bank of elevators on the opposite wall. Goslar left swiftly, his footfalls quiet. He hadn't had time to glance at Paula. She lay still, her eyes almost closed as the Ape ambled after Goslar, his huge shoulders lifting and falling, as though walking on the deck of a boat in a swell. Apelike in every movement. She watched him from behind her lashes, to conceal her hatred.

She remained motionless for a few seconds. Her acute hearing caught a whirring noise, the gentle click of elevator doors opening, closing. Then she got to work with the piece of rounded glass.

She had plenty of illumination from the fluorescent

tube attached to the ceiling. She used her right hand to quickly saw through the section of rope between her wrists. Once it was cut she eased each hand out of the rope round her wrists. She was sitting up now, leaning against the wall behind her.

She leaned forward, cut herself free from the ropes binding her ankles. She stood up carefully, not sure how strong her legs might be. Finding she could walk easily, without much hope she peered under the bed, saw both her boots lying beside the revolting bedpan.

Hauling them on quickly she walked quietly over to a cupboard in the wall. She opened it, without much hope again. Her shoulder bag lay on the floor. Opening it she realized they had not even examined it. Everything was in place. She took out her Browning .32 automatic, checked it, was both surprised and relieved to find it had not been tampered with. Very quietly she slid back the magazine into the butt. Gripping the weapon in both hands, she tiptoed to the open door, listened. A heavy silence, broken only by the whine of the descending elevator.

She stepped out into a large empty hall, luxuriously furnished with blue tiles. It had an atmosphere she had come to associate with an empty building, closed down for the night. She ran across to the elevator, which was still going down. It had reached the fourth floor. She waited.

It arrived at the ground floor. She still waited. If she tried to use one of the other elevators too soon Goslar and Abel, presumably outside the elevator, would see the light showing it was descending. A minute or two later through the open window in the room she had left she heard the sound of a car starting up. Moving to another elevator, she pressed the button, waited again as it came up.

The waiting was getting on her nerves. There is

35

something eerie about being trapped inside a large building you hope is empty. The elevator seemed to take for ever to reach her. When it stopped and the doors slid back she stood braced, her automatic aimed in case someone was inside. It was empty.

Diving inside, she pressed the button for the third floor. She had noticed beyond the elevator bank a flight of stairs leading down. If they were waiting for her downstairs she needed to surprise them. *Hurry! Hurry!* Watching the numbers above the closed doors she realized now she had been on the thirty-second floor. She shuddered at the memory of the drop from the open window.

The moment the doors opened she pressed the button for the thirty-eighth floor, darted out just before the doors closed and the elevator began its ascent. If they were waiting on the ground floor that would give the bastards something to think about.

Her rubber-soled boots made no sound as she ran down the first flight, pausing to peer round the corner. Reaching the ground floor she ran into a dim-lit vast hall. She whipped to left, to right, to left again, Browning held chest high, her finger on the trigger. No one. Ahead of her on the far side was the exit door. Crouching low, she ran, zigzagging. Next to the door, on the right, a box was attached to the wall. It had a series of digits. Oh God! She didn't know the combination. Then she saw the door was partly open. Goslar and Abel had left in such a hurry they hadn't bothered to close it.

She peered out into the moonlit night. A vast smooth space where the police car had appeared. Opposite, the building she had seen from the window soared up. No lights. To her left she saw what appeared to be a small park with trees and public seats. She walked along the side of the building she had just left, in the narrow shadow it cast on the smooth area.

Without seeing a soul she reached the park, looked round, then sank onto a seat facing the way she had come. By the light of a nearby lamp, perched on a post, she checked her bag thoroughly.

Again she was surprised to find it had never been opened. A woman knows when her bag has been searched by a man. However carefully he replaces its contents he never manages to put everything back exactly as it had been. Her passport was in the special zip-up pocket. Inside a similar pocket she found all the money in several currencies Tweed insisted everyone carried. Wads of Deutschmarks, French francs, Swiss francs, English money. A woman appeared from nowhere. Paula froze.

An old woman, poorly dressed in black, walking with a stoop, her head down. She never even saw her. Paula watched her walk to the end of the park, then suddenly vanish, as though walking down steps. Looking round again, listening, Paula got up and followed her.

Once she looked up at the colossi which loomed above her – a whole series of modern monoliths towering above her. The sight gave her a feeling of vertigo. She looked down and reached the entrance to a wide flight of steps leading down. She stopped briefly to stare in disbelief at a large illuminated sign above the steps.

Métro.

She wasn't in New York. She was in Paris.

3

Newman drove Tweed back to London through the late night. They reached Park Crescent well after daylight. George, the ex-army sergeant who acted as doorman and guard, let them in. Tweed ran upstairs to his first-floor office overlooking Regent's Park. He found Monica, his faithful assistant, a woman of a certain age, her grey hair tied in a bun, seated at her desk. She jumped up the moment he entered.

'Am I glad to see you back! I called Gidleigh Park but they said you had left.'

'Why? Has there been a development?'

'We've had a weird phone call. Came through at 4 a.m. Luckily, I recorded it.'

'Switch it on, then, please.'

Newman had followed him into the office. Tweed took off his coat, carefully placed it on a hanger and hooked it over the coat stand. His normal iron self-control had asserted itself. He sat down in the swivel chair behind his desk to listen.

'The voice is very strange,' Monica warned.

'Let us hear it, then.'

My dear Tweed, you should really look after your staff more carefully. It is becoming a real hazard to work for you. Perhaps you ought to find a replacement for the lovely young lady. As ever, H. Goslar.

The voice sounded robotic. It spaced out each word and had a low twangy screech. To Newman it sounded like a voice from hell.

'That's it,' Monica said as she switched off the recorder. 'It scared the wits out of me when I first heard it.'

'He's used a voice-changer to make it impossible to hear his real voice,' Tweed said quietly. 'Monica, would you say that is man or a woman speaking?'

'It could be either sex. Very creepy. What does it mean?'

'Brace yourself. Paula has disappeared, kidnapped on Dartmoor.'

'Oh, no!' She was going to burst into tears, but managed to subdue it to snuffles. She blew her nose. 'That horrible man!'

'We need reinforcements. Contact Marler. Then Harry Butler and Pete Nield. I want them here fast.'

The door opened and Marler walked in as soon as Tweed finished speaking. A slim man, five feet seven tall, he was smartly dressed in a Prince of Wales check suit, and a crisp white shirt with a blue Chanel tie. His feet were clad in handmade shoes with rubber soles. He spoke with a drawl.

'Mornin' all.'

'Play it back again,' Tweed requested Monica. 'I want Marler to hear it.'

They listened again. It sounded no less sinister. Marler took up his usual position, standing against a wall. He extracted a king-size, but didn't light it as he listened, his clean-shaven face expressionless.

'Don't like that last bit about finding a replacement,' he said. 'Is it Paula?'

'Yes, it is,' Tweed told him. 'My fault, my responsibility. She was kidnapped on Dartmoor when she was with Newman and me, checking out a mansion called Gargoyle Towers. Early in the morning. She took a different route through a forest. Probably took her away in a helicopter.'

'That could be tracked,' Marler observed.

'I've done more than that. When we got back to the hotel I phoned the air controller at Exeter airfield. Not knowing me, he refused to give me any information. I called Jim Corcoran at Heathrow to contact Exeter. Unfortumately Jim wasn't there. Driving back, we stopped at a phone box near here and I got Jim. He'll be calling back.'

'Surely there's more we can do to find her,' Marler insisted.

'Before we left Gidleigh Park,' Tweed went on in full flood, 'I managed to phone the local police inspector at Appledore, chap called Crake. I asked him to get a search warrant for Gargoyle Towers. Told him why, that the place was empty. I want his men to check for fingerprints.'

'Gargoyle Towers? Funny name,' Marler queried.

'So now for your benefit and Monica's I'll brief you on exactly what happened at Appledore.'

Tersely he started with the message from Goslar. He paused and asked Monica to play it again on the recorder. Then he went on, explaining their whole experience at Appledore, and later at Gargoyle Towers. Normally he would have sat behind his desk but as he spoke he was pacing round the office. Monica realized it was a sign of the acute anxiety he was feeling for Paula. He completed his explanation, sat down again behind his desk. The phone rang, Monica answered, looked at Tweed.

'It's Jim Corcoran . . .'

'Any news, Jim?' Tweed asked the Security chief.

'Quite a lot. Don't know what to make of it. I contacted my opposite number at Exeter. He told me a big private jet, a Grumman Gulfstream, so a long-range job, was parked at Exeter. In the middle of the night an ambulance arrived, drove up to the jet. Paramedics hauled out a stretcher with someone on it, took it aboard the machine . . .'

'Could anyone see who was on the stretcher?'

'No. The patient was well muffled against the cold. A medic said the patient had a broken leg, compound fracture, was being flown to a private clinic in London.'

'They named the clinic?' Tweed demanded.

'No. Let me finish. There's more. The pilot had already filed a flight plan for Heathrow. It all happened very quickly, I gather. The Grummann took off—'

'You intercepted it?'

'Tweed, if you'll just hold your horses until I finish. You keep firing at me like a machine-gun. No, we didn't intercept the Grumman. The reason is the pilot changed his flight plan soon after leaving Exeter. He's permitted to do that just so long as he gives sufficient notice of the change.'

'What change of plan?'

'I *was* going to tell you. He changed his destination. Instead of Heathrow he was proceeding to Rome . . .'

'Rome!'

'That's what I said.

'Can I check on the Grumman's progress?'

'You could try – by calling Paris Air Traffic Control. Although just how long it would take you to make the contact is anyone's guess. The pressure on flights and air space is growing.'

'Thank you, Jim. Thank you very much.'

'Tweed, is something wrong? I've never heard you so tense.'

'Nothing to worry about.'

Tweed placed the phone back gently. He looked round the office, told the others what he had heard. They stared at him. Marler was the first to react.

'Why would they be taking her to Rome, of all places?'

41

'I have absolutely no idea. Monica, get me René Lasalle in Paris on the line. Urgently.'

'Why call him?' Marler enquired. 'The head of the DST, French counterespionage?'

'Because he's a friend, as you know. And he co-operates. He'll be able to contact the French air traffic controllers.'

As he spoke Monica was obtaining the number. She was signalling to Tweed that she had Lasalle on the line when George knocked on the door, entered. He carried a batch of newspapers under his arm which he laid on Tweed's desk.

'Sorry about the delay. It's a late edition. They held the presses, apparently, to change the main story.'

'Thank you, George ... René, I need your help urgently – very urgently. A private Grumman jet took off from Exeter early this morning. The pilot filed a flight plan for Heathrow. Then in midair he gives a different flight plan, says he's headed for Rome instead of Heathrow. Did you get that? I'll repeat it.'

'Not necessary,' Lasalle said quietly.

'I want you to contact your Air Traffic Control, to find out where that machine is now. I need the answer in five minutes.'

'May be difficult,' Lasalle continued in perfect English, his tone still cool, almost distant. 'We have a crisis here. I'll deal with your request as soon as I have the time.'

'But this is terribly urgent!'

'I heard you the first time. I must go now.'

Tweed stared at the phone. Lasalle had broken the connection. He replaced the phone. He looked at the others.

'What *is* going on? He's usually so very cooperative.'

He told them the gist of his conversation. Then he

42

unfolded a copy of the *Daily Nation*, London's leading newspaper. He gazed at the screaming headline.

POISON SEA NORTH OF DARTMOOR
Special report by Sam Sneed

The text below was long and detailed. Tweed scanned it swiftly. Then he handed a copy of the newspaper to each member of his staff. Monica watched him, saw Tweed settle back in his chair, relaxed now, a look of extreme concentration on his face. His normal icy self-control had returned. Newman reacted first after reading his copy.

'What the hell's going on? This is a report by Sneed of exactly what happened at Appledore. He even hints that Whitehall is concerned about the invention of a new secret weapon. "Far deadlier than the hydrogen bomb", he reports an unnamed government source as saying.'

'He made up that last bit,' Tweed told him. 'To give his story an extra edge. My guess is that by now copies of his report will have been wired to Washington, Paris, Berlin and Heaven knows where else. It's created an international crisis. On the instructions of Goslar, of course.'

'Goslar?' Newman queried.

'Well, you see the splashy pictures of what we witnessed happening on the beach. The dead fisherman, dead fish, dead seal. I think on his first trip on that motorcycle – after making copies – Sneed delivered the original of his video to a prearranged rendezvous outside Appledore – to whoever was inside that Daimler with the tinted windows. You remember the oil patch we found in the road. Then – I'm guessing – a second helicopter picked him up with the copies, delivered him to Exeter airfield where another chopper was waiting to fly him to Battersea Heliport. From there he was driven to the *Daily Nation*, where he typed his story. It would all fit in with our past experience of Goslar. I told you he was a brilliant planner. He hasn't lost his touch.'

'But who will believe this?'

'The people we didn't want to hear about it. Washington, Paris, etc., probably contacted the police in Appledore. Crake would give them a "no comment". That response would convince everyone the story was true.'

'What is Goslar up to?'

'He's creating panic, advertising a weapon "far deadlier than the hydrogen bomb", to quote Sneed – who undoubtedly has been well paid to meet Goslar's wishes.'

'How does the disappearance of Paula fit in?'

'Goslar is manipulating me, trying to throw me off balance. I suppose that's a backhanded compliment. But that is my great worry – Paula's safety.'

'This Sneed report will set the world alight,' said Marler.

'One thing I forgot to include, Marler, when I explained the events at Appledore. The trigger was this note from Goslar. Newman and Monica have seen it.'

He handed Marler the weird note which had arrived through their letterbox during the night. While Marler read it he gazed at the phone.

'I wish Lasalle would call me back. I can't think of any other sound way of locating that aircraft. Paula must have been alive when they carried her on to it on a stretcher.'

'You don't think they'd . . .' Newman began sombrely.

'Don't say it,' snapped Tweed.

He had just spoken when the door was pushed open.

44

Paula, clothes crumpled but hair freshly brushed, walked into the office with a spring in her step.

4

Tweed jumped up, rushed forward and hugged Paula. She rested her head on his shoulder, squeezed him with both arms. She whispered in his ear, 'God, it's wonderful to be back.'

'We've been going nearly out of our minds with worry,' he told her.

'I'd like to sit at my desk again.'

She hugged them all, then settled herself behind her desk. Monica made the suggestion, 'How about a cup of tea, well sweetened?'

'A cup of tea would be great, but no sugar.' She grinned. 'I'm sweet enough as I am. And I had breakfast on the plane back from Paris.'

'*Paris?*' Tweed exclaimed. 'Not Rome?'

'No.' She looked puzzled. 'Paris. I've had an adventure. But I'm so sorry I caused you all anxiety. I did think of phoning, but when I grabbed a taxi from Madeleine and arrived at Charles de Gaulle airport there was a flight for London just about to leave. To reach Madeleine I'd caught the Métro from La Défense.'

'La Défense?' echoed Tweed. 'That's the amazing French business centre well west of the Arc de Triomphe. Incredibly tall buildings.'

'Which is why, for a while, I thought I was in New York. You're an angel,' she told Monica, who had brought her a cup of tea. She took a sip. 'And I can describe the mysterious Dr Goslar. Oh, I'm not telling this well. I'm going to slow down and start from the beginning.' She looked at Newman. 'I was an idiot. You did warn me not to go up that path through the forest on Dartmoor on my own. I'll start from there . . .'

'Do you want to go home and have a rest first?' Tweed suggested.

'Not yet. Later I'd like to go back to my flat and have a shower. But first you should have the information I can provide. Now, I'll go back to where I stupidly left Bob and went up that path . . .'

She recalled concisely every single event, this time in sequence. Nobody spoke, giving her their full attention. Tweed sat leaning forward, hands clasped on his desk, his eyes never leaving hers. His mouth twisted grimly as she described being held out of the window, thirty or so storeys above the ground. Newman muttered under his breath.

'The bloody swine . . .'

'So,' she eventually concluded, 'I said I could describe Goslar – and, incidentally, Abel the Ape. Is Richard, the artist, here?'

'Yes, he is. But—'

'I insist on having a session with him now. While my memory of what those two men look like is fresh. I know where his office is upstairs. I'm on my way.'

She was out of the office before Tweed could protest, suggesting again she went to her flat first to get some rest. He looked at everyone.

'Well, what do you think of that? Typical of Paula to refer to it as an adventure.'

'I tell you what I think,' growled Newman. 'Sooner or later I'll meet the Ape. I'll break both his arms. Then I'll do his legs. And that will only be for starters.'

'Paula has pulled off a coup,' drawled Marler. 'We've identified Dr Goslar.'

'Maybe,' replied Tweed. 'And don't tell Paula I said that. I'm just so relieved she's back in one piece.'

He stopped speaking as the phone rang. He let Monica deal with it. Quickly she called across, 'Lasalle's back on the line . . .'

'Good of you to call back, René. Any news?'

'Tweed, I'm not in my office. I'm calling from an outside phone. Is your end secure?'

'Yes. What is the problem, René?'

'First, you asked me to check on that plane. I found out that a Grumman Gulfstream jet landed at Charles de Gaulle early this morning – in the middle of the night, actually. An ambulance was waiting. Two paramedics carried someone off on a stretcher, drove away. Later the ambulance – stolen – was found abandoned in a side street. After that I drew a blank.'

Once again Tweed marvelled at Lasalle's command of English. He also detected Lasalle was under pressure, in a state of tension. Normally he was one of the coolest men Tweed had ever met.

'René, I can tell you now Paula was the so-called patient. She had been kidnapped from Dartmoor—'

'Did you say Dartmoor?'

'Yes. Why?'

'Doesn't matter. Do go on.'

'She was transported to a building in La Défense. She had been drugged during the flight. When she woke she was subjected to a terrifying experience while two men questioned her. She was suspended by her feet out of a window over thirty storeys up.'

'Oh, my God! Poor Paula. That's fiendish . . .'

'They eventually hauled her back again into the room. Briefly, they left her when a patrol car appeared below the building. She escaped and she's now back here with me. Do you know what happened to that Grumman jet?'

'Yes, it took off for Geneva. That's all I know.'

'Is it? Ever heard the name Goslar?' Tweed enquired.

'Did you say *Goslar*?' A brief pause. 'I can't help you with that.'

'Which means the name does mean something to you. We've known each other a long time. This is the first occasion you've felt it necessary to use an outside phone to call me. What is going on, René?'

'You'll keep the fact that I phoned you within your closed circle?'

'Only if you tell me why,' Tweed replied grimly.

'Tweed, the Élysée is on my back. Signing off now . . .'

Tweed put down the phone, then told the others the gist of his conversation. There was silence for a short time. Then Marler spoke.

'That's not the René we used to know. Why?'

'The last thing he said. The President of France has involved himself. Goslar is spreading a vast net. As I remarked earlier, this thing is global.'

While he had been speaking the phone had rung. Monica, looking furious, gazed at Tweed.

'Trouble. Two men from Special Branch tried to storm their way past George and up here. He's holding them at bay with his revolver.'

'Tell George to escort the gentlemen up here.' He looked at Newman. 'It is starting. Why do my thoughts run to the Prince, otherwise known as Aubrey Courtney Harrington, newly apppointed Minister of General Security, member of the Cabinet?'

Two unusual men entered. One was over six feet tall, upright as a Douglas fir, in his late fifties, his rugged face wearing an aggressive expression, his hair grey, his clean-shaven face pink, his ice-blue eyes swivelling to everyone in the room. His manner exuded domineering self-confidence. He wore an expensive camelhair coat and he was removing expensive pigskin gloves, exposing large hands with thick fingers.

'I'm Jarvis Bate, Acting Head of Special Branch. Too many people in here. Need to see you alone, Tweed.'

'First I'd like to see some identification.'

'Identification?' He rumbled the word. 'Damnit, I've shown that to the cowboy you have on the door. I suppose he has a permit for that revolver. I've a good mind to report that.'

'I'm waiting.'

Bate extracted an ID card from his wallet. He dropped it on Tweed's desk. Then he gestured to the small man who had come in with him.

'This is Mervyn Leek, my assistant. Show the man your ID, Merv. He has a bureaucratic mind.'

Newman stared at the small man. No more than five feet six tall, he was dwarfed by his superior. If anything, Newman disliked the look of Leek even more than he did of Bate. He had shifty grey eyes and a perpetual smile, which was more a smirk. He had a pale face, his eyes hooded frequently, his manner was deferential to the point of creeping. His voice was public school and quiet, in contrast to Bate's grating delivery.

'I'm sure you will wish to see my ID also,' he said, placing it carefully on the desk. 'It really is a pleasure to meet you, Mr Tweed. I have heard of your great accomplishments in the field. It is an honour.'

'Sit down and shut up, Merv,' ordered Bate.

He had already seated himself, sitting erect in an armchair. Leaning forward, he grabbed hold of the ID card Tweed had examined, then exploded.

'I did say there were too many people here.'

'I heard you the first time,' Tweed replied mildly. 'No one is leaving. They are part of the core of my organization.'

49

'Then be it on your own head. We're taking over here. Dartmoor. Know what I mean? We'll need an office where Mervyn can work on the premises. Everything about Dartmoor passes through his hands. You're out of that neck in the woods. Got it?'

'For one thing we don't have any office space available.'

'I don't think you understand the situation. I have a document here from the Minister of General Security. Be pleased to read it,' he said, handing over a large sheet of paper folded once.

'The Prince,' Newman said half aloud.

'What?' Bate swung round to gaze at Newman. 'For your information the Minister intensely dislikes that insulting nickname coined by the press.'

'Poor old thing,' Newman remarked, staring straight at Bate.

'This document has no meaning to me,' Tweed said, handing it back.

'It gives full authorization for Special Branch to take over all general security matters,' Bate said furiously.

'But it doesn't make any mention of the SIS . . .'

'That can be remedied,' Bate almost shouted.

'Are you sure about that?'

For once Bate looked uncertain. He made a great performance of refolding the document before returning it to his pocket. Then he took a deep breath.

'You can rest assured that I shall be back.'

'Perhaps,' Leek began, looking more sneaky than ever, 'I could be permitted to wait here while Mr Bate regularizes the situation. I have no doubt you could park me in a cubbyhole.'

'When Bate leaves, you leave. And I've run out of the amount of time I can devote to both of you. I would appreciate it if you left now.' Tweed stood up. 'We are rather busy.'

Paula came in. She stopped with the door still half open. Two heads swung round to stare at her.

'Who is this?' demanded Bate.

'The tea lady,' Monica called out.

Paula withdrew, closing the door quietly. Bate obviously felt compelled to stand up. Leek, like a marionette, followed suit. Everyone could see Bate was having trouble controlling his temper. He looked even less pleased when Tweed asked him his question.

'On the odd occasion previously when I've communicated with Special Branch I've always dealt with the head of your outfit, Caspar Pardoe. Where is he?'

'I've taken over from him for the time being. Pardoe is overseas, taking a rest.'

'Whereabouts overseas?'

'I really have not the slightest idea. Nor have I any interest in the wanderings of Pardoe. I am in charge now.'

'Don't have a breakdown,' Tweed said with the ghost of a smile.

'I really can't imagine why you have a newspaper correspondent sitting in on a conference like this,' Bate exclaimed, glaring at Newman. 'Sloppy security, in my book.'

'Then get another book,' Tweed suggested amiably. 'Newman was vetted years ago and, as I'm sure you do know, works closely with me on difficult cases.'

'The sooner Merv is installed here the better, I'd say.'

'I had the impression you were on your way out, Bate.'

'Oh, I'm going. I shall give the Minister a full report of the state of affairs I found here. He won't be best pleased.'

'Poor old thing,' Newman repeated.

'If you ever want to see me again,' Tweed said,

'please be so good as to phone and make an appointment.'

Bate transferred his glare from Newman to Tweed. Opening his mouth, he thought better of what he'd been going to say, closed it again and left. Leek turned at the door, smirked all round, bobbed his head, followed his lord and master.

Paula returned almost at once, hurrying into the room. She let out her breath.

'I hope you don't mind, Tweed, but I was listening outside the door. What a ghastly couple. The tall and the short. Almost more than Bate, I detested Leek – a real creep.' She went back to her desk, sat down. 'Well, we won't have to worry about them any more.'

'You could be wrong there,' Tweed warned.

'Why do you say that?'

'The arrival of the present top man from Special Branch shows how seriously the government is taking the Appledore incident. I'm sure Harrington discussed this with the Cabinet before he sent in his two lapdogs to us. On top of that the French are taking an interest.'

He told them about his strange conversation with Lasalle, the unique change in attitude on the part of his old friend. He was repeating the story for the sake of Paula, who had been absent earlier. Under her arm she carried a large blue folder of the type used by Richard, the artist, expert at creating Identikits.

'Get me the PM on the phone, please, Monica,' Tweed went on. 'I want an appointment with him later today.'

Sam Sneed walked quickly along Fleet Street, his deer-stalker hat perched at a jaunty angle. He had left the headquarters of the *Daily Nation* half an hour earlier. En route he had called in at his bank, had paid in £2,000 in cash into his account. This was the money he had been handed in an envelope by the chauffeur of the Daimler when he'd handed over the original video outside Appledore.

His gnomelike head was bent forward and he felt like dancing. He was on his way to his favourite London pub to celebrate. At this hour in the late morning it would have just opened, so he was counting on it being quiet. He could sit by himself with a beer in front of him, dwelling on his victory. At long last he was on the escalator, moving up.

He had a copy of the newspaper tucked firmly under his arm. Sneed couldn't read his long article again too many times. On the front page – with his byline. The editor had been pleased, had even hinted he was thinking of taking Sneed on the permanent staff.

'Mr Sneed? Mr Sam Sneed?'

He was being accosted and it annoyed him. He wanted to revel on his own. The voice was cultured. He looked up, studied the man who had stopped in front of him. Late thirties, early forties? Good-looking cove. Yellowish hair, a smile on his clean-shaven face. He was clad in a smart military-style trench coat with wide lapels, and he held a carrier. *Aquascutum* was printed on the carrier.

'What do you want?' Sneed demanded. 'I'm in a hurry.'

'His Lordship – the boss – was pleased with the way you handled your first assignment. A couple of grand for that, which we gave you. How would you like to earn double that amount?'

Double £2,000. Another £4,000? Out of the blue?

'What would I have to do for that?' Sneed asked, his manner more friendly.

'It's a bit public – the two of us standing here in the street. And you're a public figure now. That paper under your arm has a small photograph of you. You'll get people asking for your autograph.'

'Do you think so?'

'Don't forget,' the man in the trench coat grinned, 'charge them a fiver. Now, we need somewhere quiet where I can give you the details. My club is very close. Let's repair to it.'

'I was on my way to my favourite pub.'

'The club will be safer. I have to show you a plan. This way.'

They walked a short distance and then Trenchcoat stopped. Leading off Fleet Street was a narrow alley which turned a corner a short distance inside. Trenchcoat gestured with his gloved hand down the alley.

'After you, sir. The entrance is the door on the left just beyond the corner.'

The adrenalin was pumping inside Sneed as he made his way down the deserted alley. After all these years of living with his unpleasant sister – who paid the rent on the house – he was in the money. He'd buy himself a good car, sell the motorbike, and some good clothes. He turned the corner, looking for a door on his left.

Behind him, Trenchcoat glanced back. No one about. Rounding the corner, he took out a long black wire with wooden pegs at either end. He swung the arc of wire over Sneed's hat down to his throat. Gripping a peg in each hand, he twisted the wire at the back once, tightening it with all his strength. The wire bit deep into Sneed's throat. He gurgled, hands reaching up. Trenchcoat continued tightening the wire, even though Sneed, already dead, had sagged to his knees.

5

Three hours later Tweed returned from Downing Street. He found everyone present who had been in his office earlier. Removing his coat, he looked at Paula.

'You're supposed to be home at your flat in Fulham, resting.'

'I've been there,' she told him with a smile. 'Bob insisted on driving me there as bodyguard. He waited in my sitting room while I had the most glorious hot, then cold, shower. Felt so much better. The Ape had his hands over me – I felt grubby and soiled. Then I had a complete change of clothes and Bob drove me back here. We stopped on the way for a snack. I'm ready for anything now. How did your meeting with the PM go?'

'Very well. He was annoyed when I quoted him the wording of the document Bate shoved at me. Said Courtney Harrington had no authority over the SIS. Situation remains as before – I report only to the PM. And, of course, he knows Harrington is after his job.'

'Any reaction about Appledore?' Newman enquired.

'Yes, he's very worried about the whole business. Strictly between these walls, I think everyone is jumping the gun.'

'Which means?' queried Marler.

'We don't know yet that the sea was poisoned. I used a phone box on the way back to call Professor Saafeld. He has performed the autopsy on the dead fisherman but wouldn't tell me his conclusions. Wants to see me at his place in Holland Park this evening at nine o'clock. He's also called in an expert on fish to dissect the seal – and the fish. You know him, Paula, so you can come with me if you want to.'

'Of course I do. Any chance of my showing you the Identikits of Dr Goslar and Abel the Ape? Richard and I work quickly together.'

'Now would be a good moment. Gather round my desk, everybody.'

'This is Dr Goslar,' said Paula.

They all stared at the charcoal sketch. It showed a small thin man, clean-shaven and with a high forehead. His face was long and he wore rimless glasses. Unpleasant, shrewd eyes gazed out from behind the glasses.

'It's pretty accurate,' Paula told them, 'thanks mostly to the skill of Richard.'

'And your powers of observation,' Newman added. 'I wonder if he always wears a bow tie?'

'Possibly,' said Tweed.

'What was his voice like?' Marler wanted to know.

'Precise,' she replied. 'He speaks perfect English, but with a slight lisp.'

'Does he smoke?' Monica broke in.

'Good question,' Paula responded. 'No, at least not during the short time I saw him. And there were no ash trays in the room, nor any smoke fumes.'

'Everybody got him?' Tweed asked.

Heads nodded and Tweed knew they had all memorized the essentials. Had imagined what he'd look like without glasses or a bow tie, and wearing quite different clothes. Paula removed the sketch and replaced it with another.

'Abel the Ape,' she announced.

'What a horrible menacing creature,' Monica exclaimed. 'He is huge, almost looks like a gorilla.'

'If I met that on a dark night,' Marler commented, 'I'd kick him in the crotch, stick a gun in his thick-lipped mouth – and then ask questions.'

'Voice?' Tweed queried.

56

'Growly,' Paula replied. 'Growly, aggressive, hostile. Sure that he can cope physically with almost any man on earth. At least that was my impression.'

'And you heard him called Abel. What about a surname?'

'Nothing. Just Abel.'

'And you heard this Abel call the other man Dr Goslar how many times?'

'At least twice. Quite clearly. In a loud voice.'

'You've done well. Very well, Paula.'

'Now, I think,' she said, gathering up the sketches, 'I'd better get copies made of these for everyone.'

'Including Harry Butler and Pete Nield. Yes, please.'

Tweed waited until she had gone. Then he looked at the others and lowered his voice.

'So, there we are. What do you think?'

'It's a huge step forward,' Newman commented, 'since we now have for the first time a clear idea of what Goslar looks like.'

'Have we? We don't pass on to Paula this part of our conversation. She has tried so hard, endured so much. And, Bob, your memory isn't too good.'

'What do you mean by that?'

'One of Goslar's many tricks, years ago when you and I were tracking him during the Cold War, was to get someone to impersonate him, to use the name Goslar. When whoever it was completed his mission, he usually ended up dead. And on occasion it was a woman who impersonated Goslar. He believes in shooting the messenger.'

Tweed broke off as the phone rang. Monica told him Superintendent Buchanan was on the phone.

'Roy, Tweed here. Anything happening?'

'You could say that. Sam Sneed has just been murdered. It was a brutal job. His body was found in an alley off Fleet Street. Killer used a wire round his neck.

He had been decapitated. The head was missing. Found later inside an Aquascutum carrier along with the wire which did the job. Together with a trench coat spotted with blood. We'll do a DNA test – but my bet is it will turn out to be Sneed's blood.'

'Any clues as to the assassin?'

'None. No witness. Nothing. A very professional job. Imagine what the press will do with this tomorrow – maybe earlier if the *Evening Standard* picks up on it. Must go.'

'Thanks for informing me . . .'

'One more thing. That Inspector Crake at Appledore phoned me. A team has gone over Gargoyle Towers for fingerprints. Not even one print. The place was cleaned out.'

'Which is what I expected. More of Goslar's technique. Bye . . .'

He had just replaced the phone when Paula returned. She sat at her desk, saw his expression, asked if something had happened. He told her about Buchanan's call.

'That's horrible,' she said. She shuddered. 'I feel even more lucky to be alive.'

'As you described it those two men were in a heck of a rush to get away. Lucky, as you said.'

Tweed didn't think he wanted to explain to her the real reason. That she had been left to return to London with her description of the alleged Dr Goslar. There had been no need for Abel to use his name in front of her – unless deliberately.

'Why would they murder Sneed?' she asked.

'I was reminding Bob that Goslar always shoots the messenger when he – or she – has done their job. That way no one can be interrogated and reveal what instructions they were given – even by an invisible Goslar over the phone. Incidentally, I've sent the recording of his phone call down to the boffins in the basement, on the off chance they can recover the real voice.'

'You think they'll manage that?'

'No, I don't. Goslar will have used the most sophisticated voice-changer in the world. But we have to try.'

'So what next?'

'As soon as we can we're going to Paris.'

'We are?'

'So everyone should have their bags packed for the trip. I'll be taking a heavy delegation. Everyone here except Monica, of course, who will hold the fort. Contact Butler and Nield, who will be coming too. Monica, book seats for us on a flight late tomorrow afternoon. Make separate bookings, so it's not obvious we're together, and don't use our real names. Paula and I can travel together.'

'And,' Newman said firmly, 'I want the seat behind you. Also we'll come with you when you visit Professor Saefeld this evening.'

'That's going over the top. It's only Holland Park.'

'It was only Fleet Street where Sneed lost his head.'

Marler had left Park Crescent to visit the East End. He was going to contact some dubious characters he knew to see if anyone had heard a whisper about the murder of Sam Sneed.

'I'll probably have more luck in Paris,' he said when he was going. 'I have a real underground network there . . .'

Earlier Tweed had remarked they needed reinforcements. He'd asked Marler to locate Alf, the Cockney cab-driver with a number of other chums, also cab-drivers. He wanted them to keep cruising past Park Crescent to see if anyone was watching the building.

Paula had been disturbed by his request, to the

extent she had stood up to peer through the heavy net curtains over the windows. She voiced her concern when she sat down again.

'I've never heard you take that precaution before. Are you worried about Dr Goslar? You think we could be under surveillance?'

'I'm not worried, Paula. I'm just not underestimating my ancient adversary. He always operates with a vast organization. He has the resources – all the money he obtained from the Americans and the Russians during the Cold War. Plus the ten million he grabbed from selling his plant in New Jersey. Before he blew it to kingdom come, together with everyone inside.'

'He sounds so incredibly brutal and evil.'

'What we have to remember is he is so very *thorough.*'

The phone rang. Monica looked puzzled when she'd answered it. She asked the caller to repeat the name, then put her hand over the mouthpiece.

'There's a strange woman on the phone. Gave the name Serena Cavendish. No, she won't talk to you, sounds in a rush. She wants you to meet her at Brown's Hotel in the tea room. She said you should be able to pick out her table. She has very dark hair. She also said it was about Appledore . . .'

Tweed travelled in a taxi. Paula had insisted on accompanying him. He'd agreed, provided she kept in the background. Newman had said he would follow them in his car. Tweed decided he hadn't the time to argue with him. On the stairs Newman had encountered Harry Butler and Pete Nield. He had told them to come with him.

Arriving at Brown's, Tweed paid off his taxi and cautiously entered the hotel. The tea room was on his right, shielded from the hall by a thigh-high panelled wall. Above it were windows of thick glass, enabling him to scan the people taking tea. A large number of fashionable women chatted to each other as they consumed the famous and excellent meal.

Paula had picked up a magazine, moving away from Tweed so she stood near the dining room entrance as though waiting for someone. Tweed quickly spotted the striking woman with very black hair. She was sitting by herself facing him, long shapely legs crossed at a table for two. Then he saw something odd.

By himself, with his back to Tweed, sat a man with yellowish hair. In his late thirties, Tweed estimated. Very smartly attired in a blue bird's-eye suit. He sat reading a newspaper, the paper above his eye level. A smart business type entered, looked around, went over to the elegant lady with black hair. He bent down to ask her something. She smiled up at him, shook her head, and he walked on into the second room where they were serving tea.

While this was happening, Yellow Hair lowered his paper slowly to a level where he could gaze across at the glamorous lady during her brief exchange with the business type. Then he slowly elevated the paper to its original position. The head waiter had come out into the lobby. His face lit up in a pleased smile.

'Mr Tweed. How are you, sir? It's a while since we've seen you here.'

'I want you to do me a favour. Discreetly. You see the lady with the black hair? The one sitting by herself.'

'Yes, sir. I don't think she's been here before.'

'This is for you,' Tweed continued, handing over a banknote. 'I want you to be very discreet, as I said a moment ago. Go to her and whisper that I'm waiting here and want her to come out to me. *Whisper.* Get her bill quickly.'

'She's already paid, sir.'

'Good. I don't want anyone else in the room to hear you.'

'I'll deal with it now, sir . . .'

Tweed moved swiftly. First he beckoned to the head porter, who had just appeared.

'John, I need a taxi urgently. Now, in fact. If anyone asks where I've gone you don't know.'

'I wouldn't tell them anyway, sir. I'll get on it now . . .'

Tweed looked across at Paula who had heard every word. He shook his head, indicating he didn't want her to come with him. The dark-haired woman wrapped a fur coat round herself, then quickly walked into the lobby. He took her arm gently.

'You are Serena?' he said in a low voice.

'Yes. Serena Cavendish. You're Tweed . . .'

'Excuse the hustle. We're getting out of here quickly. Have tea elsewhere. Get in the cab.'

He saw Newman behind the wheel of his Merc, parked near the cab. Glancing back, he saw no one beyond John, the porter. He dashed to Newman, who had lowered the window.

'Yellow hair, smartly dressed . . .'

Darting back to his own taxi he sat next to Cavendish, who was already inside. He gave the destination to the driver.

'Fortnum's. We're in a hurry.'

'Who isn't these days?' the cabbie responded with a grin.

He moved off immediately. Glancing back through the rear window, Tweed saw Nield jump out of the back seat of the Merc. Paula slipped in to occupy it, next to Butler. What was going on? Then he saw Yellow Hair emerge with brisk steps, his hand up to flag a cab.

At the entrance to Brown's Pete Nield, slim, with a trim moustache and snappily dressed, also had his hand up. He handed John two one-pound coins as the cab pulled in to the kerb.

'I was first. This is my cab,' Yellow Hair snapped in an uppercrust voice.

'Sorry, old man,' Nield responded, his hand on the door's handle, 'but I was just before you.'

'Damned well weren't!'

'Plenty more cabs coming,' Nield said amiably, jumping in and slamming the door.

'Where to, sir?' asked the driver.

'Follow that Merc, please,' Nield whispered. 'There's a fiver in it for you.'

Newman had already driven off after Tweed's taxi. Butler showed Paula the very small camera he had dropped in his lap. She raised an eyebrow.

'Got a pic of Yellow Hair,' Butler told her. 'At least I hope so. I was just snapping him when he looked my way. Camera may have wobbled. Hope for the best.'

Paula reflected again on the contrast between the two men who so often worked together as a team. Harry Butler had no interest in clothes. In his early forties, five feet eight tall, heavily built, he wore a shabby anorak and equally shabby corduroy slacks and his shoes hadn't seen polish in ages. He had thick dark hair in need of a comb and his large face had a stubborn nose and a formidable jaw.

On the other hand Pete Nield took almost as much care of his clothes as Marler. He had a handsome face, rather longish, but like his partner his eyes were quick-moving and missed nothing. As a team they worked together brilliantly and ruthlessly when the occasion demanded it.

'I wonder what all that was about,' mused Newman.

'Incidentally, Yellow Hair got a cab but three cars and a van are now between him and us. Anyone hear where Tweed is going with his femme fatale?'

'Fortnum's,' Paula said promptly.

'Drop you off there, then I'll cruise round the block. No place to park, of course . . .'

Fortnum's restaurant on the top floor was crowded but Tweed managed to obtain a table at the far end. He sat with his back against the wall. It would give him a perfect view of anyone else entering the place.

'Now, why did you want to see me so urgently?' Tweed asked when they had ordered tea.

'Let me just compose myself first. I suppose you're not going to tell me what happened at Brown's?' his guest enquired.

'Had you a bodyguard with you?' Tweed suggested, adjusting his napkin.

'I most certainly had not.'

Tweed swivelled in his chair to give her his full attention. He had noticed when they came in several men had gazed at her with longing. No wonder, he thought. About five feet seven tall, she had a well-rounded figure in a green dress with a slim gold belt. At her throat she wore a Hermès scarf and above it her calm face had a superb bone structure. It was her eyes which held his. Greenish, they exuded intelligence. Her glory was her hair, cut so it hung in a carefully arranged disarray, ending above the collar of her dress. She used her left hand to pull her fur coat more securely on the back of the chair.

'You'll see there's hope for you yet,' she said with a smile.

'Pardon?'

'You were looking at the third finger of my left hand. No ring.'

'I think you ought to tell me, Miss Cavendish—'

'Serena, please.'

'I think you ought to tell me now, Serena,' he said firmly, 'what you wanted to see me about.'

'You'd better look at this.'

From her Gucci handbag she took a neatly folded copy of the *Evening Standard*. He waited patiently while she unfolded it and placed it before him. The huge headline jumped at him.

'POISON SEA' REPORTER MURDERED

He scanned the text quickly. It reported the discovery of the headless body of Sam Sneed, discovered in an alley off Fleet Street. No mention of the fact that the head had been found. Tweed felt sure Buchanan was holding that back in the hope of locating the killer, then tripping him up – using information that had not been published. He handed the paper back to her.

'Very strange,' he commented.

Tea had been served and Serena was eating a sandwich. Tweed sipped from his cup, then looked at her. He gestured towards the newspaper in her lap.

'Could you tell me something?' he asked with a smile. 'How did you get my phone number?'

She shook her head. Using her napkin she wiped her lips delicately. She drank some more tea. He had hoped to catch her off guard but it hadn't worked.

'That's a secret,' she said with a ravishing smile.

'We don't seem to be getting anywhere,' he remarked abruptly.

'Patience, Tweed.' She touched his arm. 'I don't think you've realized it but I'm scared stiff.'

'Why?'

'Because I was involved in the Appledore business.'

'In what way?'

'A Mr Charterhouse asked me to go to Appledore two weeks ago. I had to photograph the whole front, then the sea front further out beyond the estuary – where it flows into the sea. He phoned me at my flat here in London, gave me instructions, said there would be a fee of £3,000. He also said if I'd go to my front door I'd find an envelope with half the fee inside. The balance would be paid as soon as he had the photographs. I went to the front door when his call ended and found thirty £50 notes in an envelope.'

'Posted from where?'

'No postmark. It had obviously been hand delivered while I was on the phone. I'm short of cash, so I drove to Appledore and did the job for him. When I got back another blank envelope – with £1,500 inside it – was lying on the doormat.'

'Mr Charterhouse, did you say? Have you met him?'

'Never. His only communication was the weird phone call.'

'Weird in what way?'

'It didn't sound like a human being at all. More like one of those talking robots you see on TV.'

'And why would he choose you for this assignment, I wonder?'

'You're interrogating me. I can't blame you. I turn up out of nowhere. I can only assume he chose me because I'm a professional photographer. Not all that well known. But I have had lucrative assignments for society weddings, for magazine features. I have a reputation for reliability.'

'And when you'd taken these photos at Appledore how did you deliver them to the elusive Mr Charterhouse?'

'That was weird. I did what he'd told me to do over the phone. Two days later, after I'd developed and printed the pics, I put them in a large plain envelope. Then at exactly 10 p.m. I left the envelope in a phone box in Curzon Street, got back into my car, drove away.'

'Did you see anyone in Curzon Street?'

'Only a man in the phone box as I drove towards it. Later I decided he'd held the box until I arrived. He came out before I reached it, got into a car and drove away.'

'Can you describe him? And the car? Did you note its registration number?'

'Heavens, Tweed, which question first?' She smiled at him invitingly. 'The man who'd occupied the phone box was medium height, wore a dark overcoat and a Borsalino hat. I never saw his face. No one else was about. I did what I was told, dropped the envelope inside the box, got back into my car and drove straight off. I'm a good girl.' She was gazing round the restaurant, which was still busy. 'If you'll excuse me I'm going to the ladies'.'

'One brief question while I remember. Why are you scared stiff? I think that was the phrase you used.'

'Well, wouldn't you be? I did a job in Appledore. Then this Sam Sneed does another job in the same place – and ends up headless.'

Grabbing her coat, she threaded her way through the crowd to the cloakroom. The door was opposite to their table in the far wall. Tweed paid the bill, then sat thinking about her. On their way in, as she had walked in front of him, he had observed not only her elegant movements, but that she walked with a steely tread. Not a woman to scare easily.

After waiting ten minutes he began to worry that she was feeling ill in the cloakroom. He had watched

67

the cloakroom exit but there had been a lot of to-ing and fro-ing. A waitress came up to him.

'Excuse me, sir. A lady asked me to give you this message.'

He took the sealed envelope, sniffed at it. He caught a trace of the perfume she'd been wearing. He opened the envelope, unfolded the sheet of good quality paper. No address at the top. Just the message, written in an educated hand which had character.

Tweed, thank you for the tea. Sorry to leave you.
But I saw someone in the restaurant. Love, Serena.

Now he knew why she had taken her fur coat with her. Standing up, he looked round, then walked at his usual deliberate pace, gazing round all the time. No sign of Yellow Hair. In the open room beyond the elevators he saw Paula, pretending to examine an antique. He went up to her.

'Where is your stunning companion?' she asked.

'She gave me the slip. We'll go down and find Newman and his Merc.'

'What's next?'

'Our appointment with Professor Saafeld in Holland Park this evening. We should know then whether what we saw at Appledore is a storm in a teacup, the result of an oil slick, or something extremely dangerous.'

6

The large house in Holland Park – a small mansion, in fact – was situated back from the road, three storeys high. Tweed and Paula had reached it by opening a tall wrought-iron gate and walking up a very short drive. On either side were rhododendron shrubs which gave Saafeld's house even more privacy. They mounted steps leading up to a massive front door, flanked by ancient lanterns which gave illumination.

'It's very quiet here,' Paula commented. 'I remember thinking that when we were last here.'

Tweed was pressing digits in a box attached to the wall. Then he waited. Paula commented on the amount of security. Floodlights, operated by sensors, had come on, blazing down on them. Normally she would have been facing the small garden, checking their safety. But she knew Pete Nield, who had followed them in, was hiding somewhere in the shrubs. Newman was in the road, standing behind his Merc. She had no idea where Butler had disappeared to.

A Judas flap in the door slid aside briefly, then closed. They next heard someone turning keys in the single Chubb and two Banham locks. The door swung inwards and a large man told them to enter. Once inside, in a small hall paved with a woodblock floor, the door was closed, the locks turned.

Charles Saafeld was an imposing figure. Taller than Tweed, he was wearing a white smock buttoned to the neck. His build suggested a bon vivant, fond of his food and wine, which Tweed knew to be the case. In his sixties, his round, plump face had a pinkish complexion and he exuded an air of authority. He looked at Paula over his half-moon glasses.

'How are you? You look fit. I recall you're not squeamish. Welcome to the Chamber of Horrors. Let's get on with it.' He looked at Tweed. 'Something very odd here.'

He spoke in staccato bursts. His manner was courteous but he didn't like wasting time. His movements were quick and he led them briskly to a slablike door at the rear of the hall. His right hand started tapping digits in a box similar to the one outside the front door.

'You have a lot of extra security since I was last here,' Paula remarked. 'And why "Chamber of Horrors"?'

'Phrase used once by a tabloid paper. Cranks had the idea I was experimenting on corpses. Too many idle people with crackpot notions. Down we go. Mind the steps. Hold on to the rail.'

The slab had opened. Saafeld led the way, followed by Paula and Tweed, down into the large basement, a very large room, temperature-controlled. At first glance it looked like a laboratory. A system of perspex pipes ran across the ceiling, illuminated by fluorescent tubes. From the pipes ran more of the same, attached to chemical retorts and other equipment on white plastic tables. On the far wall Paula saw large metal drawers built into the walls, the containers for bodies.

A small man with beady eyes, agile, with a nut-cracker jaw and also wearing a white smock, looked at the newcomers as though they might be potential specimens.

'This,' said Saafeld, 'is Dr Fischer, expert on all forms of life inhabiting the seas and rivers. No pun on his name.'

'The number of times idiots have made that pun,' Fischer said, lips pursed.

'We'll start with the dead fisherman,' Saafeld continued. 'A chap called Gravely, so Roy Buchanan tells me. Again, no pun. I've completed the autopsy. Gather he fell overboard from a fishing vessel. He was dead before he reached the water – or the moment he did so.'

'Heart attack?' Tweed queried.

'Definitely not. He stopped breathing. Lack of oxygen.'

'I assumed he'd drowned,' Paula ventured.

70

'Definitely not. No water in the lungs. The only conclusion I've come to is he was asphyxiated – suffocated, if you like. No oxygen.'

'Strangled?' Tweed suggested.

'Definitely not. No such marks on the neck.'

'I don't understand,' said Tweed.

'Join the club. We don't either. Won't show you the corpse. Might spoil your dinner. I've removed several organs for fresh examination. Don't expect to find anything more. Listen to Fischer. You still won't understand.'

They moved further into the basement. Fischer was standing by another table. It held tanks of fish swimming around and canisters of transparent liquid. Paula thought she recognized them as the canisters used at Appledore to take samples of the sea.

'If you don't grasp something I've said, tell me,' Fischer began, addressing his remarks to Paula. 'I'll rephrase what I've said. It's complicated, but I'll try and keep it simple. You know how fish breathe?'

'Through their gills.'

'Correct. A fish has no lungs. It breathes through what we call gills, a complex system for filtering oxygen out of the water. There's only a small amount of oxygen in the sea – far less than on land. That's all they need to survive. Put a fish on the beach and it expires – even though it's surrounded by huge amounts of oxygen. The gills can't cope, don't work. So the fish dies.'

'Buchanan,' Saafeld interjected, 'told me they've found tons of dead fish at Appledore. So many they've used giant mechanical scoops to clear the beach.'

'Did you understand me so far?' demanded Fischer, obviously annoyed at being interrupted.

'Yes,' said Tweed and Paula together.

'In other words,' Fischer went on in his lecturer's

71

manner, 'the fish were asphyxiated. No oxygen at all in the sea.'

'Like the fisherman,' Tweed suggested.

'Yes and no. As I've explained, the breathing systems of men and fish are very different. Now we come to the seal, which makes everything even more mysterious. I've carried out an autopsy, let us say . . .' Fischer's eyes kept staring at Paula's, then at Tweed's. As though he was checking their concentration to make sure they understood. 'It was quite a job but I've done it.'

'You know how the seal died?' asked Tweed.

'I know *why* it died, which is a different matter. First, you'd better know how seals function, how they breathe. Unlike fish, seals have lungs. Also, again unlike fish, they are covered with fur and have a system circulating warm blood. Their lungs give them the ability to store oxygen which they can use over a period of time. A kind of reserve supply, if you like. Which is why they can exist on land. Saafeld, could you tell our visitors the incident Superintendent Buchanan related?'

'There was a witness,' Saafeld began brusquely. 'An inhabitant of Instow, a hamlet on the river shore opposite Appledore. He saw the seal surface, start to climb a rock, then immediately collapse back into the river. That must have been before you and Paula saw it drift ashore,' he explained, turning to Tweed.

'What is the significance of that?' Paula enquired.

'Significant is the word,' Fischer agreed. 'There was not only no oxygen in the water – hence the thousands of dead fish – but there was also no oxygen in the air above the water. That is why the seal died instantly – it came up to replenish its oxygen supply in its lungs and there wasn't any.'

'Which I find disturbing,' Saafeld interjected. 'I think it's time to show them your experiment, Fischer.'

'It's fortunate,' Fischer said, 'that someone thought

72

of taking water specimens as the dead specimens came ashore – and then a bit later when the tide turned. You see what is on this table.'

'Tanks of fish – a lot I don't recognize, and herring. Then two canisters which look like the ones used at Appledore to collect water,' Paula said.

'Correct.' Fischer picked up a transparent scoop with a long handle and a mesh cap which he opened by pressing a trigger. 'Your two canisters,' he went on, moving down the bench.

'Labelled, for some reason,' Paula noted.

'For a good reason,' Fischer told her. 'This one contains water taken after the tide turned. Now watch.'

He used the scoop to dip in the large tank and capture a herring. He quickly held the scoop over the canister, used the trigger to lift the mesh lid, dropped the contents into the canister. The fish began swimming rapidly inside the canister, touching the transparent walls, swimming on.

'Seems quite happy,' Paula commented.

'It's normal environment. Sea water. Now watch what happens when we perform the same experiment with the other canister – which contains water collected as the dead fish were still coming ashore.'

Paula clutched the strap of her shoulder bag more tightly. An atmosphere of tension had suddenly gripped the laboratory. With the same care Fischer used another scoop to capture a herring from the large tank. He removed a lid from the second canister, dropped the fish inside quickly, clamped the lid shut. The fish hit the water, struggled for a second, turned over, slowly sank to the bottom.

'Dead as the dodo,' said Fischer. 'The gills tried to take in air – oxygen, dissolved in the sea – and there wasn't any. Almost instantaneous death.'

'That's horrible,' exclaimed Paula.

'I think,' Saafeld said decisively, 'you've had enough of the unfamiliar atmosphere of a laboratory. We'll repair back up to the hall. I'll be back, Fischer . . .'

'I don't like what you showed us,' Tweed said when Saafeld had closed the slab door and they stood in the hall.

'You're going to like it even less. There's something else.'

Reaching inside his pocket, he brought out a transparent sample envelope of the type used by the police. He opened his hand and inside the envelope Paula saw a tiny transparent perspex cylinder. She estimated it was no more than a quarter of an inch in diameter, hardly more than half an inch in height. She had never seen such a small container.

'This was discovered, obviously washed ashore, among a mess of dead fish by some policeman at Appledore. Crake, I think his name was. Buchanan had it flown to him in London, then loaned it to me – knowing you were coming.'

'You think the poison was emptied out of that container?' suggested Paula.

'Don't use the word poison. Agent is the word,' Saafeld told her.

'We heard a powerboat disappearing out to sea,' Tweed recalled. 'Someone aboard could have emptied the contents of that tiny phial into the sea. Possible?'

'I'm a scientist,' Saafeld said abruptly. 'I never speculate.'

'If enough of this agent filled one of those canisters down in the lab,' Tweed mused, 'then it was introduced into the water supply of a country, what would be the effect?'

'Millions and millions would die, I suppose,' Saafeld replied. 'There you go, catching me on the wrong foot – speculating.'

74

'Any chance of identifying the agent which caused the havoc?'

'I would have you know – ' Saafeld gazed at Tweed grimly – 'we have analysed for hours and hours. Using every known test to identify the agent. The result? Nothing.'

'Goslar has invented the ultimate weapon of war,' Tweed said half to himself. He looked at Saafeld. 'If you do identify the agent I'm sure you'll phone me. If I'm away speak to Monica. Use just one word. *Breakthrough.*'

'Don't hold your breath for that call.'

7

The next development in the growing crisis hit Tweed the moment he walked into his office, followed by Paula, Newman, Butler and Nield.

'You'll be pleased,' Monica greeted him as he took off his coat.

'Please me, then.'

'While you were out this evening Cord Dillon phoned. To tell you he'll be aboard a flight from the US of A tomorrow. He expects to arrive here before lunch. He also emphasized it was a private visit, and he'd appreciate it if you kept it that way.'

'I see,' Tweed replied, looking anything but pleased as he relaxed in his chair.

'You don't look very happy,' Paula commented. 'The Deputy Director of the CIA is an old pal of yours. Again, I'm confused. What is happening?'

'What is happening,' Tweed said grimly, 'is Goslar is orchestrating his master plan step by step. I've said before, he really is a brilliant planner.'

'Explanation, please,' Paula pressed.

'First – if she was telling the truth at Fortnum's – he organizes Serena Cavendish to go down and photograph the whole scene of his future action from the shore. Because he knows he'll only see it from the sea when he arrives in his powerboat. That is a guess.'

'Why lure you there?'

'Two reasons. One, he knows I'll bring in some heavy talent from the police. Buchanan will swiftly inform the Home Secretary who, in his turn, will inform the Cabinet. A menacing cat among the pigeons. Two, he's confident he'll beat me again, as he did all those years ago. That should ruin my career. It's personal. That's just the beginning of the orchestration.'

'I'm all ears – that's why I look so funny,' she said, deliberately trying to reduce the teasion building up in the office. 'Now, go on.'

'His next move – a key one – is to hire Sam Sneed to video what happened. The original is handed to an emissary from a powerful and hostile state which is now controlled by fundamentalist Muslims. He'll also have had a copy of the *Daily Nation* sent to the head of that state by a fast international carrier.'

'Why?' asked Newman.

'I'll come to that later. Next he shoots the messenger, his normal technique. In this case Sam Sneed, who ends up decapitated. He knows this will hit the press. The *Evening Standard*, as you've now all seen, has splashed the story. Naturally – it's sensational news. The momentum of Goslar's orchestration balloons.'

'But, as Bob asked, why?' enquired Paula.

'All in good time. René Lasalle phones me from an outside call box, warns me the Élysée is interested. The President of France, no less. My bet is one of Sneed's copies of that video was sent to the Élysée. He'll have seen the *Daily Nation* too.'

'I won't say "why" again,' Paula promised.

76

'Don't. Now we hear Cord Dillon is en route to see me. With a request that his visit be kept quiet. Echoes of Lasalle asking me not to report his phone call. So I'm sure another video was sent by fast international carrier to the Oval Office. For the President of the United States. For all I know another one went to Berlin and to Tokyo. No, not to Tokyo – they haven't got the money.'

'The money?' Newman queried.

'Yes, the money. Goslar is going to make a killing – no pun intended, as Saafeld would say. The money to buy this ultimate weapon which makes the hydrogen bomb passé.'

There was a heavy silence in the room as they absorbed what Tweed had said. He asked Monica to be kind enough to fetch him something to eat and drink from the nearby all-night delicatessen. Tweed took off his hornrims, extracted a clean folded handkerchief from his pocket, polished them, replaced them on the bridge of his nose. Then he leaned forward, hands clasped on his desk.

'Whichever country buys that hideous weapon is automatically the leading power on the planet. It can threaten larger states, bend them to its will. In short, rule the world. We do have rather a lot on our plate.'

'What's the next move?' Newman wanted to know.

'I have no idea. Yet . . .'

As he spoke the door opened and Marler walked in. Paula blinked. For a moment she didn't recognize him. On the bridge of his nose was perched a strange pair of glasses, with large squarish lenses and thin rims. They were pushed back close to his eyes, gave him an aggressive look, menacing. He was clad in a foreign-looking anorak, zipped up to the neck, foreign-looking slacks and shoes.

'What on earth have you been up to?' Paula asked.

'Been to Paris and back, haven't I? Caught a flight out by the skin of my teeth. Same thing coming back. Hired a car at Charles de Gaulle. Drove French drivers mad as I cut them off, missed others by inches. Their cry, *Merde!*, *Merde!* must have been heard in Marseilles.'

'The object of this exercise?' Tweed demanded.

'To visit my top contact in Paris. A jewel in the underworld. You have to meet him very soon. You're almost as fluent in French as I am. These damned glasses.' He took them off, sighed with relief, looked at Paula. 'The latest thing – made of Flexon, very flexible metal frames. This pair is Calvin Klein. I got them to put plain glass in quickly. Do that a lot, I gather. Frenchmen find they make girls swoon into their arms.'

'This contact you met,' Tweed said impatiently. 'He gave you information?'

'Yes and no. He insists on meeting the top man. Which is why you have to go and see him.'

'We're going to Paris – after I've met Cord Dillon, who is flying over to see me tomorrow. Unofficially. So officially he never came to London. Now, this contact. What is his name? What does he do? Where will I meet him?'

'That's wicked of you,' Marler said with mock severity. 'You do know I keep their identities secret – all my contacts, I mean.'

'But if I'm meeting him I'll know who he is, where he is.'

'True.' Marler paused, then walked over to the wall close to Paula, turned, leaned against it. 'You remember the Île de la Cité, of course?'

'Of course. We could have a meal at that marvellous Restaurant Paul on the Place Dauphine. Superb food. Go on.'

'You'll also remember the footbridge linking Cité to another island in the Seine – the Isle St-Louis.'

'Yes. Do get on with it.'

'My contact's bookshop is in a side street off the Rue St-Louis en Île.'

'Name of contact?'

'You're interrogating me.'

'He's in that mood,' Paula commented.

'Vallade. Étienne Vallade. He deals in very rare books. That gives him entreé to some pretty high-up people in the security services – and the government. But I emphasize he'll only talk to you.'

'Did you mention the name Goslar?'

'I did. That's when he closed down. He looked frightened. He then said – I quote him, "I'll only discuss this with your chief, Tweed."'

'That's interesting. He knows my name.'

'I told you he was a jewel.'

'Now, Marler,' Tweed said, his tone serious, 'I'd better brief you on everything that's happened so far. The others will have to put up with hearing it twice – but it may hammer it into their heads. The sequence is important. But first I'll jump forward and tell you about our meeting with Professor Saafeld . . .'

Marler lit a king-size as he continued leaning against the wall. His manner suggested he was hardly listening but Tweed knew he was memorizing every word.

'So,' Tweed eventually concluded, 'you've heard about Saafeld and Fischer, and my analysis of the brilliant way Goslar has orchestrated this business. One more thing – ' he became very emphatic, his eyes moving from one member of his team to another – 'this is going to be the most dangerous assignment we have ever undertaken. We are up against Goslar and his vast organization, but on top of that I'm sure Bate and his

Special Branch, a rough lot, will appear on the scene as rivals sooner or later. And, as though that isn't enough, the French security services, their police and Lord knows who else over there are the enemy.'

'And all of them after the Holy Grail,' Marler remarked. '"The Holy Grail" – not really a good description of the most devilish weapon ever devised.'

'We need more people,' Paula said quietly. 'I think that has already been said.'

As though on cue, the door opened and the Director, Howard, sailed into the room. A plump-faced man, over six feet tall, he had a build which suggested he liked gourmet food and wine – and didn't hesitate to indulge in what he liked. He had a lordly manner and an upper-crust voice.

'Great news for you, Tweed,' he announced as he occupied an armchair and placed his right leg over the arm. 'I have reinforcements. Two chaps – both out of the top drawer. I'm sure someone will have heard of the first one. Captain Alan Burgoyne, ex-military intelligence. Gulf War and all that.'

'I've heard of him,' said Newman. 'What he found out in Iraq changed the whole Allied strategy.'

'Ah!' Howard swung round the face Newman. 'The filthy rich, world-famous international correspondent. Expect a wallah like you to get the message.'

'A wallah like me reported the Gulf War,' Newman retorted with an expression of distaste as he gazed back at the Director.

Howard, in his sixties, had greying hair, was clean-shaven and, as always, impeccably – expensively – dressed. He wore a blue Chester Barrie pin-striped suit from Harrods, a cream shirt, blue Chanel tie and gleaming black shoes.

'Burgoyne has got fed up with the army, retired recently of his own volition.'

'Probably,' drawled Marler, 'got fed up with taking crackpot instructions from superior officers with plummy voices. The type that always sports the old school tie.'

Howard frowned, stared hard at Marler, as though he didn't like the description. Marler transferred his king-size to his left hand, gave Howard a mock salute with his right, grinned.

'Despite his record,' Tweed broke in quickly, 'I can't take him on until he's been thoroughly vetted.'

'Already done, old chap,' Howard assured him. 'By myself. And I really put him through the hoops. Then checked independently. Isn't that the way you'd have proceeded?'

'Something like that.'

'Come on, boys and girls,' Howard protested. 'Show us a bit of enthusiasm. I've pulled off a coup . . .'

'I'm not a girl any more,' Paula said icily. 'I'm thirtysomething, in case you'd forgotten.'

'Oh, my dear,' Howard faced her, 'I wasn't referring to you. Just a mode of expression. I know you went through hell in Paris. You do have all my sympathy.'

'Ancient history,' she said.

'And who is the other candidate?' Tweed asked.

'Candidate?' Howard was indignant. 'I've taken him on.'

'I haven't. Not yet. Who is he?'

'Evan Tarnwalk. From Special Branch. He resigned.'

'This sounds very tricky,' Tweed warned. 'Why did he resign?'

'Because he couldn't stand Bate any longer. No one can stand Bate. Swaggering around like a company sergeant-major, bullying his way to the top, stabbing subordinates in the back if they look like rivals.'

'I think you're going to say he had to be vetted to join Special Branch. That won't do for me. We'll have to do our own vetting.'

'Already done. Again by myself personally. You don't think I'd just accept the chap at face value, do you?'

'I'll have to talk to him.'

'He's a wizard at disguises,' Howard snapped.

'Then maybe we won't recognize him at a vital moment,' Newman suggested with a straight face.

'*God in Heaven!*' Howard exploded. 'Is that supposed to be funny?' He glanced at Paula. 'Do excuse me, my dear.'

And I wish you'd shut up callling me 'my dear', Paula thought.

'What other qualifications does this Tarnwalk possess?' Tweed enquired.

'He's a wonderful tracker. Can follow a target for hours without being spotted. Hence his flair for disguises.'

Howard turned to look at Newman, ready for another comment. Newman, studying a file, didn't look up. Tweed pursed his lips, then stretched his arms. He could take only so much of Howard.

'Where are these two candidates?'

'Alan Burgoyne is coming to see me in about an hour. Shall I send him down to you?'

'Phone me first. I may be up to my eyes in something.'

'Some people don't get any thanks for what they do,' Howard said resentfully and left the room.

'There,' said Monica, 'you've spoilt his surprise. Now he's disgruntled.'

'I'll thank him when I've seen them. Ever met this Burgoyne, Bob?'

'He was always elusive. Probably part of the secret of his success. Because successes he certainly had. And no, we've never met.'

Tweed looked at Butler and Nield. Ever since they

had sat down neither had said a word. Butler had listened to Howard without showing any reaction. Several times Nield had raised his eyes to the ceiling, as though to ask how much longer they had to stand Howard prattling on.

'What do both of you think of what Howard told us?' Tweed asked.

'I'll reserve judgement until I've seen them. Takes a long time to get a new addition to merge into the team.'

'Me too,' said the reserved Butler.

Tweed knew they had hit the nail on the head. Everyone in the room knew how the others would react in a dangerous situation. There were times when their swift reaction would save the lives of the other members – or even their own lives. Familiarity and trust were the key words.

'Tweed,' Paula said suddenly, 'I haven't had the chance till now. But I can tell you something about the mysterious Serena.'

'You can?' Tweed concealed his surprise. 'I'm very interested in any light you can cast on her background.'

'I'm going back to my teens, when I was a wild young thing. Only up to a point,' she emphasized. 'Lots of parties, in London and out in the country at mansions owned by aristocrats and dubious self-made men. There were coteries, groups of girls who went around together.'

'Did these coteries mingle with each other?'

'Not on your life. Sounds cliquey but that's the way it was. The Cavendish sisters were leading lights, but not in my crowd.'

'Sisters? Where is the other one now?' Tweed enquired, relaxing in his chair.

'No longer with us, I'm afraid. Serena and Davina were very much alike in appearance. Not twins, but one could pass for the other. They were devils. They used to wear each other's clothes, makeup, then one would go out with the other's boyfriend. The boyfriend rarely caught on he was taking out the sister. They were careful – no intimacy. Just for laughs.'

'Tell me about Davina.'

'She's dead, I'm afraid. She was the clever one. A brilliant mind. Had come down from university with a double first. In science and biology. It was a tragedy when she died.'

'How did it happen?'

'She was driving a sports car by herself in the country. In the middle of the night. She liked to ram her foot down. On a lonely bend she collided with a heavy truck. Her face was badly smashed up. She died instantly. Serena, who had gone to meet her, saw it happen.' Paula paused, shivered. 'Must have been terrible for Serena – and no one else was about. They never did find the driver of the truck. She's buried at Steeple Hampton in Hampshire. Serena was so upset she left the country, disappeared for years.'

'How long ago would this be?' Tweed asked quietly.

'Oh, quite a few years ago. I'm not sure how many.'

'And her parents?'

'Both died when the girls were in their early teens. Ironic. The parents also died in a car smash.'

'Anything more about Serena?'

'Somewhere abroad she took up photography, became good at it. I don't want you to get the impression Serena was dim. She wasn't. It was just that Davina was so brilliant. Her tutor once said she was well on her way to becoming one of the world's really great scientists.'

'You knew either of them – or both?'

'No, we never met. They were in a different set. Higher up the social ladder than mine.'

'Did the parents leave them money?'

84

'Not a penny. The father was an inveterate gambler. Left huge debts. A lawyer friend sorted out the estate, found a way to clear the debts. But that left them penniless. A wealthy boy friend of Davina's gave her the money for them to buy a small cottage at Steeple Hampton. That's about all I can tell you.'

'When did Serena surface in this country again?'

'I think it must have been about two years ago. She quickly established herself as a society photographer. Also she has a sparkling personality, which helps. Not a second David Bailey, but very good.'

'You must have seen her while we were having tea in Fortnum's. What was your impression of her?'

'You were quite a distance away, but she seemed animated and full of self-confidence. Very attractive. Wouldn't you agree?'

'Yes.' Tweed looked thoughtful. 'She has most unusual eyes. Several times I had the feeling she was looking straight through me. Slightly disturbing.'

'She was getting to you,' Paula said with a warm smile.

'And I think,' Tweed decided, 'it's time you went home. But not by yourself. Newman can drive you.'

'I don't think that's necessary.'

'Have you forgotten Sam Sneed so quickly?' Tweed asked ominously.

'It would mean leaving my car here,' she protested.

'I'll drive that back behind Newman,' Butler said. 'Just give me a tick to collect my kit. Never travel without it if I can help it.'

'His kit?' Paula queried when Butler left the room.

'He is an explosives expert,' Newman reminded her.

Butler parked her car behind Newman's Merc when they arrived at her flat, the upper storey of a small house in a mews off Fulham Road. Paula jumped out, with Newman and Butler close at her heels. She held the door key in her hand as she mounted the outside staircase which led to her flat.

'Don't insert that key,' Butler said roughly. 'Both of you go back to the car while I check this place out.'

'I'm not going back,' said Paula. 'I'm dying to get inside.'

Butler pushed in front of her. He looked at the front door, which had a Banham lock. Then he ran delicate fingers round the top and sides of the door. His expression became grim.

'Go back to the car, both of you. Don't argue. Stay there until I fetch you. I may be a while.'

From the car they watched Butler in the distance. Then they saw him disappear round the side. They sat chatting for over half an hour. Newman lit a cigarette. Butler had not reappeared. The next thing they knew was a heavy metal van pulling up beside them and two men in protective apparel running out to the house.

'That's the bomb squad from Park Crescent,' Paula said. 'I can't make out what's going on. The two men who have arrived are carrying a heavy metal box . . .'

'Just leave it to Harry. He knows what he's doing,' Newman assured her.

A few minutes later the front door opened, the two men came out carrying the metal box between them. Reaching the van, they took it to the rear doors, slid the box inside, locked the doors and drove off. Butler appeared, carrying his kit, walked to the car as Newman lowered the window.

'What on earth is happening?' Paula demanded.

'I'll tell you.' Butler bent closer to her. 'I think you said you were dying to get inside. That's what would have happened – you'd have died. The moment you turned your key a huge bomb planted behind the door would have detonated. It would have wrecked the house – and bits of what was left of you would probably have ended up on the far side of the street. I'm staying to double-check. Then I'll drive back to Park Crescent.'

'We'd better go now,' Newman said. 'Tweed will want to know about this.'

8

'What's happening to my bomb?' Paula asked, smiling ruefully as she gazed at Tweed.

'Your bomb,' Tweed informed her from behind his desk, 'will now be clear of London. The A3 will be quiet at this hour. They are taking it to the training mansion in Surrey.'

'I imagine they'll dismantle it there.'

'Harry phoned me while Bob was driving you back here. They will photograph the mechanism thoroughly, but no attempt will be made to dismantle it. It's an entirely new and sophisticated device. Trust Goslar to come up with an advanced variety. After it's been photographed it will be detonated in the quarry. Probably bring down half the rock face, according to Harry.'

'You'll tell Buchanan, I imagine.'

'Only after the thing's been detonated. Roy will be furious, but at least I'll send him copies of the photos – for his own Bomb Squad people to browse over.' He looked up as the door opened. 'Enter Marler and Pete Nield . . .'

Tweed quickly told them about what had happened at Paula's flat. Marler gave a slow whistle, went to Paula, squeezed her arm affectionately.

'You lead a charmed life.'

'It's my virtuous habits,' she said with another smile.

'Now, Nield,' Tweed began, 'have there been any watchers outside our building today?'

'There have,' Nield told him. 'Marler can tell you.'

'We've just come in from having a chat with Alf of the East End mob,' Marler reported. 'Alf and his buddies in their cabs have been patrolling the area at intervals. They caught some fish.'

'Tell me.'

'Early this afternoon Alf spotted a watcher. English chap, well dressed, hanging around and pretending to read a newspaper. The second time round, half an hour later, the watcher was still there. Alf pulled up, told him there'd been a lot of burglaries round here, that he'd had time to read his paper three times over, so he was informing the police. Chap swore at him foully, walked off.'

'Then there was another of them,' Nield said. 'After dark in early evening. Same technique – the watcher leaning against a wall, also pretending to read a paper. English, again smartly dressed. Bill, one of Alf's pals, saw him off.'

'And now?'

'Nobody. Marler and I have just toured round. Coast is clear.'

'Interesting,' Tweed mused, 'that he uses smartly turned out Englishmen. Typical of Goslar not to employ scruffs. I wonder where he gets them from? Private detective agencies? I think not.'

'Alf's guess,' Marler explained, 'is the watchers are men on drugs. Cocaine, probably. His chap was jittery, as though in need of his next fix.'

'Sounds likely. That type needs a constant supply of money – and Goslar was always generous with cash for services rendered. Until he had them eliminated.'

'I've been wondering about that,' Paula said. 'That business of Goslar always shooting the messenger.

Maybe I was a messenger of a sort. I brought back the description of Goslar.'

'Paula, you brought back the description of a man who called himself Goslar – or rather Abel did. If you'd been wiped out by that bomb I might have thought your description was accurate. Or that you'd been killed so you couldn't describe him. But he knows me – would assume you'd come straight here to describe him.'

'Are you saying that man in rimless glasses wasn't Goslar?'

'I'm sure it wasn't.'

'What a diabolical mind he has.'

'Well, we are dealing with the Devil himself. Oh, Monica, re-book us all on the latest flight to Paris tomorrow. Late so I can see Cord Dillon first.'

'And I'll be watching over you,' Newman said firmly.

'Then,' Tweed continued, 'book us rooms at the Ritz in Paris – in our real names. I don't want it to appear we're together when we arrive at the hotel.'

'Then,' Paula suggested, 'I'd better take turns with Monica. She books in some of us, I book in the rest.'

'Clever idea,' Tweed agreed.

'Could you tell us why we're going to Paris?' she enquired. 'I know—'

'Three things,' Tweed interjected. 'First, I want us when we arrive to go by hired car straight to La Défense. You will be able to identify the building where those thugs held you?'

'Absolutely!'

'Second, we visit Marler's contact, Vallade, rare-book dealer on the Île St-Louis.'

'Take Paula in with you,' Marler advised. 'I'll be there. Vallade may not be as young as he once was – he is still susceptible to attractive women.'

'Thank you. Third, I want a brief word with Lasalle about something.'

'Lasalle!' Paula exclaimed. 'From what you said, at present he won't give you the time of day.'

'René and I go back a long time. I think I can persuade him to tell me what I'm after. So we'll be busy in that beautiful city.'

The phone rang. Monica listened briefly, then looked at Tweed. She was grinning.

'You've got a treat. Howard says he has Captain Alan Burgoyne with him, that he could see you now.'

'Wheel him in, I suppose.'

Paula stared at the man who entered the room, her interest aroused at once. Burgoyne was of medium height, and muscular – which showed in his face and hands. In his forties, she guessed. Athletic, with a spring in his tread, and a strong face with a hint of humour in his expression. The moment he entered his clever blue eyes had scanned everyone in the room. Paula decided he already had a mental picture of everyone present.

He wore a camouflage jacket and his beige slacks had a razor-edged crease. His well-polished brown shoes had thick rubber soles. He would move as silently as a cat, she thought. Burgoyne looked at Paula, slapped his jacket twice with a tanned hand.

'Excuse this. Makes me look a bit like a thug, which I suppose I am. But there are a lot of them about these days.' He smiled at her as he spoke. 'Helps me to merge with the crowd. Which is the general idea, said he hopefully.'

'Do please sit down,' said Tweed, his tone neutral.

'Thank you. I guess you are Tweed.'

'Yes. What do we call you? Here we're on first-name terms.'

90

'Not Alan, please,' Burgoyne said. 'Never liked the name. Why not call me Chance – my nickname in the army.'

'Why Chance?' asked Paula.

'They all used to call me that.' He swivelled round to look again at Paula. 'Because I took chances a lot. Now please don't get the wrong impression. By chance I mean taking a coldly calculated risk – after weighing up the odds.'

'From your track record you weighed them up well,' Tweed remarked.

'I know a general who wouldn't agree. A stuffed shirt back at HQ. Never seen a bullet fired in anger. If you do decide to take me on, there'll be a document to sign, I imagine.'

'You've signed the Official Secrets Act at some time?'

'I have.' Burgoyne looked at Newman, grinned. 'I can recite the Official Secrets Act backwards – and it makes more sense that way.'

'You could be right.' Newman smiled back. 'We don't go in for a load of bumf here.'

Paula was watching Burgoyne closely. She liked his remark, 'If you do decide to take me on.' She detected plenty of self-confidence – but not a trace of arrogance. Burgoyne looked round at everybody again, meeting their gaze eye to eye. Behind his back Monica held up a piece of paper. On it she had scrawled, 'Paris?'

Tweed nodded. Then he stared at Burgoyne, his expression very serious. He spoke quietly.

'Chance, is there someone at the MoD I can talk to about you?'

'Colonel Bernard Gerrard. Don't expect him to be too complimentary about me.'

'I know him. I'll give him a call. Pack a small bag. And be ready here in the morning for a possible departure tomorrow. Now I suggest you return to Howard . . .'

'What do you think?' he asked everyone after Burgoyne had left. 'You're the ones who'd have to work with him.'

'I like him,' Paula said promptly.

'Looks pretty tough to me,' Newman commented.

'We could at least try him out,' Marler suggested.

'I'm not sure,' Butler told Tweed. 'He could be a loose cannon,' he added. Nield agreed.

Tweed asked Monica to see if she could get Colonel Gerrard on the phone. After a few minutes she waved her phone at him and nodded.

'Bernard, Tweed here.'

'Long time no see. I'm sure you want something from me.'

'I was thinking of using Captain Alan Burgoyne sometime. What do you think?'

'He's a wild card.' There was a pause. 'Haven't seen sight or sound of him since he retired over a year ago. Half a mo. I'm forgetting something. Seven months ago he visited Kuwait off his own bat. He went to see what Saddam was up to. Sent me a report by courier. It said Saddam was in the market for the ultimate weapon, whatever that meant. I just filed it.'

'And after that?'

'Heard he'd retired to some village on Dartmoor called Rydford. Which fitted in with his character. His pension is sent to a bank in London.'

'That's all?'

'Tweed, I haven't been very positive. Burgoyne pulled off some amazing coups. The type of thing no one else would have dared attempt. He was particularly daring – and effective – in the Gulf War. Gave us information about Saddam's Presidential Guard which changed our strategy. Can't give you any details.'

'You've heard from him since?'

'Not a dicky bird. Which is what I'd expect. He's a

loner. All right, I'll go overboard – he was a brilliant intelligence officer. Come to think of it, you're the sort of chap he would take orders from – something about your personality. Let's have a drink together one day.'

'We'll do that.'

Tweed sat back in his chair, told the others everything Gerrard had said, word for word. Newman ran a hand through his fair hair.

'I'm impressed. Those MoD types rarely say anything so positive about one of their own.'

'We need extra manpower,' Paula insisted. 'He's dynamic and, I think, very clever.'

'I agree,' Tweed told her. 'I wonder where on earth Rydford is?'

'I've found it,' said Paula. She had an Ordnance Survey map open on her desk. 'It appears to be a very small place off the main road from Moretonhampstead to Princeton. It's located just under Hangman's Tor.'

'Very encouraging,' said Butler.

The phone rang. Tweed looked at the ceiling. Monica answered, then looked at Tweed.

'You'll never guess who's on the phone wanting to talk to you urgently.'

'I'm not even going to guess.'

'Serena Cavendish. Long distance . . .'

'I'll have a word with her . . . Serena? You walked out on me,' he said, his voice cold.

'Didn't you get my note? I gave it to a waitress, with a big tip.'

'I got it. You could have come back to the table and told me.'

'I was so frightened by a man I saw watching me from another table, I panicked.'

'You didn't think I'd be sufficient protection for you, then?'

'I told you. I panicked . . .'

93

'Describe the man.'

'Not now. I'm in one hell of a rush. But I have information about Appledore. Could you pop over to Paris tomorrow? We can arrange a rendezvous.'

'Tomorrow is impossible. Maybe the day after. Or the day after that. How would I contact you – if I can make it.'

'Take down this number ... Got it? Good. A man will answer. It's a small café opposite where I'm staying. Say you're Maurice and want to speak to Yvonne. That's me. He'll dart across the road and fetch me. You shouldn't have to wait more than a couple of minutes. Try to call that number between 9 a.m. and noon, local time. You'll be glad you did.'

'Where are you speaking from now?'

'Brussels. You sound so unfriendly. You'll be glad you came when you hear what I have to tell you. Must dash. Greetings . . .'

Tweed put down the phone. He waited a moment, then picked it up again and asked for the international operator.

'Operator, I've just been speaking to someone who called me from the Continent. She gave me her number in Brussels. Unfortunately the call was broken in mid-sentence. Can you help me? The line wasn't all that clear and I must call her back.'

'Did you say Brussels, sir?'

'I think that's what she said. But there was a lot of crackle.'

'There must have been. I handled that call myself. It was from Paris.'

'It *was* a bad line. Thank you so much . . .'

Tweed looked at the others. He reported the whole gist of the phone call. He asked them what they thought.

'Serena is devious,' Paula reflected. 'Odd that she

should be in Paris, where I had my little experience. What are you going to do?'

'It's what *we* are going to do. If I recall correctly, you said the Cavendish sisters had a cottage in Steeple Hampton. That's in Hampshire. I recall seeing a turning off to the village on the A303 just beyond the Barton Stacey area.'

'You're right.' Paula had glanced at the map still open on her desk. 'You've been there?'

'No. I noticed the signpost when I was driving to the West Country over a year ago.'

'You do have a remarkable memory.'

'I need it. I rely on my memory – and my observation for detail. Did you notice Burgoyne has just a slight limp? Right leg?'

'No, I didn't.'

'Probably result of a war wound. I must phone Gerrard at the MoD tomorrow and ask him if Burgoyne was injured. Slipped my mind.'

'Is he coming with us to Paris?' Paula asked.

'I haven't decided. I want to think it over.' He looked at Monica. 'We can always cancel his air and hotel bookings if I decide against. Now, Paula, I want you to come with me to Steeple Hampton early tomorrow. A woman notices things a man misses.'

'I'll be glad to join you. Why are we going there?'

'I want to get all the background I can on Serena. There may be people in the village who knew the sisters.'

'You have to be back for when Cord Dillon arrives,' she warned.

'I know. If we start early we can do it easily. Not all that long to get there.'

'With you driving like the clappers it won't be long.'

'So, I think,' said Tweed, 'you ought to go home, get

95

to bed in good time. I'll call for you at seven. Not too early? Good.'

'I'll drive Paula home,' Newman decided. 'We can get a bite to eat on the way. I could stand guard over her during the night – considering what has happened.'

'I'd be grateful for that, Bob,' Paula agreed. 'And you could sleep on the couch in the living room.'

'Then let's get cracking,' said Newman, standing up. 'Tweed, I think I should come with the two of you tomorrow.'

'Won't be necessary. Enjoy your meal . . .'

He waited until they had gone, followed by Marler, Butler and Pete Nield. Then he asked Monica to scribble the MoD number on a bit of paper. She did so and handed it to him.

'I'll phone Bernard Gerrard from my flat before I leave in the morning. He's an early-bird-catches-the-worm type. Always in his office from 6 a.m. onwards.'

'He ought to work for us,' Monica commented with a wicked smile.

'What glorious countryside,' Paula enthused the following morning as Tweed drove along the A303. 'It's good to get away from town.'

The sky was overcast with grey clouds scudding east but there was a fresh breeze. Tweed, behind the wheel, had his window open. On either side of them fields stretched away into the distance. Many had been ploughed and brown clods of earth were covered with frost. When a shaft of sunlight broke through it gave the fields a crystaline appearance. Paula glanced at Tweed.

'I could have sworn you're carrying a gun in a hip holster.'

'I am.'

'That's very rare for you. And we are in England.'

'Sam Sneed was beheaded in England. Also, we are being followed,' he said with mock seriousness.

'I know.' She glanced again in the wing mirror. 'By Newman in his Merc. Against your orders.'

'I think he'll keep well away from us in Steeple Hampton. And we're very close to the turn-off. Yes, here it is.'

He slowed down, swung off the highway down a narrow lane after passing a signpost. *Steeple Hampton.* The lane twisted and turned. Tweed had slowed to a crawl. Paula expressed approval.

'Well,' he explained, 'you never know what's round the next bend. Maybe a whacking great farm tractor which assumes it has the right of way. I suppose it does – it belongs here, we don't.'

'Do you think we may be too early? I imagine you'll want to talk to some locals.'

'Too early?' Tweed chuckled. 'In these isolated villages they live as they did long ago. Early to bed, early to rise. Farm workers want to make use of all the daylight. And here we are – what there is of it.'

Steeple Hampton was one street of old cottages. Near the end a church spire like a spike bisected the sky which was now blue and cloudless. Small gardens, neatly kept behind gated walls, fronted the cottages. There was a pub, the Black Bull. Outside, a white-haired man was sweeping a paved area.

'That's the chap we need,' Tweed said, pulling up and getting out.

'What a lovely morning,' Tweed said cheerfully.

'If it lasts.'

'Nice-looking pub.'

'We're not open till twelve – if it was a pint you wanted.'

He had gnarled hands gripping the bristle broom. His skin was weatherbeaten, his shoulders stooped, his voice had a tinge of some local accent. He managed a smile at Paula, who had alighted with Tweed.

'Come the wrong way, 'ave we? Lots of folk do, specially in summer. Where you 'eading for?'

'We're where we wanted to come to,' Paula replied with a warm smile. 'Steeple Hampton. I had two girl friends who lived here years ago. The Cavendish sisters . . .'

'Ah! Davina and Serena. Nice ladies. Always 'ad a word for me when they came into village.' He paused. 'Suppose you know? The tragedy? Davina's gone.'

'Yes, I do know. Died in a car crash.'

'Shockin' business. Drivin' back to the cottage at three in the mornin' and hit by a truck. Musta been the size of Exeter Cathedral. I've only been here forty years. Comes from West Country, I does. Truck driver was an 'it-and-run. Police never did find 'im. The cottage is still 'ere.'

'It's years since I knew them,' Paula went on. 'Some- one told me Serena still lives in the cottage. I'd like to see it.'

'See the church? The cottage is just beyond it, on its own. Hedgerow, it's called.' He was warming up. 'Serena still owns it. Hardly ever see her, though. Mrs Grew looks after it for her. Her husband tends the garden. A cheque comes regular for them. But it's ages since we've seen 'er.' He gestured with his free hand to the open countryside beyond the pub. 'See all that land? Once belonged to their father, Sir Osvald Cavendish. He gambled it all away on the 'orses. The big 'ouse, the land – all went to pay off his debts. Suppose that's why those sisters bought the cottage. Near where they was brought up.'

'Did you say Sir Osvald?' Tweed enquired.

'I did. Father was German.' He looked at an old fob watch he took from his pocket. 'If you goes up to cottage now you'll probably find Mrs Grew there. She could tell you more. The sisters were so alike. Clever too. But the really clever one was Davina. Became a scientist. Who knows what she might 'ave discovered if she'd lived? Make you a cup of tea and a sandwich when you come back – if you're peckish.'

'That's very kind of you,' said Tweed. 'Let's see how we feel later . . .'

They got back into the car and drove slowly through the village. An old woman was on her knees in front of the doorstep of a cottage. She was scrubbing the doorstep Persil white.

'They do work,' Paula commented.

'That was how England used to be. There have been great changes – some very much for the better, others very much for the worse.'

While they had talked to the innkeeper Newman had crawled past them in his Merc. He hadn't given them a glance. Now he had his car backed into a track alongside the church – so he could drive whichever way we leave, Tweed surmised. Newman had the bonnet up, was apparently attending to some mechanical defect. Tweed drove slowly past him.

'This is Hedgerow,' Paula said, pointing to a cottage standing away from the village. 'Maybe that woman weeding the garden is Mrs Grew.'

'Only one way to find out,' Tweed replied, stopping the car and getting out. 'Being a woman, you may have better luck with her,' he said quietly to Paula.

'Good morning,' Paula said cheerfully. 'Are you Mrs Grew?'

'I might be.'

The late middle-aged woman with grey hair, wearing gardening clothes, stood up from her kneeling mat. She dropped her gloves. Both hands were placed on her back as though it ached.

'I'm Paula. Years ago I knew Serena and Davina Cavendish. We met at parties in London. Days of youth. I thought I'd just call in as we were passing. Have a natter about old times.'

'Davina's gone. Her grave's in the yard behind the church.'

'I do know. It was Serena I thought I might meet. Oh, she isn't here. I gather Hedgerow still belongs to her. Does she come down often?'

'Never. At least not that I sees her. I think she does come. But always in the middle of the night. I cleans the cottage, so I knows where everything is. You can put things back thinking that's where you found them. But even a woman can get it wrong.' Her sharp eyes gleamed. 'Maybe she brings a feller. So they'd get here after dark and get away very early. Once I couldn't sleep. It was a warm night so I got dressed, came out for a short walk. All the lights were on behind the curtains in the cottage. And further up the road a car was parked on the verge. Facing the other way, which I thought was odd. Looked as though they'd come that way, then turned the car round. You can get back to the A303 that way, but it's a roundabout route. Much quicker the way you two came. I guessed they didn't want anyone to hear the car driving through the village.'

'How long ago would that incident have been?' Tweed asked.

'This is my boss,' Paula introduced. 'I work for him in London. He kindly offered to drive me down here.'

'Your boss.' Mrs Grew's eyes gleamed again. 'I see.'

Paula smiled to herself. Mrs Grew had already tagged her as Tweed's mistress. But funny things go on in villages.

'You asked how long ago,' Mrs Grew said, addressing Tweed. 'I'd say it must have been six months ago. They've been back since. I found a kitchen towel which was still damp from use. Those two sisters were as alike as two peas in a pod,' she continued. 'Davina was the clever one. Got a scholarship to Oxford to study science and biochemistry.'

'I think you mean biology,' Tweed interjected.

'When I say biochemistry I mean biochemistry.' She glared at him. 'I'd like to have had the chance to go to university. I read a lot. Every month I cycle to a second-hand bookshop in Andover. Science, travel, biography. Now I must get on.' She bent down to pick up her gloves but Tweed was quicker and handed them to her. 'Thank you.' She lowered herself back on to the kneeling mat, looked up. 'While you're here you might as well see Davina's grave. I look after it and the headstone.'

'Thank you,' said Paula. 'We've enjoyed talking to you.'

They walked back to the church. Fifty yards away Newman was still having 'trouble' with his car. He treated them as though they didn't exist.

Paula pushed open the shaky wooden gate into the churchyard. Tweed followed her as she made her way round the ivy-clad walls.

A weed-strewn path behind the church led to the graveyard. She found what they were looking for at the very back. The grave, unlike most of the others, was well tended. The headstone had been so carefully looked after it almost appeared new. They stood side by side, reading the modest wording.

DAVINA
Never to be forgotten
SERENA

9

They were driving back to London. The sun shone out of a duck-egg-blue sky. Passing the ploughed fields Paula noticed the frost had gone, exposing clearly the clods of brown earth. A flight of birds swooped above them. She looked at Tweed, who had a preoccupied expression.

'What did you think of Davina's grave?' she asked.

'Something unusual about it,' Tweed replied. 'Only a few words. No dates of her birth and death. Strange.'

'I thought so too. Was the trip worthwhile – from what the innkeeper and Mrs Grew told us?'

'Their father was German. Must at some time have changed his last name to Cavendish. Who visits Serena's cottage in the dead of night? I can't see her taking all that trouble just over a boy friend to keep the visits secret from the village. Not these days. Why should she care tuppence about what the villagers think? Then you told me Davina had studied science and biology. Mrs Grew was very emphatic it was biochemistry.'

Paula looked again at Tweed. She had the impression that he wasn't so much answering her question as thinking aloud, assembling facts, trying to put them in some sort of order. His jigsaw puzzle.

'Professor Saafeld,' he went on, 'is not only a top pathologist, the man Buchanan goes to for autopsies in difficult cases. He is also a biochemist, a biophysicist, a clinical microbiologist and a professor of bacteriology. He has no less than fourteen honorary degrees from various universities on the Continent and in the States.'

'How does he do it?'

'He has an extraordinary brain. And he never stops

working. His wife once told me she has adapted her lifestyle to his routine. She's good at embroidery and patchwork. She also reads a lot, like Mrs Grew. She listens to the BBC's World Service and keeps her husband in touch with what's going on in the world. The interesting thing about Saafeld is he has the same expertise as Dr Goslar.'

'How on earth do you know that?'

'From snippets I've picked up here and there – particularly from America. Remember Goslar, staying in the background, produced in his New Jersey plant an advanced weapon of war – a gas, or so Dillon said.'

'Then Saafeld is the ideal man to crack Goslar's secret agent.'

'You mean the agent – or ingredient – which caused havoc in the sea at Appledore. Unfortunately it's one thing to invent such a deadly agent, but quite another to detect it. I checked up again on Burgoyne early this morning. Got in touch with Gerrard at the MoD.'

'So are you going to tell me what the result was? And whether Burgoyne comes with us to Paris?'

'First question. I wanted to hear how Gerrard reacted after I had slept on our earlier conversation. I asked him to describe Burgoyne. He only met him once briefly – quite a long time ago. But he said my description fitted, especially his manner. Very buoyant and direct.'

'So that's it?'

'I'm making one more check. I phoned Marler. He'll be well on his way to Rydford on Dartmoor, the village Burgoyne was retiring to. See if he can pick up anything there.'

'Then Marler will never get back in time to catch our flight to Paris this evening,' she objected.

'Oh, yes he will. Marler can go thirty-six hours without any sleep. He drove off in the middle of the night. He could be in Rydford now. He'll be back in

103

good time for Paris – and that reminds me. I was intrigued by what we heard and saw in Steeple Hampton. So I'll be keeping an appointment with Serena. But not as early as she suggested. I'm not having her thinking I'm eager. I'm building up a picture of what is happening. The trouble is it's a misty picture. I need more data to clarify it. I just hope to Heaven that I'm wrong. If I'm not, the world faces a horrendous disaster.'

Marler drove along the deserted road across Dartmoor from Moretonhampstead towards Princeton. A mist hung over the countryside but here and there he saw the peak of a tor peering out above it. Well west of Moretonhampstead he saw a signpost to his right. *Rydford.*

He turned off the main road on to a narrow lane which began to climb. He drove slowly now. Turning a corner he saw ahead of him the village. He was about to back his car up a track with a lot of shrubbery round it – ready to leave quickly if that proved to be necessary. Then he saw in his rear-view mirrow a sports car stopping behind him. The driver, by herself, was an attractive girl with her dark hair cut short. He got out, walked back slowly, stopped a couple of yards away to avoid frightening her.

'Sorry, I was just going to back up that track, ready to leave later. You wouldn't happen to know Rydford?'

'Yes and no. Who have you come to see?'

As she spoke he realized she was assessing him. When she gave him a smile he knew he had passed muster. She had a perky nose, warm eyes – without a come-hither look, and a pointed chin which suggested determination. In her thirties, he guessed.

'I'm looking for a Captain Alan Burgoyne. I understand he lives here.'

'He does. I'm a friend of his. Coral Langley.' She extended a hand for him to clasp and he knew the confidence-inspiring exercise was over. He clasped the hand quickly, careful not to hold on too long. 'I can show you where he lives,' she suggested. 'Park your car and I'll take you there. It's a short way. It's a short village.'

'I'm David Miller. If I could just back my car . . .'

He stopped speaking. She was already reversing. He backed into the track, hauled out his golf bag, locked his car, sat next to her, nursing the bag between his knees.

'Hope you don't mind my carting this with me. Good irons cost a fortune these days. I don't want someone breaking in and walking off with them.'

'Very wise – even out here. Salesmen travel around, trying to sell household equipment. You've known Alan long? I refuse to use his nickname, "Chance". Don't like it. He's given in.'

'Known him? Off and on.'

'Same with me.'

She had a soft appealing voice. Marler now saw she was right in her description of Rydford. The cobbled street was short and steep. On either side small terrace houses, two storeys high, were built of granite. He saw a poster advertising a fair.

'Seems very quiet,' he remarked. 'Can't see a soul. Is it always like this?'

'No. I expect they've all gone off to the fair. We're nearly there.'

They had left the village behind and Marler saw the menacing bulk of Hangman's Tor looming above Rydford. No mist at its summit. Great crags protruded

105

alarmingly from it and Marler thought it looked unstable. Coral Langley seemed to read his mind.

'Don't like that tor behind Alan's place. It will come down one day. I tell Alan that and he just shrugs. Here we are . . .'

Marler prepared to hoist his golf bag over his shoulder. It contained his Armalite rifle. Dartmoor was a lonely place and he recalled Paula's grim experience near Gargoyle Towers. Burgoyne's cottage was a replica of the village houses, but larger because it was detached. Close to the lane, the front garden was a riot of gorse in golden bloom. Coral froze by her car, staring at the cottage.

'The front door's half open. That's funny. Alan always keeps it shut even when he's inside. Very security-minded.'

'When did you last see him?'

'About two months ago. He roams about a lot. A legacy of his military career, I suspect.'

'I suggest you wait here while I check the place out.'

'Would you? It's very odd . . .'

Marler glanced up at the tor. Out of the corner of his eye he had caught movement. He paused to take a better look. A precipitous path wound its way up towards the summit. No sign of anyone now. He put his right hand under his anorak, gripped the butt of the small Beretta 6.35mm automatic tucked inside the top of his slacks. He walked up to the door, shoved it open with his foot, listened. No sound. No giveaway creak of a foot on the plank floor. He used his foot to push the door flat against the wall. No one waiting behind it.

He walked into a large living room, modestly furnished with a wooden table and chairs arranged round it. Two chintz-covered armchairs on either side of the inglenook fireplace. A wall-to-ceiling bookcase. Beyond, a door opened into the kitchen.

106

A narrow curved wooden staircase led upwards out of sight. He peered into the kitchen. Empty. The back door was half open. He strolled across, first looked out of a window. The back garden petered out into the moor. He walked out, looked up at the tor. No sign of the intruder.

He had explored upstairs, checked two bedrooms, a shower and a toilet, was walking down the stairs when he saw Coral standing at the open front door. She had a club in one hand, presumably kept in her car.

'Are you all right, Miller?'

'I'm afraid there's been a break-in. Someone picked the lock on the front door. Scratches round it. Come in. Is anything missing?'

Coral surveyed the living room, opened a few drawers. He was watching her, wishing she wasn't attached to Burgoyne. He'd have waited his moment, asked her out to dinner in London. She went into the kitchen. He had closed the back door, using his elbow. He had long ago been trained not to leave fingerprints in suspect situations. He heard her exclamation.

'Damn him! He's taken Alan's photo.'

'Where was it?' he asked as he followed her into the kitchen.

'On that shelf. In a silver frame. Alan, like a lot of people, including myself, didn't like his picture being taken. I took one, bought a silver frame. He put it on that shelf. Used to say it gave him something nice to look at when he was preparing a meal.'

'That's a shame.'

'And the old copy of the *Daily Nation* which had his picture in it has gone. Used to wrap up the silver frame, I suppose.'

'Petty thieves will take anything.'

'With no thought of other people's sentiments. I used to spend time with him here.'

107

And probably nights – lucky Alan, Marler thought.

'Want to check upstairs?'

'Nothing up there.' She was opening another drawer. 'He also whipped Alan's old army paybook. The things they take.'

'Probably a market for army paybooks. Forgers use them. This is bad luck for you, Coral.'

'Never mind. The photos are gone. I'll take another of him when I can.'

'How did you two first meet?' Marler asked.

'At a dance in London. We took to each other right away. He may have been a soldier but he was such a gentle man. I'll call him again at his London flat. I did so before I came up here. No reply. That often happens.'

Marler would like to have asked for the number. He desisted – it would seem strange to her that he didn't know it. She said she needed some fresh air. She moved quickly. Before he could stop her she had opened the back door, walking into the garden. He was following her when he heard the shot.

From the back door he saw her collapse. He unzipped the pocket in the golf bag hiding the Armalite, ran out, looking up at the tor. A man stood on the crag projecting high up. He held a rifle. When he saw Marler he raised the rifle. Marler aimed his Armalite, caught him in the cross-hairs, pressed the trigger, firing an explosive bullet of great power.

The man was perched near the edge of the crag. Marler fired again. The explosive bullet hit the crag where it joined the mass of the tor. He saw the man start to topple, screaming as he cartwheeled down the long drop. Then the whole crag gave way, parting from the tor as tons of rock plunged down. Then there was a heavy silence.

Marler ran to Coral. She had fallen on her back. He

only needed one look to know she was dead. Half her face had been blown away. He didn't even check her pulse.

'*Bastard!*' he said aloud. 'Used a dumdum bullet.'

He ran to the base of the tor. He half-expected to find he was looking down at Yellow Hair, the man Tweed had seen at Brown's Hotel through the window. If there was any trace visible of the killer.

There was. He stopped running when he reached the edge of the rock fall. Only the killer's head was visible, dead eyes staring at the sky. The rest of his body was hidden beneath a massive boulder which, Marler thought with satisfaction, must have crushed every bone in his body. The hair was thick, black. Again he didn't bother to check the neck pulse. He had to get away quickly . . .

He ran round the end of the cottage, peered down the street.

Still empty. No one about anywhere. He slid the Armalite back inside the special pocket, walked rapidly back to his car. As he drove out and reached the highway he thought how lucky it was that the fair had cleared the village out. Then it struck him the killer might never have broken into Burgoyne's cottage if there had been people about.

He felt rotten about leaving Coral Langley lying there in the garden. But Tweed had always emphasized to his team they must never get mixed up with the police – especially during an operation.

Well on his way from Dartmoor, Marler stopped at an isolated phone box. He asked Directory Enquiries for the number of the Exeter police and called it.

'I'm reporting the murder of a girl. You'll find her body behind a cottage near the tor in Rydford on Dartmoor. I said Rydford, spelt . . .'

He put down the phone when the man who answered asked for his name. Then he drove – just inside the speed limits – back to London.

10

Only Tweed and Paula were in the office when Marler arrived back after dark. He sat down in an armchair, lit a king-size. Paula brought him an ashtray, perched it on the arm of his chair.

'Nothing ever turns out the way you think it will . . .' Marler began in a distant voice.

He then proceeded to report every detail of his trip to Rydford. Tweed listened without interrupting him, absorbing every word, imagining the scenes Marler was describing graphically. He had just recalled the death of Coral Langley when he stopped his account.

'Any hope of a drink?'

'Brandy and soda?' Tweed suggested.

Marler nodded and Tweed leaned down, opened his deep bottom drawer. He produced a glass, a bottle of good brandy and a soda siphon. Planting them close to Marler he let him fix his own drink. Marler fixed a stiff one, drank half, placed the glass within reach. Paula squeezed his shoulder. He looked up at her, winked.

'That's better. I just had a flash of what Coral's face looked like after the bullet hit her. Now, to continue . . .'

He ended by recalling his phone message to the police. Gazing at Tweed, he raised an eyebrow.

'I felt I couldn't just leave her there. She might not have been found until tomorrow morning.'

'I think,' Tweed said, 'you acted correctly and very sympathetically. And you were right. If you'd got caught up in a police investigation they might have forbidden you to leave the country, even treated you as a suspect. And you've given me a big piece to help me build up the picture I'm forming. I am grateful.'

'Is Burgoyne coming with us to Paris?' Paula asked.

'I told you in the car this morning that I had made a second call to Gerrard at the MoD.' As he spoke he was staring at the ceiling, which struck Paula as curious. 'I also told you that he'd given Burgoyne a very positive assessment.' He looked down at both of them. 'Since he's new, I will be the only one to give him orders when we are on the move. Marler, you might pass that bit of information on to all the others before we go.'

'Will do.'

'Now we have something to tell you – about our visit to Steeple Hampton . . .'

Tersely he described every detail of their experience. Marler sat very still, watching him. Tweed ended with a flourish of his hands.

'Paula,' he went on, 'thinks there's something strange about what we heard – and saw. Any comment?'

'I find the wording on that headstone on Davina's grave quite bizarre. And I gather Serena's hardly ever there – apart from those secret visits to the cottage at night. So where does she go to, what does she really do?'

'Our own reactions. She called me from abroad, wants me to meet her when we're in Paris. I shall meet her. I shall want to know a lot more about her. Where she goes to. Where the money comes from – her clothes are very expensive.'

'Her fur was sable,' Paula remarked. 'But some of the questions you're going to put to her are pretty personal.'

111

'She approached me. She must expect searching questions.'

'I sense there's something you haven't said,' Paula told him.

'She has jet-black hair. She admits being in Appledore, albeit at an earlier date – when she carried out her commission to photograph the area. Buchanan reported that the chauffeuse, who drove a Middle Eastern diplomat on the night we were in Appledore had jet-black hair tucked under her peaked cap . . .'

He looked up as Monica, red-faced, hurried into the office. She settled herself behind her desk and spoke apologetically.

'Hope you haven't had a lot of calls. I rushed out to get a quick meal. Couldn't face the deli.'

'No calls at all,' Tweed assured her. 'And I wish you'd go out for a meal more often. You need to keep up your strength, the way I work you.'

'I've just remembered something else about my trip,' Marler reported. 'I was driving back along a deserted stretch of the A303 when a motorcyclist came tearing up behind me, then slowed down. I thought that was odd. Those chaps usually overtake with a roar. I drove with one hand, had my Beretta in the other. Thought he might have a present for me – like lobbing a grenade through the open window. Then a police car appeared in the distance, coming towards us. Motorcyclist roars straight past me, never to be seen again.'

'He could have been working in cahoots with the man on Hangman's Tor,' Tweed mused. 'Went back to Rydford to pick him up after delivering him there. Saw you leaving.'

'Then I was lucky he didn't arrive when I was inside the phone box calling the police.'

'From what you told us, he'd have to find his villainous chum. That probably took a while. I said Goslar has a huge organization.'

'Have I got time to dart back to my flat?' Marler asked, standing up.

'Bags of time,' Monica told him.

Marler had just left when the phone rang. Monica answered, then called across to Tweed.

'Our transatlantic visitor has arrived. Cord Dillon is downstairs.'

'Tell him to come up now. I'm intrigued by this visit. Why do I have the strong feeling that what he is bringing us is bad news?'

The door opened and Cord Dillon strode in. The Deputy Director of the CIA wore a duffel coat, fastened up to the neck, a pair of blue denim slacks and loafers. His large craggy head always reminded Tweed of one of the Presidential heads carved out of rock at Mount Rushmore. Clean-shaven, his thick hair was turning white. In his fifties, he moved like a man twenty years younger.

'Hi, Monica,' he greeted her as she took his coat. 'Paula, you look younger than ever. Can't say the same about you, Tweed,' he said with a weary grin.

'Welcome, Cord. What have you been up to? We expected you earlier.'

'At Dulles Airport I spotted a tail. Lost him and booked on a flight to Canada, then flew on here.'

He was sitting upright in one of the armchairs. He refused the offer of a drink from Monica. Earlier Tweed had put away the brandy bottle and siphon. Paula had taken away the glass Marler had used.

'You did that?' Tweed remarked. 'I hope you're not in bad odour in Washington again.'

'Far from it. I'm running Langley myself for weeks

on end. My chief keeps getting recurring bouts of flu. It was another lot I was keeping away from.'

'I sense that what you're going to tell me is secret. Do you mind if Paula stays?'

'Hell, no.' He looked across at her. 'Last time I was here she saved my life. That business in Albemarle Street. As for Monica . . .' He swivelled to grin at her. 'She's been with you for more than a few years. If Bob Newman turns up he can also listen in. But no one else, if you don't mind.'

'So what is the secret?'

'You're not going to like this. I don't think you're going to like it one little bit. And you're going to have to watch your back over this Goslar thing.'

'Tell me, Cord. I'll try not to tremble.'

'That will be the day, when you tremble.' The American paused as though gathering his thoughts. 'I'm talking about Unit Four. A body of highly professional agents who answer only to the President's right-hand man, Vance Karnow. A tough guy if ever there was one – like his subordinates. Here's a pic of Karnow.'

He handed Tweed a photo he'd extracted from an inner pocket. The photo was protected by a slim plastic folder. Tweed handed it back to him without comment. Dillon passed it to Paula, his long arm just reaching her desk.

'Like your reaction, Paula. You're good at weighing men up.'

She studied the pic, taking longer over it than Tweed had. She pursed her lips.

'Photos can be so misleading.'

'I think you formed an impression,' Dillon insisted.

'A strange face. You can see the European origins. Probably from a few generations back. Prominent cheekbones. A long face, long nose, thin lips, pointed jaw. A lot of smartly brushed dark hair. Eyes like bullets. Hard, ruthless, amoral. I'm guessing,' she concluded, handing back the photo.

'On the button,' Dillon said approvingly.

'What is the function of Unit Four?' Tweed enquired.

'The dirty work they'd sooner not hand to the CIA – because we have such a large organization. Also, Unit Four prides itself on doing its job underground. They dress in suits, like respectable businessmen. Often pose as just that – businessmen.'

'Do they work on direct orders from the President?'

'Not on your life. Officially he isn't aware they exist. The orders always come from Karnow. But my guess is the President makes an off-the-cuff remark to Karnow about someone who is worrying him. Result, Karnow and his men see that the someone is not walking the earth much longer.'

'Why are you telling us about Unit Four?' Tweed wondered.

'Because an informant – very reliable – told me they were coming over here.'

'With what purpose?'

'To grab off you – if you get it – the ultimate weapon of war invented by Dr Goslar. My informant told me the President sees it as ensuring America remains the top world power.'

'Cord . . .' Tweed leaned forward over his desk. 'You and I know about the mysterious Dr Goslar – but how come the President also knows about him? If he does?'

'He does. Recently – very – the Oval Office received a video showing what happened at Appledore. Also he received a recorded phone call from Goslar. I gather in that weird screechy robot-like howl he speaks in. He said he might consider selling the formula and a specimen to the States for three hundred million dollars. The President would go berserk at the idea of paying that sort of money – even for world supremacy. Hence his using Unit Four. A copy of that article by Sneed in the *Daily Nation* also reached the Oval Office. Unit Four could already be here – which is what I came to warn you about.'

'That would be quick.'

'There is Concorde. What is it? A three-and-a-half-hour trip from Washington to London. Unit Four is a squad of élite killers. Karnow himself could be in London now.'

'Cord, I really appreciate your coming all this way to warn us.'

'One huge favour deserves another. You hid me away down in the Romney Marsh when a gang of thugs were after my hide. But you must understand these people in Unit Four are not thugs scooped up out of the underworld. They are educated, clever and sophisticated. Far more dangerous. Maybe a dozen of them. Maybe more. I just don't know.'

'Have you time for a drink at a nearby bar?'

'No.' Dillon checked his watch. 'I have to catch a flight back to Washington. I know the pilot of the plane. I'll leave it at Dulles dressed like an officer of the crew.'

'Have you any information on Goslar, no matter how vague?'

'Well . . .' Dillon settled back again in his chair. 'I started to read a file on Goslar before I came over. There's a second file on him I have to trace when I get back. I'll contact you when I've located and read it.'

'What about the first file you were reading?' Tweed pressed.

'That had a weird report in it. All based on rumours – so I can't vouch for its authenticity.'

'I'd still like to hear it.'

'It's about the Galapagos Islands – way out in the

Pacific off the coast of Ecuador. They belong to Ecuador. It sounded like a fairy story to me, Tweed.'

'I like fairy stories.'

'I'm sure you know that in the sea around the Galapagos there are huge turtles. Occasionally wealthy tourists go there to see these strange creatures.' He looked at Paula. 'You're probably wondering where I'm going.'

'Then let's go there, Cord,' she encouraged.

'They're a kind of protected species – because they're unique in the whole world. A fisherman from Ecuador was in the area. He saw a giant seaplane moored offshore. Later, apparently, he heard it belonged to a Dr Goslar.' Dillon waved a dismissive hand. 'I stress this is all nothing but rumour. I didn't believe a word of it myself.'

'Let's see if I believe it,' Tweed suggested. 'Do give us all the details you have.'

'And you were talking about a fisherman from Ecuador,' Paula reminded the American.

'This fisherman – if he ever existed – had a pair of high-powered glasses. He used them to check on what was going on. There were very big dinghies drawn up on the beach. The fisherman saw a landing party capturing two turtles, lifting them into tanks of water. Then the crates were transported to the dinghies, presumably on their way to the seaplane. The sail of the fisherman's boat was very distinctive. That is important later. A red sail with a white half-moon on it.'

'How long ago was this?' asked Tweed.

'Date's obscure. Within the last year. The fisherman returns to Guayaquil, Ecuador's port. Tells his story in a waterfront bar crowded with people. Tells it to a freelance agent of ours – who sends off this report. A copy goes to our main agent in Quito, capital of

Ecuador. He decides to check, goes down to Guayaquil. Finds the fisherman and our freelancer have both been murdered. That's it, for what it's worth. I must catch my flight now.'

Tweed had gone over to the windows. He pulled aside a gap in the closed curtains, peered out into the night. Below a taxi waited. He came back to shake hands with Dillon.

'No watchers that I can see out there. Safe flight back. Oh, how were those two men murdered?'

'Beheaded. Tough place, that port. Be in touch. If you ever get hold of that nightmare weapon of Goslar's, destroy it. Destroy him too . . .'

'That is encouraging,' Paula commenced.

'Unit Four arriving on our doorstep? Isn't it,' Tweed agreed.

The door opened and Newman walked in, carrying a bag. Dumping it against a wall, he sat down. He looked first at Paula, then at Tweed.

'You two look as though a bomb had dropped on you.'

'It has,' said Tweed. 'Where are Butler and Nield?'

'Downstairs in the waiting room with their bags. They're playing poker.'

'Monica, get them up here right away.' He looked at Newman. 'Any idea where Burgoyne is?'

'Having a good old chinwag with Howard in his office.'

'We'll leave him there. Howard is very good at getting people into the atmosphere of how we work.'

He waited until Butler and Nield appeared, each carrying a bag. They dropped them alongside Newman's, sat down. Nield studied Tweed before he made his remark.

118

'You look godawful serious.'

'Pretty much what I've just observed,' agreed Newman.

'Pay attention, everyone,' Tweed said. 'Cord Dillon has been in to see us. Flew over for that express purpose. Now he's flying straight back to Washington. He brought interesting news . . .'

Concisely, his manner grave, he gave a résumé of what the American had told him. They sat very still as they listened. Marler had arrived just before Tweed began explaining. He took up his normal stance, leaning against a wall. Tweed concluded his résumé. Nield was the first one to react.

'We're going to have fun. First we'll be up against the invisible Dr Goslar. Then we'll have to keep a sharp lookout for Bate and his Special Branch thugs, who don't play by the Queensberry Rules. The French security services, and maybe the police, will be hostile. Now, on top of all of them, we have Unit Four Yanks on the prowl. Yes, it should be fun.'

'If you like to describe it that way,' Tweed remarked.

'One important point,' Marler spoke up. 'We can't take weapons on the plane, which is why I've been back to my flat so I could be on my own. I contacted a friend in Paris who sells every type of gun – for a price. I told him I'd see him tonight, and he'll wait for me. I'll hare off to him in one of the cars hired by Monica over the phone and waiting for us at Charles de Gaulle. But everyone should be armed quickly, so where can we meet?'

'On Madeleine,' Paula suggested. 'You know the Restaurant Valais? Marvellous Swiss food. There's a bar next to it. On the right as you face Valais. It's not well lit and stays open all hours. We'll probably get a table at the back.'

'All right, Marler?' Tweed checked.

'Perfect rendezvous. Close to where I'll be coming from.'

'Then we go on to La Défense, to look at that building where you had that appalling ordeal, Paula.'

'We'll be there in no time,' Paula said. 'Go by Métro.'

'Everyone has plenty of foreign currency?' asked Tweed. 'Good.'

He unlocked a drawer, took out a long fat white envelope. He handed it to Marler.

'Underground gunsmiths come expensive.'

Marler opened the flap, glanced inside. The envelope was crammed with five-hundred-franc notes. He grinned.

'Enough to buy an artillery piece.'

'Which we may need, considering what we'll be up against,' Nield said with a smile.

'What's that bulging canvas bag you've got as well as your case?' Paula asked Marler.

'Crammed with newspapers and magazines. An empty bag might look suspicious to Customs at one end or the other. I'll dump them on my friend in exchange for the weaponry.'

'You'd better get moving to catch that flight,' Monica warned.

'Then ask Burgoyne to come down here *tout de suite.*'

11

The flight to Paris was three-quarters empty. Tweed sat next to Paula. Newman occupied a seat behind them. Further back Butler sat with Nield and, at Tweed's suggestion, Burgoyne occupied a seat on his own several rows behind them. Marler, however, had taken a front seat, nearest the exit. He wanted to be first off the plane so he could grab his hired car and drive swiftly to his gunsmith.

'I don't like night flights,' Paula remarked. 'All you look out at is blackness.'

'Luckily it's a short flight,' Tweed replied. 'I'm going back to have a word with Chance Burgoyne . . .'

'Because you were with Howard I didn't get the time to brief you,' Tweed began as he sat next to the retired officer. 'We drive from the airport to Madeleine. Marler is acquiring an armoury of weapons and will meet us there. What is your choice of weapon?'

'Sounds as though we're going to fight a duel,' Burgoyne said and grinned. 'I'd like a .38 Smith & Wesson, hip holster if possible, and plenty of spare ammo.'

'I'll tell Marler. From Madeleine – after we've met Marler – you, Paula, Newman and Butler, plus myself, will take the Métro to La Défense. You know it?'

'I know Paris but I've never had reason to visit La Défense. It's the business district, isn't it? Whacking great American-style skyscrapers. You can see them in the distance from certain parts of Paris.'

'That's the place. We want to visit the building where Paula had a bad experience . . .' Tweed briefly described what had happened to her. 'I told you about Dr Goslar when we had a few minutes on our own at Park Crescent.'

'A right swine, if there ever was one,' Burgoyne commented. 'I liked the look of Paula. Summed her up as tough. After what you've told me I underestimated her. She must be as tough as old hickory. I really admire her.'

Tweed glanced at Burgoyne. Having discarded his

121

camouflage jacket, he was now wearing a military-style trenchcoat. The change of apparel made him look much more like a soldier.

'It will be late at night when we get to La Défense,' Burgoyne observed, looking out of the window.

'That's the idea. We arrive at about the time Paula was there. Now, if you'll excuse me, I'll go and tell Marler the type of gun you prefer.'

Earlier that afternoon a huge man, clad in a grey over-coat with a fur collar, stood watching a phone box on the Île de la Cité. His brown cropped hair was protected with a beret. He needed the garb – a bitter wind was blowing down the River Seine.

A man was using the phone inside the box, had been talking for over fifteen minutes. The man in the grey overcoat checked his watch, pursed his thick lips. The phone box was not far from the HQ of Police Judiciaire, which amused him. For the third time he checked his watch. It was coming up to the hour.

He strode forward after extracting a banknote from his wallet. Opening the door of the box, he placed a large hand on the shoulder of the man inside, hauled him straight out. The victim swung round, blazing. Then he saw the size of the intruder.

'I need this phone,' the huge man said, handing a hundred-franc note to the much smaller man.

Grumbling, the small Frenchman walked away. He stared at the banknote greedily, shrugged, walked faster.

Inside the box the giant picked up the dangling receiver. He rammed it back on the cradle and waited. Once again he checked his watch. On the hour. The phone began ringing.

'Yes. Who is this?' he asked in English.

'Identify yourself,' a cool voice, speaking the same language, requested.

'Abel. I repeat Abel.'

'Hold on for a moment and then listen . . .'

Abel looked all round the outside while he waited. Two uniformed policemen walked out of the Police Judiciaire headquarters. They gave him not so much as a glance. Hunched up against the cold, they walked away, disappeared round a corner. The weird screeching voice began speaking.

'I expect Tweed, if I read his mind correctly, to visit the deserted building in La Défense. As I suggested, go there and prepare a suitable greeting for him. Go *now*.'

Abel replaced the receiver. He knew he had heard a recording, played by the man who had answered him when he first spoke. For a large man he moved swiftly after leaving the box. The equipment would be waiting for him inside the building. As he walked he repeated to himself the correct sequence of digits he must press on the combination device on the outer door of the La Défense building.

They had the Métro coach to themselves as the train rushed through the tunnel. Tweed sat with Burgoyne on one side and Paula on the other. Facing them were Newman and Butler, who carried his kit inside an airline bag. Butler had had to open the bag at Security, and had explained he was a plumber. The tools had the outward appearance of what a plumber would use.

Paula slipped her hand inside her shoulder bag, into the special pocket. She felt confident as her hand gripped the butt of her Browning .32. They had met Marler at the bar on Madeleine and he had distributed his purchases.

Newman and Burgoyne had their hip holsters, each

with a .38 Smith & Wesson. Butler and Nield had been provided with 7.65mm Walther automatics. Everyone, except Tweed and Paula, had an additional armoury of stun and smoke grenades. Marler was equipped with an Armalite rifle and a .455 Colt automatic pistol. Only Tweed carried no weapons.

After leaving the bar at Madeleine, Nield had driven the hired estate car to the Ritz. Marler had followed him in a Renault. It was the estate car which had transported Tweed and those who accompanied him from the airport to the bar. As the Métro train sped endlessly through a long tunnel – next stop La Défense – Paula was aware of nervousness and the pumping of adrenalin. She became calm and cold as they alighted and, with Burgoyne on one side, Butler on the other, she mounted the steps she had run down when escaping so recently.

Emerging into the night near the small park, she saw the seat she had sat on for a short time. She checked her watch. It was 10.30 p.m. – just about the time when she had endured her ordeal.

'Which building?' Burgoyne asked, his tone commanding and crisp.

'I'll lead you to it – but first let's make sure there's no one about . . .' Paula responded.

They waited in the shelter of the park. Paula stared up at the blue, glass monsters shearing up above them. The wide forecourt spaced out between the buildings was eerily quiet and apparently deserted. Tweed, hands in his coat pockets, glanced at her to see how she was reacting. He was impressed by her calm, purposeful look.

'I can see the building,' she said suddenly. 'Let's get on with it.'

Under her windcheater she wore an extra jumper, remembering the cold. She was also clad in leggings and rubber-soled boots, which made no sound. Burgoyne marched alongside her with Butler escorting her on her other side. Behind them Newman followed, his Smith & Wesson in his hand, concealed under a trenchcoat he wore not unlike Burgoyne's. Paula began to walk forward as she reached the entrance to the door leading into the vast hall beyond.

'The door's open a bit,' she said. 'It was when I left.'

'*Get back!*' ordered Burgoyne.

Butler repeated the same instruction almost simultaneously. He grabbed one of her arms as Burgoyne grabbed the other. Acting in unison, they turned her round, pushed her away, told her to return to the park.

'Something wrong?' Tweed's quiet voice enquired.

'Plenty,' said Butler. 'You all go back to the park. You, too, Newman. That's an order.' He had pushed Burgoyne aside and was reaching up to the top of the door, his sensitive fingers tracing the course of the wire, painted blue to merge with the building.

'I saw it, too. Remember?' grated Burgoyne. 'I've seen rather a lot of boobytraps – just in time.'

'Doesn't take two of us to do this job,' Butler snapped. 'In fact two fiddling with this apparatus could end up with us both being blown to kingdom come. For Pete's sake, let me concentrate.'

'It's all yours,' Burgoyne replied calmly. 'I'll just stay and watch. You want me to give a hand, just ask.'

'I'll do that thing.'

From a distance, standing between Tweed and Newman, Paula had a strange sensation of déjà vu. She recalled how, sitting in Newman's car outside her flat, she was waiting while Butler did what he was doing now. But this wasn't Fulham Road – this was a hell of skyscrapers and she'd been dangled from that floor halfway to heaven. No, heaven was hardly an appropriate word.

'I have to get inside some other way,' said Butler. Picking up his kit case, he left the door, walked to a nearby ground-floor window. Standing with a small torch clenched between his teeth he peered inside, saw only a vast hall stretching into infinity. He took out a special cutting tool after checking round the window. He used the tool to trace out a large oblong area near the lower ledge. His other hand held a powerful sucker at the tip of a wooden handle. He had the sucker pressed against the middle of the loose sheet of glass. Very slowly he withdrew the sheet, laid it on the ground, releasing the sucker.

'I'll go in first,' Burgoyne snapped.

'I don't think so. Just keep well away from that damned door.'

Butler crouched down, stepped slowly inside, Walther gripped in his right hand. He waited in a crouched position until his eyes were accustomed to the darkness of the interior. While he did this he listened. He might have been inside a tomb. No sound. No movement anywhere.

Walking slowly towards the door, he held his torch so it scanned the floor. He found what he'd expected behind the partly open door, in a position so that as the door was opened wide enough for someone to enter it would detonate. Same device as they'd used in Paula's flat back in London.

Down in Surrey, when the bomb squad had taken the previous device, they had done more than photograph it. After examining the photographs an expert had carefully studied what they had. He had taken a chance, pressed a switch. It had turned off the bomb mechanism.

'The green switch, not the red one, as you might imagine,' they had reported to Butler over the phone.

'Know what you're doing?' a soft voice asked behind him.

'You would follow me in,' Butler told Burgoyne. 'Now you can just hope I know what I'm doing. Where are the others?'

'Well clear. Back at the park.'

'Hold your breath, Burgoyne.'

Butler bent down, his torch illuminating the device's innards as he raised the lid. He shrugged, pressed down the green switch. Small illuminated bulbs inside the metal casing went out. He had done the right thing.

Butler severed the wire running along the top of the door, down the hinged side, connecting up with the bomb. He then lifted the metal casing containing the bomb, put it down against the wall well away from the door. He didn't want Paula to see it. Going outside, he waved to the others to tell them the coast was clear.

'Chance,' Paula said when she arrived, 'you saved our lives. Thank you.'

'Harry spotted the wire a split second after I did, called out a warning.'

'So thank you both.'

They were talking in whispers. Burgoyne followed suit.

'Can't understand what's going on. I'd swear this whole building is empty. No sign of a guard behind that counter with a phone.'

'Phone's dead as a doornail,' Butler told them after picking it up.

'Goslar's normal procedure,' Tweed explained to Burgoyne. 'He leases a base for longer than he thinks he'll need it. Just as he did at Gargoyle Towers, his temporary base on Dartmoor. He has vast sums at his disposal.'

'I'd like to go up to that room where they held me,' Paula suggested. 'They might just have left something. The thirty-second floor.'

'In that case,' Burgoyne said, 'Harry and I will go up to the thirty-third floor in another elevator. We'll check it out quickly, then come down those stairs I see to join you. Just in case. Agreed, Tweed?'

'Yes, do that.'

Newman asked his question while he was travelling up in their elevator with Tweed and Paula. He noticed she looked tense again as the elevator ascended.

'Maybe, Tweed, we'll find another pair of gloves. What did you do with the pair we found at Gargoyle Towers? He slipped up there – Goslar. A boffin back at Park Crescent could measure those gloves, come up with some idea of the wearer's weight and height.'

'I threw them into my wastepaper basket. You're forgetting, Bob. Goslar likes to leave false clues, hoping we'll waste so many hours coming up with useless ideas. I'll go into the room with you, Paula. Bob can watch our backs . . .'

Like Newman, Paula had her gun in her hand as she stepped out of the elevator. She walked slowly to the room where the door was still open, as she had left it. Tweed glanced round the spacious hall, his hands still in his coat pockets.

'This place must have cost him a packet,' he remarked. 'That wouldn't worry him for a second . . .'

Paula paused at the open door. The lights were still on. She gripped her Browning with both hands, peered inside, sweeping the interior with her automatic. Then she walked inside with a firm step.

'It's just as I left it. That's the bed they threw me on – and the window they dangled me from is still open. No one has been here.'

'Someone has,' Tweed corrected her. 'At least on the ground floor. To fix up the boobytrap bomb.'

He walked over to the open window, peered down at the moonlit area thirty-plus floors below. His mouth tightened. He turned and looked at Paula.

'What an appalling experience you endured.'

'I'd just as soon not have to repeat the performance,' she replied with a wan smile.

'I've found something,' reported Newman, who had been searching under the bed. 'An unsmoked cigarette. Does Goslar smoke?'

'He did. Menthols. St Moritz brand.'

'Well, I've found one which must have rolled under the bed.' He was dropping it inside a transparent specimen bag. 'We can, in due course, have it checked for fingerprints.'

'Then that man with rimless glasses I described could have been Dr Goslar,' Paula said.

'Sorry to disappoint you,' Tweed told her, 'and don't waste your time, Bob. Just another false clue. I'm sure Rimless Glasses, using latex gloves, placed it there while the Ape was suspending Paula from that infernal window. The idea was she might find it when the two men had gone.'

'Then why did they go to all that trouble of scaring the wits out of me and asking useless questions?'

'I'm sure they meant to let you go all the time. It was another of Goslar's elaborate plots to lure me back here so I would be blown to pieces.'

'Goslar is incredibly subtle and devious.'

'Something we must not forget. But one day he'll accidentally leave a real clue. Then I can track him and find the fiendish weapon he tried out at Appledore. Also he's repeating some of the tricks he used over ten years ago. Remember, Bob? That may lead to his eventual destruction . . .'

129

He became silent. Newman had crouched just inside the open door, his Smith & Wesson aimed at the foot of the staircase leading down from the floor above. He had heard a faint footstep.

'Don't shoot the postman. He's doing his best,' Butler called out as he appeared at the bottom of the staircase.

'Nothing up there,' Burgoyne called out as they walked to the room. 'Place is as clean as a new pin. No furniture, not anything. Just as though the building was never occupied for weeks.'

'Dr Goslar's trademark,' Tweed said, looking at Burgoyne. 'He is the most careful man I've ever encountered. Yet there are times when he takes risks. *Toujours l'audacité.* One of his favourite maxims. He used it twice when he called to taunt me in his – or her – disguised voice. I'm talking about years ago. He repeated it at the end of the second call. *Toujours l'audacité.*'

'Interesting.' Burgoyne frowned briefly, a crease appearing in his tall forehead. 'Napoleon, isn't it? Napoleon said it first.'

'He did,' Tweed replied. '"Always audacity." Either he or – more likely – one of his thugs was, I'm sure, in the building opposite this one. When I looked out of the window the moonlight was shining on it. I saw a shadow behind an unlit window.'

'Then let's get over there,' said Newman.

'Pointless. It's a huge building. The door is certain to be locked. The shadow figure will have gone by now. We'll take the Métro, make our way to the Ritz.'

'I'll put in an anonymous call to the police about that bomb,' Newman decided as they walked out of the building.

He was the first to go outside, followed by Tweed and Paula, with Butler and Burgoyne bringing up the rear. Tweed looked to his left, saw a uniformed guard with a peaked cap strolling out of the next building. The guard, obviously emerging for a spot of fresh air, stretched his arms. Tweed walked swiftly towards him with Paula by his side. He spoke in French.

'Excuse me. I came here to meet someone but the building is empty. Do you know when they left?'

'About a week ago. A convoy of big vans turned up well after dark. I watched from a window. A large crew spent half the night carrying out small containers and loading them into the vans. I could see a number of the containers were marked "fragile". I was curious so I approached them when a lot of them were loading. Only one man spoke French, so he told me. Said he'd been hired because he was also fluent in Serbo-Croat.'

'So the rest of the crew were Croats?'

'Yes. So were all the staff in that building. They were escorted everywhere, only got out for the occasional meal. The Frenchman told me he didn't fancy moving to Annecy – he was Parisian – but the pay was good. Then the big man came out and all hell broke loose.'

'The big man?'

'Big as a giant. When he walked he padded like an animal. His shoulders – they were huge – dipped up and down when he moved. Had cropped brown hair.'

'Sounds like an ape,' Paula interjected in French.

'You've got it!' The guard clapped his gloved hands together. 'I wondered what he reminded me of.'

'You said all hell broke loose,' Tweed reminded him.

'The giant was furious because the Frenchman had been talking to me. Practically dragged him away. Heard him swearing foully. I know enough English to recognize swear words.' He grinned. 'Particularly the

131

foul sort. I heard the Frenchman protesting that all they'd been talking about was the weather. Then there was something else . . .'

'Annecy,' Burgoyne's voice said behind them. 'Could that be significant?'

Tweed waved at him to keep quiet. He returned his attention to the guard.

'You said there was something else?'

'A whacking great limo arrives. A woman dressed like a man comes out. She hurries into the back, slams the door shut, the limo takes off.'

'How can you be sure it was a woman?' Tweed pressed.

'Wears trousers, men's shoes, long man's overcoat, a Borsalino hat, brim pulled well down.'

'Sounds as though it could have been a man,' Tweed insisted.

'I'm French.' The guard laughed. 'A Frenchman can always detect a woman. Body language.'

'Of course.' Tweed chuckled. 'Any idea who owns the building?'

'That was strange too. Leased by a company in Luxembourg City. But when they left the lease had another three months to run. I'd better get back to my post. Hope you find your friend who worked there . . .'

'Annecy,' Burgoyne said again as the guard disappeared. 'Might that not be significant?'

'Maybe. Let's leave this weird place. We'll take the Métro, make our way back to the Ritz.'

Again they had an empty coach to themselves as they travelled back from La Défense. Paula sat next to Tweed and Butler faced them two seats further back. Further along the coach Newman sat with Burgoyne, engaged in conversation as the two men got to know each other.

132

'Chance was very quick,' Paula recalled. 'I mean spotting the wire along the top of the door.'

'He was,' Tweed agreed. 'He is most promising material.'

Paula glanced at him. What he had said was the highest praise he could bestow on a new addition to the team.

'Howard's other reinforcement, Evan Tarnwalk, never appeared,' she remarked.

'Ex-Special Branch. We can do without him. You realize that we were followed from Heathrow?'

'No!' She was startled. 'What makes you say that?'

'There were two people on our flight. One, a woman by herself in a seat well behind us. Several seats behind her, across on the other side of the aisle, was a man, also by himself. They rushed into the final departure lounge at Heathrow – separately – waving their tickets when we'd started boarding. When we left Marler and Nield at Madeleine to drive the cars to the Ritz, I saw the woman hail a cab and follow Marler. Then, when we got into the Métro coach for La Défense I saw the man dive into the last coach. He skipped out again at La Défense just before the doors closed.'

'This is very serious. Alarming. It has to mean that Goslar knows where we are.'

'Which suits me to the ground. I know now we're in the right place – on his track. That puts pressure on Goslar. People under pressure sooner or later make a mistake. I'm waiting for him to do just that.'

'You're as manipulative as he is,' she commented.

'More so, I hope. The interesting thing is the couple following us made their actions obvious. No attempt to conceal the fact they were following us.'

'Why would they do that?'

At that moment Burgoyne turned round. He waved buoyantly at Tweed and grinned. Tweed beckoned for him to join them. Burgoyne sat on the facing seat, looked at Paula.

'I reckon a good night's sleep will do you no harm at all when we get to the Ritz.'

'Sounds like a good idea,' she agreed. 'You look as though you could go on for hours. How do you manage it?'

'Clean living.' He grinned again. 'At least that's my story and I'm sticking to it. You need stamina prowling around in the desert.'

'Chance,' Tweed said, leaning forward, 'tomorrow I have to go and see someone. I want you to stay inside the hotel with Nield as backup. Stay there all day. They have more than one restaurant.'

'What do we do – Nield and me?'

'You're on the lookout for any odd characters – men or women. I need to know if anyone starts making enquiries about me. Paula and I will give Pete Nield keys to our rooms.'

'Why?'

'So you can both check them at regular intervals. I don't want to open a cupboard door when I get back and get blown to pieces all over the room.'

12

After breakfast the following morning Tweed called Lasalle. He used a public phone box on rue St-Honoré. Outside, at intervals on both sides of the street, Paula, Newman, Butler and Marler waited – and watched.

Rush-hour traffic had evaporated, and the street was quiet. It was too early for the wealthy ladies to be strolling, looking in expensive shop windows. Spasmodically the pavements were wet where shopkeepers had hosed them. The sun shone out of a clear blue sky but there was a chill wind. It was still almost the end of March. A few optimistic shopkeepers had lowered striped blinds but there were no tables outside.

'Tweed here, René. In Paris.'

'Go back to London.'

'I appreciate the warm welcome. I have to see you urgently – we may be working on the same thing. An exchange of information might help us both. You owe me.'

'I knew you would say that.' A pause, a sigh. 'What you said is true. Where are you?'

'In the rue St-Honoré.'

'In thirty minutes I'll meet you. Facing Madeleine there's a brasserie, a bar. Le Colibri. Just the two of us. Don't come with your team, which I'm sure you have with you. Thirty minutes from now.'

The connection was broken. Lasalle had not even bothered to say goodbye. A man under great pressure, Tweed said to himself. There was tension in Paris in certain quarters. When he emerged Paula and Newman strolled across the street, joined him, one on either side.

'Marler and Butler are providing backup,' Paula said.

'I suppose it's necessary,' Tweed grumbled.

'It's not necessary,' Newman said grimly. 'It's essential. Or have you forgotten Sam Sneed, Coral Langley, who had her face blown away when Marler visited Rydford, the bomb waiting for Paula in the Fulham Road, the bomb waiting for you at La Défense?'

'You have a point,' Tweed conceded.

He was walking slowly, glancing in shop windows. Once he looked back quickly, but there was no sign of Marler or Butler. They would be there, he knew, but both were experts – not only at tracking but also at remaining invisible to whoever they were following. Tweed told Paula and Newman the gist of his conversation with Lasalle.

'Doesn't sound like him,' Paula commented.

'Goslar is brilliant at creating an atmosphere of uncertainty – and tension. He's succeeding.'

'Why?' asked Newman.

'To push up the bidding sky-high.'

'The bidding?'

'Yes, for the ultimate weapon he's invented. Sooner or later he'll get large offers from America and France. I'm convinced he's determined to sell it to the Arab Fundamentalists. They now have vast resources. He – Goslar – will use the bids from other countries to squeeze far more from the Arabs.'

'Will Britain make an offer?'

'Not if I have anything to do with it. Why should we play his hideous game? As I said before, we have to find him, to destroy this maniac and all his works.'

As Tweed entered, Le Colibri had the usual curving bar on his left. To the right and deep inside were round glass-topped tables with wicker chairs. No sign of Lasalle. Tweed checked his watch as he made his way to the back, where the tables were empty. Nearer the front, groups of workmen and the odd couple chattered non-stop over drinks or coffee and croissants.

Tweed was early and had come in by himself. When the apron-clad waiter arrived he ordered a Pernod. A moment later Paula came in, chose a table at the front with its back to the wall. Tweed pursed his lips. At least the others had dispersed somewhere in the vicinity outside.

The waiter brought his Pernod. Tweed sipped at it for the sake of appearances. Paula had not even glanced in his direction. She appeared to be reading a copy of *Le Monde*. She ordered something from a waiter, which he guessed would be coffee. Tweed took off his horn-rims, cleaned the lenses on a new handkerchief, put them on again.

A small man with a trim moustache entered. For a moment Tweed didn't recognize him. Lasalle wore a shabby anorak, buttoned to the neck, equally shabby denims and shoes. A stained hat with the brim pulled down covered his head.

His normal brisk step was absent. He slouched between the tables, his head moving from side to side. Checking on everyone in the place, Tweed knew. He chose a chair close to Tweed with its back to the wall. The waiter appeared.

'I will have one of those,' he said in French, pointing at the Pernod in front of Tweed.

'Thank you for coming,' Tweed said in a quiet voice.

'I took a chance. Remember that,' the Frenchman said, speaking English. 'And why is Paula sitting at that table?'

'She has a mind of her own. I told her to stay outside.'

'She looks after you. That is good. You first. Thank you,' he said to the waiter who had just returned. 'How much? I'm paying for both drinks . . .'

'I'd like to know where the Grumman aircraft that I spoke to you about from London is now.'

'That private jet intrigued me, so I made enquiries. First, as you know, it flew from Exeter to Charles de Gaulle – where an ambulance was waiting to take away a patient on a stretcher.'

'The so-called patient was Paula – who was kidnapped on Dartmoor, drugged, transported to Exeter Airport and then flown here. She had a bad experience. At the hands of Dr Goslar's thugs.'

'Then thank God she looks her normal fit self. To continue, the pilot filed a flight plan for Geneva, then changed it at the last moment. The private jet flew straight back to Heathrow.'

'That's strange.'

'I thought so. Maybe to pick up a passenger – to deliver one to London. Who knows?' Lasalle drank half his Pernod. 'From Heathrow it then flies straight to Geneva. I contacted Swiss friends. They tell me the aircraft is parked in an area reserved for private aircraft at Cointrin, Geneva's airport.'

'You said a private jet. Any idea who owns it?'

'A company called Poulenc et Cie, registered with a company in Liechtenstein at Vaduz. You know it is impossible to penetrate that place. So the trail ends there.'

'Meantime the jet is sitting on the tarmac at Geneva.'

'Yes.' Lasalle removed his hat, placed it on a chair. His dark hair was lank and greasy. The Frenchman saw Tweed's glance. 'I used plenty of oil on it – to merge with the background.'

'You're wearing your undercover work gear?'

'Yes. Awful, isn't it?'

'Changing the subject,' Tweed began, 'I suspect you have heard the name Goslar. Is that so?'

'Ah!' Lasalle shrugged, paused. 'I think we now come to what you call the nitty-gritty. You mentioned that name earlier.'

'And you didn't react. Which told me you'd heard of him.'

'I know you are a master interrogator. Slipped up there, didn't I? What I am going to tell you is so confidential I would lose my job if anyone came to hear of my talking to you. We are both referring to a strange incident at Appledore. Have I pronounced that correctly?'

'Yes. Please go on.'

'The Élysée received a video of that affair. You understand me?'

'Perfectly.'

By 'Élysée' Lasalle meant the President of France. He was being as frank as he dared. Lasalle took out a coloured handkerchief, mopped his forehead before he went on.

'The Élysée also received a recording made by someone with the most doctored voice. The message said the sender would consider sending his device – then he said *selling* his device – to France for eight thousand million francs.'

'That's roughly eight hundred million pounds. Didn't want much, did he?'

'There was an explosion of fury inside the Élysée at the amount. The security services were immediately ordered to track down the speaker, to get hold of the device with extreme urgency. So...' Lasalle looked embarrassed, 'I fear that we are rivals, fighting each other.'

'At least we can be civilized about this.'

'You must be careful. We believe the enemy has employed a very dangerous assassin. The Yellow Man. So called because he is believed to have yellow hair.'

Nothing in Tweed's expression betrayed the fact that he was startled by this information. He nodded to encourage Lasalle to keep talking.

'A few months ago a very rich man, a friend of a Cabinet Minister, was murdered horribly by, we believe, the Yellow Man. The victim was found decapitated in his apartment.'

'I think it made the English papers.'

'This assassin is so reliable the underworld believes that he was paid a million francs for that job.'

'Which is roughly a hundred thousand pounds.

139

Thanks for the warning. So on this Goslar business we're on opposite sides.'

'I'm afraid so, my friend. Expect no help from France. Take care.'

Tweed watched Lasalle putting on his old hat, pulling down the brim. Then he slouched away, head down. As he passed Paula's table he took no notice of her. She didn't look up, was apparently reading her newspaper.

There was a phone on the bar. Tweed stood up, went over to it. He called the number Serena had given him. A rough voice demanded in French who the hell it was.

'Maurice, a friend of Yvonne's,' Tweed replied, using the same language. 'I believe you can contact her. I can wait while you—'

'Not available!'

The phone was slammed down. Tweed walked slowly out of the brasserie. A few yards along the street he gazed round as though not sure where to go next. As Paula joined him a minute later Marler appeared out of nowhere.

'We'll go now and visit your rare-bookseller friend,' Tweed told Marler. 'Where are the others?' He had just spoken when Butler and Newman walked up to them. 'No point in going back for the cars,' he decided. 'We'll take a taxi.'

He hailed one. The driver pulled in to the kerb with a screech of brakes. He looked ahead, conveying the impression that passengers were a nuisance.

'Please take us to the Île de la Cité. We're in a hurry.'

'You always are,' the driver responded rudely. 'Traffic today is terrible. We get there when we arrive . . .'

'I think we're being followed,' Paula said after looking back.

140

'We'd better get used to it,' Tweed replied calmly. 'Is it,' he whispered, 'someone in another cab?'

'Yes.'

'Get a look at the passenger?'

'I'm afraid I didn't. But back at Madeleine I saw, out of the corner of my eye, someone flag down another cab as we got into this one. The same cab keeps following the route that we are taking.'

'Try and see who is inside if it stops when we do . . .'

Despite what the driver had said, once they had left Madeleine the traffic was light. Following Tweed's instructions the driver crossed a bridge over the Seine onto the Île de la Cité, then stopped outside the Palais de Justice. Paula got out quickly, looked back. She saw the cab which had tailed them pulling up. Then a huge truck stopped in front of it, blocking her view.

'Here you are,' said Tweed, handing the fare over plus the tip a Frenchman would have given him. The driver held out his hand with the money in his palm. He glared at Tweed.

'Is this all?'

'Fare with normal tip,' Tweed told him.

'Tip? Is this all? You are a miser.'

'Drop dead!' Paula snapped in French.

The driver stared at her as though unable to believe a woman had answered him back. He shrugged, drove off.

'Couldn't see who got out of the cab which followed us,' Paula said. 'A truck got in the way.'

'It doesn't matter. We'll walk past Notre-Dame.'

As they approached Notre-Dame Tweed stared up. Each time he saw it it always seemed larger, more massive. There were hardly any tourists about – it was the time of year and the weather. At the end of Cité they saw the Île St-Louis, the smaller island with the Seine swirling round it.

They came to the narrow bridge linking Cité with St-Louis. It was just wide enough for a car to cross but a barrier prevented wheeled traffic. As they walked round past the end of the barrier Marler caught up with Tweed.

'When we're the other side of the bridge take the right turn – along the quai d'Orleans. Vallade is in one of the narrow streets off to the left.'

'And I'm sure we're being followed,' said Paula.

'You warned us of that earlier,' Marler recalled, 'but neither Newman or Butler – or I for that matter – have spotted anyone. If Paula is right it must be someone very clever.'

'Paula is right,' Paula said obstinately. 'I can sense it. I just hope it isn't the Yellow Man.'

Earlier, while walking across the Cité, Tweed had told them about what Lasalle had said concerning the now notorious assassin. He felt he was not breaking his word on this subject. On the other hand he repeated not a word Lasalle had told him about the Élysée.

'We'll stroll along the embankment,' Marler suggested. 'I will tell you which is Vallade's street but it might be better if we continued on past it. That will give Newman and Butler an opportunity to check our rear. Paula's shadow has to cross the bridge to keep after us.'

'Except,' said Paula, after glancing back, 'a tour party has appeared. It is about to cross the bridge. An assassin could easily mingle with them . . .'

They continued along the *quai*. To their right the Seine flowed swiftly, a dark green current. A stone wall, roughly three feet high, separated them from the river below. On their left were ancient buildings five storeys high, also built of stone and with an appearance of having wealthy occupants.

As they strolled on Tweed was aware of an atmosphere of tension building up. They had been convinced by Paula's assertion that they were being followed. They all resisted the temptation to look back – which would have given the game away. It was up to Newman and Butler, somewhere behind them. They arrived at the first street leading straight down on their left. Tweed peered at it.

'Not that one,' snapped Marler.

'If there is a watcher,' Tweed pointed out, 'and I look down each street we come to, it will tell him nothing.'

'Hadn't thought of that.'

They kept walking and the wind was growing stronger. When they came to a certain side street Tweed peered down it. Marler spoke quickly.

'That's the one.'

Like all the streets on St-Louis the street was narrow, dark. On the ground floor there were shops, and above, Tweed assumed, would be apartments. They walked a short distance further and the *quai* curved round a sharp corner. There was a large gap in the embankment wall where a wide stone ramp led down to the water's edge. Tweed stopped.

'What is it?' Paula asked.

'There's a very modern powerboat moored to a bollard down at the bottom of the ramp. No one about. Interesting.'

'Why?'

'We'd better get on with it, Marler. Time to visit Vallade and see what he can tell us.'

'I hope he's still alive,' Paula said.

13

In his suite at the Hôtel Crillon in Paris Vance Karnow, aide to the President of the United States, sat in a carver chair and stared at his guests with hard eyes. Tall and thin, with a long face which had prominent bone structure, his mouth was wide with twisted lips. Below the mouth his jaw was pointed.

'Everyone present and here on time,' he said in his harsh voice. 'You know I demand punctuality on the rare occasions when I call a full meeting.'

Including Karnow, there were eleven people in the luxurious room. All were members of Unit Four. Ten men and one woman. They sat spread round the room, seated in armchairs or on sofas. The woman sat in her own carver chair close to Karnow.

'We now know,' Karnow continued, 'that Tweed is in Paris, staying at the Ritz. Thanks to Trudy.' He turned to her. 'Show them the photo of Tweed.'

Trudy Warnowski was an attractive woman in her late thirties. Her blaze of soft red hair was perfectly coiffeured and she wore just enough makeup on her cheerful face. She had a good figure, and was clad in a fashionable and expensive black suit.

From a folder she produced a photograph. Walking elegantly to one of the men she gave him the photo.

'Hand it round, Brad,' she told him. 'After you've memorized Tweed. That's important.'

Karnow gave her a verbal pat on the back when she had returned to her chair.

'You should all know that Trudy followed Tweed to Paris on his late flight last night. She then drove after him from Charles de Gaulle in her hired car. During the

144

flight she saw Tweed speak to another man sitting by himself further down the aircraft. At Madeleine she had to take a quick decision. She saw the man Tweed had spoken to getting into another car. She decided to follow him, thinking he'd lead her to where they were staying. She had parked her car by a meter. She hailed a cab, wanting a different vehicle so she wouldn't be spotted. She was smart. She waited inside the reception area and later Tweed himself arrived, booked in.'

'Nothing to it,' Trudy said in her soft voice.

By this time the photograph had passed round the room. A short, heavily built, fat man with a large round face ambled over to Trudy, handed back the photo. She knew he had been gazing at her legs as he approached her.

'You did a good job,' he said in his hoarse voice.

'I've just spent time telling everyone that,' Karnow said coldly. 'Weren't you listening, Bancroft?'

The fat man was the only member of Unit Four Karnow always addressed by his surname. He knew Bancroft was the only man present who wasn't frightened of him.

'So I paid her my own compliment,' Bancroft retorted, staring at Karnow. 'Anything wrong with that? And where's Milt? Not here.'

'Milt,' Karnow replied through lips which had almost vanished, 'is following Tweed Inc. at this moment.'

'Waiting for an opportunity to use his knife?'

'Anybody ever tell you that you talk too much?'

'Lots of people. I do it all the time. Milt's going to carve up Tweed if he can?'

Bancroft was referring to the fact that Milt Friedman always used a knife to persuade men – or women – to talk. He had once used an axe to kill a target.

145

'Milt will use his own discretion. Subject closed. Although if any of you get Tweed on his own he is *very, very* embarrassing.'

Translation: kill him. Karnow used a number of careful phrases to explain what was needed. *Very embarrassing* meant beat up the named subject. *Lose him* meant cripple the subject, man or woman.

Bancroft grinned at Trudy, gave her a mock salute, ambled back to his sofa.

Trudy recalled that, despite his fatness, Bancroft was a winner with women. She knew he'd had a number of successes – often with classy ladies. Something about his personality. Then she recalled the strong thin piece of rope he had once carried. It was attached by one end to his belt while the length dangled down inside his left trouser leg. He had strangled two women with that piece of rope. She took out a lacy handkerchief and dried her moist palms.

'Your task is simple,' Karnow began again. 'All members of Tweed's team – when we have identified them – are *very, very* embarrassing. You circulate round the Ritz, inside it. First you identify his team – I suspect there are a number of them.'

And they could do that, he thought as he paused. Because they were all well dressed in good suits. They were all educated – even Bancroft. He had recruited Unit Four with great care. No thugs from the back streets of Chicago.

Several had been trained as lawyers. They had then found it would take years to earn big money. Some were from Harvard and thought the world was their oyster. They'd had a shock when they discovered the lowly jobs, the low pay, the endless hours they'd be expected to work for years.

Karnow had looked for frustrated men. Those who

would never get anywhere – and knew it when they started exploring the jungle of the real world. Karnow had looked for those with a streak of amorality, brutality. He had offered them regular money they'd have taken years to get near in any profession. Generous money. Paid in cash – so they could forget about forking out tax. He looked at Brad Braun, a good-looking man in his late twenties.

'Brad, you book yourself a suite at the Ritz. Keep an eye on Tweed and see who he mixes with. Circulate descriptions to the rest of the unit.'

'A suite at the Ritz will be expensive,' Brad observed as he stroked his thick black and well-groomed hair.

'You all have a load of dollars. Brad, when you pay you just tell the desk you've lost your credit card. They're French,' he said with a note of contempt, 'they'll grab your dollars. Oh, there was a woman travelling on the plane with Tweed.'

'Great!' Bancroft grinned. 'Do I get a description?'

'Only a vague one,' Trudy informed him. 'Thick black glossy hair. A looker. Slim, in her thirties would be my best guess. About five feet six tall. That's it.'

'That's enough,' Bancroft said with another suggestive grin.

'Move,' Karnow said. 'All of you – except Trudy.'

'Have a cosy get-together,' Bancroft said as he was leaving the room with the others.

Karnow caught his eye, the fact that he was still grinning. His expression would have scared the daylights out of any other member of the unit. Bancroft just went on grinning until he shut the door and disappeared.

'He's a character,' Trudy said, lighting a cigarette.

'Do you have to smoke?' Karnow asked.

'We're not in America now. Thank God. I like

147

Europe. I knew a Frenchman who told me over here they think political correctness is treating a woman friend generously.'

'Do you think they got my message – the unit?'

'Hardly fail to – the extremely diplomatic way you put it across to them.'

'Nobody talks back to me the way you do,' he commented with a grudging note of admiration. 'But I meant it – when I said you'd done a good job tracking Tweed.'

'Oh, I think there was another man with him. A military type. I couldn't be sure. It would have meant turning my head round and staring.'

'You rescued your parked car?'

'Took a cab back to pick it up after Tweed arrived. A piece of cake.' She went silent for a short time, then glanced at Karnow. 'I thought the object of this exercise was to locate Goslar, to grab this new weapon.'

'It is.'

'Then I think it was a mistake to order them to eliminate Tweed. You got someone to ask Cord Dillon about Tweed. Dillon said he was the most formidable security officer in Europe.'

'So?'

'Keep him alive. Follow him. I think eventually he'll lead us to Goslar. This is his back yard.'

'You could be right.' Karnow pondered briefly. 'I think you are right. I'll put that order on hold.' He picked up the phone, called a room number. 'Brad, I imagine none of our associates have left the hotel yet? Good. Get them all back up here in ten minutes from now . . .'

He clasped his cruel, long-fingered hands, looked at the woman sitting next to him with what passed for a smile.

'How about having dinner with me tonight?'

'Vance, I made it quite clear when you hired me the

148

relationship must remain strictly professional. You agreed. The agreement still stands. I must go now.'

'Anything you say,' he responded as she was leaving the room.

He sat ruminating. His first meeting with Trudy had been at a Washington party. She was English, which, added to her appearance, he knew would make most American men a pushover for her. He had been looking for the right woman to add to Unit Four and she fitted the bill. He had just finished talking to Bancroft when he had encountered her.

She had told him she was a widow. He had told her he was the right-hand man to the President. It hadn't seemed to impress her. He had arranged several lunches with her – while he instructed a detective agency, through an intermediary, to check on her. Vance Karnow was a careful operator.

The agency had confirmed what she'd told him during the lunches. She was employed by a top security outfit, handling difficult assignments brilliantly. She'd had a two-year stint in New York. She lived alone in an apartment in Washington after her transfer. The one item the agency couldn't come up with was the identity of her late husband. He had casually asked her about him over lunch.

'We lived in a very different part of the States,' she told him. Gazing straight at him, she went on. 'It's a painful subject and I don't want to talk about it. Don't ask me again . . .'

He'd glossed over that. His next move was to offer her a highly paid position with 'a confidential organization not so different from the one you're working for now'. He had emphasized that the difference was the work was absolutely top secret.

'If you think by now that I can't keep my mouth shut, forget it,' she had told him.

He had hired her for three times the salary the security agency had been paying her. She had accepted, but had refused point-blank to sign any kind of contract. He had reluctantly agreed to the condition, so impressed was he by her personality.

Taking his time, he had gradually revealed to her the function of Unit Four: that it was to protect state secrets. He had not told her that it was in any way involved with the Oval Office – which, in a way, put her on a level with the President.

When Karnow had come up with the idea he had no more than hinted about how Unit Four would operate. He had been vague when he had talked to the President. First, he had laid the groundwork.

'Neither of us are very happy about the leaks which filter out of the FBI and the CIA,' he had suggested. 'I've been thinking that we need a small, tough group of élite men to handle sensitive situations . . .'

'You mean "I" not "we",' the President had corrected him.

'Yes, I do,' Karnow had agreed. 'A slip of the tongue.'

'Very unusual for you, Vance. I have so much to do I must leave decisions like that to your discretion.'

The President had winked at him.

Karnow was recalling that wink when Brad Braun walked into the suite, followed by Bancroft and the others. The nine men sat in the same places they had occupied earlier.

'Trudy,' said Bancroft, 'isn't coming. Said she wasn't needed for this conference.'

'She has something to attend to,' Karnow improvised.

Mentally he gave her top marks. She had thought it tactful to stay away, to give him the floor.

'I have been thinking about what I said to you earlier

concerning Tweed,' he began. 'We let him walk the face of this planet. It has struck me . . .'

Long ago Karnow had learned to take the credit for other people's ideas. It comfirmed his own cleverness.

14

Tweed and Paula managed to walk side by side down the meagre width of the pavement. Marler walked alongside them in the narrow street. The area was deserted and Paula had a claustrophobic sensation as the old buildings on either side seemed to close in on them. It was too quiet and there was no wind.

'There's the shop,' Marler said.

'I've seen it,' replied Tweed. 'Looks pretty rundown.'

He could just make out the name in crumbling gold paint on the fascia above the grimy windows. The name, *Vallade*, hadn't been repainted for ages. Quite a narrow frontage with a warped wooden door which had pebble glass windows in the upper half. Tweed paused by the first window. He could see ancient volumes in worn leather bindings.

'He speaks English,' Marler said. 'You two go in to get the feel of the place. I'll come in when I've checked the street.'

The door creaked when Tweed turned the old-fashioned handle and he had to lift and push to get it open. With Paula he walked inside and immediately met a musty smell. The shop was narrow and long, went back further than he'd expected. On a counter was a huge glass dome housing a large stuffed owl. Paula stared at the left-hand wall facing the counter. From floor to ceiling were glass-fronted bookcases crammed with old books side by side.

Tweed was walking further down the counter. Behind it stood a small plump man. Everything about him was plump. His plump face was a surprisingly healthy pink colour and his grey hair was brushed neatly back from his forehead. He wore a shabby velvet jacket with gold buttons and a pair of corduroy trousers which had seen better days. Perched on his short nose were half-moon glasses. He peered at his visitors over the top of them.

'Have you a copy of Hogarth's *Characters in My Times*?' asked Tweed.

'No, sir. And no one has. Such a title does not exist.'

'Just checking,' Tweed said with a smile.

'I do know books, sir,' Vallade replied with a smile which included Paula.

'It's like *The Old Curiosity Shop*,' Paula whispered to Tweed.

'Charles Dickens,' Vallade called out.

Paula then realized the Frenchman had exceptional hearing. When he smiled his chubby red cheeks seemed even plumper. At that moment Marler entered.

'Ah!' Vallade commented. 'When Tweed appears Marler is not far behind.'

'How do you know my name?' Tweed enquired.

'I presume you have come for any information I can provide. So I know a few things about this jungle of a world we live in – including the existence of Mr Tweed.'

'What is that ferocious-looking thing hanging from the wall near the door?' Paula asked.

She was looking at a long curved oriental sword. The handle was large and decorated with strange designs. There were more weird symbols on the blade.

'That is a Japanese . . .' Vallade paused – he had been going to say 'execution sword' but because she was a lady he changed it – 'ceremonial sword. The Japanese

152

pay a lot of money for such articles. We don't see Japanese much these days – now their economy has collapsed.' He looked at Tweed. 'I said the world was a jungle. Now the Americans drop 2,000 pound bombs from a height of 15,000 feet on Serbia – killing many women and children. This is mass murder. I fear your government trots along behind Washington. Excuse me, I digress. How can I help you?'

'I am hoping you can tell me something about a man called Dr Goslar.'

'He is a client of mine. Not in person. He phoned me with a screeching voice and wanted me to find a copy of a book on the Galapagos Islands in the Pacific, the home of giant turtles. It is a rare medical book on these strange creatures.'

He paused and came through a gap in the counter. He had noticed Paula peering into the glass bookcases against the opposite wall. Producing a bunch of keys he opened a bookcase, took out a small black cardboard case, handed it to her.

'You may find this interesting . . .'

Tweed intervened quickly, realizing he had not introduced her to the bookseller. Vallade shook her hand, smiled again.

'Inside the case is a first edition, illustrated, of J. M. Barrie's *Peter Pan*. I think you will like it.'

He shuffled back behind his counter. His visitors saw he wore a pair of slippers. He gazed at Tweed.

'Excuse the interruption. I told this Goslar I had one copy but it was expensive. He asked how much and told me to keep it for him.'

'He came to collect it himself?' enquired Tweed.

'No, as arranged on the phone, he sent someone to pick it up. A good-looking red-haired lady.'

'She gave a name?' Tweed asked casually.

'No. She said she had come to collect the book Dr Goslar had called me about, paid me, took the book away.'

'Could you describe her?'

'About as tall as Miss Grey. Another beautiful lady. Her eyes were grey-blue. She wore a scarf round her head. I only saw the lovely red hair because when she opened the door to leave the wind blew the scarf off her neck. The hair was long.'

'How long ago was it since she collected this book?'

'My memory is not good these days for time lapses. I would say about ten days ago. Maybe a little longer.'

'One other point, Étienne,' interjected Marler, 'do you know anything about the Yellow Man?'

'Oh dear.' For the first time Vallade's expression became grave. 'That terrible assassin. He has killed three important men so far. One in Germany, another in Switzerland – and a wealthy man here who lived in a big house just along the *quai*. They say he receives a million francs for an assassination. He is so efficient but no one ever sees him. Certain top informants I know in the underworld tell me it is rumoured he has yellow hair. Which is why he is called the Yellow Man.'

'Any clue as to his whereabouts?' Marler suggested.

'None at all. Another rumour is that he is English. But he is invisible. Please do not tell anyone what I have told you.'

'We wouldn't dream of ever mentioning your name,' Tweed assured him. 'And you really have been most helpful.'

Tweed was hesitantly reaching for his wallet when Marler nudged him. Tweed withdrew his hand. Vallade did not expect any payment. The plump little man shuffled through the gap in the counter to Paula, who had been admiring the *Peter Pan* book.

'This is quite beautiful,' she said, handing it to him after carefully placing it back in the case.

'It is for you, Miss Grey.'

'But this is a first edition. I couldn't possibly . . .'

'It is a present.' He squeezed her hand. 'You cannot refuse a present from Vallade.' He turned to Tweed, shook his hand.

'Always be on the lookout for a man with yellow hair. Take great care.'

'Thank you so much for the magnificent present,' Paula said. 'Your English is perfect. Where did you learn it?'

'Thank you.' Vallade beamed at her. 'As a young man I studied my profession with a rare-book dealer in a street off Piccadilly. I go back to London when I can to listen to how they speak English today. Languages change. You also take great care. You are a nice lady . . .'

He closed the door behind them gently as they stepped onto the pavement. Marler glanced to his right.

'We're nearly at the end of this street. We could go into the main thoroughfare, the rue St Louis en l'Île.'

'No,' Tweed decided, 'we'll go back the way we came. I'm hungry and that is the direct route to the Restaurant Paul on Cité. We'll get an excellent meal there.'

Newman appeared. He walked slowly alongside Tweed as they proceeded to the *quai*. He had his hand over his mouth as he took his time lighting a cigarette.

'Coast appears clear. Neither Butler nor I have seen anyone following us. Hard to be sure. Several individuals have wandered down here while you were inside.'

'They went past the shop?'

'Some did. Others disappeared into houses. I'll walk ahead. Harry is bringing up the rear . . .'

They had reached the end of the street, and were

about to turn right on to the *quai*, when Tweed looked back, stopped, hesitated, then walked on slowly. He had his head down, hands inside the pockets of his grey overcoat. Paula kept quiet. She guessed he was turning over in his mind what Vallade had told them.

When they reached the bridge he paused again. He was staring at the River Seine, which was less choppy. Paula wished he'd get moving. She was starving. After a minute or two he looked at her.

'We're going back to Vallade's shop. At the top of his street I thought I caught a glimpse – out of the corner of my eye – of someone walking into one of the buildings near the bottom of the street. It could have been Vallade's bookshop.'

'Something up?' asked Newman who had walked back to them.

'Tweed thinks he saw someone going into Vallade's place,' Paula told him.

'We'll go back now,' Tweed decided. 'Peripheral vision can be deceptive, but I thought I caught a glimpse of yellow hair.' He began stepping it out. 'Move, everyone.'

They were halfway down the street when Tweed paused. He looked back, listened. There was the distant sound of an engine starting up.

'Sounds like that powerboat we saw,' he said. 'I don't like this . . .'

Butler had moved ahead of them. His right hand was tucked inside his anorak, gripping his Walther. He arrived at the bookseller's shop. Paula, close behind him with Tweed, was about to enter when Butler grasped her by the arm, pulled her back.

'You stay outside while I check the place.'

He entered, opening the door slowly. Tweed was at

his heels. Newman remained on the pavement, restraining Paula, who snapped at him. He tightened his grip on her arm, glancing up and down the street.

'Our job is to keep an eye open for watchers.'

Butler, Walther in his hand, had gone into the shop in front of Tweed. He stopped suddenly. Turning round, he gazed at Tweed.

'Better prepare yourself,' he whispered.

'What is it?'

'Stay where you are while I search the back.'

Tweed waited where he stood. He was not able to see much inside. Butler ran to the back, crouched down. He tried a door at the end, found it was locked. His expression was grim when he walked back. Tweed walked further in, stopped. For a few seconds he was in a state of shock.

The large stuffed owl was no longer inside the glass dome. It lay on the floor on his side of the counter. In its place he found himself staring at the head of Étienne Vallade, perched upright inside the dome. The eyes were open and he had the odd sensation that the bookseller was staring at him. Lying on the counter was the Japanese sword, its blade smeared with blood. More blood coated the rim of the dome inside. The bookseller's half-moon glasses were perched on the nose, a hideous insult.

'No one here,' Butler reported. 'The rest of the body is lying on the floor behind the counter. Whoever did it must have come in, seen the sword, snatched it off the wall and beheaded Vallade with one savage sweeping blow. Then he lifted the glass dome, threw out the owl, replaced it with Vallade's head. Some nice people in this world . . .'

He had just spoken when Paula broke free from Newman's grip and rushed inside. She stopped suddenly. Tweed tried to shield her gaze from the thing inside the dome, but he was too late. She stood very still, all her colour vanished from her face, in a state of deep shock, Tweed assumed.

'Get out of here,' Butler ordererd. 'All of us. If the French police catch us we'll be interrogated for days.'

Tweed turned to leave, pulling at Paula, but she wouldn't move. Butler also took hold of her. Between them they pushed her back to the doorway. Her reaction astounded Tweed. She stopped in the open doorway, had snatched her Browning from her shoulder bag. She hissed the words as the others stared at her.

'If I meet whoever did this I'll empty all nine bullets into them. Vallade was such a lovable character,' she gulped.

'Put the damned gun away,' Butler growled at her. 'If anyone in the street sees you like that—'

She slid the Browning back inside its pocket, walked like a robot into the street. Tweed called out to Newman quietly that Vallade was dead. Newman put his arm round Paula while Butler joined them. Tweed still had his wits about him. He took out a handkerchief, wiped fingerprints off both sides of the handle to the door, then closed it, his hand wrapped in the handkerchief.

'We go left, back to the *quai*,' he said calmly, decisively. 'At the end of the street we turn left. I want a second look at the ramp where that powerboat was moored. Don't hurry. Walk at a normal pace. Stay with Paula, Bob. Let's spread out a bit.'

Paula was breathing heavily but refused the offer of Newman's arm. She walked stiff-legged, one foot in front of the other. At the end of the street she took a deep breath of air off the Seine. Tweed, after glancing left and right, walked quickly to the left. Paula and Newman had to hurry to keep up. Behind them, a number of yards away, Butler brought up the rear.

Reaching the gap in the embankment wall where the ramp ran down to the river, Tweed looked down. No sign of the powerboat. It might never have been there. He looked round for witnesses but there was no one. Normally, he recalled from a previous visit, men with rods had fished from this ramp. They were either away at lunch or – more likely – had not fished this morning because of the bitter wind.

'We'll go to lunch at the Restaurant Paul,' he decided. 'I'm anxious we get off St Louis and onto the Île de la Cité.'

'It was the Yellow Man,' Paula said quietly.

'I think so. Then he darted to the end of the street, along the rue St Louis en l'Île, turned down another side street to the ramp where he had that powerboat waiting. He'll always have his escape route planned.'

'The Yellow Man,' Paula repeated, almost to herself.

15

The Restaurant Paul on the Île de la Cité is curiously situated. It stretches from the triangular *place* Dauphine, invisible from the Seine, like a wide corridor to a street overlooking the river embankment. It was very crowded but the manager found a table for the five of them at the river end. Marler had appeared from nowhere as they'd crossed the bridge linking the two islands.

'I don't want anything to eat,' Paula said, putting the menu aside.

'Then I'll order something for you,' said Tweed. 'You must keep up your strength.'

'Then I won't eat it . . .'

When their orders came they all started except Paula. They said nothing important because they were surrounded with other diners. Suddenly Paula picked up her knife and fork and attacked the fish on her plate, devouring it. Tweed looked across at Newman, who smiled and surreptitiously gave a thumbs-up signal.

'We'll get back to the hotel,' Tweed said as he paid the bill. 'Maybe someone will have something to report.'

He was referring to Burgoyne and Nield, who had been left behind to check on the other guests. During the taxi ride back Newman diverted the cab driver into a side street. He had spotted an isolated phone box. With his back to the taxi he took out a silk handkerchief, held it over his mouth to blur his voice as he called police headquarters. He reported a murder at Vallade's bookshop, slammed down the phone when asked for his name.

He whispered to Tweed what he had done as the cab continued to the Ritz. Tweed merely nodded his approval. Newman then passed the same message to Paula. She looked relieved. The thought of Vallade's remains staying in the shop had revolted her.

The first people they saw when they entered the hotel were Nield and Burgoyne, seated in the lobby apart from each other. Tweed collected his key and, with a little wave of his hand, indicated they should both join him. Marler took off his coat, folded it over his arm, began strolling round the ground floor.

'I suppose nothing has happened,' Tweed began the moment they were inside his suite.

'It has,' said Nield.

Paula glanced at Burgoyne, who smiled, nodded agreement with what Nield had said. Newman sat in an armchair, lit a cigarette. Butler had gone straight to his room.

'The Americans have arrived,' Burgoyne announced. 'In force. Here in the hotel. Pete told me about Unit

160

Four. We do have distinguished company. Pete, I'll leave you to tell them.'

'The early indication I had that they were on their way here was not conclusive,' Nield began. 'A well-dressed American – expensive suit – arrived, booked a suite. Chap by the name of Brad Braun.'

'How did you find that out?' asked Tweed.

'Heard his American accent when he spoke to the doorman as he walked in. He goes up to reservation so I join the queue, standing next to him. Saw his name when he registered. He goes up to his suite. Soon he comes down, has a late breakfast. I go into the dining room, get a table close to him, order a second breakfast of coffee and croissants. Braun is joined by another American, a short fat character with wide shoulders and large hands. Smiles and laughs a lot, though his eyes never smile. While talking he's scanning the other guests in the place. I hear his name when Braun calls him Bancroft. Very tough, this Bancroft, I'd say.'

'Chance,' Tweed said, addressing Burgoyne, 'you referred to distinguished company. Who was that?'

'Hold on to your hat. None other than Vance Karnow, chief aide to the President. I saw a picture of him in the paper once. A striking-looking man.'

'Sell his own mother if the price was high enough,' Nield added.

'I wonder who is running the Oval Office in his absence,' Tweed mused. 'From what I've heard Karnow handles all the tricky situations. Advises the President how to react – or how not to react.'

'The Oval Office must be taking what happened north of Dartmoor pretty seriously,' Burgoyne commented.

'Yes,' Tweed agreed, 'sending a big gun like that over here.'

161

Before leaving Park Crescent he had privately briefed Burgoyne on aspects of what he had called the Appledore 'trigger'. He sat back, drummed the fingers of his right hand on the arm of his chair.

'I have to find a way of getting the French and the Americans off our backs. I believe I now know where Goslar's main base is. Something Lasalle said to me.'

'So where is it?' asked Burgoyne.

'I could be wrong. I need more confirmation. Where are our transatlantic friends now?'

'In the bar, last time we saw them,' Burgoyne told him. 'I think I should check the streets near here – see if they have any reinforcements waiting in cars or whatever.'

'Good idea. Nield, you check inside the hotel again.'

Burgoyne was sitting relaxed in an armchair. Paula had been watching him with interest. Catching her gaze he gave her a wink and she smiled back. When they had left the room, Burgoyne following Nield, there was a knock on the door. Newman went to unlock the door. Marler stood outside, came in, then stood against the wall.

'You've probably heard the Yanks are here.'

'We have,' Tweed said.

The phone rang. Paula answered it. She frowned, covered the mouthpiece with her hand.

'We have company. Lasalle is on the phone, calling from downstairs. Wants to see you urgently. *Now*, he said.'

'Ask him to come up.'

'I think,' Marler decided, 'I'll hide myself in your bathroom. Otherwise with all of us here Lasalle is going to feel outgunned.'

'Good idea . . .'

Newman again attended to the door. Paula's eyes

162

narrowed as Lasalle walked in with another man. Lapin, his assistant. A small thin man, he had a face like a monkey. He wore a neutral-coloured raincoat, denims and shoes with thick rubber soles. Newman frowned. He had seen this man recently.

'Sit down. Make yourself at home, René,' Tweed greeted their visitors.

'This is an official visit,' Lasalle said stiffly,

'Sit down, stand up – whichever you prefer.'

They perched together on the edge of a sofa. Lapin's ferret-like eyes switched from one occupant to the other. He had a sallow complexion and always looked as though he'd come to work after having a row with his wife. Tweed said nothing more, waited.

'Were you on the Île de la Cité earlier this morning?' Lasalle demanded.

'As a matter of fact, we were. Why?'

'And then on the Île St-Louis?'

'What is this all about?' Tweed asked mildly. 'I suppose your associate, Lapin, followed us for some reason?'

'Do you know a seller of rare books called Vallade?'

'How do you spell that name?'

'Is Vallade a friend of yours? Someone you have known for quite a while?'

'No,' said Tweed, answering the second question.

'Why were you on the Île de la Cité this morning? Please don't say you were taking the air.'

'We wanted to see if we would be followed, wherever we went to. Obviously we were. By Lapin.'

The monkey-faced assistant had the grace to stare at the floor. He moved his feet uncomfortably.

'So you have no information to give me.' Lasalle had stood up, obviously annoyed. 'In that case we will leave.' Newman had unlocked the door, opened it. Lapin walked into the corridor as Tweed spoke.

'René, I do have some information which is confidential.'

Lasalle shut the door, leaving Lapin outside in the corridor. His previously stiff demeanour changed and he became more like his normal self. He walked over to Tweed but did not sit down again.

'I'm listening,' he said.

'You might like to know this place – this hotel – is crawling with Americans. I'm sure they're on the same mission you and I are. From what I've heard they're a team of sophisticated thugs – well dressed, well spoken. And this is the clincher – their leader is a certain Vance Karnow, who is probably still downstairs in the bar.'

'Karnow?' Lasalle was startled. 'The American who runs the White House? Probably the second most influential man in the whole world? Here in Paris?'

'I just told you – he was downstairs in the bar. With some of his very tough and sleek-looking associates. One of them, a Brad Braun, has actually taken a suite here. The Americans have a lot of money. Neither of us wants them to reach Goslar first.'

'True. The source I spoke of earlier when we met – the one where the video and message was sent to – will be enraged.'

Tweed knew he was referring to the President of France. He made his suggestion in an off-hand manner.

'Would it be in the interests of France if you harried these Americans? Threw them off balance, so to speak. You might even be able to charge them with some offence.'

'You know me. I'll think of something. I'd better get moving. And thank you for the information . . .'

'What is the plan?' Paula asked as Marler came out of the bathroom.

'Up to the moment of Lasalle coming to see us,' Tweed began, 'we were fighting too many outfits. Goslar's vast organization. On top of that the French security services. And on top of that the American contingent. With just a few words to René I've simplified the situation. The French security services will be paying attention to hassling the Americans. I'm sure that when the President in the Élysée hears what Lasalle tells him he'll order all firepower to be turned on America. That gets Karnow and his men out of our way. It also concentrates the focus of the French security services away from us. That leaves us free to concentrate *our* efforts on what matters. Locating and destroying Goslar.'

'That was a clever gambit,' Newman commented.

'Just a thought on the spur of the moment. A tactical move.'

'That is a real plan,' Paula agreed. 'Top marks. I thought it strange that Lasalle didn't tell us what had happened to poor Vallade. He didn't even tell us he is dead.'

'He's trying to keep the story out of the press as long as he can. Imagine the panic in Paris when it comes out. Vallade was not a famous and powerful politician. In the eyes of the public he'll be an ordinary person – so everyone will feel at risk. I wonder if the Yellow Man really has yellow hair? I was inches away from him in Brown's Hotel in London. It struck me he had very thick hair. Could it be a toupee?'

'I hope not. In that case we'll never recognize him. Why do you think Goslar had Vallade killed?' Paula wondered.

'I think because he used his name, Goslar, when he phoned Vallade about the book on Galapagos turtles. He used to do that on rare occasions in the old days of the Cold War. Remember, Bob? It's a form of bravado.

Then he regrets having done it. So he shoots the messenger, so to speak.'

'Why would he want a book on Galapagos turtles?'

'I've no idea,' Tweed admitted. 'But remember the so-called fairy tale Dillon told us in London? A fisherman with a distinctive red sail and a half-moon. Therefore easy to track him down after he'd landed in Ecuador. He was killed – together with the freelance agent he spoke to. Both beheaded. Shades of the Yellow Man?'

'Weird,' Paula ruminated aloud. 'So what's next?'

'You and I, with Bob, go down to the bar to see if the Americans are still there. Marler, trail us down there, then stay outside the bar. Just in case of trouble.'

They were still in the bar. Vance Karnow sat upright with his back to a wall. Next to him sat an attractive red-head. On his other side sat a good-looking man Tweed thought could be Brad Braun, the American with the suite. The fourth member of the party was short and wide-shouldered, and was grinning. Fatso, Paula thought – probably Bancroft.

Tweed chose a table not too close to them, which gave him a sideways view. As he walked towards it he saw out of the corner of his eye Karnow staring straight at him. He sat down as Karnow nudged the red-head, who glanced up at Tweed.

They had ordered their drinks when Braun gazed at them. Soon afterwards Bancroft took his time observing them. Taking a sip from his glass of wine, Tweed looked at the Americans, making no attempt to conceal his action. Karnow, his eyes hard, stared at him again. Tweed looked back at Karnow point-blank. It was the American who turned away first.

166

'They know who I am,' Tweed remarked. 'And look who's in the corner to the left of us.'

Paula looked over the rim of her glass as she also sipped wine. Sitting by himself, pretending to read *Figaro*, was Lapin. As she watched a much larger Frenchman came in, went to Lapin's table, shook hands with him and sat down. As soon as the newcomer had ordered his drink the two men engaged in a close conversation.

'Lasalle doesn't waste much time,' Paula observed.

'He doesn't,' Tweed agreed. 'And my guess is that by now he's got men covering every exit, including the one onto the side street. Men equipped with motorcycles in case any American leaves by car or taxi. Now Lapin has produced a mobile phone, is talking into it. Giving a description of every man – and the woman – at that table.'

'I like the look of her,' Newman commented, after drinking more of his double Scotch. 'How old would you say she is?'

'Late thirties, early forties,' Paula told him.

'I think there's someone else she's interested in,' Newman replied.

While Karnow was deep in conversation with Braun, the woman was gazing straight at Tweed. He looked back at her and she held her gaze. He had the impression she was weighing him up. As he watched her she glanced at Karnow, saw he was looking the other way, then gazed back at Tweed and gave him a half-smile.

'You've struck lucky,' Paula teased Tweed. 'Why would a nice-looking woman like that be mixed up with a mob of Americans who look as though they'd snatch a dollar out of a beggar's hand?'

'Maybe I'll get the chance to find out,' Tweed joked back.

'You'd better keep your mind on why we're here,' she teased him again.

'That's why I said what I did.'

'Is it really a good idea to be here?' Paula wondered. 'It gives them an opportunity to recognize us.'

'That works in the opposite direction,' said Tweed. 'Know your enemy. And now, if everyone's ready, I think we ought to go . . .'

He signed the bill, added his suite number, and they left the bar. No one at the Americans' table gave them a glance. They met Marler outside, perched on a chair, a magazine in his lap. He joined them.

'I want to try and contact Cord Dillon,' Tweed decided.

'I peered in through the door,' Marler reported. 'Got a good look at them. Nice people.'

'Fatso looks rather jolly,' Paula remarked. 'A nice smile.'

'Bancroft,' said Newman. 'They all probably thought he looked rather jolly – with a nice smile. I'm talking about his previous victims. They thought that, and then it was too late. He is the most dangerous. Think I'll patrol round the hotel.'

'I'll do that thing also,' Marler remarked. 'See if we've missed anything. Anyone . . .'

Tweed and Paula had just sat down in his suite when the phone rang. Nearest to it, Tweed picked it up.

'Yes?'

'Mr Tweed?' a soft feminine voice enquired.

'Speaking.'

'This is Trudy Warner. We looked at each other long enough in the bar. Could we meet and have a talk? I do know your suite number.'

168

'Then why not come up now? You'll be on your own?'

'I promise. And will you be on your own? I really do want to talk to you alone.'

'There is no one else in this room as we speak.'

Tweed was telling the truth. Paula had slipped into the loo in his bathroom. The door was closed.

'Could I come up now, then? I don't often get the opportunity to do this.'

'Yes, come now . . .'

Paula came out of the bathroom. He told her quickly what the phone call had been about. He added that Trudy Warner was very anxious to see him on his own. Paula looked worried, spoke rapidly.

'I don't like that at all. Look what's happened. Sam Sneed murdered in London, my experience at La Défense, the murder of Coral Langley when Marler visited Chance's place Rydford – and Vallade. I could hide in the bathroom. No, she might want to use it.' She walked to a tall cupboard, opened both doors. 'If you don't mind, I could hide in here. Plenty of space next to your clothes.'

'Get in quickly, then. She'll be here any moment.'

She took out the key and, with her shoulder bag over her arm, she stepped into the closet. She shut the doors from the inside, peered through the keyhole. She could clearly see Tweed seated on the sofa. She opened the door again.

'Get her to sit next to you. Then I can see both of you.'

Less than half a minute later there was a light tapping on the main door. Tweed jumped up agilely. He positioned himself to the hinged side of the door, reached across, unlocked the door, leaving it on the chain. He didn't think it a sound idea to be standing in front of the door if bullets came flying through it.

169

'Who is it?'

'Me. Trudy.'

Silently, he walked past the door, unlocked it with the chain in place. She stood outside, alone. She looked nervous. While he removed the chain she had glanced up and down the corridor. She came in quickly and he relocked the door, replaced the chain.

'Come and sit with me,' he said. 'Tell me what this is about.'

Following Paula's suggestion, he occupied the same seat on the sofa and she sat beside him. Seen close up she was very attractive. Her long red hair, just touching her shoulders, framed a face with a good complexion, pencilled eyebrows above grey-blue eyes which stared straight into his, as they had done in the bar. He sensed that she was unsure what to say first. He waited.

'I know about you, Mr Tweed,' she said.

'You do? How?'

He was still wary. On previous missions he had encountered several murderesses. The breed seemed to be growing.

'I listened in – on an extension – to a call Vance Karnow made to Cord Dillon, Deputy Director of the CIA. Karnow wanted to know who was the toughest man among the security services in London. Dillon was very abrupt in his reply. I can quote his exact words. "A man called Tweed. The most formidable of them all. And, Karnow, he's as honest as the day is long – a very long day. So you won't be able to practise your tricks on him." Dillon then slammed down the phone and I replaced my receiver at the same moment – so Karnow wouldn't hear the click.'

'May I ask why Karnow is over here? Why are you with him?'

'Let me tell the story in my own way, please. I've spent five years in the States . . .'

'You're English, aren't you?'

'Yes. I married an American called Walt Jules Baron. Jules is pronounced Jewels over there. He was an accountant, told me he worked for a security outfit in Washington. It was a good marriage and I knew it would have lasted. We'd been married eighteen months when one night Walt drank a lot, which was unusual. He said he was worried about the outfit he worked for. He told me its name. He had realized he was being used to launder huge sums of money to finance the outfit. He was thinking of contacting the FBI.'

'Did he do that?'

'Wait, please.' Her hands were folding the top of her handbag, her knuckles white. 'The following evening ... The following evening, after dark, a car pulled up outside. We lived in a house outside a small town in Virginia. The only other property near was a house next door. Walt peered through the net curtains, then ordered me to stay out of sight. I went into the kitchen. It had an oval window which was open to the living room, masked by a heavy net curtain. The visitor was a fat man I'd never seen before. He told Walt to sit down. Walt did so. The fat man didn't say much.'

'Can you remember what he did say?'

'Every word,' Trudy said tensely. ' "Walt, you've been checking bank statements which are confidential. Open your mouth – you have a cyanide capsule on your tongue." Walt looked astounded, said that was the most ridiculous thing he'd ever heard. At that moment the fat man shoved the muzzle of a gun into his mouth and pulled the trigger. I went into shock.'

'Would you like something to drink? Coffee? Water?'

'Water, please.'

She drank the glass Tweed had poured from a carafe, thanked him, continued talking.

'The fat man wore gloves. He took hold of Walt's

171

dropped hand, pressed it on the gun, let it fall. I was in a trance but I knew I had to leave – so I could identify the killer later. I went out the back way, closed the door quietly, rushed to the house next door. The couple who lived there were away and the wife had given me a key. I went inside, locked the door, and didn't put any lights on. A few minutes later I heard the fat man rattling the handle of the locked front door. It was a nightmare. Then I heard him drive away.'

'Can you describe the fat man?' Tweed enquired gently.

'Wait.' She checked her watch. 'I'll have to tell you the rest later. I told Karnow – he's the head of the outfit I'm working for – I was going to the Hôtel Crillon, where they're staying, to get a shower. I must be back when he returns. Could I come and see you again between seven and eight tonight? They'll be having dinner at the Crillon.'

'Yes, I think that would be all right.'

'Must go.' She stood up and Tweed accompanied her to the door. She put a hand on his to stop him unlocking it. 'They're after you – they were going to kill you. Now Karnow has decided not to. Yet. The name of the man who murdered my husband is Bancroft. I'm going to kill him at the first opportunity. Now, could you let me out, please . . .'

16

'What do you think of her?' asked Tweed when Paula had emerged from her closet.

'At first I was suspicious. I thought Karnow was trying to put a plant inside our team. Then I changed my mind. What about you?'

172

'Same reaction to begin with. What convinced me she might well be genuine was that last remark, just before she left. The fact that she named Bancroft.'

'She sounded very bitter, very determined, from the way she expressed herself.'

'I think the same. You didn't see the expression in her eyes as she said that. Her eyes narrowed and were full of pure hate.'

'So we assume she is the genuine article?'

'Not yet,' Tweed warned. 'Let's hear what else she has to say, when she comes back this evening.'

'I was going to have dinner with Chance Burgoyne. He invited me out while we were downstairs. I agreed.'

'Then I insist you keep your dinner engagement. It will give you the opportunity to get to know him better, to help him merge in with us. One proviso. I'm going to ask Nield also to have dinner wherever you're having it. Being on his own he will be more alert – when you two are involved in conversation. Dinner here?'

'No. Chance suggested Maxim's.'

'Better still. I'll get Nield to book himself a table. He'll be difficult to recognize.'

'We're not sure about Trudy. Shouldn't I stay here, hide again in the closet?'

'Newman will take your place.'

The Yellow Man sat in a swivel chair inside his attic flat at the top of an old building overlooking the Bastille. He liked the hideaway. The Bastille was not in the most upmarket arrondissement in Paris. The message from Goslar had come through over the phone earlier.

'Is that Mr Danton?' a cultured voice had asked in English.

'No,' the Yellow Man had replied, 'this is Marat.'

'Then kindly be so good as to listen carefully.'

173

He'd had to wait while the unknown caller put on the recording. It was the usual screeching voice.

Your next assignment is to eliminate Tweed's assistant, Paula Grey. Lure her to a quiet place. This will devastate Tweed, make his mind go round in circles. Timing is your choice. I have deposited half the usual fee in your Swiss bank. You can confirm that. The balance paid on results.

'Tweed must be getting too close,' the Yellow Man said after hearing the recording once more. He spent so much time on his own he often talked to himself. 'This little device should do the job. All women like jewels,' he commented later.

After receiving the message he had bought a string of pearls from a jeweller in the Rue St-Honoré. Returning to the attic flat, he had detached the pearls from the rope which had held them, then fed the pearls carefully onto a long length of razor-sharp wire.

The wire was spring-loaded. Holding it up to a desk light in the gloomy attic, he admired the way they hung close together. Then he gripped both ends of the large clasp he had attached. His fingers had a firm hold on the clasp ends as he pulled hard. Substantial lengths of the wire were exposed. Enough for him to pull it tight round a neck – tighter and tighter. Until a head rolled onto the street.

He looked up at himself in a mirror perched on the desk and smiled unpleasantly. The dark wig he wore completely covered his own hair. At about midday he wore black tie and a dinner suit. He stood up to look at himself critically in a cheval glass. The effect was of a smart man about town out for an evening's entertainment.

He slipped the pearls into a pocket of his dinner

jacket. Now all he had to do was to watch and wait. He tried on a woollen scarf, which hid his black tie, then a black overcoat. Now he could almost have been wearing day-time clothes. All he had to do when the time came was to lose the woollen scarf. He was confident that Tweed and Paula would dine outside the Ritz in the evening.

Leaving his attic room, he walked along a short corridor, opened a door to an ancient fire escape, walked down the metal steps carefully and into the Bastille. He hailed an empty cab, rare in this district, but the Yellow Man was always lucky. He told the driver to drop him in the rue de Rivoli, close to the Ritz.

After telling Paula that Newman would replace her in the cupboard when Trudy arrived for her second visit, Tweed stood up and stretched. He checked his watch.

'I think that was a good idea of Burgoyne's to check up on what is going on outside,' he said to Paula. 'I feel the need of a bit of fresh air myself. Let's go out and see for ourselves.'

In the foyer they met Newman, wearing his overcoat and just back from a swift surveillance. He spoke quietly when he saw they were both dressed for going out.

'What do you think you're up to?'

'Taking a spot of fresh air.'

'Then I'll come with you. Don't argue. Paula can walk between us.'

'I'm beginning to feel overprotected,' she joked.

'For a very good reason,' Newman said grimly. 'I haven't detected any watchers, any Americans.'

They spent some time walking.

Tweed moved slowly. He kept stopping, gazing round, looking up at buildings like a tourist. He saw no one – and nothing – suspicious. For a while they encountered men and women hurrying, obviously office workers making the most of their lunch hour. Then the streets became quiet, hardly anyone about.

They completed a wide circuit along the streets round the Ritz. Back at the entrance to the hotel, Tweed stood for a few minutes. He seemed to be in a dream, Paula thought.

'It has to be somewhere close,' he said half to himself. 'We will now walk up to the Opéra.'

'What has to be close?' Paula enquired.

But Tweed was off again, heading for the street leading up to the Opéra. Paula felt frustrated. What was the bee Tweed had in his bonnet? They began walking up the street to the Opéra. Tweed stopped again.

'There is the fox on the trail.'

'What?' asked Newman.

'Ahead of us. Walking towards us. Chance Burgoyne.'

Paula and Newman then saw him. Burgoyne was wearing a shabby raincoat, had his hands in his pockets as he strolled. He was looking to left and right as he came nearer. Tweed had again stopped when he reached them. He was staring down a side street. Burgoyne withdrew both hands, spread them in a gesture of resignation.

'I'm puzzled,' he said. 'No sign of the enemy. No sentries on guard. No skirmishers.'

Paula thought it was typical that he had reverted to employing military terms. Burgoyne noticed Tweed's fixed gaze, looking down the side street. He looked in the same direction.

'Chance,' Tweed said urgently. 'See that small furniture van? The two men have just carried out a modern swivel chair, put it inside. Try and find out where that furniture van is off to. Who employed them. Quick, they're leaving . . .'

176

Burgoyne took off like a rocket. His legs loped like a tiger who has sighted prey. They began to follow him, saw him arrive just too late. The van – no name on it – was driving off. Chance turned round, again spread his hands in a gesture of resignation. When they arrived at the building, which needed a coat of paint, a woman had emerged from the open front door, had hung from a railing a crude notice painted on a sheet of cardboard. *À Louer.*

'Good morning,' Tweed said in French, smiling.

'It's afternoon,' she spat at him.

She was plump, wearing a dress which had a washed-out look. Her eyes were greedy, her thin mouth tight. She glared at Tweed from the top of the steps.

'So it is. Afternoon. You're right,' he said, smiling again.

'People are crazy,' she snapped. 'They pay to rent a room for a month and in twenty-four hours they're gone. You want a room?'

'I'm police,' Tweed told her. He took out his forged Special Branch identity, flashed it in her face, put it away. He hoped she wouldn't ask to examine it more closely. She didn't. 'We need to look at the room which has just been vacated. You saw the tenant?'

'Only once. Then I didn't really see him – or her.'

'Why do you say that?' Tweed asked as he mounted the steps.

'Very early this morning the tenant is walking up the stairs to the room – on the third floor. I was in the hall. I only saw it from behind. It wore black trousers, a black cape and a Spanishlike hat. Big brim, well pulled down. I called up and it hissed "thank you" back at me without turning round. Then it was gone.'

'I need to see the room,' Tweed repeated. 'That furniture van which just left took away an office swivel chair. What else?'

'Nothing. The chair was delivered late last night. Why I can't imagine. The room is let furnished. The door's still open. I'm not climbing all those stairs again. Here's the key. Lock it when you've had your look-see.'

'Anyone else up there?' Tweed asked.

'I told you. The tenant has gone.'

'I didn't mean in his flat. I meant the others. Or aren't they occupied?'

'Gone to work. People have to work to live. Or didn't you know that? With the cushy job you've got.'

Tweed shrugged. Burgoyne went up first, with Newman on his heels. As soon as they turned a corner, out of sight of the irate old woman, both men had their revolvers in their hands. Tweed went next, holding Paula back so she brought up the rear.

The staircase was narrow, with a moth-eaten strip of carpet laid in the middle of each tread. The landings were equally narrow. When they reached the second floor the strip of carpet vanished. They mounted the last flight and one door stood wide open. Very slowly, Burgoyne, gun held at chest level, peered inside, then entered.

'Nothing much here that I can see,' said Newman. 'A few sticks of furniture only good for firewood.'

Paula thought it an apt description. She stroked her gloved finger along a section of a chest of drawers against one wall. It was covered with dust. The room was a small oblong. Standing by a wall below a grubby window was a wooden table with a wicker chair shoved under it.

'Where does that door lead to?' Paula asked.

'Let's see,' said Burgoyne.

He opened it cautiously and an unpleasant latrine smell drifted into the cell-like room. Burgoyne peered in, then took two paces forward and was inside. He came out, wrinkling his nose.

'Toilet and a rusty shower. Hardly able to close the

door when you're inside. What a shower – and I'm not referring to the one inside.'

'I think this is a bed let into the wall,' Newman said. He took hold of the apparatus at the top to haul it out.

'Careful,' Burgoyne warned. 'Might be a body inside.'

Paula tensed but kept her expression neutral. Holding the mattress firmly in position, Newman lowered it. The bed stretched the full width of the apartment, squeezed at the end against the opposite wall. Whatever bedlinen was laid on it was covered by a stained duvet.

'No one has slept in that,' Tweed observed.

'What are you doing now?' Paula asked him.

Tweed had pulled out the wicker chair, was sitting on it with the table in front of him. He wriggled as the chair wobbled. One leg was shorter than the other three. He pulled a face as he rocked on the chair.

'Damnit!' he said quietly.

'I'll fix it,' Paula said. 'Get up for a moment.'

Taking a notebook from her shoulder bag, she tore out a number of sheets of blank paper. Folding them, she bent down, tucked her improvised wedge under the short leg. Tweed sat down again and the chair was firm.

'Thank you,' he said.

He then began performing a strange pantomime while Paula, fascinated, watched him. He cupped his right hand to his mouth as though speaking into a trumpet. His left hand reached out to poise over a section of the table and he pretended to be turning a dial.

'What on earth are you doing?' Burgoyne enquired.

'Demonstrating why Goslar needed this room, how he used it. My right hand is holding a very advanced form of voice-changer. My left is adjusting a recording machine. There's an oblong outline in the dust where the recording machine was placed. "It,"' he said in

179

French, mimicking the landlady, 'used this out-of-the-way apartment to record – in a screeching voice – either one message or several. He then took everything away, including the cassette – or cassettes. They would be hidden in a prearranged hideyhole, maybe a loose brick with a space behind it, for an accomplice to collect later ready for playing it back over the phone.'

'So Goslar is still in Paris?' Burgoyne suggested.

'I wouldn't bank on that now. He moves around a lot.'

'Look at this – on the floor near the toilet door,' Burgoyne said suddenly.

'Don't touch it!' Tweed warned. 'Bob, use tweezers to pick it up and pop it in a sample envelope.'

Newman bent down, used tweezers he'd extracted from a small case he carried, carefully picked up what Burgoyne had pointed out. Straightening up he held them to the pallid light penetrating the room from the window.

'It's strands of hair,' Newman reported. 'Yellow hair.'

'The Yellow Man,' Paula said quietly.

'Goslar tripped up this time,' Newman remarked. He looked at Tweed. 'You said he would, sooner or later.'

Tweed stood up. Paula collected her home-made wedge, stowed it away in her shoulder bag. Never leave anything behind to show you've been somewhere outlandish was one of Tweed's instructions, delivered long ago.

'That explains the expensive-looking swivel chair,' he explained. 'Goslar came prepared. He needed a firm stance to produce his recordings. Nothing more here. Let's get back downstairs. The aroma is beginning to get me down. Plenty of places like this back in London. And I want another word with Mrs Cheerybye.'

The landlady stood at the bottom of the stairs, her arms akimbo, her expression sneering as she watched them descending the last flight.

'Finished messing up my place?' she demanded.

'Just a few more questions before we go,' Tweed said, smiling at her. 'What is your name?'

'Antoinette Markov, if you must know. My grand-parents escaped from Russia when the Revolution came.'

'Good for them. Good for you, too. This mysterious tenant. How did it pay you a month's rent in advance?'

'Phoned up first, didn't it? Funny voice. Then sent a month's rent by cash in a blank envelope. And, before you ask, the money was delivered by courier on a motorcycle. Don't know which outfit.'

'Surely you can give it a better description since you saw it walk upstairs,' Tweed persisted.

'Told you before all I saw.'

'And was that really the only occasion when you observed it?'

Tweed was standing close to Markov and gin fumes assailed his nostrils. Rather early in the day to start on the bottle. She was probably sozzled by midafternoon. So her reply in no way surprised him.

'I've already told you it was. How many times do I have to repeat myself before it sinks in?'

'Thank you, Madame Markov. We'll leave you in peace now.'

They had reached the street when she shouted down at Tweed, in a voice which was part wheedling, part sarcastic.

'Don't you want the flat, then? It's a two-minute walk from here to the Ritz.'

'If you're an Olympic sprinter,' Newman said *sotto voce*.

'I don't understand it,' Paula whispered to Tweed as

Burgoyne walked ahead of them, with Newman behind. 'You said Goslar used the apartment but Chance spotted those yellow hairs. He was quick. How does that link up with the Yellow Man?'

'I've no idea. I'll phone Lasalle when we get back to my suite. I'm sending him those yellow hairs Burgoyne spotted on the floor of that flat – for analysis. Butler can take them to the rue des Saussaies.'

'Are you building up your jigsaw?'

'I need more pieces. I may have them after my talk with Trudy Warner this evening at seven. I'll also try again to contact the elusive Serena Cavendish. She fits in somewhere.'

As they entered the street leading in the opposite direction to the Opéra, Newman and Burgoyne followed them. Newman suddenly looked back, stopped. His right hand slipped inside his raincoat to grip his Smith & Wesson. The action was not lost on Burgoyne, who also stopped and gazed back.

Two hundred yards behind them a giant in a dark coat padded towards them. His huge head was cropped with a fuzz of brown hair. He fitted perfectly Paula's detailed description of the Ape, who had kidnapped her on Dartmoor. The Ape stopped, hailed a cab moving towards the Opéra, climbed inside. The cab moved away.

'Who was that mountain of flesh?' Burgoyne asked.

'Tell you later. Let's keep up with Tweed and Paula . . .'

They were close to the entrance to the Ritz when a man walked to the end of the rue Castiglione, which gave a good view of the entrance across the rue St-Honoré and the *place* beyond. He wore a dark overcoat, had a woollen scarf wrapped round his neck and his hair was thick and black. He stood on the kerb, rocking back and forth, as though waiting for traffic to clear. Hands in his pockets, he watched Paula as, with Tweed, she came close to the entrance.

'Well, at least we've seen no one menacing,' Paula remarked.

'Maybe we just didn't see them.'

17

Vance Karnow sat at one side of a long table in his suite at the Hôtel Crillon. The only other person in the room sat facing him. Bancroft, as usual, was grinning. His fat hands were clasped on the table top.

'What's up? Got a job for me, Chief?'

'Yes. Tweed is sitting back in the Ritz. Waiting for something to happen, would be my guess. I don't think this Goslar is in Paris. I want to get Tweed, Inc. moving so we can follow them.'

'So how do we make that go down?'

'I want you to scare the living daylights out of Paula Grey. I think that might do the trick. The only problem is she could so easily recognize you – she saw you in the bar at the Ritz.'

'Can I use your bathroom for a minute?' asked Bancroft.

'Hurry it up, then.'

Karnow's expression was bleak, his mouth no more than a thin line. At the American Embassy he'd answered a call from the White House. The aide he'd left temporarily in his place had told him the President wanted a progress report. Yesterday would do. Karnow had told the aide he was expecting developments very shortly – anything to keep the Oval Office off his back.

He was thinking sourly about that phone call when Bancroft, who had gone off carrying a large shopping carrier, emerged from the bathroom. Karnow stared.

Bancroft now wore a dark blue French raincoat, a beret and large horn-rimmed glasses with plain glass lenses. When he sat opposite Karnow again he had a cigar clamped in the centre of his mouth. His thick lips gripped the cigar so tightly his normally plump cheeks had sunk.

'Not bad. Not bad at all,' Karnow commented. Always sparing with praise.

The fact was that, without this preview, he would not have recognized Bancroft had he seen him in the street. He sat erect in his, chair, gazing at his deputy.

'Follow her,' he said eventually. 'Wait your opportunity, then frighten the hell out of her. Mess her up a bit.'

'You mean – ' Bancroft leaned forward with an eager look – 'I go all the way with her?'

'Godamnit, no!' Karnow exploded. 'And don't put her in hospital. You do that and I'll never get Tweed off my back. He'd never give up until he'd smashed us.'

'Tweed worries you?' Bancroft enquired softly, grinning.

'Of course not. And take that smirk off your ugly face.'

The truth was Tweed did worry Karnow. First of all, Dillon had told him Tweed was formidable. But second, Karnow, good at assessing men, had been impressed and uneasy when he'd studied Tweed in the bar at the Ritz. Beneath the apparent placid manner he had detected an aura of power, of immense stamina. He would never have admitted it to anyone, but Karnow had no intention of tangling face to face with Tweed.

'Be careful,' he warned. 'Just frighten her.' He leaned close to his deputy. 'Bancroft, do you understand me?'

184

'Perfectly. It's a soft job – but I have to make her want to leave Paris, hoping Tweed will agree. Then we follow them.'

'Then get to hell out of my suite . . .'

Tweed stopped after walking a few paces into the lobby of the hotel. He looked up at the tall man with the aggressive manner who had appeared. Jarvis Bate, Acting Head of Special Branch in London.

'Oh, no. Not you,' Paula said under her breath.

'Tweed, my dear chap. What a pleasure to meet you again.'

Bate held out a paw to shake hands. Tweed ignored it and stood staring at this unexpected arrival, who was smiling wolfishly. It was probably the only way he could smile.

'Follow me,' said Tweed. 'There's a quiet lounge where we could talk. Paula, please join us.'

Paula saw Bate frown at the suggestion. She had the impression Bate regarded women as an inferior species. He had not even had the courtesy to acknowledge her presence. She followed Tweed and Bate was compelled to stride after them. Tweed mounted several steps and there was no one else in the small lounge. He sat down on a sofa, patted the seat behind him for Paula to occupy. Bate picked up a carver chair, carried it over to face the sofa so he looked down on them.

'How did you know we were here?' Tweed demanded.

'Pure coincidence.'

'Coincidence my foot. Was it the man or the woman aboard our flight from Heathrow? I think it was the woman. She hailed a cab at Madeleine, followed one of my people here.'

'Do we have to discuss this in front of a junior

185

member of your staff? Discretion, Tweed. These are policy matters which go right to the top.'

'She happens to be one of the most senior members of my staff. She stays. Or our conversation ends now.'

'I just thought that as you are almost the top SIS man—'

'That's right. Shout it from the rooftops.'

Paula knew that he was referring to Bate's mention of the SIS. Bate swallowed, adjusted the points of the silk handkerchief in his top pocket.

'Sorry,' he said more quietly. 'Perhaps I was a bit out of order.'

'Why are you here?' Tweed repeated.

'Well . . .' Bate leaned forward, lowered his voice. 'I assume you were at Appledore in north Devon.'

'I was there six or seven years ago.' Tweed waved his arm in a wide circle. 'Roaming round on holiday. I thought the place was rather boring so I moved on after an hour or so.'

'I'm referring to the story which appeared in the *Daily Nation*. Written by a certain Sam Sneed, if I recall correctly. Harrington, the Minister of External Security, is very concerned with what took place there – when the dead fisherman, and shoals of dead fish came ashore.'

'I don't work for Harrington. You do. I have no further comment, Bate.'

'Actually,' Bater responded, smiling again, 'it's Jarvis Bate. Jarvis. Surely we can converse on first-name terms.'

'We have nothing to converse about,' Tweed said, standing up.

'You can't just walk out on me like that,' Bate rumbled.

'I have things to attend to. Where are you staying?'

'At a small hotel in rue St-Honoré.' His mouth curled in a sneer. 'We don't have the funds you have at—'

186

He stopped suddenly. Followed by Paula, Tweed descended the steps into the lobby, walked along it so they could collect their keys. At the bottom of the steps a small sneaky-looking man sat in a chair on the other side of the lobby. He kept his eyes hooded, staring at the carpet, careful not to look at them.

'Did you notice that little man sitting in a chair?' whispered Paula. 'Bate's sidekick, the little wretch he brought with him when he visited us in London. Mervyn Leek. Straining his ears to try and catch a snatch of our conversation, I expect.'

'Yes, I did see him.' They collected their keys. 'Now let's go up to my suite. Plenty to think about . . .'

'So now we have more rivals to watch out for,' Tweed said. He drank some of the coffee Paula had ordered from room service, put down his cup, counted them off on his fingers. 'First the Americans, who may – or may not – have been neutralized by Lasalle. Then we have the French security services who may – or may not – have turned their full attention to the Yanks. Now, on top of that, we have Bate and his Special Branch gang. I'm sure Bate will have brought over a team with him. Far more than just Mervyn Leek.'

'And we want to concentrate our full attention on Goslar,' she said.

'Which we will do. But warn everyone when you can of Mr Jarvis Bate's arrival on the scene. Now I must contact Lasalle and ask him to analyse the yellow hairs from Mme Markov's flat. Newman slipped the sample envelope into my pocket as soon as we'd left. Could you find Harry Butler so he's here for me to give him the envelope . . .'

He phoned Lasalle. As soon as he mentioned the Yellow Man the Frenchman agreed to cooperate. Paula came back with Butler and handed him the envelope. Paula had already told him about the situation. Butler left at once with the sample envelope . . .

He had only just gone when the phone rang. Tweed had perched himself on the edge of the king-size bed. He knew that getting out of a chair would help him to think. Paula answered the phone, put her hand over it, called out to Tweed.

'It's *him.*'

Tweed picked up the bedside extension while Paula listened in. He just caught the closing words of the cultured English voice.

'. . . a message for you which is important. Please hold on just a moment.'

While whoever had spoken switched on the recording, Tweed thought. The next thing he heard was Goslar's screeching voice.

Not getting very far with your mission, Tweed, I gather. You are walking round in circles. I thought you might appreciate a tip. Aniseed. I repeat, Aniseed. Good luck.

Tweed put down the phone. The recording had ended. He swivelled round to look at Paula.

'Well?'

'Aniseed. Sounds very much like Annecy. The place the guard at La Défense told us one of the furniture remover crew had said they were going to. Or could it be a trap?'

'We'll walk into it – after taking certain precautions. I need to discuss this with Marler. You're having dinner with Burgoyne tonight. Tomorrow we'll leave Paris and head south.'

He stopped speaking as there was a knock on the

door. Paula opened it cautiously, then wide. Burgoyne walked in, raincoat over his arm, smiled.

'Hope this isn't an inconvenient moment? I've been on my feet trawling the area and could do with a sit-down. There isn't a drink, I suppose?'

'Yes, there is,' said Paula, taking his raincoat, settling him in an armchair.

Tweed watched with amusement. These two were getting on like a house on fire. Paula produced a bottle of vodka, a glass and ice. Burgoyne relaxed in his chair, grinned at her.

'Just the job. You've got a secret bar?'

'No. The waiter who brought coffee also brought this. I think it was for someone else but I hung on to it. Just in case.'

'Make it a stiff one, please.' He raised the glass she had filled. 'Cheers! And damnation to our enemies.'

While they sat chatting Tweed used the phone to call Monica. She answered immediately.

'Tweed, it's great to hear from you . . .'

'I'm calling from my suite at the Ritz,' he warned.

'Understood. Saafeld hasn't phoned, so no break-through. Also the boffins working on that strange conversation have not broken it. Sorry, that's all the news I have. And none of it good.'

'Not to worry. Monica, we may be leaving Paris during the next few days. I'll contact you wherever we end up. Nice to hear your voice . . .'

'Anything happened?' Paula asked.

'Two negatives. Which is what I expected. No news from Saafeld. No success by the boffins in trying to extract Goslar's real voice from the machine he uses.'

There was a knock on the door. When Paula opened it Newman entered, looking as fresh as though he was starting a new day. The stamina of the man, Tweed thought.

'We kept out of the way,' Newman said, nodding towards Burgoyne as he flopped in a chair. 'I thought you'd sooner tackle that hyena on his own – on *your* own, I mean, with Paula.'

'That was very sensible of you.'

'Well, I don't think Goslar will ever return to Mme Markov's flat,' Newman ruminated. 'So no point in my going out and watching it. After all—'

'Mme Markov!' Tweed had jumped up, was grabbing his coat. 'I should have thought of her. My God! I hope we're not too late. We're going back there now.'

Once outside, Tweed was walking so fast he was half-running. He was near the turning into the side street when Paula caught up with him.

'What's the matter?'

'I just hope to Heaven I haven't killed someone else . . .'

18

Burgoyne overtook them as they hurried down the side street, again loping like a tiger. He paused at the foot of the steps leading up to the Markov apartment to let the others catch him up. Tweed paused as he reached him. Paula was by his side and Newman, who had protected their rear, stood behind them.

'That front door's half open,' Tweed observed. 'I'm sure Mme Markov always keeps it locked. We must be careful. The Yellow Man might be inside.'

Burgoyne leapt up the steps, his revolver concealed under his poloneck sweater. Tweed was the only one who had grabbed a coat before leaving. Newman followed Burgoyne, his Smith & Wesson in his hand. Burgoyne paused at the half-open door, pushed it quietly back against the wall. Newman knew why he'd taken that precaution – in case someone had been hiding behind it. The ex-intelligence officer knew his way around.

The hall was empty. While Burgoyne, with Newman following, crept up the winding staircase, Tweed slowly turned the handle of the only other door in the hall. Mme Markov's living room, he felt sure. Paula stood with her Browning in her hand as he turned the handle until it stopped, then pushed gently.

'The door's locked,' he said. 'She'd do that before she went upstairs to check the flat we'd been inside. We'll go up now.'

'I'll go first . . .'

'No, you won't.'

'Then take my Browning.'

To please her Tweed took the gun, automatically checked it, began to mount the stairs. On the third floor the door to the flat was still open. Paula pushed past him, entered the room. Then she stopped.

'Oh, no!'

Newman swung round, gripped her by the forearms, gently guided her back onto the landing. But she'd had time to glimpse what was inside. The wall bed had been pulled down. Stretched along it was the prone body of Mme Markov, on her back, a pillow over her head and neck. Newman released her by Tweed's side, but he still blocked the entrance to the flat.

'She's been smothered,' she said in a choking voice. 'But why all the blood on the pillow? It's stained red.'

'Stay with her,' Tweed ordered Newman.

He walked inside. Apart from the bed and what lay on it everything looked as they had left it. Burgoyne's expression was grim. He took Tweed by the arm, led him to the far side of the table Tweed had used to conduct his pantomime.

'It's in the metal wastepaper basket,' Burgoyne told him.

Tweed walked round the far side of the table, stopped. Inside the metal bin was Mme Markov's head, her eyes open. Her hair was dishevelled. The killer had lifted the head by the hair to carry it to the bin. Blood everywhere. Tweed swivelled round. Now he saw spots of blood leading from the bed to the bin.

'Don't touch anything,' he warned. 'We don't want to see what's under the pillow. We know. Let's get out of here fast.'

On the landing Newman offered to help Paula down the staircase, suggesting she took his arm.

'I don't need any bloody help,' she flared. 'I'm not feeble yet. And don't warn me about leaving finger-prints. I'm wearing gloves.'

Newman didn't reply as she moved steadily down the steps, one hand holding the banister. When she reached the hall she walked straight out into the street. Tweed followed, looking to left and right. The street was deserted.

'Back to the hotel,' he said.

Paula didn't answer him but walked alongside him. Newman came behind them while Burgoyne moved ahead. As he walked, Burgoyne glanced at all the windows they were passing. Tweed realized he was check-ing to make sure they weren't being observed by a nosy neighbour.

'I'm all right now,' Paula said as they left the side street.

Burgoyne dropped back to speak to Tweed. He was not smiling.

'I'm staying out here for a little while, keeping an

eye open. There's a little shop near the Opéra where I can get a newspaper. Good cover. Be back soon.'

'We'll see you then,' Tweed replied in a strange voice.

Paula glanced at him as Burgoyne left them. Tweed's expression was like that of a man walking in a trance. His complexion was ashen. She put her arm through his, squeezed it.

'Are you all right?'

'Of course I am.'

Newman had heard the exchange of words. He came alongside them, peered at Tweed, then looked away. He said nothing until they were about to enter the hotel.

'I'm going to my room to freshen up. Maybe take a shower. I'll come along to see you later.'

'I'll get the keys,' Paula said when they were inside the lobby.

As she returned with the keys an expression of fury crossed her face. Tweed had been stopped by a tall man with a wolfish smile. Bate. She heard the brief exchange of words.

'Tweed, my dear fellow. I have some questions for you which I simply must put to you. We are on official business, if I may remind you. They'll serve us a snack, and a drink, in the bar.'

'To hell with you, Bate,' Tweed snapped. 'And to hell with your silly questions!'

'You saw the hyena off,' Paula said with a smile as they entered Tweed's suite and she locked the door.

'Bate is someone I can do without any time. Particularly now.'

'You're shaken by what happened to Mme Markov,' Paula observed. 'You could never have prevented it.'

'I could, if I'd had my wits about me. Asked Lasalle to send her a guard . . .'

'Which she probably wouldn't have accepted inside her property.'

'A plainclothes man could have been stationed outside.'

'Tweed, stop it. Feeling guilty. When we left the hotel you said you hoped you hadn't killed someone else. You haven't killed anyone.'

'There's Vallade. Poor devil.'

'He'd have been killed anyway – even if we hadn't visited his shop. You said yourself Goslar was shooting the messenger again – all because he used his own name when ordering that book on turtles . . .'

'There's someone else I should have thought of,' Tweed exclaimed. 'Pray God I'm not too late.'

Again he had perched on the edge of the bed. He grabbed the phone and from memory called Roy Buchanan's number at the Yard. Paula watched him anxiously.

'Roy? Thank heavens. Tweed here, speaking from the Ritz in Paris. I think Miss Sneed, Sam Sneed's sister, out in Appledore, could be in grave danger of being murdered. Take my word for it. Could you contact that Inspector – Crake wasn't it? – and ask him to check immediately that she's safe? Then get him to move her miles away at once. She may have relatives or friends in the West Country. She must not stay in that house a minute longer than is necessary. Can you call me back when you know the situation? My suite number and phone number are . . .'

'Deal with it immediately. Then come back to you.'

Buchanan was gone before Tweed replaced the receiver. Paula had had something on her mind for a while. She decided to come out with it to give Tweed something else to think about.

'You may think I'm crazy but I've been pondering something and I think I ought to bring it up.' She paused. 'How much do you know about the background and previous life of Bate?'

'Not much. What I do know Howard told me. Bate has only been with Special Branch for two years. He rose very rapidly to his present position. By climbing over other people's backs. Someone else gave me that titbit. Prior to then he'd been with some international security organization. I suppose that's what gave him clout in getting the job with Pardoe, the head of the outfit, who is away on holiday. Bate's earlier experience was mostly in the States, I heard. He's away from Special Branch's HQ, travels a lot. That's it.'

'Not a lot, is it,' Paula commented. 'Bate,' she said. 'Bate,' she repeated.

A few minutes later Cord Dillon was on the line, speaking from the States.

'I'm talking from a hotel,' Tweed warned quickly. 'Good to hear from you. How did you reach me?'

'Called Howard. I'm talking about the subject you're most interested in now.' Tweed knew he meant Goslar. 'I decided to go through some old files. You might like to know the subject spent a couple of years or so in Britain.'

'I see. Doing what, do you know?'

'I do. He controlled a very profitable security organization in Germany. No description, of course. Of the subject, I mean. I guess it was some kind of tax dodge – owning a company abroad and living in Britain.'

'Which two years was this?'

'No information on that.'

'Switching to another subject, ever heard of a Jarvis Bate?'

195

'That tough. Met him once. His technique was to impress people out of their crazy minds. "What wonderful people you Americans are. You deserve to rule the world. Such dynamism. Such know-how, can-do. Love that phrase." And so on – and on and on. It went down a storm. He had key people, hard people, in the palm of his hands.'

'Where was he based?'

'In New Jersey. Except he was hardly ever there. Flitted about like a goddamn mosquito. Disappeared off the face of the earth for long periods. I thought he was a phoney.'

'Thank you. I find what you've said intriguing.'

'Any time. That's it?'

'It is.'

In typical American fashion Dillon ended the call abruptly. Tweed looked at Paula, who had just put her phone down.

'I hope you don't mind,' she said. 'I listened in.'

'I'm glad you did.'

'You look tired. How much sleep did you get last night?'

'Not a lot. I was up, pacing round while I recalled everything that's happened, trying to link up factors, but they didn't fit together. I could do with a drink.'

'Vodka any good?'

'Sounds tempting. Make it weak.'

He got off the bed and the phone rang again. They both picked up their phones at the same moment.

'Yes?' Tweed answered.

'Roy here. All's well. We got lucky. Crake just phoned, said a patrol car was near Miss Sneed's house. She's all right. She agreed to go to stay with an aunt elsewhere. Crake said she was packing. He'll have an unmarked car, no uniforms, to collect her. One of his men is inside the house while she packs.'

'I'm very relieved. Can't thank you enough.'

'Then don't try . . .'

Tweed again got up off the bed. He walked over to an armchair, sank into it. Paula was mixing his drink. She spoke as she handed it to him.

'There. You don't have to worry about Miss Sneed. And, by the way, Chance told me he couldn't get a decent table at Maxim's. Full house almost. So he's taking me to Sandolini's. The new in-place, he said. Then he chuckled. At least for the last couple of years, I heard.'

'Where is it?' Tweed asked after sipping his drink.

'In a street leading off this side of the rue St-Honoré. We get there at 8.30 p.m., leave here in a taxi at 8.15.'

'I think it's a good idea that you get away from it all for an evening out. Enjoy yourself.'

'I think I will. Chance is fun. When you've finished your drink I suggest you get some sleep.'

'I have Trudy Warner coming back to see me.'

'That's not until seven o'clock. Don't forget to get Newman to hide in the closet. Do you believe Trudy's story?'

'I'll tell you when I've heard Chapter Two. Then I must phone that number Serena Cavendish gave me again. I might fit her in before it's time for Trudy.'

'Just so long as you get some sleep first. You've finished your drink. To bed before I go and have a shower, then try to decide which of two dresses I'll wear. That will take hours.'

Tweed got up, walked slowly to the side of the bed with the phone. He couldn't be bothered to take off more than his jacket and his shoes. Paula took his jacket, hung it inside the closet. Tweed sat up in bed under the duvet. He didn't want to fall asleep yet.

'You might call Newman – if he's in his room, will he pop over for a moment.'

197

'On his way,' she said after using the phone. 'Sleep well – you have bags of time. Make the most of it. You don't look comfortable.' She walked over, adjusted his pillow. 'I'll just wait to let Newman in.'

Newman arrived quickly. Paula frowned, signalled with her eyes that Tweed was washed out, then left. Newman, freshly showered and shaved – his first effort had been a rush job early in the morning – played it softly.

'What can I do for sir?'

'Sir? Didn't know I'd appeared in the New Year's Honours List.'

'Would you take it, if they offered you a K?'

'No. Not my style. Bob, has Paula told you Trudy Warner will be back here at seven this evening for a second session with me?'

'Yes. I don't like it – or her sob story. She's Karnow's girl.'

'Maybe. Paula hid in that closet while Trudy was here last time. Would you do the same thing? Paula insisted on it.'

'Good for Paula.' Newman walked across to the closet, opened it, pushed some clothes aside, shut the door. 'I'm bigger than Paula. I can't hide in there. The bathroom's the answer.'

'Supposing she asks to use it?'

'Tell her it's out of order. Management is sending up someone to see to it. She can use the one downstairs.'

'All right. I agree, then. I'll know if she's genuine when I've heard what more she tells me this evening. Before you go, could you call Nield, ask him to come here now? And I haven't seen Harry Butler for hours.'

'Because he's cruising the whole area on a motorbike. He told me he'd peered into the bar while we were there. He saw Vance Karnow glaring at you. I later told

198

him who he was. A few minutes ago Harry popped in here, told me Karnow is staying at the Crillon.'

'Harry has covered a pretty big area. Oh, have you seen Bate anywhere? I suspect he has more than Mervyn Leek with him. A team of six or seven, would be my guess.'

'Saw two of them downstairs. Easy to spot them. Amateurs.'

'How did you recognize them?'

'They always wear grey suits, well-polished black shoes. And they can't hang around like normal visitors. They're too obvious.'

'I have heard they can be rough.'

'We can be rougher. I'll call Nield. Mind if I leave him with you? I'm keeping an eye on Bate's gnomes.'

'You get off when Nield arrives . . .'

Newman put a finger to his lips as he ushered Nield in, warning him not to linger any longer than he needed. Nield nodded. When Newman had left he walked to Tweed's bedside, held out his hands in a what-can-I-do? gesture.

'Pete, there's been a change of plan. Chance Burgoyne couldn't get a good table at Maxim's, so instead he's taking Paula for dinner to Sandolini's. It's somewhere off—'

'I know where it is. I'll be there to back up Burgoyne, to look after Paula. Same time? 8.30 p.m.? Piece of cake. I'll book a table from my room.'

'Might be awkward, being on your own,' Tweed ruminated.

'I won't be on my own. I'll find a nice lady as my dining companion. Not off the street, of course.' He used his index finger to stroke his moustache. 'It will be easy. I'm off now. But what about the door?'

'Lock it from the outside, take the key with you. I have a spare in the bedside table. Look after Paula.'

'Nothing will happen . . .'

Tweed thought his last words had an ominous sound as he pushed down the pillow. He went into a deep sleep the moment his head rested on the pillow.

19

'We're going to war,' Bate announced in his dominating voice.

He sat in a tall, hard-backed chair in his room at the hotel on the rue St-Honoré which was his temporary base. He was addressing four members of his team who sat on sofas the Ritz wouldn't have accepted for its staff.

'What does that mean?' asked a slim man in his late thirties. He spoke in an upper-crust voice.

'Clive.' Bate paused, his ice-blue eyes glaring. 'If you will kindly listen without interrupting you may learn something.'

Clive Marsh, almost as tall as Bate, was the maverick in the team. He adjusted his tie, stared back at his boss, raised his eyebrows. Bate might be his superior but Clive would interrupt him whenever he felt like doing so.

'We're going to make our presence felt to Tweed,' Bate went on. 'Put the pressure on him. At the moment Leek and Prendergast are stationed inside the Ritz, both armed with mobile phones so they can report the moment they see Tweed & Co. are on the move.'

'And then?' Clive enquired.

'We have six cars, so you all have transport,' Bate thundered on as though he hadn't heard the question. 'I have worked out that Tweed will move either east into Germany or south into Provence – and maybe beyond.

You take it in turns to overtake him. In that way he will not realize he is being followed. Get me?'

'Quite clear,' answered Wilbur Jansen, a small, plump man with a toothbrush moustache. 'Quite clear,' he repeated unctuously.

'You are all armed by Leek, who obtained your weapons here in Paris from some source I don't wish to know about. But on no account are you to engage in a shooting match unless it becomes inevitable.'

'When does it become inevitable?' Clive enquired, suppressing a yawn.

'My God! Sometimes I think you are thick. If – or when – they start shooting at us first.'

'It helps if we do know when,' Clive commented. 'And has this authority behind us back home? Shooting, I mean.'

'One more interruption from you,' Bate snarled, almost with a screech of rage, 'and I'll send you back home.'

He knew he would never do that. Unfortunately, Clive Marsh was his most efficient and reliable operative. He glowered at the offender before continuing. Clive again adjusted his tie. All the men present wore grey suits and gleaming black shoes.

'I am leaving on my own in a few minutes,' Bate informed them. 'In my absence Mervyn Leek is in command. You take your orders from him. He, in turn, will be in close touch with me. You may not hear from me for some time but, I repeat, in my absence Leek is running the show. Also, none of you leaves this hotel without an instruction to do so from Leek. You eat here, sleep here, stay put. Understood?'

'Quite clear,' said plump little Wilbur Jansen. 'Understood.'

'Go back to your rooms, then,' Bate ordered, standing up and donning his camel-hair coat.

On his own, Bate took from a cupboard his packed bag. Going down to the desk, he wrote out a cheque backed by a bank card, handed it to the desk clerk.

'That will cover everything. If expenses go beyond that then my associate, Mervyn Leek, will deal with any extras. Now, if the concierge will bring round my Renault, wherever he has hidden it, to the front . . .'

When Paula, after tapping on the door, unlocked it and walked into Tweed's suite, she stared in surprise. Tweed was fully dressed, his eyes and movements the peak of alertness. She'd seen this transformation once before. No longer exhausted, he was a dynamo of energy.

'Newman will be here in a moment,' he said briskly.

There was a tap on the door. When she opened it Newman walked in. Tweed stood, hands clasped behind his back.

'Those two snoops, Bate's underlings – are they still here?'

'Yes, sitting in the lobby where they can watch the exit and the elevator.'

'I want them out of here. Is Pete Nield about? Good. Both of you find seats opposite them, as close to them as you can. Sit there and stare at them. Keep on staring. Make them feel nervous. It is a tactic we've used before.'

'On my way.'

'Before you go, is Bate still patrolling down there?'

'No. He seems to have disappeared. Some time ago. No sign that he's coming back.'

'Interesting. Start the staring match. Is Burgoyne about? Good. Ask him to come here ASAP.'

Paula smiled after Newman had left. She perched herself in a carver chair, quickly adjusted her skirt, which she preferred to her leggings.

'You've meditated,' she said. 'Now suddenly it's all go.'

'Can't hang around here for ever. Goslar could be miles away by now. Probably is.'

Paula jumped up as there was another tap on the door. Burgoyne strode into the room, grinned at Paula, looked at Tweed.

'You've come alive. Haven't seen you like this since we flew in from Heathrow.'

'Chance, I think we should move to Annecy. I've spoken to Marler and he's geared up for a swift departure. In the middle of the night.'

'Could I make a suggestion?' Burgoyne enquired, folding his arms.

'Make it.'

'I think I should go on ahead of you ...'

He stopped speaking as the phone rang. Tweed, who was pacing restlessly, answered it.

'Yes?'

'It's Serena. You're going to want to shoot me. I'm awfully sorry but I can't come and see you this afternoon. Something has cropped up which I must see to. Could I come at four o'clock tomorrow afternoon instead? I do need to see you. What I have to tell you is important. But not over the phone. Can you make it then?'

'Yes. But be sure you do.'

He put down the phone. Picking up a carver chair he placed it close to Burgoyne, who had sat on a sofa.

'You were saying?'

'I think I should drive down ahead of you after Paula and I have had dinner this evening. I want to make a recce along the route you'll take.'

'Why?'

'To forestall your being ambushed. I'll check out the locales where Goslar's thugs could set up an ambush.'

203

Behind Burgoyne Paula nodded. Then she mouthed 'yes.'

'It might be wise,' Tweed agreed after thinking for a moment.

'Which route will you follow?'

'From here we'll drive first to Geneva. Then on from there to Annecy across the border. You know the area?'

'I do. Not so long ago I did an extra job for the MoD. Drove to Aix en Provence, a walled city. I was looking for an Arab agent. Found him.'

'An Arab?' Paula queried in surprise.

'Job's done, so no harm in telling you. In Aix there is a scribe, an Arab. He occupies a hut in a small square for his business. There are – or were – a lot of Arab refugees from North Africa. They only spoke Arabic and they'd want to send a letter to their relatives back in Algiers, Constantine, or wherever. Couldn't pen a word. They'd tell the scribe what they wanted to say in a letter and he'd write it for them. It wasn't the scribe I was after.'

'Annecy is further north,' Tweed commented.

'I know the place. What do you think?'

'You'll be driving through the night. Less traffic. I agree. How do we communicate with you?'

'Via my mobile.'

Burgoyne took out a pad, scribbled a number on it, handed it to Tweed.

'You can reach me at any hour of the day or night. If I find anything suspicious, I'll contact you. Marler thinks it a good idea. I have his mobile number. Now, I'd better pack – ready for a swift departure late tonight. After I've delivered Paula safely back here, of course . . .'

Tweed resumed his pacing when Burgoyne had left. His head was bowed in thought.

'It is a good idea,' he said eventually. 'Paula, why were you so approving?'

'Chance is used to operating on his own. Prowling through the desert. He's a good precaution . . .'

She went to the door as someone tapped. Marler strolled in, leaned against a wall.

'Burgoyne wants to drive off ahead of us tonight. I thought it a sound move.'

'Except,' Tweed told him, 'we're not leaving until tomorrow night.' He looked at Paula. 'That phone call was from Serena. Can't get here until four in the afternoon tomorrow. It delays us but I want to hear what she has to tell me. She did have arm's length contact with Goslar when he hired her to photograph the Appledore area two weeks before the night the sea was poisoned.'

'If it was arm's length contact,' Paula commented.

'You suspect everyone.'

'You trained me to do just that. Hadn't you better tell Marler about the route to Annecy?'

'Just about to do so. Marler, we'll be going via Geneva, then across the border to Annecy.'

'Why Geneva?' Marler enquired.

'To check something. You don't sound very happy.'

'Just thinking. From Geneva we'll pass through a Swiss checkpoint. That should be all right. Then comes a French checkpoint. We'll have to be careful with the armoury we're carrying. I'll manage it somehow. I've hired a third car.'

'Why?'

'We'll be travelling in convoy to Annecy. I'd worried about an ambush before Burgoyne raised the possibility. If there is an ambush the enemy will expect you to be travelling in the middle car. You won't be. You'll travel in the last car.'

'If you insist.' Tweed checked his watch. 'I'm expect-ing a visitor. I want to see them alone.'

'And I want to check that third car thoroughly . . .'

At about the time Marler left Tweed it was dark outside. In a side street, leading off the rue St-Honoré down to the rue de Rivoli, a very large man pressed the button on an entryphone. Alongside the button a card gave the occupant's name. *Serena Cavendish.*

When no one answered he looked up and down the street. People were hurrying past. No one took any notice of him. The French, released from their boring jobs, were on their way home. He was on the verge of pressing the button again when he saw a curtain on the ground floor pulled aside, then closed. He waited.

The front door was unlocked, opened. The concierge, a tall thin woman in her sixties with bright pink hair, stood looking at him. She wouldn't have opened the door but it was rush hour. Plenty of people about.

'What you want?' she demanded in English.

She could see this big brute was English from the style of his clothes. A long dark overcoat, pigskin gloves over his huge hands.

'I have come to see my friend, Serena Cavendish. She doesn't answer the entryphone.'

'Then she's not in.'

'She's expecting me. Which room?'

'Flat Two, first floor. Come later . . .'

'I said she's expecting me. Probably taking a bath.'

He pushed into the lobby, pressing her aside. Then he mounted the staircase as the concierge called after him in French. He turned, dropped a banknote over the banister. She picked it up. A hundred-franc note. She looked up but he was gone. Shrugging, she tucked the note into the purse concealed under her apron.

The big man walked along a narrow corridor on the first floor. He saw the figure '2' attached to a door. The next door further along had a '3' screwed to it. Taking out a square of metal with one serrated edge, he eased it between lock and the wooden frame. He twisted hard, damaged the frame but opened the lock. He walked inside.

He had checked the living room, the small kitchen, the bathroom, had found the flat was empty when he heard someone behind him. The concierge was glaring at him, one bony hand tapping the damaged frame. She was staring hard at him, memorizing his appearance. She would have no difficulty describing him.

'You pay damage,' she snapped. 'It cost lot of money. New lock. New everything. Who are you?'

He walked to the window of the living room he had entered direct from the corridor. A surge of people below, hustling along the pavement. The gridlocked traffic began moving again. No sign of a police car. He looked at her, staying where he was.

'Who are you?' she repeated. 'I call police.'

He took out a wallet. From it he extracted three five-hundred-franc notes. He held them in his gloved hand. Irresolute, she licked her lips, walked towards him, towards the banknotes. A third of that amount would repair the damage.

'Of course I pay,' he said, his voice hoarse. 'I push the door too hard. Don't know my own strength.'

He held out the banknotes. As she extended her hand he dropped one. He apologized and she bent down to retrieve it. As she straightened up one large hand grasped her by the throat, the other gripped the back of her neck. His movement was a swift jerk. Her neck was broken. To make sure he grasped her throat in both hands, squeezed in a vicelike grip. She sagged and he let her go.

He stooped, picked up the banknote he had dropped, then extricated the two notes still clutched between her dead fingers. He looked out of the window again, moved towards the door and looked back once.

'I am Abel. You shouldn't have opened the door to me.'

Newman was inside the suite's bathroom, the door almost shut, his foot against the bottom when Tweed ushered Trudy Warner in. At his suggestion she occupied a sofa while he sat in an armchair, facing her. She had taken off her fur coat, laid it across the back of the sofa.

'Can I get you something to drink?' Tweed asked quietly.

'No, thank you.'

Second impressions of a person are sometimes more powerful than the first. Trudy was a very striking woman, Tweed was reflecting. Her glorious red hair rested on her shoulders, but it was her nose which caught his attention. It was strong, but not so prominent that it spoilt the perfect symmetry of her features. Trudy was a beautiful woman and he was sure she had turned the heads of many men. Behind this façade he detected an inner strength.

'I'll go on from where I left off,' she began. 'The brutal murder of my accountant husband, Walt – by Bancroft, when he shoved his gun into Walt's mouth and pulled the trigger. Bancroft left when he'd tried to get into the house next door where I was hiding. I knew I also had to leave immediately. That Bancroft would come back. After packing the things I liked most I drove – my car had been locked in the garage – to New York. Leaving Virginia behind for ever. To cut a long story short, I got a job with a big security outfit in New York. Being English helped.'

'What sort of work?'

'Tracing – following – men and women who had embezzled quite large sums from their firms and then done a bunk. I was so adept at the work I was promoted to run their Surveillance Division. Then I was posted to Washington – which was just what I wanted.'

'Why?'

'Because I knew Karnow and his secret outfit, Unit Four, was based there. I'm sure that's why they murdered Walt. He knew so much about how Unit Four was financed, and was thinking of contacting the FBI. Once settled in Washington I went to a lot of parties – I was hoping to bump into Vance Karnow. I'd almost given up hope, then one evening Karnow was at a party I attended. I even saw him first talking to Bancroft. I was stunned. Later Karnow came over to me, said he'd heard of the efficient Trudy Warnowski. He ended up offering me a job. I played hard to get, told him I was a widow and only accepted when he asked me at the third lunch. I was on the inside of Unit Four.'

'What about your name? He must have known your husband had a wife.'

'It isn't my real name. As soon as I got to New York I visited a man Walt had told me about, an expert in creating a new identity. I had enough money to buy a driving licence in the new name I'd invented, social security number, passport and all the other papers. I did this before I applied for the job I got.'

'May I ask what was your real name, your married name?'

'Petula Baron. My husband was Walter Baron. My friends back in England called me Pet – rather like the singer's name.'

209

'But surely – ' Tweed's tone was sceptical – 'the Unit Four people must have seen you while your husband was their accountant.'

'Never. Walt was suspicious early on about what he'd walked into. He told them I suffered from a mild case of agoraphobia, that I'd break down among a crowd, so I was never asked to Washington. And none of them ever saw me. Walt thought it would be safer if he kept me hidden away in the little town in Virginia. He was right.' She swallowed. 'It was awful. I didn't even dare attend his funeral, which I still regret terribly. But it wouldn't have been safe.'

'And your maiden name is?'

'Petula Pennington. The girls at school in Surrey used to call me Pippy. The two "P's" – the ones who didn't like me. You can check that. I was at Ramstead.'

'And why did you join Unit Four?' Tweed asked casually.

'I told you.' Her voice was quiet, steady, but there was a glitter in her grey-blue eyes. 'I'm going to kill Bancroft when I get him on his own. I loved Walt very much,' she said calmly.

'Bancroft – I've seen him – is very tough.'

'I'm tougher. What happened made me that way. You want to know what Karnow plans for you?'

'It would be interesting.'

'First, he was going to have you killed. Then he changed his mind. He wants you alive – so you can lead him to Dr Goslar.'

'Dr Goslar?'

'You know who he is.' She leaned forward and Tweed caught a whiff of expensive perfume. 'He's the Invisible Man who's invented a world-beating weapon. The Americans will do anything to get their filthy hands on it. No one seems to know even what he looks like.'

'So Karnow intends to follow me?' Tweed remarked, still playing it coolly.

'He has men in this hotel waiting for you to move. One, Milt Friedman, has a suite here. He's tall, clean-shaven, in his late thirties with weird eyes. Then they have another one here, also in a suite. A Brad Braun – German spelling. He has thick black hair, takes a lot of trouble over his appearance, has a long nose which twitches when he's nervous. Yes, he intends to have you followed. He's convinced that you'll leave Paris, that Goslar isn't in the city.'

'Why are you telling me all this?'

'Because of what I overheard Cord Dillon saying about you – I told you about that when I was here before. I'm confident you will destroy Unit Four. I want to help you – so I can reach Bancroft.'

'If I did leave Paris how would we keep in touch?'

'Could you give me your mobile phone number?'

'I'd sooner you gave me yours.'

'Here it is.' She had it already written on a card she handed him. The numbers were written in a refined script. 'If, when you call me, I'm with people I'll say "wrong number". It will then be up to you to try again later. When I'm on my own I can tell you where we are.'

'I fear you're putting yourself in great danger,' Tweed warned.

'I don't give a damn. I can cope. I've had the training. Can I rely on you? Do check me out at my old school, Ramstead.'

'Can I, discreetly, check you out at the security agency you worked for in New York?' he suggested, watching her closely.

'National Intelligence and Security, Inc. Known as NISI. Don't forget I worked there as Trudy Warnowski.'

'I'll be careful. Incidentally, when you escaped from Virginia didn't you leave photographs behind?'

'I did not. I grabbed every photo of myself, of myself and Walt, and shoved them in my case. Then I called on my neighbour who had come back that evening. We got on well together. I told her what had happened, said Walt had found out he was working for the Mafia, that he'd been killed. I would be next, so I was flying back to England.'

'Anyone else in the States Unit Four might have contacted?'

'Yes.' She smiled grimly. 'I phoned my widowed sister living in San Francisco, told her the situation, that she might be contacted. She said she'd tell them I had visited her and then flown on to Seattle. If they asked for my description she'd tell them to go to hell and slam down the phone.'

'They might have asked your neighbour for a description.'

'I covered that. If they did she was going to describe a friend of hers, a Mrs Cadwallader who lives in Richmond.' She paused. 'I hated leaving Walt behind in that room – but I knew he'd have told me to run for it.'

Tweed stared at her and she tilted her nose cheekily. He was full of admiration for how she had handled a situation most would never have coped with. She checked her watch.

'I'd better get back to the Crillon. Karnow has a habit of checking up on where his people are. I'll use my mobile to take messages from you. If possible – if I'm alone – I'll reciprocate by keeping you informed of Unit Four's movements. I really must go.'

'Isn't there a risk you might be spotted by Milt Friedman or Brad Braun, since they're both staying here? On your way out, I mean.'

'Watch me.' She stood up, took a cap she'd hidden

under her coat. Using a mirror on the wall, she adjusted the hat, tucked her hair under it, dropped a black lacy veil over the upper half of her face. She slipped on her fur. 'Imitation,' she told Tweed. 'What do you think?'

'I wouldn't have recognized you,' Tweed said, standing up to let her out. 'Now you take great care. No risks. You're dealing with killers.'

She threw a kiss at him and then was gone.

20

'Well, what did you think of Trudy Warner?' Tweed asked as Newman emerged from the bathroom.

'My money's on her.' Newman was grinning. 'What a looker – saw her through the keyhole.' His expression became serious. 'What hell she's been through – seeing her husband shot in the mouth by that bastard, Bancroft. Good job you briefed me earlier. I was able to follow every word. And the way she covered her tracks. We could use her on the team – we really could.'

'Well, maybe she is on the team. But I want her checked out. I would like you to contact her New York employer, National Intelligence and Security. You could say she's been recommended to you for security work and ask their opinion.'

'I'll go back to my room. I'd like a quiet few minutes to work out how I'll handle it.'

He opened the door and Paula was standing in the corridor. She whispered, 'Coast clear?'

'Yes, I'm just leaving.'

'Musical chairs. One out, one in.'

'I forgot to tell Tweed something.' Newman went back into the suite with her. 'We've shifted those two Bate snoops,' he told Tweed.

213

'Good. How did you manage that?'

'Pete and I just sat on the other side of the lobby and stared straight at them nonstop. They didn't like it. Then Butler arrived back – he'd had the sense to take off his motorbike gear and leave it behind. Underneath he was wearing a business suit. He caught on immediately to what we were up to. So he plonks himself down in a chair next to me and stares at Mervyn Leek. I think he did the trick – when Harry stares at someone they get very uncomfortable.'

'They've left the hotel?'

'They have. It was comical. Watching them try to get up casually as though they'd just been resting. Made a real mess of it. I don't think Special Branch training comes within a mile of ours.'

'Good work.'

'Now I'm on my way back to my room to do that check on Trudy.'

'What check?' Paula asked when he had left. 'I'm back early because I decided quickly what I'm wearing tonight for my evening out with Chance. I'm wearing my black number. I rejected the frilly job – a bit too exotic. Now, what check on Trudy?'

Tweed told her about his second meeting. From memory he recalled every word that had been said. Paula, serious-faced, leaned forward, tucking away in her mind every detail.

'Newman thinks she passes muster,' Tweed concluded, 'but I asked him to check with the New York security agency she says she worked for. He's doing that now. You've heard of Ramstead, the school she says she attended in Surrey?'

'That's like asking if I've heard of Roedean.'

'I want you to phone Ramstead, try to get through to the headmistress, check her out as best you can. Might be difficult.'

214

'No, it won't be. I've just had a baby, a little girl, want to get her a place at Ramstead when she's old enough. A friend of mine, Petula Pennington, recommended it to me. I'll see if the name strikes a chord. I won't ask what the fees are. If you have to do that you can't afford Ramstead. I'll do it now.'

While Paula was getting the number, then started talking to the headmistress, Tweed had taken a pad of blank paper from his briefcase. He began writing names, trying to link them up with loops. Bate, Karnow, Mervyn Leek, Milt Friedman, Brad Braun, Lasalle, Bancroft, Goslar, the Yellow Man . . .

He easily looped up the Yellow Man with Goslar. He had more people looped up with a query when Paula finished her conversation, came over to sit with him, a Ritz notepad in her hand.

'I got lucky. Spoke to the headmistress, who is retiring soon. She was working late. She remembers Petula Pennington well. We got chatting. She said Petula got on well with most other girls, then chuckled. Said the ones who didn't like her called her Pippy.'

'Sounds as though she checks out.'

Paula went to the door, let in Newman, who was nodding. Tweed asked him what the nodding donkey act meant.

'I was quick,' Newman reported. 'Got straight through to the agency, found the man who employed Trudy Warnowski. It's early afternoon in New York. He said she was very good, that I'd be wise to grab her.'

'Checks out on both fronts, then,' Paula commented. 'I'm off now to change.'

'You've had a bad time,' Tweed told her. 'Have a relaxing and fun evening. You should enjoy it. Peace for a few hours.'

*

A well-built man with thick dark hair walked into Sandolini's. He handed his black overcoat to the hat check girl as the manager greeted him.

'Pierre Martin. You have a table reserved for two.'

'I cannot find the booking,' the manager said after checking his register.

'Then I'll take that table in the corner at the back.'

The manager was about to say it was taken when he was discreetly handed a banknote. I can shift the tables about, the manager said to himself. He led the guest to the table. As he sat down the dark-haired man looked at him.

'I'll start my meal now. She's always late, my companion . . .'

When he ordered a lock of hair fell across the side of his face. He left it there. Feeling in a pocket of his jacket his hand touched the string of pearls with the razor-edged wire. He took from another pocket a copy of Marcel Proust, began reading. Occasionally he glanced across the restaurant where Paula chatted with Burgoyne.

In the bar, Pete Nield sat on a stool next to an attractive woman with a sophisticated appearance. Reaching for a menu, he knocked over her drink.

'A thousand apologies, madame. You must let me order another,' he said with a smile as the barman mopped the counter. 'I'm on my own. Business in Paris. I'm sure I'm not lucky enough for you to be on your own.'

'Actually I am,' she said, after a good look at him. 'I found my boy friend in a compromising situation. I've just ended the relationship. I came out to be among people.'

'You are. You're with me. I think dinner here would cheer you up . . .'

At their table Paula was finding Burgoyne animated,

amusing. He told her jokes which, at times, had her almost in hysterics. She asked him about his experiences in the desert and then sipped at her champagne.

'Had to disguise myself as a baby camel once,' he said seriously. 'Very difficult, getting the arms and legs moving like a camel.' His fingers did an imitation on the tablecloth. 'Arabs stared at me then looked away. It was hard work – moving on all fours for hours.'

'You are an idiot,' she chaffed him, enjoying herself.

'Then I had coffee with Saddam.'

'Saddam Hussein? How did you manage that?'

'Saddam Ali, a bazaar contact,' he told her. 'Very fat.' His arms described a huge circle. Burgoyne moved constantly on the banquette. He blew his cheeks out, mimicking the fat man. 'He told me where secret missiles were hidden.'

'And did you find them?'

'When I arrived at the location, disguised as an Arab, they were already moving them on transporters. A load of medieval cannons. That was all the armoury he had,' he said solemnly. 'Which is why we won the Gulf War. All he fired at our troops was cannon balls.'

'I don't believe a word of it.' She chuckled. 'You really are a fool, you know.'

'I know,' he agreed amiably. 'When I was in Kuwait . . .' he began.

Sitting at a table in a niche, Nield could just keep an eye on Paula and Burgoyne. She was so absorbed, so relieved to have an enjoyable evening, she hadn't seen Nield with his temporary woman friend.

The dark-haired man watched their progress with the meal carefully. As they finished their coffee he paid his bill, walked slowly out.

'Care for a short walk before we ritz back to the Ritz?' suggested Burgoyne.

'I could do with some fresh air. I saw some interesting shops in a side street opposite. The windows are illuminated.'

'Closed, I hope. Diamonds cost a fortune . . .'

The street was narrow, the lighting dim except for the shops with glares of light in their windows, protected with grilles. Paula had walked a distance when an American, lost, asked Burgoyne how to get to Concorde. Burgoyne had to explain his directions three times. Paula reached a corner, turned into a small square in a direction she felt confident would lead them to the Ritz. Dimly lit, it had a number of alleys leading off it. In an alcove the dark-haired man waited.

She paused in front of an illuminated window so Burgoyne could catch her up. The round end of the barrel of a gun was rammed into her back. Behind her a short plump-faced man wearing a beret spoke with an American accent.

'Don't move or I'll blast you to hell.'

She felt him take hold of a handful of her hair. He began pulling her hair backwards. Bancroft was grinning. This was just the kind of sport he revelled in. Then he felt a gun rammed into his back.

'Take your hand off her hair,' Nield ordered. 'Or I'll blow your spine to bits.'

'Stand-off,' Bancroft snarled, not turning his head. 'Do that and by reflex action I'll shoot her.'

'Then the only thing to do,' Nield said calmly, 'is for both of us to drop our guns on the pavement. On the count of three.'

Bancroft backed a short distance away from Paula. His gun was still aimed point-blank at her. As he backed, Nield also retreated, his Walther still pressed into Bancroft's back.

'Here we go,' he said in the same calm voice. 'One . . . two . . . three.'

Bancroft let go of his gun and it hit the cobbles a millisecond before Nield dropped his own weapon. The American swung round, lowered his shoulders, charged to head-butt Nield in the face. Nield darted to one side. Bancroft ran, disappeared round a corner just before Burgoyne appeared.

The shadow of the dark-haired man slipped out of the alcove. Burgoyne raised his Smith & Wesson, fired. The bullet chipped stone from a corner of the alcove. Burgoyne fired again, chipped more stone off the corner of an alley the dark-haired man had vanished down. Burgoyne ran like a greyhound, stopped at the entrance to the alley, walked back.

'He'd gone. The alley went round a corner. He could have been waiting for me. Paula, are you all right?'

'I suggest we escort her straight back to the rue St-Honoré,' Nield said firmly. 'Grab the first taxi and go back to the Ritz.'

'Have a nice evening?' Tweed asked as he let Paula into his suite.

'Super. Until two thugs tried to do me in.'

Her tone was brittle. Tweed sat her down when she'd thrown her coat onto a sofa. Someone tapped on the door. When Tweed opened it Burgoyne stood outside.

'Paula will tell you what happened. I've got to drive like hell down the route you'll be following tomorrow night. Geneva first, then on to Annecy. I'll keep in touch – when I can . . .'

'You look shaken,' Tweed said when Burgoyne had gone. 'Room service can bring up some tea and plenty of sugar.'

'Don't want tea.'

Tweed was already ordering it. Paula sat very still and erect, so Tweed said nothing until the waiter arrived. He poured a cup of tea, added a lot of sugar. She lifted the cup and saucer and her hand shook. She swore, tried again, holding the cup in both hands. When she had emptied it he was going to pour a second cup but she shook her head. She began talking calmly, describing what had happened in detail. Tweed's expression was grim as he listened.

'So,' she concluded, 'Nield grabbed us a taxi and we all came back here.'

'Then it was Bancroft who put a gun in your back before Pete sorted him out. I expect the thug in the alcove was the Yellow Man. Pity Burgoyne missed shooting him.'

'He did try. It all happened so quickly.'

'How are you feeling now?'

'Very tired. The tea was a good idea. Settled me. You look livid.'

'I've had an idea to eliminate the Americans. You go to your room, get some sleep. We're not leaving until midnight tomorrow. You can sleep all day.'

'Lovely idea . . .'

She bent down, kissed him on the cheek. She had just gone when the phone rang. Tweed answered. It was Trudy.

'The whole unit has left the Crillon for another posh hotel nearby. I don't know why. I'm in my bathroom with the shower running. Here are the details, including Karnow's suite where they all dine in the evening at nine o'clock . . .'

'Do you dine with them?' Tweed asked after he'd noted her data.

'No. It's a men only thing. I eat by myself in the dining room.'

'On no account dine with them tomorrow night.'

'I won't. Must go now. Bancroft keeps bothering me,

trying to get into my room. I always open the door on the chain, keep him out.'

'Don't ever let him in. He's a very savage piece of work – but you know that . . .'

Tweed summoned Newman and Marler to his suite as soon as he'd ended Trudy's call. They listened as he gave them the data Trudy had provided. He then outlined a plan, to which Marler added a few touches. Tweed asked him if he could get the equipment for the operation.

'Easily,' Marler replied. 'I have a contact who stole a load of police equipment. I think we should bring Nield and Butler in on this little shindig.'

'Agreed,' Tweed responded. 'And when Paula eventually appears I will get her to type out the documents. Hit them hard. Have you heard what Paula went through this evening?'

'Pete told us a few minutes ago,' Newman said. 'We will hit them very hard. It will be a pleasure. Haul down the Stars and Stripes.'

The following afternoon, when Paula arrived in Tweed's suite, he told her that all the members of his team were packed, ready for departure.

'I'm packed too. I slept nonstop. Now I'm ready for anything.'

'Then could you type out something for me on blank paper?'

'The Ritz can supply anything. I'll get them to send up a word-processor. What do I type?'

'Head the first page *Direction de la Surveillance du Territoire*. Put in brackets D.S.T.' He asked if he was going too quickly as she scribbled on a pad. She shook her head. 'Next line should read Director, René Lasalle.

Then, Assistant, Lapin. In brackets First Name Unknown. Next line, Function of Organization – Counterespionage. Then, Address – rue des Saussaies . . .'

Tweed continued dictating. When he had finished he smiled without humour.

'When Lasalle finds that he'll go berserk. He'll arrest the Americans, probably get an order for instant deportation once he's consulted the Élysée. The French President will blow his top. When you have it ready put it inside a blank file. Scrawl on the front *Vance Karnow. Top Secret.* Then give it to Newman.'

'You're hatching plots. I'll get the word-processor sent up now. This won't take me long.'

'It's a new kind of bomb,' Tweed told her.

At 8.55 p.m., Marler knocked on the door of Vance Karnow's suite in the hotel he had moved to. He wore a white jacket, taken off a waiter who was now unconscious in a service elevator. Brad Braun, the tall, dark-haired American, unlocked the door, opened it.

'Room service,' Marler announced.

'It's already been delivered—' Braun began.

He never finished the sentence. Marler had kneed him in the crotch. As Braun groaned, bent over, Marler stood aside. Three men, wearing gas masks and carrying tear gas pistols, burst into the suite. Eight members of Unit Four sat eating dinner at a long table. The three attackers fired their bulky-nosed pistols. The suite became a fog of tear gas as Marler, now also wearing a gas mask, entered. The Americans were choking, couldn't see, some collapsing with their heads in their plates. The four intruders moved swiftly. They circulated the suite, hammering each American unconscious with a blow from their pistol muzzles. Marler had shut the door to stop fumes leaking into the corridor. New-man produced Paula's file, looked round, hid it under a leather blotter on a desk. All four men left the room, closing the door behind them. Butler and Nield ran to the service elevator they had ascended in. As soon as Newman was inside Marler pressed the button, and the elevator descended to the ground floor. Newman stooped, inserted a five-hundred-franc note between the fingers of the unconscious elevator operator lying in a corner.

Before the door opened they had replaced their gas masks and pistols inside strong carrier bags from a well-known London store. They had only a short distance to walk in the open air. Then they dived inside the waiting car they had parked earlier. On their way back to the Ritz, they stopped once in a side street. Newman ran inside a public phone box, rang Lasalle on his private number. He made no attempt to disguise his voice.

'Lasalle, better get over to this hotel with a strong team. A lot of mayhem. The Americans in suite . . .'

'He sounded alarmed and almost on his way before I broke the connection,' he told Nield, who was driving.

21

At five minutes to midnight three cars left the Ritz. The front vehicle was driven by Marler with Butler hunched by his side. The second vehicle was driven by Pete Nield, travelling by himself. In the third car Newman was behind the wheel, with Tweed and Paula seated in the back.

There was so little traffic that after leaving Paris behind the cars spread out, but not so far away from each other that they could not see the car ahead of them. It was a cold, brilliantly starlit night with the moon casting a glow over the countryside to left and right.

'Sorry it was a last-minute pickup,' Newman said, 'but we were checking the cars thoroughly.'

'An excellent precaution,' replied Tweed.

'I wonder if we'll find Goslar?' Paula mused.

'Eventually, yes,' Tweed assured her. 'He's started making mistakes. Leaving his signature behind.'

'His signature?'

'Yes. Repeating himself. At Gargoyle Towers, way back on Dartmoor, he leased the place for three months, then moved on after two or three weeks. Then at La Défense he leased the whole building for a long period and cleared out after a month or whatever it was. We know he leased Mme Markov's flat for a month. He's out of the place in twenty-four hours.'

'Why did he get the Yellow Man to kill poor Mme Markov?'

'Because she saw him climbing the stairs to the flat. The cloaked figure. Doesn't take any risks, our Dr Goslar. Lasalle called me while you were asleep, about the yellow hairs Burgoyne spotted on the floor inside the flat. Told me his analyst said they were definitely a woman's hair.'

'That's strange,' Paula commented.

'Another phoney clue. Like the gloves he left behind at Gargoyle Towers, then another pair at La Défense. He was always doing that even in the Cold War days. To confuse us.'

'Unless the figure on the stairs wearing that cloak Mme Markov saw was a woman.'

Paula opened her holdall, which was divided into sections. It held a variety of grenades. Marler had come to her room at the Ritz just before they left. From a deep canvas bag he had produced more grenades.

'Take these. They're firebombs.'

'I've already got shrapnel and stun grenades,' she'd protested.

'And now you've got fire-bombs,' he'd replied.

'What about a machine-pistol?' she'd joked. 'I shall be protecting Tweed.'

'Here you are,' he'd said, handing her the deep bag.

Inside it she'd found a machine-pistol with plenty of spare ammo. It was now lying on the floor at her feet. As Marler was leaving she'd joked again.

'You must be expecting the grandmother of all battles.'

'I am,' Marler had replied, not smiling.

Her brain was working overtime now as the convoy of three cars sped along the autoroute through the night. Moving at just inside the speed limit. She nudged Tweed.

'Serena Cavendish never turned up. She was coming to see you.'

'She did, while you were asleep. She wanted to tell me she'd seen the messenger who delivered the second payment to her flat. You remember? She was paid to photograph Appledore and its surroundings two weeks before Goslar poisoned the sea. She was paid half before she did the job, the balance after she'd left the photographs in a phone box in Curzon Street.'

'So what did the messenger look like?'

'She happened to look through her net curtains when the delivery was made. It was after dark but she got a good look at him by the light of a street lamp. A very big man with hair like stubble in a wheatfield. She's flying ahead of us so we can pick her up when we reach Geneva.'

'You can phone her to warn her where we are? Maybe now?'

'Yes. I have her mobile phone number. But not yet. From what you told me,' he went on, addressing Newman, 'you cleaned up the Americans at their new hotel.'

'I loved that,' said Paula, almost hugging herself. 'So they at least are out of the picture.'

'Not quite.' Newman paused, knowing the news would not be welcome. 'Trudy wasn't there, thank Heaven. But neither were Vance Karnow – or Bancroft.'

'Then Bancroft is still roaming around,' Paula commented quietly.

'He is. Somewhere.'

Paula felt a frisson of apprehension. To take her mind off it she gazed out of the window. France, by moonlight and at night, was a dream landscape. Across a peaceful field she saw, stepped down a distant hillside, a grid of vineyards. Next summer's wine was coming. There was very little traffic on the autoroute, most being huge juggernauts lumbering south, which they overtook, and others heading north, for distant Paris.

'You tried to make two calls,' she said to Tweed.

'Yes, to Burgoyne. No answer. You know I mistrust wretched mobiles. They don't always work.'

'Probably he hasn't found any ambush sites. Could be good news. Actually, he was going to call us. So he's found nothing so far. I imagine he's passed through Geneva now, is on his way to Annecy. You know something, that description Serena gave you of the messenger who delivered the balance of her money sounds to me like the Ape.'

'I think you should know,' Newman called back to them, 'that we are being followed. From the moment we left the Ritz. I expected that. I wonder who our friends are? We were driving round a long curve a while ago and I'm sure I saw not one, but two cars, tagging along on our tail. They've dropped back quite a bit but I'm sure they'll still be there. I wonder which lot it is?'

Had there been a pilot flying a plane above the auto-route he'd have seen the traffic far below. In front, well spaced out, was Tweed's convoy of three cars, appearing to move slowly even as they raced along the auto-route. Some distance behind he'd have seen another car.

Behind the wheel sat Abel, the Ape, his eyes glued to the distant red lights of Tweed's car. He was alone. Back in Paris he had waited in an all-night café, drinking coffee, his car parked outside. From his window seat he had a view of the exit from the Ritz. He had seen Tweed leave with Paula and Newman. What he hadn't recognized the significance of was Marler and Butler strolling out first to their car parked in the street leading to the Opéra. Nor had he taken any notice when Nield had followed them to pick up his own car.

Earlier, in another message from Goslar in his screeching voice, Abel had been given the mobile number of a certain Gustav Charles. He had been told to report Tweed's progress to Charles at regular intervals. Goslar had given him no idea of the location of the mysterious Charles. When he called him, Charles confirmed his name, listened, then gave only one answer.

'*Merci.*'

The Ape, often operating on his own, had a habit of talking to himself. He was doing so now.

'The end of the line for you, Tweed. Somewhere ahead a gang of storm troopers is waiting to blast you to hell.'

Abel was looking forward to this. His only anxiety was that he was sure *he* was being followed.

*

227

Inside the car which worried Abel were two men. The driver was Mervyn Leek. Beside him, a map open on his lap, sat Bate.

The warning that Tweed was leaving had come from one of Bate's men planted inside the Ritz. They had driven into the *place* outside the Ritz just as Tweed's car was leaving.

'There should be more of us,' Leek said nervously.

'Just keep your eye on the road,' Bate had snapped. He opened the glove compartment, took out a gun. 'When they eventually lead us to Goslar we'll use his girl friend, Grey, as a hostage while we take Goslar. Too many of us could have been noticed, I decided.'

'If you say so.'

'Damnit, Leek, I just did say so.'

Inside the last car a pilot would have seen, sat Vance Karnow. By his side Bancroft gripped the wheel. Karnow also had a road map open on his lap. He was an excellent navigator and knew exactly where they were.

Bancroft, wearing a beret and an anorak, had waited inside the same all-night café the Ape had used. Bancroft had taken no notice of the huge man. The café was full of French people, catching up on their drinking, smoking Gauloises.

Bancroft had been cleverer than the Ape. He had recognized Marler from the brief glimpse into the bar at the Ritz when Marler had glanced in. That had been on the occasion when Tweed, with Paula and Newman, had watched Karnow and his henchmen drinking with Trudy. Bancroft had immediately left the café, had seen the first car. Walking back, slouching with a bottle in his hand, he had then seen Nield get into the second car. On his mobile phone he had called Karnow as

Tweed had emerged with Paula and Newman to get into their car.

Karnow had been sitting earlier in a nearby night-club. Bored stiff, he had watched the scantily dressed French girls performing. He'd thought they did it much better in Vegas. In fact they did everything much better in the States, in his opinion. He had joined Bancroft as soon as his call had come through, thankful to get out of the nightclub.

Earlier, from outside, he had called his suite at ten o'clock to tell them he'd be late for dinner. A waiter had answered.

'There's been an attack on that suite. Everyone arrested . . .'

Another voice suddenly took over the conversation.

'Who is this?' Lasalle, furious with the waiter, had enquired. 'Please identify yourself!'

Karnow had broken the connection, had told Bancroft they would eat in a small restaurant near the Ritz. Later, Bancroft had moved by himself to the all-night café while Karnow wandered into the nightclub, after paying an extortionate entrance fee.

As they continued along the autoroute Karnow checked his map yet again. Bancroft was hunched over the wheel as he followed the red lights of the car ahead.

'Two more cars behind the first three,' he reported again.

'They'll be more backup,' Karnow said coldly. 'Shouldn't cause us much trouble when the time comes, when Tweed contacts Goslar.'

'We'll blast them all off the planet,' Bancroft growled.

'You mean you will,' Karnow told him.

'We – I – have a load of firepower,' Bancroft said with eager anticipation.

He was right. An executive case perched on the floor held an incredible variety of handguns. Plus the three machine-pistols stashed away in the boot. He had once gunned down fifteen men.

Dr Goslar wore whites, similar to those worn by Professor Saafeld when Tweed had visited him in his Holland Park mansion in London. The whites skirted a table as Goslar walked to a Norman-style window and peered out into the night.

There was deep snow on the steep slope running down from the old castle to the lake below. The moonlight reflected off ice rimming the lake's edges. No sign of lights in the distant village on the far side of the lake. Goslar returned to work in the room at the top of the castle.

The laboratory was nothing like a scene from a science fiction film. It was also totally different from a scene in a Frankenstein movie. Despite the intense cold in the mountains outside, the room was warm. In the centre stood an ancient stone chimney-like structure, thigh-high above the floor, about six feet in diameter at its open top. A blazing fire burned thirty feet down, well below floor level. The fire was so strong it warmed the room.

It had a dual purpose. It not only heated the stone-walled room, it was a useful place to throw in unwanted material. The ferocity of the fire was such that it immediately consumed whatever might be tipped into it. The heat was so intense that the large section above floor level was hot. Goslar's hand held the whites close to avoid them touching the chimney.

Overhead was a series of transparent glass tubes leading from one large globelike container to another. As liquid left one globe on its way through tubes to another, it passed through a filter. This process continued until, finally, the treated liquid dripped into a large canister placed on one of the laboratory tables. The canister was barely a quarter full. It would take some time before the canister was full.

On another table stood two canisters already filled with the liquid. The canisters were made of the very strong perspex used to create the pilot's cabin in a helicopter. Almost unbreakable. Each of the two filled canisters was sealed with a screw-top cap. There was enough liquid in them to kill at least fifty million people instantly if it was introduced into the water supply of a largely populated country – or dropped as a spray from a missile.

In essence, the laboratory was a large distillery, distilling the liquid into its final deadly state. The figure in whites checked a watch on its wrist. Time to leave. Goslar checked a door in the wall which led to an outside fire escape. It was locked. Goslar took one last look round. On another table lay a dead turtle, at least four feet long. At an early stage it had been injected with a hypodermic, dying instantly. The shell had been carefully cut open, exposing its inside. Goslar had extracted a rare ingredient, the key element in producing the weapon.

Satisfied that the third canister would take plenty of time to fill up, Goslar left the laboratory, stepping carefully down a circular stone staircase to the next level. This room was comfortably furnished. Goslar spent time in the bathroom, then emerged in warm outdoor clothes.

Descending another staircase, the doctor opened the door to a garage housing a car with snow tyres. Now for the tricky drive to the city. All the lights had been left on so the villagers in the distant hamlet would assume the castle was still occupied.

The moonlight glittered on the heavy fall of snow covering a small mountain above the castle. A few hundred yards below the summit towered a monstrous crag, projecting like a huge platform. There was hardly any snow in the cave underneath it.

22

The motorcyclist, crash helmet pulled well down, visor closed, masking the face, roared down the autoroute. It overtook the car with Bate and Leek inside, raced on. It sped past the Ape's car, reduced speed as it approached the next car. Tweed, seated on the right, lowered his window. Paula gripped her Browning, aimed it out of the window.

'Don't react,' Tweed warned. 'Not unless it makes a hostile move.'

He looked out as the rider drew alongside. There was now no glove on the rider's left hand. He caught sight of a varnished thumb gesturing back, then three fingers raised, then the cyclist sped ahead. Paula frowned as Tweed closed the window, keeping out the icy night air.

'Did he make a rude gesture?' she asked. 'Or was it a she?'

'You were right,' Tweed called out to Newman, 'there are three cars following us still.'

'How do you know that now?' Newman enquired.

'Just trust me,' Tweed replied.

Ahead of them the motorcyclist roared past Nield's car, drove on towards the first car. Butler saw the motorcyclist coming in his wing mirror. Agilely, he climbed into the back seat, grabbed a machine-pistol off the floor, lowered the left-hand window, perched the barrel on the window's edge.

The motorcyclist saw the muzzle protruding in the moonlight. Slowing down, the rider saw a petrol station ahead. Slowing even more, the rider turned into the station, stopped, then wheeled the machine round the back. When the rider appeared again it walked into the ladies'.

Trudy had thrown her crash helmet into the ditch where she had dumped her machine. In no time at all she brushed her hair, applied lipstick, went outside. It had been a long and tiring trip from Paris. Standing in a shadow she counted Nield's car flashing past, then Tweed's. The Ape raced past next and a minute later Bate's vehicle drove by. Trudy then walked out and stood where she could easily be seen, clad in her leather motorcycle gear. She had gloves on both hands now.

Bancroft reduced speed, then stopped on Karnow's order. Trudy opened the back door, stepped inside, closed the door. As the car began moving again she revelled in the pure pleasure of its warmth. She let out her breath in a sigh of relief.

'What have you got to report?' Karnow demanded.

'Tweed is in car number five ahead of us,' she lied.

'So, when the time comes, that's the one we blast,' Bancroft said enthusiastically.

'You've done well,' Karnow said in a burst of rare praise.

Yes, I have, Trudy thought. Car number five looked by far the most dangerous. Two men inside, one armed with a machine-pistol. Walk into it, Bancroft. Walk into it.

'Trudy did well in the States,' Karnow recalled. 'She put three men we were after in a compromising position.'

233

'She went all the way,' Bancroft said, licking his lips as he leered.

In her rear seat Trudy managed to keep the fury out of her expression at Bancroft's filthy remark. She started removing her boots, replacing them with fur-lined shoes.

'Actually,' Karnow corrected Bancroft, 'she did no such thing. The mere fact that she was alone with each man in a hotel room was all we needed to put pressure on them. All were married.'

'So she says,' Bancroft sneered.

'Bancroft.' Karnow's tone was savage as he looked at the driver. 'Are you questioning what I just said? We had a video in each hotel room. She did not go anything like all the way at all. You underestimate her cleverness, you stupid schmuck.'

'Sorry, Chief,' Bancroft mumbled.

Some time later, following Nield, with Marler ahead of him, they had turned off the autoroute, had passed through Belfort, and were travelling along a country road lined with trees. They had passed through several small French villages without lights and drove more slowly.

This was one of the very attractive areas of France, with cultivated fields beyond the trees on both sides. The villages consisted of old houses built long ago, their walls covered with plaster and colour-washed in different pastel tones. They had intriguing names like Ranspach Bas and Chavannes sur l'Étang.

In places the road became a series of switchbacks. In others there were long ruler-straight stretches. Newman was whistling to himself, enjoying the change from the endless autoroute.

'We're now on Route D419, heading straight into Geneva,' he called out.

He had just spoken when Tweed's mobile started buzzing. He answered cautiously.

'Yes?'

'This is Serena. Lovely to hear your voice. I'm in a motel on the edge of Geneva. I've hired a car. Where are you now?'

'Approaching the suburbs of Geneva. We should be in the city in twenty minutes. Half an hour at the most. No traffic. Meet you at the main station.'

'Then I'll drive to the station now. I can wait in the buffet. I should warn you there's been an exceptionally heavy fall of snow here. From what I can see the mountains behind Geneva are thick with it. Of course the Swiss are saying it's most unusual at this time of the year.'

'You had a good flight?' Tweed asked.

'Smooth as silk. I got a shock when the plane was coming in. It flew over the mountains and then I saw the snow. Specks of it glittered like diamonds in the moonlight. I'd better get moving now. See you . . .'

'That was Serena,' Tweed told them. 'She'll be waiting for us at the main station in the buffet.'

'And I thought it was Burgoyne,' Paula said with disappointment.

'No call from him, no ambush,' Newman said cheerfully. 'Yet.'

'Did you talk about anything else when Serena visited you at the Ritz?' Paula asked. 'Besides identifying the Ape?'

'We had quite a long chat. She talked for a while about biochemistry. That led on from our recalling Appledore. She's really pretty bright – at least from what I could gather with my limited knowledge of the subject,' Tweed mused.

'But I thought her sister, Davina, was the scientist.'

'Sisters pick up things from each other. She was very relaxed, had several glasses of wine. She was speculating on what the key ingredient could be in whatever poisoned the sea. Couldn't come up with an answer. Some of it was too technical for me.'

'Sounds more like Davina who, I gathered, was brilliant in her subject,' Paula observed.

'As I said a moment ago, sisters – especially when they're lookalikes – talk to each other a lot. I found Serena much brighter than I'd realized.' Tweed looked out of the window as they passed through another village, then glanced at his map. 'I meant to ask you, did you really have a good evening with Burgoyne before it all turned hideous?'

'Wonderful. He kept telling me jokey stories. I'll give you an example . . .' When she had finished she pursed her lips. 'You may not think it all that funny from the way I told it – but he has this flair for acting out what he's describing. That's what makes it hysterical. He's a natural born actor.'

'We'll probably hear from him soon.'

'Incidentally,' Newman broke in, 'we are still being followed – the car behind us had to close up nearer on this road. It will be interesting to see what they do when we reach the main station. Nowhere for them to hide in the middle of Geneva. And I'm calling Nield and Marler to warn them to head for the main station.'

Earlier, while still on the autoroute, Paula had more than once detected the sound of a helicopter. She had mentioned it to Tweed, wondering if it was checking traffic speeds.

'More likely to be checking a juggernaut they suspect

of collecting drugs across the Spanish border. Small boats come into isolated coves, deliver the drugs, collect their money, then return to their mother ship well offshore – which sails back to Colombia.'

In fact, aboard the chopper a well-built man with thick dark hair sat in the pilot's cabin. He had a pair of night-vision glasses screwed to his eyes, focused on Tweed's vehicle. He kept warning the pilot to keep his distance.

He watched Tweed's car all the way to Geneva and then to the main station. Only then did he lower his binoculars.

'Land me at the airport quickly,' he ordered. 'In addition to the agreed fee there's a bonus if you land within three minutes.'

Close to the main station, they drove a short distance along the promenade with the wide River Rhône on their right. Paula gazed at the furious surge of lime-coloured water.

'It's an odd colour,' she remarked.

'As you know,' Tweed replied, 'the Rhône starts miles and miles away to the east at the glacier near Andermatt. Maybe the temperature has risen in that area, melting snow. That would account for the exceptional height of the river. The colour comes from melted snow . . .'

They arrived at the main railway station, Cornavin, just in time to see Serena, muffled up against the bitter cold, hurrying inside. In front of the station there was a wide open area surrounded by buildings. They passed the entrance to a large underground garage.

'I see Marler, Butler and Nield are parked in their cars,' remarked Tweed. 'We'll go into the buffet and pick up Serena.'

237

'I'm going to stay outside,' Newman decided. 'I want to see what happens if our camp-followers arrive. They won't know what to do.'

'I think I'll stay with you,' Tweed replied. 'Paula, could you go in and find the buffet. You'll be able to spot Serena easily – with her jet-black hair. You saw her at Brown's Hotel, then at Fortnum's when I had tea with her. Tell her who you are, keep her company. I'll join you in a few minutes.'

Tweed, who had listened to weather forecasts for the Continent in his suite at the Ritz, had warned everyone to wear plenty of clothes. Newman, clad in fur-lined boots, two pullovers and his overcoat, was thankful he had listened. As he waited, he slapped his arms round his body.

A car appeared. Shadows made it impossible to see who was inside. The driver reacted quickly – probably after seeing who was standing outside the station. He drove straight for the entrance to the underground car park. Newman caught a glimpse of the make and the colour of the vehicle as it vanished down a sloping ramp.

'That was one of them,' Newman commented. 'A very distinctive green Citroën, I saw it way back on the autoroute as we came round a long curve. Don't ask me which one it was.'

'That underground car park is vast,' Tweed told him. 'I used it once. It covers almost the whole area under the square.'

'Here comes Number Two. A Renault, again of an unusual colour.'

This car paused in the shadows.

'No way of seeing who – or how many – were inside . . .'

As he spoke the car suddenly shot forward, headed

238

for the ramp, slowed, then vanished like its predecessor. Tweed turned his gaze in a different direction.

'I'm watching the pedestrian exit. No one has appeared yet.'

They waited a few more minutes in the bitter cold. No one else was visible. Behind them the station was dead. The Swiss, Tweed thought, were sensibly keeping indoors. He checked his watch. It was nearly eleven o'clock. Geneva had gone to sleep.

A third car, an Audi, then drove into the square. The driver of this new arrival was decisive. He must have just had time to see the two men standing outside the station before he increased speed, flashed out of sight down the ramp into the garage. Again Newman couldn't see how many people were inside.

'That's Number Three,' he said. 'I do remember seeing an Audi among the three cars following us – when we were on that narrow country road passing through French villages. But don't ask me the sequence. I was absorbed on driving.'

Newman was concentrating so hard on watching that entrance to the square where the vehicles appeared he completely missed something. A hired Renault, which had been waiting at the airport, had driven into the square from another direction. Behind the wheel sat a man with thick dark hair. He drove into a side street, parked his car, got out, fed a meter with coins.

The Yellow Man then strolled back into the square, walked into a hotel and asked for a room overlooking the station. He paid for the room in advance, using cash. He didn't like credit cards – they could leave a trail which might be followed.

'A lot of snow seems to have fallen,' he remarked amiably to the night receptionist.

'It's terrible. Never happened before like this. Tons

239

of it have come down on the mountains. If the temperature suddenly rises there will be avalanches . . .'

'Strange,' Newman commented, outside the station. 'You'd expect at least some of the people inside those cars to either walk out by the pedestrian exit or drive out again.'

'I've got an idea,' Tweed said. 'I'm going to that phone box to call Arthur Beck.'

'But he's in Berne!'

Newman shrugged. Tweed was already inside the box. Marler and Nield got out of their parked cars and wandered over to him.

'Just what is going on?' Marler asked.

'No idea. Did either of you recognize anyone inside those three cars?'

'No,' they both replied in unison.

'They're in a huge underground garage – vast,' Tweed said. 'Can't imagine what's happening down there.'

'Sounds to me like an ideal place to take out the lot,' Marler suggested.

'We do nothing until Tweed gets back. He's phoning Beck in Berne. Can't imagine why . . .'

Several minutes later Tweed came striding briskly back from the phone box. He had his hands inside his coat pockets.

'We're in luck. Beck is away – at some security conference held in Chicago. Expected back any moment. I got hold of his chief assistant, a woman who knows me. She gave me the number of Captain Charpentier, based at police headquarters here in an odd building with walls which look like plastic. Just on the other side of the Rhône. I know Charpentier well, explained the situation we have here. He's heard of Dr Goslar. Every-

240

one has now. This is Goslar's doing – publicizing what he has for sale to the highest bidder.'

'So what is Charpentier doing?' Newman asked impatiently.

'Sending across the river to here a whole fleet of patrol cars. I warned him not to let them arrive with screaming sirens and flashing lights. He's got plain-clothes men coming too – so they can walk down into the garage and check out what's going on.'

'Then what happens?'

'We'll know soon enough now.'

The atmosphere seemed full of menace. The silence in the square was disturbing. Then patrol cars began to pour into the square from every direction. Several stopped, took up a position in front of the entrance ramp. Others circled the exit ramp. A man in a business suit climbed out, walked down the entrance ramp. Charpentier told Tweed later what happened next.

The man in the suit, a Sergeant Davril, stood at the base of the ramp, looked at the cars parked everywhere. Charpentier explained that there were no tourists at this time of the year, in this weather. The parked cars belonged to Swiss businessmen, some sleeping in their nearby apartments while others, often bankers, were there to visit their mistresses.

Davril walked further in. Without warning a machine-pistol began to chatter. One bullet chipped his arm, a second one passed straight through his left shoulder. He sagged between two cars, hauled out his automatic, fired back several times where he thought he saw a figure. Then all hell broke loose.

Guns were being fired all over the garage. At least two machine-pistols rattled away. Handguns opened up. A bullet struck the petrol tank of one parked car. It

241

exploded with a roar, ignited the car next to it, which also detonated. Then other cars blew up. Flames soared to the ceiling. Smoke began to obscure what was happening, blossoming in great clouds. Uniformed, armed police rushed down both ramps. The whole garage was beginning to explode. The fire brigade arrived, unreeled great snakelike hoses, flooded the whole interior. Chaos and confusion everywhere. Many cars had become burnt-out wrecks. It was Dante's Inferno.

23

Tweed, realizing he could do nothing, had told Marler and Nield to go back to their heated cars, to wait and report later. With Newman he went into the station, found the buffet. The only two occupants were Paula and Serena.

Paula was chatting animatedly to Serena, in fact telling her nothing, when Tweed and Newman arrived. The sole waitress was asking them if they would like more coffee.

'I think we're swimming in it, thank you.' Paula smiled at the waitress. 'Thank you also for letting us stay so late.' She looked at Tweed and Newman.

'This kind lady has stayed open just for us. I think it's because we're English.'

'You're welcome,' the waitress replied with a warm smile.

'Hello, Serena,' Tweed said quickly. 'Sorry to rush you both but we're staying at the Hôtel Richemond for the night. We can talk later. Oh, this is Bob Newman, my staunch protector. Bob, meet Serena Cavendish. I think we'd better go now.'

Paula gave the waitress a generous tip, thanked her

again, then they were outside. Paula stopped. All the police cars. From below the rumble of gunfire. She stared at Tweed.

'What is happening? Sounds like the end of the world.'

It will be for some people, Newman said to himself. Charpentier, a tall, handsome man in his forties, was introduced briefly. He nodded, shook hands, turned to Tweed.

'This is sensible of you to go to the Richemond. I will come over later to have a word with you.'

Paula and Serena occupied the back of Newman's car while Tweed sat in the front next to Newman, who drove the short distance to the Richemond. The night manager was waiting for them as they walked into the luxurious surroundings. He gave them the good news as they registered.

'Captain Charpentier phoned to say you would be coming. The chef has agreed to stay on to provide you with a meal. After you have settled in your rooms please come down at your convenience. You can choose whatever you want from the menu . . .'

Tweed was about to join the others on their way to their rooms when he heard a noise. He turned round and saw, almost hidden behind a corner, Trudy.

'I'll follow you up,' he told the others. When they had gone he turned to Trudy.

Her hair was dishevelled, quite unlike her normal coiffeured appearance. Her clothes were rumpled. She carried a shoulder bag over one arm.

'What are you doing here? You look as though you've been in a war.'

'I have. Come into the bar. I'll tell you . . .'

'Nice of you to stay open,' Tweed said to the barman when he brought their drinks.

'We knew you were coming, sir,' the barman replied with a smile and left them.

'*I* was in that underground garage,' Trudy began. 'Hence my appearance.'

'You look OK to me. Your makeup's perfect.'

'I rushed into the bathroom as soon as I'd walked here, then dashed down so I could catch you. I'm lucky to be alive.'

'Take it slowly. Start from the beginning.'

'You understood my hand message when I signalled to you back on the autoroute? I was the motorcyclist. All the way from Paris.'

'You must be exhausted. Are you sure you want to talk now?'

'I won't sleep if I don't. Vance Karnow suggested I travel that way. He wanted to know how many of you there were in different cars. I agreed. Anything rather than travel with Bancroft as the driver. There were just the three of us. Something happened to the other lousy Americans back at the hotel in Paris. When I'd checked up on you I dumped my machine behind a petrol station and I was picked up by the car. Then the world blew up in that underground garage.'

'Want to tell me what did happen?'

'Karnow couldn't make up his bloody mind what to do next. So we sat in the garage. Then a man in a business suit walked down the ramp and inside. Bancroft thought it was Newman – the man did look a bit like him. He went berserk, grabbed a machine-pistol, got out of the car and opened fire, shooting all over the place. That's what started the holocaust, if I can use that expression. Shooting everywhere, bullets flying all over the shop. Cars exploding. I got out, ran for it, crouching down . . .'

'What happened to Karnow? To Bancroft?'

'Karnow was still in the car when it caught fire. There was a lot of smoke. I saw in a blur a figure climbing a ladder by the wall. I ran to it. I heard in a brief pause in the mayhem the sound of something metallic. It was just an ordinary aluminium ladder. I think it was lowered by pulling a lever on the wall. I shinned up it – whoever had gone up first had vanished. At the top I realized it was a ventilation shaft. The cone protruding above the ground had been knocked off. I scrambled out, saw you talking to another tall, good-looking man. He had raised his voice to be heard above the noises below ground. I heard him say something about going to the Hôtel Richemond. I know Geneva, so I walked here, avoiding the station. I still can't believe I got away.'

'But you did.' Tweed squeezed her round the waist and she nearly burst into tears, but stopped herself. 'Have another drink,' he said, summoning the waiter.

'I'll be drunk.'

'Doesn't matter.'

Normally he would have suggested sweetened tea, but he could tell she was not in a state of shock. Relating to him what had taken place had calmed her down. He asked the question when the second drink had been served.

'Was Bancroft in the car when you fled from it?'

'No. I don't know where he was. He started it all, by opening fire with his machine-pistol on the man he thought was Newman. When I scrambled out of the car he'd disappeared in the smoke.'

'You could catch a flight back to London from here in the morning.'

'Can't I stay with you? You're still after Goslar, aren't you? I would like to see where it all ends – remember, I was the motorcyclist who tried to warn you. Did you understand my signal? I asked you earlier and you didn't answer.'

245

'Sorry, I should have done. Yes, I did understand. You indicated there were three cars behind me. Thank you for—'

'I also lied to Karnow – told him you were in the first of the three cars. I'd seen two men in that one and the barrel of a gun protruding from a window. Bancroft was going to blast the front car when the time came, as he put it. I thought when he did carry out his threat two men would be more than a match – even for Bancroft. I'm determined to see this through, Tweed.'

He thought about it, looked at her, looked away. She was intense but, despite her ordeal, now quite calm. He sipped at his drink before he spoke.

'Let's both sleep on it after a good dinner. I don't imagine you are carrying a weapon?'

She glanced round. The barman had his back to them, was polishing glasses. Slipping her hand inside her jacket, she produced a 6.35 mm automatic from her hip holster.

'I can use it. When I was in New York I took shooting lessons in my spare time. I shouldn't say it, but I was a crack shot. I was keeping it in case I ever encountered Bancroft. When I did, I never got the opportunity to use it.'

'Hide it now. My team will be coming down for dinner. Everyone will be ravenous – including yourself, I'm sure. I'll introduce you to them as Trudy Warner, if that's all right by you.'

'I'd like you to go on calling me Trudy.' She smiled. 'You have always known me as Trudy during our brief acquaintance. And I do want to come with you wherever you're going.'

'Tell you my decision in the morning. Now we'll go into the dining room. I have a Captain Charpentier of the Swiss police coming to see me later. I want food first before he arrives.'

After a sumptuous dinner they all realized they were very alert and didn't feel like going to bed yet. Tweed invited them to his suite to drink their coffee. He had taken one sip from his cup when the phone rang. It was Captain Charpentier downstairs. Tweed asked him to come up to the suite.

Charpentier frowned when he entered and surveyed the gathering – his gaze fixed on Paula and Trudy. They were seated together on a sofa. During the dinner they had got on very well with each other. Tweed invited the Swiss police officer to sit down, to have coffee. Charpentier remained standing.

'Something wrong?' Tweed enquired.

'I was going to describe what we have found in the garage,' their visitor said in impeccable English. 'Some of it is grisly.'

'You're thinking of the ladies.' Tweed introduced Trudy. 'I can tell you both have seen some pretty grisly things. Like the rest of us they will want to hear this.'

'If you say so.'

Charpentier took off his outdoor coat and sat down. He accepted a cup of coffee, drank it greedily.

'Then I won't pull any punches. We found several corpses, burnt to a shrivel almost. Behind the wheel of a Citroën was a big man. Very big. An odd thing had happened. His body was badly burnt but the upper part of his head was intact. We think while he was on fire foam was flooded over him by the fire brigade, then later he was hosed down. He had very close-cropped brown hair. Like stubble. The fire hadn't reached it. He must have had it cut that way.'

247

'The Ape,' Paula said to herself, but still aloud.

'You knew him?' Charpentier asked.

'Yes. Briefly and unpleasantly. One monstrous thug.'

'Could you give me his name?'

'Abel. I'm sure that was his Christian name. No idea of what his surname might have been.'

Paula felt no regrets at the news. After her experience of being suspended by him from a window up thirty floors she experienced only relief that he was no longer walking the planet. Tweed had been watching Trudy closely. She had shown no signs of distress at the description. Instead, she was leaning forward, watching the Swiss closely.

'I'll go on,' Charpentier continued. 'Inside a Renault, well away from the Citroën, we found what must have been a tall man in the front passenger seat. He was a black stick. His door was open and we think he tried to escape. On the concrete floor of the garage near the open door we found his passport.' He consulted a notebook. 'Jarvis Bate. Officer, Special Branch.'

'Was there anyone else in that car?' Paula enquired.

'Yes. A much smaller man behind the wheel. Burnt almost down to a skeleton.'

'Mervyn Leek,' Tweed said. 'Also an officer of Special Branch, for your records.'

'Thank you, sir.' Charpentier made a note in his little book. 'Lastly there was a corpse in a third car, again well away from the other two vehicles. An Audi . . .'

My car, thought Trudy, leaning forward further. What's coming now?

'With this one,' Charpentier went on, 'I'm glad my chief, Arthur Beck, arrived in Geneva an hour ago on a much-delayed flight from America. It has delicate international implications. The body in the front was charred to the waist. Again, the brigade had pumped in foam, which saved the top half of the corpse. And it was later hosed down. Features singed but clear. A fireman emptied his breast pocket, gave me the contents. They included a passport. The dead owner was Vance Karnow, top man in Washington.'

'Was there any other body in the car?' Trudy asked.

'No.' Charpentier looked surprised at the question after what he had just told them. 'Why?'

'I just wouldn't expect a man like that to travel alone. You did say the body was in the front of the car,' she continued. 'What about a driver?'

'No sign of one. But two people escaped.'

Trudy concentrated on straightening a crease in the slacks of her trouser suit. When she looked at Tweed her eyes were like stones. They'd both had the same thought.

Bancroft.

'Escaped?' Tweed asked. 'How did they do that?'

'Climbed up inside one of the ventilator shafts, knocked the top off, vanished. I saw them running.'

Tweed and Trudy again exchanged glances. He knew what she was thinking. He wasn't far off. She recalled the figure she'd seen disappearing above her. Had she known she could have shot Bancroft in the back with her Beretta.

'Any evidence of anyone else shooting?' Tweed enquired to divert the attention of the Swiss from the ventilator shaft. 'I mean, any sign of weapons?'

'Yes. Inside the Renault,' he said, 'Bate had an automatic clenched in what was left of his right hand. 'In the first Citroën – the one with the man you called the Ape – there was a machine-pistol on the floor. Both weapons had been fired.'

'So it was a shoot-out,' Tweed commented. 'Made far worse when bullets hit petrol tanks, which promptly exploded.'

'That sums it up.' Charpentier was standing. 'I think

that is enough for tonight. We'll know more after the autopsies – I don't envy the pathologists their job. Beck will be coming to see you at eight o'clock in the morning, Mr Tweed. I'd better get back. I suggest you all try to get a good night's sleep . . .'

Tweed looked again at Trudy. When he saw the steely look in her eyes he had no doubt she would be coming with them to Annecy.

24

From his front-seat view the Yellow Man had watched it all with interest. Careful not to turn on any lights in his bedroom, he had carried a chair, placed it behind the thick net curtains across a window, had sat with night-vision glasses.

He had seen Tweed and Newman standing in front of the station, the arrival of a horde of patrol cars which had formed a cordon round entrances and exits. Soon he had heard the muffled sound of gunfire from inside the underground car park. It hadn't meant a thing to him.

Later he had focused his glasses as another woman and Paula had joined Tweed and Newman. With his free hand he had felt the string of pearls with the razor-edged wire, had imagined placing them round Paula's neck from behind her.

Later still he had gone to bed, setting his alarm clock for an early start. After using room service to have a 6 a.m. breakfast he had left the hotel, walked to his car through deserted streets. Patrol cars were still parked barring entrances and exits to the car park.

Getting inside his vehicle parked in the side street, he had taken off his suit, then donned a dark blue uniform. He took off the black wig, which he was fed up with. Quickly he rammed a peaked cap over his hair. He then drove into the square and parked where he could see the entrance to the Richemond. He had, before leaving his own accommodation, phoned several hotels asking for Tweed before a temporary receptionist informed him Tweed was at the Richemond. He had broken the connection before the receptionist could say any more.

Dissatisfied with his viewpoint, he drove closer to the hotel, parked. Slumped in his seat, pretending to read an old newspaper, he looked like a chauffeur waiting for his employer to arrive.

As arranged the night before, Paula arrived at Tweed's suite in time to have breakfast with him. She thought Tweed looked amazingly alert. He thought she looked tired. They were just finishing their meal when Beck arrived.

The Chief of Federal Police hugged Paula when he entered the room. They had always liked each other. Beck, in his late forties, was of medium height, slim, had greying hair and a neat trim moustache. He had a paper under his arm and he handed it to Tweed.

'*Le Monde.* Flown in by express from Paris this morning. The headline is interesting.'

AMERICANS DEPORTED
ACCUSED OF ESPIONAGE

Tweed scanned the text underneath. The gist was that incriminating documents had been discovered in the suite of a top-class hotel where an American delegation was staying. Vance Karnow was involved, but had gone missing.

'Interesting, as you say,' Tweed agreed, handing the newspaper to Paula.

'And where was your last port of call?' enquired Beck, settling himself in an armchair. 'That is, before you arrived here.'

'Paris.'

'So you wouldn't know anything about René Lasalle and his team finding the Americans tear-gassed and recovering consciousness?'

'I wasn't there.'

'As always, a devious answer,' Beck commented, his expression quizzical.

'You've heard about a Dr Goslar?' Tweed responded, changing the subject.

'Heard about him! All the security services in Western Europe – and the States – are talking about nothing else.'

'That will be Goslar's network – spreading the news as a prelude to raising the bidding sky-high for his fiendish new weapon. Anything in the press about what is really going on?'

'Not a peep so far. The security people, who do know, are so scared they have kept their mouths shut outside their own circles. This has caused them to create a miracle for the moment – keeping it out of the press. Of course here we have something else to think about which will make the headlines in tomorrow's papers.'

'The devastation in the underground garage?'

'Yes.' Beck paused. 'You wouldn't have been involved in that in some way, I suppose?'

'Indirectly, we were. Three cars followed us from Paris. Newman, standing outside the station, watched as at intervals all three cars entered that garage.'

'Why is it, Tweed, that when you arrive somewhere the whole city blows up?'

'Obviously I'm mixing with the wrong people.'

'You do that all the time. To be fair it's your profession, rather like my own job. Washington is already screaming about what has happened to Vance Karnow.'

'Let them scream. Arthur . . .' It was Tweed's turn to pause. 'Can I ask you a favour?'

'I knew that would be coming. Just when I'm up to my eyes in my own problems. Tell me the worst. What is it?'

'Goslar has a habit of leaving what I call his signature when he moves on. It's his great mistake. He needs a base, wherever he happens to have alighted. So he leases a large property on a long-term agreement. Then, when he's ready, he leaves while the lease still has weeks – or months – to run. He has tons of money to operate in this way. It means he can dart on elsewhere the moment he wants to. Do I make myself clear?'

'Yes. But what do you want me to do?'

'With your authority, could you approach the two top estate agents in Geneva? I want to know if an expensive property has been leased recently – within, say, the last three months.'

'Oh, that's easy,' Beck said sarcastically. 'This is Switzerland.'

'I hadn't finished. The property will be fairly large – but not a Blenheim Palace. Essentially it will be in a remote location, but within one hour's driving distance from Geneva. I emphasize it will be remote. And on its own. No neighbours. It could have been leased in the name Charterhouse, but I very much doubt that. Also within driving distance of Geneva's airport.'

'Could be anywhere. You think Goslar is here?'

'I haven't a clue. It's a long shot. While I think of it, could Charpentier contact the airport, ask them if a private jet registered in Liechtenstein – under the company name of Poulenc et Cie – is still waiting there. A Grumman Gulfstream jet.'

'That's the easy one. I may phone you before you leave. When are you going – and where? If it isn't a state secret, which it probably is.'

'As soon as possible we leave for Annecy. This morning definitely.' Tweed reached for a hotel notepad. Tearing off a sheet he placed it on the cardboard back, scribbled, handed the sheet to Beck. 'There's my mobile phone number. I want us to keep closely in touch.'

'Thought you didn't like mobiles.'

'I don't. Mistrust them. They can be intercepted. But it's the only way we can contact each other this time. All my team have them.'

'What do you expect to find in Annecy?' Beck asked. 'Maybe Goslar.'

'Isn't he wonderful?' Beck said, turning to Paula. 'He asks me to contact estate agents here, then says Goslar could be hiding in Annecy.'

'In addition,' Tweed went on, 'we don't even know whether Goslar is a man or a woman. There are indications both ways.'

'He's looking for a phantom,' Beck commented, standing up. 'I'll check with the estate agents myself. This afternoon I'm flying back to Belp, the airport for Berne. Then I'll be locked up in my HQ. You have the number?'

'In my head. Always.'

'Have a nice quiet trip to Annecy. The weather will be better down there. I must go.'

'I expect that trip to be anything but quiet. Take care, Arthur.'

'You two are the ones who should take care. Goslar, I suspect, is one of the most dangerous men in the world . . .'

*

Marler arrived with a canvas holdall soon after Beck had departed. He walked over to Paula.

'One Browning for my collection, please. We'll pass through one of the French checkpoints. Thank you,' he said as Paula reluctantly handed over her gun, holster and spare ammo. 'I had trouble with Trudy Warner, getting an automatic off her. Had to promise to give it back once we're over the border. See you.'

'Hello, Bob,' he said as he opened the door and Newman walked in. 'Feel naked without your Smith & Wesson? Thought so. I'm off . . .'

Paula got up, picked up her fleece from a chair. She explained when she'd put the garment on, 'Poor Trudy. All her clothes were in a case inside the trunk of the Audi, which is a wreck. We're going shopping to get her something to wear. I loaned her a nightdress after we'd left this suite last night, plus a few other things. Serena is coming with us.'

'Don't be too long,' Tweed warned.

'Why do men always say that when women go shopping?'

'What do you think of Serena?' Tweed suddenly asked.

'Mystery woman,' was Paula's reaction.

Newman threw his coat on a chair, dumped his bag beside it. Then he settled himself in an armchair, lit a cigarette.

'What is the situation now?' he enquired. 'After last night.'

'Simplified,' Tweed assorted. 'Up to a point. Don't think me callous, but Goslar is the target. Now Bate is out of the way, no longer following us, that's one less enemy to think about. The same applies to the late Ape. All we have to worry about is Goslar – and his huge organization. There is one other highly lethal danger.

255

Bancroft. When I saw him at the bar in the Ritz back in Paris he struck me as a thug, but a very dangerous thug with brains.'

'He may have caught a flight back to the States.'

'No. He'll still be around,' Tweed said grimly.

'Still no word from Burgoyne?' Newman asked. 'That worries me.'

'It shouldn't. Burgoyne is used to operating on his own. And he is not a man to waste time just keeping in touch. When he finds something we'll hear from him.'

'Let's just hope it's in time. When do we leave?'

'As soon as the ladies get back. I hope Marler has hidden all the armoury properly.'

'He has. I helped him tape weapons under the chassis of his car. He wants to lead the pack again – says when the French checkpoint people see three cars they're liable to let the first one through without much bother.'

'Let's hope he's right.'

Newman had spent some time explaining Marler's plan of manoeuvre – if they ran into an ambush – when the door opened. Into the suite trooped Paula, Serena and Trudy, with carrier bags.

'I see,' said Tweed, 'you've bought up half Geneva.'

'Why do men always say that when women go shopping?' asked Paula, repeating her earlier remark.

'And from the names on the carriers you've spent a fortune,' Tweed continued.

'Same reply as the one I've just made,' Paula responded. 'Trudy is fixed up now. As you see, we managed to find her a fleece. And a nice fur cap. Don't take it off yet, Trudy. Circle, let them admire you.'

'I'd say,' Newman commented with enthusiasm as

Trudy swivelled round, 'that you look rather more than terrific.'

'Thank you, kind sir,' Trudy replied, curtsying.

'Serena also has a few new things – including a really warm coat,' Paula pointed out.

'And fashionable new boots,' Newman observed. 'She also makes me wish we were staying in Geneva. Then I could take the three of you out on the town.'

'You can forget that,' Tweed said severely. 'We have a job to do.'

He had just spoken when the phone rang. He grabbed hold of it, sat back.

'Yes?'

'I have the answers,' Beck's voice told him. 'First the private jet at Cointrin. Charpentier has two men out there at the airport permanently – to check on who is arriving. The news is the Grumman is kept fully fuelled, regularly maintained, ready for instant departure. Furthermore, there are eight-hour shifts on round the clock, three teams of air crews, who take it in turns to occupy the cockpit. That jet could take off for distant points at any moment. Most unusual. Most expensive.'

'Then I could be right about the Geneva area.'

'You could. I've also contacted the two top estate agents. They are checking on leases on the type of property you described, going back three months. Charpentier will get their reports later. I gave him your mobile number. Hope you don't mind.'

'I agree. And thank you for taking action so quickly. I believe we're now facing a race against time.'

'You've had that in the past. You coped. Must go now to catch my flight to Belp. Again, take great care . . .'

Everyone in the suite was seated. They had all kept quiet during the conversation, something Tweed appreciated. These were women with heads on their shoulders.

'A race against time?' Paula enquired.

'Yes. I've paid the hotel bill. I can give you five minutes to get yourselves organized. Then we leave.'

'You look very grim,' Newman remarked when they were alone.

'I feel very grim.'

'Your old adversary from all those years ago. He managed to get away then. We don't want a repeat performance.'

'My old adversary,' Tweed repeated.

Much earlier, the Yellow Man had been slumped behind the wheel of his hired Mercedes when the door to the hotel he was parked outside opened. A small business-man, wearing an astrakhan coat, walked briskly down the steps.

The assassin straightened up, adjusted his peaked cap. The businessman spoke as the 'chauffeur' lowered a window.

'You're my car for Stuttgart? I am early, I know.'

'*Yes sir!*' The Yellow Man was out of the car, opening the rear door with a flourish. He bowed his head as the businessman handed him his case, then stepped into the rear. He closed the door. Then he opened the boot, deposited the large case inside, shut the lid.

Returning to his place behind the wheel, he caught the eye of the man in the back. The businessman wore rimless glasses, exuded an air of wealth and success. He spoke English with an accent.

'I know I'm three hours ahead of schedule. I phoned your firm this morning but no one answered.'

'Staff comes on duty later, sir,' the Yellow Man replied.

'My meeting in Stuttgart has been brought forward. I'd like to stop somewhere for breakfast later. Just a quick one.'

'That can easily be arranged, sir.'

The Yellow Man was scanning the street. It was totally deserted at that hour. He started the engine, cruised forward slowly a short distance, then stopped. He scanned the street in his rear-view mirror, in his wing mirror, ahead of him. His hand reached under a newspaper spread out on the seat beside him. He turned round.

'I don't think the lid is locked. I must protect your—'

As he was speaking he aimed the gun with the silencer he had in his hand. He shot the passenger once. A red patch like a flower blooming appeared on the businessman's chest as he slumped down. The Yellow Man jumped out of the car, unlocked the boot, took out the heavy case. Then he opened the rear door, placed the case next to the dead man. He wrapped the white silk scarf the corpse was wearing in such a way that it concealed the bullet hole.

He then swiftly lifted the body so it was upright against the seat. The corpse looked as though it was sleeping, head resting against the back. He wedged in the case to prevent the body slipping sideways. Satisfied with his exertions, he sat again behind the wheel. Then he steered the car forward until it was close to, but not opposite, the Richemond.

He waited.

When, eventually, Newman drove a car to the hotel entrance, the Yellow Man started his engine. Again he waited. He watched as Tweed, with three women, emerged and entered the car. Two women squeezed into the back with Tweed. The third woman – he recognized her as Paula Grey – sat next to Newman.

As Newman drove off the assassin drove after him.

In his rear-view mirror he saw a limousine pull up in front of the hotel the dead businessman had come out of. The Yellow Man smiled callously. He was leaving the area just in time.

25

As they left Geneva behind, heading for the French border, Tweed sat with Trudy on his right and Serena on his left. The original plan had been for Serena to travel in Nield's car, seated beside him. Serena had not liked the idea at all.

'I want to travel with you,' she had told Tweed firmly. 'I'm going to feel much safer that way.'

'Why shouldn't you be just as safe with Nield?' he'd asked.

'After what happened last night in that underground garage I will feel safer with you,' she had repeated.

'Then I'll sit in the front next to Newman,' Paula had decided.

She had been watching Serena, had seen the upward tilt of her nose and the determined expression on her face. She was puzzled as to why Serena was so insistent. During the previous evening Paula had again watched Serena when they were all assembled in Tweed's suite.

Paula had observed that Serena had shown no signs of fear – or distress – when Charpentier had described in gory detail the condition of the corpses found inside the garage. She had almost seemed to take it as all in the day's work.

Reaching her hand back over her seat she now called out to Tweed.

'Could I have that map you've been studying? Sitting where I am makes me in an ideal position to act as navigator.'

'You're quite right,' Tweed agreed, handing her the map. 'In any case, I have the route in my head now.' He looked to his left. 'Are you comfortable, Serena? We have just enough room, I think.'

'I'm very comfortable,' Serena assured him with a warm smile. 'I hope Nield didn't think I was avoiding him.'

'No, he wouldn't. In fact, I'll tell you now – he prefers to be on his own. If trouble comes he won't have to worry about you.'

'Are we expecting trouble, then?' she asked casually.

'Hard to say. Depends on whether Goslar knows where we are.'

'How could he know that?'

'I've no idea,' Tweed lied.

He was thinking of the weird phone call from Goslar when he had given a 'clue'. *Aniseed.* Which Paula had interpreted as Annecy.

He felt fairly sure they were heading into a trap – an ambush. But Marler had outlined a reaction to such an eventuality which he had approved with Newman. Which is why it was important that on a straight stretch of road he could see Marler's car leading the way. Followed by Nield's vehicle, then his own. So far it was their only possibility of contacting Goslar's men – of capturing one of them. If they were successful Harry Butler would persuade a captive to talk – and he could do that without resorting to the brutal methods of torture used so widely these days.

'We are going to Annecy, aren't we?' Serena asked. 'Paula told me she thought we might be going there but she wasn't sure that it might not be somewhere else.'

Good for Paula, Tweed thought. A very discreet

261

response. But Paula trusted no one except the members of the team.

'What is your working method when grappling with a man like Goslar?' Serena enquired.

'Well, when the Duke of Wellington was fighting the Peninsular War, in Portugal and Spain, he said that his method was like tying knots in a length of rope. He meant he reacted as the situation developed. My method is similar. Of course he was a long way from becoming Duke of Wellington at that time.'

'Sounds to me as though you haven't got a plan,' she suggested with a hint of humour.

Tweed was saved from answering as Newman glanced once again in his rear-view mirror. Then he called out to Tweed.

'I've been wondering whether we were being followed by a limo with a chauffeur behind the wheel. Seemed unlikely. He had a passenger in the back. And there was always one car between us and them. Now he's disappeared. Won't be long before we're at the border.'

The Yellow Man's quicksilver mind had moved at its normal speed when he had shot the businessman in the back of his car. He had been worried that after the devastating events at the garage there would be patrol cars swarming round the area the following morning.

A lone chauffeur driving a Mercedes might have been stopped for questioning. He would present a much more normal image with a passenger in the back. He had been right.

As he had followed Tweed's car through the city numerous patrol cars had appeared. None of them had given him more than a fleeting glance when they saw the 'sleeping' passenger in the back. But now he had a serious problem. He knew the French checkpoint was coming up at the frontier. He couldn't risk arriving with a corpse in the back.

Knowing the route he was taking, he kept glancing in his rear-view mirror, saw nothing behind him. Suddenly he swung off the road along a track strewn with small rocks. He drove slowly, passed a big sign with the word 'DANGER' in large red letters.

He was out of sight of the road when he stopped the car near the edge of an abandoned quarry. Moving swiftly, he jumped out of the car, leaving the engine running. Opening the rear door, he was strong enough to have no difficulty lifting out the dead businessman. He carried the body close to the brink of the quarry, hurled his burden over. It slithered halfway down the quarry face, came to rest on a ledge. He then collected the suitcase, carrying it with gloves on his hands, hurled it down. His last task was to throw the gun and silencer he had used into the quarry.

The loss of the weapon didn't worry him. He had two more handguns taped under the dashboard. Getting back behind the wheel, he managed to turn the car in a circle and return to the road. He was confident he would soon catch up with Tweed's car.

Paula worried about Marler as she saw his car stop in the distance at the border post. She knew he spoke fluent French – what she did not know was that before they left the hotel he had dashed out and bought himself a French suit and a pair of shoes.

As the French guard approached him he switched off his engine. He had his window lowered as the guard peered in, checked the empty rear.

'Where are you going to?' the guard demanded.

'To Annecy. I hope the weather is better there than it was back in Geneva,' he replied in his perfect French.

'On business or pleasure?'

'Officially on business.' Marler looked straight at the guard. 'Of course, if a little pleasure is offered by an attractive lady who am I to refuse it?'

The guard smirked. He waved him on and prepared for the next car, which had Nield inside it on his own.

From a distance Paula watched as first Marler, then Nield were waved through. She heaved a sigh of relief. Taped to the chassis under Marler's car was an armoury large enough to start a war. Tweed had lowered his window as they stopped. As he anticipated, the guard peered in at the rear.

'A short holiday,' Tweed explained in English. 'Switzerland is so stuffy. In your country it is so much more relaxing. If the weather is better then we shall have a most relaxing time.'

'The weather is much better,' the guard told him. 'None of that snow the Swiss seem to love so much, although they deny it. So,' he smirked at Trudy and Serena, 'enjoy your holiday.'

He waved them on with a flamboyant flourish of his hand. He was still smirking.

'Unpleasant type,' snapped Serena.

'He has a boring job,' Tweed said placidly, 'therefore he varies it with his idea of a joke.'

'I thought it was strange the way we passed through the Swiss checkpoint,' Paula commented, 'only a hundred yards back. The barrier was raised, no officials came out.'

'There's a difference. We were *leaving* Switzerland so why should they worry about us. Entering a country is a different matter.'

'Well, thank Heaven Marler got through all right.

And that saucy guard was right. The weather is much better, even though it must have been raining earlier.'

She was referring to two things: the sun was shining down on them out of a clear blue sky, and the road was damp from recent rain. They were out in the country now with rolling hills stretching away into the distance like a huge green sea. Here and there trees had a sprinkling of leaves on them. Spring was arriving.

They were driving along a rare straight stretch with hill slopes rising on either side when Tweed saw Marler's car stop. Nield drove closer to him, then he also stopped. Newman had glanced in his rear-view mirror again.

'Nothing coming. That chauffeur-driven limo must have turned off somewhere. I know why Marler has stopped. He's going to distribute his armoury. Think I'll go and give him a hand.'

'I'd like to stretch my legs,' said Paula. She turned round and gave Tweed a certain look. 'Care to accompany me?'

'Good idea. We'll climb this slope. I don't think it goes up very far.'

As they began the climb they heard Trudy and Serena start chattering to each other. The grass beneath their feet was short and firm. Arriving at the top of the ridge they had a panoramic view. Distant villages huddled inside deep valleys. It was a scene of perfect peace.

'You know,' Paula began as they admired the view, 'I've been thinking. In the past you've chivvied members of the team for never noticing the absence of something. Well, I've noticed something like that which I find odd.'

'Tell me.'

'You've said Goslar always shoots the messenger, as you put it. He eliminates anyone he's had a connection with, however remote. He had that reporter from

Appledore, Sam Sneed, murdered in an alley off Fleet Street. Seems ages ago now. Then poor Vallade, the rare-book seller on the Île St-Louis was also decapitated. Finally, Mme Markov's head ended up in a waste basket in the flat near the Opéra. A pretty hideous roll call of murder.'

'What's your point?'

'That there's been no attempt to kill Serena Cavendish. Yet she took photographs of Appledore for him. She saw the Ape deliver the balance of her fee through her letter box.'

'I had noticed that fact myself . . .'

'It's that helicopter again,' she interjected. She swung round. 'There it is. It's a distance away and flying at about five hundred feet.'

Tweed had turned round with her. The machine was flying parallel to the ridge on the far side of the road. Too far away see what markings were on its fuselage.

'I don't like it,' Paula went on. 'When we were leaving the Richemond I heard a chopper circling – as though it was above the square with the underground garage underneath.'

'I heard it too. That one was probably from a TV station, shooting the scene they'll feature on their next news programme. The one over there could be a different job. Quite a lot of businessmen use helicopters these days to get fast from A to B.'

'Then there was the helicopter we heard while we were driving down the autoroute from Paris to Geneva,' she persisted.

'Don't worry.' He looked down the slope. 'I think Newman wants us. Time to get back to the car.'

Newman met them halfway down the slope. Keeping his back to the car parked below, he handed Paula her Browning and spare ammo. She quickly hid them inside her shoulder bag.

'Funny we still haven't heard from Burgoyne,' Newman remarked as they came close to the road.

'He'll call us when he has something to report,' Tweed replied.

He was within thirty feet of the car when his mobile started buzzing. He looked at Newman as much as to say, I told you so.

'Hello?' he said, stopping.

'Monica here. Thank God I've reached you. I've had another of Goslar's weird screechy messages. Quite short. He said, I quote, "If you wish us to meet, Tweed, try the Château de l'Air." That was all. Do you know where it is?'

'No idea. It's possible you've told me just in time. All is well. Do not hesitate to contact me again. Take care.'

'*You* take care . . .'

Staying on the slope, Tweed beckoned to Marler and Nield to join him. When they were gathered round him he told them about Monica's message. He reminded Marler to tell Butler who had stayed with their car.

'I've handed back the armoury to everyone,' Marler said. 'Here is Trudy's automatic and spare ammo. She'll raise Cain if she doesn't get those back.'

'I think we should proceed,' Tweed ordered.

'You've seen that helicopter, I'm sure,' Marler remarked.

'Yes, we have. Paula pointed it out to me. It seems to be heading south now. Off we go. Warily.'

Marler passed Paula a canvas holdall. He opened it so she could see inside. He pointed out the three compartments it was divided into.

'Stun grenades in there, firebombs here and shrapnel grenades in this one.' He looked at Tweed. 'Warily is

267

the watchword. Since we left Geneva it's been rather too quiet for my liking.'

Inside the helicopter, flying south towards Annecy, Bancroft sat next to the pilot. The previous night he'd had no idea, as he climbed the ventilator shaft to escape the inferno in the underground garage, that someone was coming up behind him.

After prising off the louvred cone at the top he had emerged into the night. He had crouched low, keeping in shadows, as he left the square after spotting Tweed and Newman standing outside the railway station. Darting into a side street he had waited by the corner where he could see the two men.

Bancroft had caught a glimpse of a blurred figure climbing out of the shaft he'd used. Since Trudy was dressed in a trouser suit he couldn't make out whether it was a man or a woman. Then the vague figure, also keeping in the shadows, had disappeared.

He was still standing by his corner when he saw Tweed, Newman, Paula and another woman get into a car. He thought he had lost them as, boldly, he had hurried after the car. He had arrived just in time to see them disappear inside the Richemond.

Bancroft had then walked into a nearby hotel and reserved a room for the night. In a money belt wrapped round his waist under his coat he was carrying hundreds of dollars. The only similarity between Vance Karnow and Tweed was they both provided members of their teams with plenty of money. The hotel – typically Swiss – had provided him with a shaving kit, toothbrush and a pair of pyjamas.

He had risen early the following morning and a department store had opened its doors as he was passing. Inside he had purchased a leather coat, heavy motoring gloves and a fur hat, Russian style. Leaving the store, he had hailed a cab, asked the driver to take him to the airport. There he had found a company which hired out helicopters with pilots.

Bancroft had flashed in front of the pilot a card which had proved effective before. In large letters were printed the words *State Security*.

'I'm cooperating with the Swiss Federal Police,' he had told the pilot. 'We're on the track of terrorists who blew up the garage last night.'

What turned the trick was the sheaf of dollars Bancroft agreed to pay. The pilot followed his instructions, circling for some time high above the underground garage. Bancroft's eyes had almost popped out of his head when, using binoculars he had bought, he saw Trudy Warner leaving the Richemond with Tweed and Paula.

So now I have three targets, he decided. The traitor, Trudy, Paula Grey and Tweed.

Also in the forefront of his ambitious mind was the memory of seeing Karnow's dead body, hit by two bullets in the shooting, in the front of the car. Bancroft saw the opportunity to let Tweed lead him to Goslar – to seize the secret weapon for Washington.

He would be the new chief of Unit Four.

Now he was gazing through the binoculars at Tweed and Paula, perched on the top of a hill. He couldn't see anything that was down on the road.

As Newman drove his car behind the two spaced out in front, Tweed was recalling Monica's message. Where was the Château de l'Air? He sensed a trap, but sooner or later Goslar had to commit a major error. When he did that would be the moment to pounce – with ferocity. No holds barred.

Seated beside Newman, Paula was studying her map. She glanced up as the road suddenly started to wind, to go steeply downhill. Then she stared. At the bottom of the hill, where she knew the road curved round a sharp bend, a curtain of white mist was rising. Due, she guessed, to the brilliant sun shining on the damp road surface. It was more like a fog.

Tweed's mobile buzzed. He grabbed it, pressed it to his ear.

'Hello?'

'Marler here. Prepare to go into the planned manoeuvre. Nield has been warned.'

Marler was obviously bothered by, even suspicious of, the heavy mist. Tweed passed on the message to Newman.

His phone buzzed again as they came close to the fog.

'Hello?'

'Tweed?'

'Speaking.'

'Burgoyne here. Potential ambush point at bottom of road near Choisy. Ambush warning . . .'

'Ambush!' Tweed said urgently into his mobile, first contacting Marler, then Nield. Newman had heard him anyway.

It all happened so quickly it was like a fast-forwarded film. Marler swung off the road up a track, turned his car to face the way he had come. Nield reversed, backing towards them, then turned his vehicle sideways on, lowered his window. Newman backed, drove into the entrance to farmland, smashing a gate. He left the front part of the car exposed, lowered his window at the same moment as Paula lowered hers, grabbing the canvas holdall.

Paula sucked in her breath as she saw what was coming out of the mist curtain. Tweed put an arm round

270

both Trudy and Serena, pushing them down as he shouted, 'Keep your damned heads down as far as you can!'

Through the mist curtain a small army of strange men was advancing. Their faces and bare arms were tanned a dark brown. Round their heads they wore green cloths. Each man carried a machine-pistol aimed at two cars – Nield's and Tweed's. They hadn't noticed Marler parked in his niche. Tweed's voice was grim.

'Arab Fundamentalists . . .'

One group came walking rapidly along the side of the bank to the right. They ignored Nield's apparently empty car. A rattle of bullets hit the road in front of Newman's car, became a hail of gunfire. Four men were suddenly very close. Paula hurled one of her firebombs. It burst at the feet of the attackers. A sheet of flame enveloped them. They screamed, running in all directions, their clothes on fire, flaming torches rolling on the ground, running up the bank before they collapsed.

A much larger body of men burst through the curtain. Marler's machine pistol opened up, catching them in the rear. They fell like ninepins. Paula threw a second firebomb, further this time. Its flames consumed mist, exposed a pick-up truck with its back towards them. In the open back a man stood holding a bazooka, aimed at Newman's car. Nield sat up, fired three times. The Arab with the bazooka staggered, jerked his weapon upwards, fired it by reflex. The shell soared high into the air, exploded harmlessly.

Marler was firing his machine pistol at random into what remained of the mist, traversing it as he pressed the trigger. There were shrieks, then silence. A few moments later an enormous Arab appeared, armed with a machine-pistol. He advanced towards Newman's car. Newman fired at him once. Hit him. The Arab continued to advance. Newman threw open his door,

271

jumped out, emptied his Smith & Wesson at point-blank range. The Arab looked surprised, tottered briefly, then fell forward on the weapon he had never fired.

A heavy silence descended as Newman swiftly reloaded. The mist evaporated, particles of it glowing like diamonds in the sun.

Parked by the bend which could now be seen, were several trucks, the vehicles which had brought the killers to this point. Marler jumped out of his car, held his machine-pistol ready as he walked slowly forward, checking each truck. All empty. Weapons scattered on their floors. He walked back, called out, his voice cool as a cucumber, 'All clear!'

'That was something,' Paula said quietly. 'Burgoyne warned us just in time.'

'Except Marler smelt danger first,' Tweed reminded her.

'Are you all right?' he asked the women on either side of him.

'I'm OK,' said Serena, sitting up and adjusting a crease in her trousers.

'Nothing wrong with me,' replied Trudy, slipping the automatic she had been holding back under her coat.

Marler appeared at the open rear window. He looked quickly at everyone. They looked back at him as he gave a snappy salute.

'Time we got moving. Don't drive over anything in the road.'

'Does this often happen?' Serena enquired very quietly.

'Nield has just said this must be the first of them.'

'Hurrah for Pete!' Paula said ironically. 'I really do love an optimist.'

26

They were driving along another stretch of country road, the carnage of dead Arabs well behind them. There had been no difficulty passing along one side of the pick-up truck where the Arab with his bazooka had stood. Paula sensed that the atmosphere of tension inside the car was gone. The scenery beyond hedges on both sides of the road was beautiful and the sun was a warm glow.

'I wonder where Burgoyne is now?' Paula mused aloud.

Probably locating the site of the next ambush, Newman thought, but he kept the idea to himself. Time enough to worry about that when it happened.

'Probably somewhere ahead of us – could be any distance away,' said Tweed, answering Paula's question. 'We'll hear from him when he's ready.'

'We must keep a lookout for this Château de l'Air,' Newman reminded them.

'I have been looking for it ever since we received Monica's phone call,' Paula retorted.

'Pardon me for speaking.'

'Do you expect to find Dr Goslar at this Château de l'Air? Sounds in English like "lair".'

'Very apt,' Tweed commented. 'As for finding him there, maybe.'

They were travelling along an unusually straight stretch in their same formation – Marler leading in the distance with Nield behind him – when Newman peered in his rear-view mirror. A car was coming up behind them at great speed. As it came closer he thought it was the Mercedes they had seen earlier with a chauffeur behind the wheel.

'This one is ramming his foot down,' he remarked.

The car, moving like a rocket, overtook them, sped on. Newman caught only a blur of the driver, but enough to see it was not the chauffeur. Instead of a peaked cap he thought the driver wore a beret. At the same speed he overtook Nield and raced on to roar past Marler.

Earlier, the Yellow Man had started driving over a hilltop, then stopped when he saw what lay well below. With nothing in sight behind him he had backed swiftly. He had caught a glimpse of heavy mist rising at the bottom of the hill, of Tweed's scattered convoy, of figures advancing out of the mist. He had heard the first sounds of gunfire.

Parking his car on the grass verge, he had waited a long time. He had eventually walked cautiously to the top of the hill, peering down. Everything had gone. The mist. Tweed's cars. Only bodies strewn along the sides of the road remained. He had then driven on, hoping he had not lost Tweed.

At the bottom of the hill he had hardly given the bodies a glance. He had, however, been careful not to drive over one. Not from any compunction – such emotions were alien to the Yellow Man – but he did not want any remnants attached to his tyres which might catch the eye of the police.

Before starting up again, he had taken off the chauffeur's cap, had hurled it way into the undergrowth. He had then replaced it with the beret he had worn in the dark square in Paris when he had come so close to killing Paula. Having got rid of the cap he now wanted to get rid of the car.

It was a relief when he saw, ahead of him, Tweed's cars driving along a straight stretch. He pressed his foot down, hunched over the wheel. Marler's car had disappeared in his mirror when he reached the turn-off to

Choisy. At this point a magnificent old bridge, still intact, crossed a deep gorge. It was no longer part of the highway – a new stretch had been built over a new bridge. But the road swung in a sharp curve.

It was as he approached this point that he saw a car parked by the roadside. It was pointed in the direction of Geneva and beside it stood an erect man, hands on his hips. He had the impression the man was staring hard to see who was behind the wheel of his car. He increased speed. It was almost his downfall.

Pressing his foot down even further to avoid the man's gaze, he began to swing round the sharp curve. He felt his machine skidding. He kept his nerve, went with the skid, straightened up, continued along the road to distant Annecy.

He drove at speed for about fifteen minutes. There was no other traffic on the road when he pulled up, parked his car on the edge of what he knew was a steep slope. Getting out, he lifted the bonnet, pretending to fiddle as if the engine had broken down.

A large truck and several cars passed him. He was hoping for a car with only the driver inside. Then he saw a Peugeot coming towards him at thirty miles an hour. Behind the wheel was a white-haired man, smartly dressed. He stood up, waved both hands in a gesture of despair. The driver stopped, spoke through his window.

'Do you speak English?'

'I am English,' the Yellow Man said with a broad smile, thankful that he had left his beret under a newspaper in the car. 'And I am no mechanic.'

'Let me have a look,' the man said, getting out. 'I used to run an agency for selling Rovers before we retired to Annecy.'

The assassin stood back as the Englishman bent over to peer inside. Glancing up and down the empty road, he whipped out a knife from a curved sheath concealed under his coat. The blow was so strong and savage that it completed the job instantly. He lifted the severed head by the hair and hid it behind a clump of shrubs.

He was wearing leather gloves and had no trouble lifting the dead body into position behind the wheel of the Mercedes having had the foresight to leave the door open. His coat was covered with blood but this didn't worry him. He quickly searched his victim's pockets, took out a wallet from one pocket, some letters from another. He stuffed the letters inside the wallet. Checking the road in both directions again, he walked to the edge of the steep slope, hurled the wallet, watched it sail through the air and land in a tangle of wild shrubbery.

He next checked to make sure, as he'd observed, that the elderly driver had left his keys in the Peugeot's ignition. Returning to the Mercedes, he adjusted the gears so it would roll freely. He then slammed the door shut and pushed. The car began to roll backwards. He took off his blood-soaked gloves, used the one which was least affected to clean his knife. He returned it to his sheath.

The car was still rolling slowly backwards as he took off his leather coat – which was too warm for this climate anyway. Stuffing it inside a large carrier bag, he added the gloves, keeping his hands away from streaks of blood. He then picked up several small rocks and dropped them inside to give weight. He looked up, stared.

The Mercedes had reached the edge of the slope and stopped there, a rear wheel wedged against a small rock. He looked up and down the road once more. He put the fingers of his left hand in his mouth and frowned. It was one of the few times in his life when he had felt nervous.

Pulling his fingers out of his mouth he rushed forward. He used his right foot to kick at the offending rock which was spoiling the whole scenario. The rock dislodged. The Mercedes started rolling backwards at speed down the shale slope. It charged inside a forest and was lost from view amid dense shrubbery.

'Do better next time,' he said aloud as he climbed behind the wheel of the Peugeot.

He had remembered to throw the head into the forest.

27

They had driven further towards Annecy when Paula saw Marler's and Nield's cars parked close together. They had got out of their vehicles and were talking to a man who stood very erect, hands on his hips. He wore tropical kit – beige trousers, a jacket and shirt of the same colour. His shirt was open at the neck.

'It's Burgoyne!' She almost shouted, she was so pleased to see him again.

Butler, who had travelled with Marler, sat on the verge. By his side, half-hidden in grass, was a machine-pistol. Butler never let down his guard.

'You survived the ambush, I gather,' he said, grinning at Paula.

'You warned us just in time.'

'I was beginning to give up hope,' he said to Tweed. 'I'd tried to call you several times. No response.'

'Mobile phones,' Tweed replied with an expression of disgust. 'I never trust them. As you see, we brought two attractive ladies along for the ride.' He introduced Trudy and Serena to Burgoyne, who shook hands and eyed both of them appreciatively. 'Welcome to the party,' Tweed concluded.

'"Along for the ride,"' snorted Serena. '"Welcome to the party." Some ride, some party. A delightful delegation of Arabs came to meet us.'

'Arabs?' queried Burgoyne.

Tweed explained tersely details of their encounter in the misty hollow. He left out some gory details since he didn't think either Trudy or Serena would appreciate too vivid a description.

'I drove all the way to Annecy and back,' Burgoyne told them. 'I didn't see this gang of cut-throats. My guess is they must have assembled at Choisy, only a few miles up that side road.' He pointed to a road leading off the main highway. 'They must have emerged soon after I'd driven past it. I can guess where they came from.'

'And where would that be?' asked Paula.

'A number of Arab Fundamentalists are regularly smuggled across the Med from Algeria into France. They come in by night aboard small fishing boats, are landed at remote coves near Marseilles. They have transport waiting to get them away from the coast. Goslar has worldwide connections, I've heard. He'd pay them well and they are used to killing. Heaven knows they've done enough of that back in Algeria.'

'I find that interesting,' said Tweed.

'I find *that* interesting,' Trudy remarked.

She was gazing behind Burgoyne at the ancient bridge which spanned a gorge. Paula also was gazing at it. A stone-paved approach led to a curved arch. On either side of the arch enormous old stone pillars, at least three feet in diameter, reared up a great height.

278

Cables, anchored to the ground near them, sloped up and disappeared inside huge cavities near the tops of the towers. The tops were castellated and gave the impression that they guarded the approach to a great castle. They looked as though they had stood there since the beginning of time.

'That is the Pont de la Caille,' Burgoyne explained. 'It's a suspension bridge which once carried the highway across the valley – hence the huge cables.'

Trudy walked rapidly along the paved area and when she stepped on to the bridge she felt a faint tremor. She walked on, staring down into the incredibly deep gorge with a small river running along it – in a cutting which seemed miles below her as she paused and gazed over.

'What interests me is *that*,' Tweed said emphatically.

'What is that?' Paula enquired.

'That old noticeboard across the road by the entrance to a track with old rusty gates wide open beyond.'

'*Château de l'Air*,' she said half to herself. 'Is it possible Goslar is still inside? Look up there, where the hill rises beyond the trees.'

They were standing less than a hundred yards from where the track on the far side of the road began winding its way upwards, through the open rusty gates, then disappearing round a bend. Tweed walked forward, stood in the middle of the road. He appeared to be looking at the mildewed board, perched on a post, where the name of the château could just be made out. Actually he was staring at an estate agent's board which had toppled, face up, into the grass.

À Vendre. For sale. Below the words were the estate agent's name. C. Periot, Annecy. Then a telephone number. The sun almost burned the back of his neck. Paula joined him, began to walk further to explore the track.

Her arm was grabbed, she was hauled back and when she looked round she saw it was Burgoyne who had taken hold of her.

'Go back and join the others by the bridge. Don't argue. Tweed, go with her. *Now!*'

'Got a bee in his bonnet,' Paula grumbled.

'Better do as he suggested,' said Tweed.

They joined Marler, Newman and Nield, who stood chatting to Serena. Trudy was a long way off, halfway across the bridge. She was leaning over the railing, gazing down into eternity. On the grass verge Butler still sat hunched up, seemed to be asleep, but his eyes were everywhere. A car was driving slowly towards them from the direction of Annecy. It stopped near the far end of the suspension bridge.

'It's like a fairytale,' Paula remarked, calm again. She was gazing at the beautiful old bridge, which was now redundant. 'Pity they couldn't have left it as part of the highway. I love it.'

'What is Burgoyne doing?' Newman asked.

Paula swung round to look in the direction in which they were all staring. Burgoyne had walked to the edge of the track leading up to the château. He moved slowly, with deliberation, walking a few yards up the side of the track, treading down grass. Bending down, he picked up a small limestone rock, then came back along the path he had just walked over. He turned his head, shouted.

'Everyone stay where you are! Don't come an inch closer!'

They stood very still, watched as Burgoyne crossed the road, then crouched down, still holding the rock in his right hand. He swung his arm backwards and forwards, then lobbed the rock in an arc. As he did so he dropped flat. The rock landed on the track. An explosive *thump!* echoed. Huge quantities of soil and grass soared into the air above the point where the rock had landed. A lot of it showered down into the road, a mix of splintered rock and earth.

Burgoyne stood up, strolled to where the others gazed at him, then he smiled.

'Anti-personnel landmine. I saw the sun glint off it. The rain must have uncovered a section of it. Not the place for a morning's walk, wouldn't you agree?'

'And I was going to go up that track,' Paula said after swallowing hard. 'All I can say, Chance, is thank you for saving my life.'

'I've seen them like that in the desert,' Burgoyne explained casually. 'The wind blows sand off them and that same sun reflects off them . . .'

He stopped talking suddenly. Butler had rushed past them like a greyhound, racing across the bridge. Paula turned and gasped with horror. A small thickset man, who must have emerged from the car from Annecy, had grasped Trudy round the waist, was lifting her so her waist was now level with the railing between her and the immense drop behind her. She looked down at his brown face, his open mouth, exposing teeth, savage determination. Her right hand pulled out her automatic, pressed the trigger. The bullet entered the assassin's thigh. He grimaced, but was still hoisting her higher. Butler's hands closed round his neck, hauled him backwards. Trudy slid back, her feet on the floor of the bridge. Butler rammed the assassin's head down hard on the rail. Then he elevated the Arab in a business suit. He toppled him over the brink as Paula rushed forward, Browning in her hand. She stopped, watched as the Arab cartwheeled down and down, arms and feet flailing. It seemed to take a long time before he hit the bottom and Paula couldn't hear any sound as the body, tiny, lay still under a huge limestone crag on the Annecy side.

'He never even screamed,' Trudy said. 'I don't understand it.'

'Being an Arab, a Muslim,' explained Burgoyne who now stood beside Trudy, 'he had no doubt that he was on his way to the Arab version of heaven. Which is why he didn't utter a sound.'

'How far is it down there to the bottom?' asked Paula, who now stood on the bridge, with the others.

'It's two hundred metres deep. Or two hundred yards. Or six hundred feet.'

'You do hammer it home,' commented Serena. 'I can't see him.'

'He's down there somewhere,' Tweed said quickly. He could see the minute shape, but felt it better not to point it out. 'Now, I feel like a little walk before we move on to Annecy. Bob, Paula – like to accompany me?'

As they walked back along the bridge it swayed very slightly, an unsettling feeling. Looking back, Tweed saw that Burgoyne had taken Trudy's arm. So she would have someone to talk to after her horrendous ordeal.

'There's that château,' Paula said as they left the bridge. 'Do you think we should check it out?'

'No.' Tweed lifted the binoculars he had borrowed earlier from Marler. 'All the shutters are closed. I'm sure the place is empty. But if we forced a door or a window it could blow up in our faces. Remember what was waiting for us at the front door of Goslar's building at La Défense. How do you summarize the situation now?' he asked as they strolled along the road.

'Looking for Dr Goslar.'

'More to it than that. We have to check out Annecy to make sure Goslar wasn't practising a double bluff. But the main thing is I know he hasn't yet manufactured enough of that hideous poison – enough to wipe out fifty million, a hundred million, two hundred million people. Who knows how much?'

'How do you know he hasn't done that yet?' she asked.

'Because if he had, he'd never have bothered to organize such a ferocious attack on me when the Arabs came through the mist. I still bother him because I'm alive.'

'Then we have time,' Newman said.

'No, we haven't. He might complete his work at any moment. It is even more a race against time. Let's start out for Annecy now.'

At Tweed's suggestion they altered the sequence of cars. Newman's car remained at the rear of the convoy. Paula again sat next to Newman while Trudy and Tweed sat in the back.

Nield drove ahead of Newman. Alone for so long, he now had Serena for company by his side.

Marler again drove in front of Nield. And again he had Butler in the seat next to him.

Burgoyne took the lead at the head of everyone else, He drove his own hired car. Resting on the seat by his side was the machine-pistol Marler had handed him.

'I can't think of that bridge as fairyland any more,' Paula called back. 'I don't imagine you do either, Trudy.'

'Well, at least I put a bullet into the bastard,' Trudy responded grimly. 'It was him or me. I'm glad it was him.'

'All this started back in England on Dartmoor,' Tweed recalled.

'I know. I knew before I left the States,' Trudy said. 'I read about it in a Washington newspaper. It became a lead story when someone leaked the reaction of the White House. Sorry, I think I interrupted you.'

'That's all right. I was going on to say that when we reach Annecy I first want to contact an estate agent called Periot. He's the one who has the sale of that château in his hands. I want to see if Goslar is using the same technique he's used several times before, taking a long lease and then evacuating a property early.'

'Shouldn't be difficult to find,' Newman commented. 'All we need is a phone book in a telephone box.'

'There are two more factors we must not forget,' Tweed continued. 'Somewhere the Yellow Man is still on the loose . . .'

He explained to Trudy who the Yellow Man was. He turned to face her and went into detail about how the assassin operated. She listened with a serious expression but showed no sign of fear or revulsion at what he told her. She really is tough, he thought.

'And the other factor?' Paula prodded.

'The missing Mr Bancroft. I studied him in the bar at the Ritz. He's not only vicious and ruthless – he's also shrewd and has, I believe, plenty of stamina.'

'He was the worst of the lot,' said Trudy. 'I haven't forgotten seeing him shove a gun inside Walt, my husband's, mouth and then pull the trigger. I've got an automatic full of bullets for him,' she went on savagely. 'I'll only be able to forget that terrible scene in my house – when I felt so helpless – when he's dead.'

'I think you'll like Annecy – at least the old town,' Paula said to switch her mind to something else. 'I only spent a short time there but it's unique. Strange ancient buildings with waterways everywhere. I think they eventually empty into the lake.'

'It does sound interesting,' Trudy agreed. 'Is it like a rabbit warren?'

'Yes, except I doubt if rabbits could find their way round the place.'

Trudy chuckled, smiled at Tweed. He was smiling

back when his mobile buzzed. He assumed it had to be Monica – or Beck.

'Hello?'

'Wait just a moment, sir,' a cultured English voice said, 'someone wishes to speak to you.' Tweed gripped the phone tightly. 'Here we go,' the English voice, said. 'Please listen carefully. The words will only be spoken once . . .'

The screechy voice began. Tweed pressed the phone close to his ear, trying to decide whether it was the voice of a man or a woman.

'Mr Tweed, welcome to Annecy. May I suggest you cross the Pont Perrière into the old town. On a railing to your right at the start of the bridge you will see a sign for a three-star hotel. Hôtel du Palais de l'Isle. Across the bridge you will see a restaurant – Les Corbières. Go in there and you will find a message waiting for you. Do take greater care. H. Goslar.'

Tweed waited but the connection was broken. He repeated word for word to the others what he had heard. There was silence for a short time, broken by Newman.

'Where the hell is Dr Goslar?' he rasped in exasperation.

'That helicopter has reappeared,' Paula said.

28

When Tweed had described Bancroft as shrewd he was not far off the mark. Seated beside the pilot in the helicopter, Bancroft was thinking hard. He was an unusual combination of talents. Before Karnow had recruited him as a member of Unit Four he had been a semi-successful lawyer.

He had acted as defence counsel in a number of trials. He had often managed to bring in a verdict of 'not guilty' for his clients, whether they were innocent or guilty. He had studied the history of law deeply, concentrating on legal precedents. So it was not infrequent for him to challenge successfully a direction by a judge, quoting an old legal precedent the judge had never realized existed.

This had gradually made him the *bête noire* of judges in general. So they had hit back by giving him a hard time at every possible opportunity. Often a judge had overruled a Bancroft objection when it was a borderline instance. Bancroft's track record of obtaining 'not guilty' verdicts began to wither.

So when Karnow offered him the job of joining Unit Four, Bancroft, disgusted with the law, accepted. The size of the salary offered was also a factor.

Seated in the helicoper, he was now using his acute brain to assess what was happening, how he should proceed next. Also, brought up in the back streets Brooklyn, not the most salubrious district in New York, he had maimed three thugs who had attacked him on different occasions. Training with Unit Four had honed his natural flair as a fighter – as a thug.

Tweed and his team are now on their way to Annecy, he said to himself. *So Dr Goslar has not yet been found – otherwise they wouldn't be driving along the highway to Annecy*, a nowhere place he had never heard of before. *First, I have to arrive ahead of them. Second, I'll need transport to tail them . . .*

He stopped talking to himself inside his head and checked the map open on his lap. He had bought it from a shop in Geneva after stocking himself with fresh clothes. What had given him the idea of hiring a helicopter was his recollection of the chopper which had appeared to follow them along the autoroute from Paris.

'How long before we reach Annecy?' he asked the pilot.

'Five minutes. Maybe less. I can slow down a bit.'

'Wait a minute.' Bancroft raised his binoculars to his eyes, scanned the four cars proceeding along the highway, looking like toys from his altitude. 'Is there somewhere close to Annecy where you could land me?'

'The old town or the more modern area?'

'The old town,' Bancroft replied, relying on instinct.

'Then that will be easy. There's a large park at the edge of the lake. It's very close to the old town. I could land there.'

'Also I'll need to hire a car ... to follow those terrorists,' he added quickly to keep up the fiction.

'There's a car-hire place only a short walk from where I'll land you. I'll point it out to you. Will you need me later to fly you back to Geneva?' the pilot enquired.

'Quite possibly,' Bancroft replied, having no idea whether he would require the pilot's services again. 'That will mean you waiting around, so here is a bonus.'

He had already paid the pilot a large sum but he hauled a sheaf of hundred-dollar bills out of the money clip in his pocket. He was careful to keep his money belt concealed. He handed the pilot a folded sheaf of five bills. Another five hundred dollars. He had always found that money bought loyalty and reliability.

'I'll wait for you,' the pilot said. 'Our chopper still has plenty of fuel. Do I slow down?'

'No. Keep going.'

Inside the car Paula focused the bincoculars she had just borrowed from Newman. She pressed an elbow on the edge of the open window to give herself more stability. She was trying to identify who was aboard the helicopter. Like Bancroft, who had focused on the four cars, she found the distance was too great. All she could make out was a blur. She gave the binoculars back to Newman, carefully looping them round his neck.

'Any luck?' he asked.

'Can't see who is inside it. It worries me – the way it keeps flying on a parallel course to us.'

'Forget it.' Tweed called out, 'When we get to Annecy I need a local map to locate this estate agent, Periot.'

'Burgoyne may already have one,' Newman suggested. 'I think we are getting very close to Annecy. I could overtake Burgoyne and ask him if he has got a map.'

'Let's do that,' Tweed agreed.

'That helicopter is flying well ahead of us now,' Paula observed. 'I suppose it's not landing somewhere close to Annecy. It's losing height now.'

Bancroft left the helicopter which had landed in a large parklike area at the northern edge of the Old Town. He walked rapidly over the grass, glancing back at the machine. The pilot had his back to him and was starting to consume his packed lunch. Bancroft was heading for the car-hire establishment the pilot had pointed out.

He felt the sun on the back of his thick neck and realized he felt hungry. Scattered across the park were various structures for children to play on. A roundabout. A short ladder leading up to a slide. Children were yelling with delight as one of their friends swooped down the slide, landing on a huge rubber cushion at the bottom. Bancroft pulled a face.

Children screaming and rushing about reminded him of his early days in Brooklyn. But there the children had been different, growing up quickly, wielding knives

288

at an early age. These were far more civilized young-
sters, but their screams recalled to him the number of
times he'd made sure his back was to a wall as two or
three of them came at him. How he'd held them back
with a long club, then had beaten them to a pulp. It had
been the survival of the quickest.

There had been times when he had wondered
whether it would be best to settle in Europe. An idea he
had always quickly rejected. The really big money was
in the States. Away from anyone, he paused to check
which of two passports to use. The one he chose did not
show his name as Bancroft. He had it in his hand as he
crossed the road, entered the car-hire establishment.

He had a warm smile on his face as he approached
the attractive brunette behind the counter. He handed
her the passport. When she saw it she looked at him
with interest.

'We don't get many Americans in this part of the
world. Maybe a few during the season, but only a few.
What can I do for you, sir?'

'I need to hire a car for a few days,' Bancroft began.
'I've just flown in here.'

'I saw your chopper land. Have you come far?'

'From Paris.'

His mind moved fast. He decided it would be
unwise for him to be associated with Geneva. Not after
what had happened in that underground garage.

'That's quite a flight.' She opened the passport, made
notes on a form, talking as she did so. 'Mr Conroy. I see
your first name is August – the same as the month you
were born in.'

'Which is why I was christened that,' he lied. 'I'd like
a Peugeot, if that is possible. I'd prefer a grey colour.'

'There are two Peugeots available. One is grey, one
is red.'

'Definitely the grey job, please.'

Bancroft thought grey was a less noticeable colour. He paid the deposit in dollar bills. It was impossible to trace someone if they used cash. He'd made up his mind not to use a credit card while in Europe. When the formalities had been completed she led him through a back door into a small garage, showed him the car. He said it would do nicely, took the keys from her, then paused.

'You do speak good English.'

'I spent two years with a big car-hire firm in London. Thank you for the compliment.'

'I made a mistake in Paris,' he said, lingering. 'In a bar I met another American I didn't like at all. Wanted to borrow money off me. I let slip I was coming to Annecy. He said he might be coming down here. I guess he'd need to hire a car. If someone asks if there's an American in Annecy maybe you'd say you haven't met one.'

'Tried to borrow money! That's shocking.' She smiled warmly. 'I will keep quiet. You can rely on me.'

Bancroft didn't think he would be followed. But, as in the States, he always covered his tracks. She waited while he got behind the wheel when he appeared to remember something.

'I do hope to meet a friend who is driving down here today from Geneva. Is there some place I could intercept him?' He looked at his watch. 'He should be arriving soon.'

She produced a local map from a leather pouch hanging from her waist. Using the bonnet as a table, she drew a route, starting from where they were. Then she bent down, showed him the map and explained.

'Your best bet is to follow this route. It's not far. It will take you to where the highway from Geneva reaches the outskirts of Annecy. Your friend has to pass this point.'

290

'That's very good of you. You should have a sign in that window at the front. Service with a smile.'

'Thank you, sir.'

He thought she blushed just before he drove off. He looked at the park and saw the lake beyond, glittering in the sun. In the distance he could see mountains covered with snow. Above them hovered menacing dark clouds. The weather further south was looking very different from the atmosphere at Annecy.

The route he had to follow was easy. He had just left behind the outskirts of Annecy when he saw the highway leading to Geneva – a signpost confirmed the fact. He also saw a wide farm track leading off to the left. He didn't hesitate – he left the highway, drove onto the track, reversed the Peugeot, stopped, got out.

He lifted the bonnet of the car, stooped over it as though there was something wrong he had to attend to. Then he waited. He was well versed in waiting. He reckoned Tweed's convoy had to pass this point.

Earlier, the Yellow Man, reaching Annecy, had driven past the sign *Vieille Ville* – Old Town – and had continued on until, very shortly, he saw a public phone box. He was relieved. He must make a phone call quickly. There were specific hours. Parking his car, he opened his notebook and called the number, as instructed. He had no idea where he was phoning to but recognized the code as Switzerland.

'Good afternoon. Who is calling?' the cultured English voice enquired.

'Hobart. Oscar Hobart.'

'And where are you calling from, Mr Hobart?'

'Hell!' the Yellow Man exploded. 'What the devil does it matter where I'm calling from?'

'It does matter, Mr Hobart,' the voice explained

politely. 'I can only play the recording if you are in a certain place.'

'Bullshit! All right? I'm in Annecy. That's in France, in case you didn't know.'

'I do know, Mr Hobart. Please hold on a moment. I have a message for you . . .'

The Yellow Man sighed audibly. He waited for the screeching voice to start speaking. He didn't have to wait long. He held the phone hard against his ear, not wishing to miss a word.

'You are in Annecy. Proceed at once to the Old Town. You go to the Pont Perrière, a bridge leading into the Old Town. Across the bridge is a restaurant – Les Corbières. I will spell that out for you . . . Tweed will be visiting this restaurant. Get there first. Ask for the proprietor. Tell him you are Francis. He will give you a long sealed box with the label "machine tools". It contains a sniperscope rifle with ammunition. Kill Paula Grey. H. Goslar.'

29

Newman waved Burgoyne down after overtaking him. He parked his car on the verge. He got out with Tweed and Paula as Burgoyne slowed down, stopped. Nearby, a man wearing a panama hat stooped over the engine of his grey Peugeot. He had driven the car off the highway a short distance up a track. He wore large wraparound dark glasses and was peering into the interior with the bonnet up.

'French cars are always breaking down,' Newman commented. 'It is nothing to do with their quality – it's the fault of the way the French drive.'

'I need a local map of Annecy,' Tweed told him.

'Have you got one? I need to find that estate agent, Periot.'

'Easy,' Burgoyne said with a grin. 'I remembered afterwards seeing the name when I reached Annecy earlier. He's near the Old Town. Just follow me. I'll wait till you're back in your car . . .'

Because of the heat they walked back slowly. Tweed had his head bowed, an expression of concentration on his face. Paula nudged him.

'You're brooding on something.'

'Yes, I am. I have the feeling we're moving in the wrong direction. At the moment we can only follow the trail – the obstacle course – I'm sure Goslar has laid out for us. Sooner or later I hope to get a phone call which will pinpoint where we should be.'

'You're being mysterious again,' Paula chided him.

When they reached their car Trudy was swigging water out of a bottle she'd obtained from the kitchen at the Richemond before they left Geneva. She looked up as Paula stopped by her open window, wiped the top carefully with a clean handkerchief.

'Not very ladylike,' Trudy said with a smile. She offered the bottle to Paula. 'But in this heat you can get dehydrated.'

'Nice to have a good Samaritan as a companion.' Paula upended the bottle, took several swallows. 'That's much better.'

'Maybe Tweed and Newman could do with a drink,' Trudy suggested. 'I have two more bottles in my canvas bag here. I'm only charging one hundred francs a drink,' she went on as Tweed handed the bottle to Newman after helping himself.

'Cheap at the price,' Newman replied. 'Give you an IOU.'

When they were settled back in the car, Burgoyne

293

drove slowly past. Newman put his hand out of his window, waved for Marler and Nield to precede him. Marler saluted as he overtook them. Butler was peering out of his window as Nield started to follow Marler.

'Don't too much like the look of Panama Hat,' he growled as they passed the stranded Peugeot parked on the track.

'You see killers everywhere,' Nield joked.

'Well, I got his registration number,' Butler said obstinately.

They began to pass houses set back from the road. Then they were inside the town. Burgoyne slowed even more as he passed a sign pointing to *Vieille Ville*. He parked, not caring whether it was legal or not. Newman waited with Trudy while Tweed and Paula got out, crossed the road.

Periot et Cie had a modern plate-glass window. It was covered with coloured pictures of a variety of properties. Tweed scanned the photos, saw nothing which looked like the old pile he had seen, perched on a ridge, from the ancient bridge, where Trudy had been almost hurled into the valley. They went inside.

'I am looking for M. Periot,' Tweed said in French as a tall good-looking man in his thirties came forward to greet them.

'You have found him, sir. It is I.'

'I might be interested in an old mansion near Choisy. You can see it from the Pont de la Caille. Perched on the top of a ridge. It had a "For Sale" board at the entrance.'

'I see.' Periot frowned, then smiled quickly. 'There is a problem, sir. At the moment it is rented for a year. But the tenant has left suddenly. I cannot get in touch with him. Frankly, I am not sure what the position is. Will the Englishman, Mr Masterson, be coming back? I went to inspect it recently. The property had been leased unfurnished. There was nothing in the place when I arrived. Even the window ledges had been carefully washed. None of his personal possessions are in the mansion. He appears to have left for good – with seven months' rental time still left. He paid everything in advance.'

'Mr Charterhouse, Gargoyle Towers, now Mr Masterson, Château de l'Air,' Tweed mumbled to himself, but Paula caught the words.

'Pardon, sir?' Periot enquired.

'Sorry, I dropped my voice. May I ask when this Mr Masterson first leased the place?'

'Five months ago. None of us ever saw him. And – I shouldn't say this – but the whole year's lease was paid in five-hundred franc notes. Delivered in an executive case, which I had to sign for.'

'Yet you have a "For Sale" board up.'

'True.' Periot looked embarrassed. 'A form of insurance. Just in case we never hear from him again.'

'I understand.' Tweed smiled. 'But under the circumstances I had better get in touch with you later. In the meantime you may have solved a puzzle.'

'I am most sorry, sir . . .'

Tweed waited until they were outside. Periot had accompanied them and closed the door, repeating his apologies.

'It was Goslar,' Tweed said grimly. 'Same technique as at Gargoyle Towers, the building in La Défense, the flat where Mme Markov was murdered. He can afford to throw money about like confetti. He rents a place for longer than he needs it, so he can leave in the night, so to speak, with no one the wiser. I'm guessing, but I suspect he perfected his fiendish weapon at the Château de l'Air, then moved all the way to Gargoyle Towers on Dartmoor. That was his base from where he could "go public". Demonstrate openly the power of what he had invented. We'd better go to the Old Town now, cautiously.'

'Cautiously? What is worrying you now?' asked Paula.

'I'm convinced that strange phone call from Goslar, inviting me to collect another message from that restaurant, can only be a trap.'

Panama Hat (as Butler had nicknamed him), who was Bancroft, decided he had been clever, and had then made a bad mistake. He had bought the hat from a stall near the estate agent, Periot. Other people had been buying similar hats to ward off the heat, so Bancroft felt he merged with the locals.

The mistake had been to park where he had. Expecting Tweed's convoy to drive on, he had anticipated the four cars would be easy to follow. Now they were all parked a few hundred yards up the road from where he pretended to tinker with his engine. Worse still, Newman's car was backing up the entrance to a house, prior to coming back. Earlier he had seen Paula point to the notice leading to the Old Town. He must move quickly.

Slamming down the bonnet, he climbed behind the wheel, started his engine, drove back down the highway and turned off towards the Old Town. When he got there he saw it was forbidden to drive over the Pont Perrière. Pausing, he looked round, saw an area nearby next to an ancient stone wall where two cars were parked. They were also in the shade. He drove his car the short distance and parked near the other two vehicles.

Getting out, he hurried across the bridge over the river to enter a small restaurant, Les Corbières. A moment before he reached the entrance a tall, stocky man wearing a beret emerged. He was carrying a long cardboard box with the words 'machine tools' written on the outside. Bancroft walked in, sat down, ordered a drink and a glass of water. This seemed a likely vantage point if Tweed and his team were heading for the Old Town.

A short time earlier, the Yellow Man, beret rammed well down, had entered Les Corbières and asked to see the manager. A very young Frenchman with a napkin over his arm had appeared.

'You want a table, sir? Just for one?'

'My name is Francis. *Francis*. A messenger has left a box for me to collect from you.'

The Yellow Man held a hundred-franc note between his fingers. The manager glanced at the note, became voluble.

'How pleasant to meet an Englishman. I spent time in Bournemouth, training there. A delightful town. The residents were very high class. Of course tourists were a different breed, at least some of them. I had one couple coming in to the restaurant at lunchtime asking if they could just have a cup of tea. Can you believe it? The restaurant was full of people taking lunch, most of them à la carte. I just looked at them—'

'The box you have for me,' the assassin interjected, forcing himself to sound polite.

'Of course, sir. I kept it behind the counter out of sight. It says on the outside "machine tools". It is really rather heavy to contain flowers . . .'

'Thank you,' said the Yellow Man, grasping the box when it had been brought. 'Here is something for your trouble.'

He walked out just before a man wearing a panama hat came in to the restaurant. He immediately turned left along the rue Perrière. He hoped it was not going to be difficult – searching for a firing point overlooking the bridge. He soon realized there was no such convenient site and walked on, continuing his search.

Burgoyne drove into the Old Town, followed by the other three cars. On his earlier visit he had found it was forbidden to drive over the bridge. He parked alongside three other cars in the shadow of a stone wall.

As Newman parked in the same area and got out, followed by Tweed, Paula and Trudy, they saw Burgoyne standing at the entrance to the bridge, hands on his hips. He was gazing round quickly. As Tweed paused with Paula, Butler came up, lowered his voice.

'We may be walking into trouble. Panama Hat's car is parked near to ours.'

'Panama Hat?' Tweed queried.

'Just before we reached that estate agent, Periot, there was a car parked off the road. A man in a panama hat had the bonnet up, was fiddling with the engine. I told Nield I didn't like the look of him. Now his car is parked where ours are by that wall. I took the registration number earlier.'

'Could be a local,' Tweed said, only half-listening.

'So why did he suddenly get the engine working, then drive down here ahead of us?'

'Which one could it have been?' mused Paula.

'Which one?' queried Butler.

'Yes. The Yellow Man or Bancroft? Both of them are still at large.' She shrugged. 'One could have been in the helicopter, the other one may have been in that car which flashed by us at breakneck speed on the highway.'

Tweed's eyes had been staring everywhere across the river. Nowhere could he see anything that looked in the least suspicious. Burgoyne had already walked across the bridge at a fast clip. As Tweed began to follow him Newman appeared on one side, Nield on the other.

'That bridge is pretty exposed,' Nield warned.

'It may be,' Tweed retorted, 'but I'm not running across it.'

Newman and Nield still guarded him on both sides as Tweed strolled across the bridge. Paula was behind them. She was gazing round in wonderment at the bizarre beauty of Annecy. To the right of the bridge a weird triangular-shaped building reared up where the river divided into two sections, flowing on either side of it. The building had a castlelike appearance and looked as though it had stood there since the beginning of time – as did other three and four-storeyed edifices.

'This is like something you see in medieval paintings,' she commented.

Tweed was more concerned about entering Les Corbières. The restaurant had a polished wooden bar and a few tables. Some were occupied but several were empty. He asked for the proprietor.

A young Frenchman appeared, napkin over his arm. He glanced at the members of Tweed's team crowding in behind him. Raising his eyebrows he asked what they required.

Bancroft, sitting by himself at a table at the back, froze as he saw Tweed at the far side of the bridge, then saw him advancing towards the restaurant. He removed his hat, tucked it under his chair. Some of them must have seen the panama earlier as he had pretended to fix the engine of his car.

He was thankful that he had made another purchase at the stall where he had bought the hat. He now wore a large pair of dark wraparound glasses which concealed the upper half of his face. Before entering the restaurant he had seen his image, reflected in the polished glass of the window. He had also quickly adjusted the cravat under his bull-like jaw. He had hardly recognized the image which had stared back at him. Now he picked up a copy of a French newspaper someone had left behind on a chair. Opening it, he placed it beside his plate. If they were going to eat here he had the problem of leaving unseen.

'My name is Tweed,' he said to the manager. 'I believe someone left you an envelope to give me.'

'Heavens,' the manager burst out. 'We're not the Post Office.'

'I'm sorry,' Tweed replied. 'Why do you say that?'

'Not ten minutes ago someone else called for a box which has been left here for me to deliver to him.'

'A box?' Newman realized Tweed's omission. He held a fifty-franc note, which he played with between his fingers. 'Can you describe that person? Was it a man?'

'Supposing someone came in here after you have gone and asked me to describe you. Would you like it if I did describe you?' He handed Tweed an envelope. 'For you, sir.'

'I don't suppose I would,' replied Newman.

His hand holding the banknote was extended. The manager acted like a conjurer. His hand moved in a blur and the banknote vanished. Practice makes perfect, Newman thought.

'How long would you say this box was?' Marler spoke up. 'And your display handkerchief isn't quite right.' He slightly adjusted the handkerchief in the top pocket of the manager's jacket, tucking a fifty-franc note down behind it.

'About so long,' the Manager said promptly.

He held his hands wide apart. Then extended them a little further.

'Marksman's rifle?' Marler whispered in Tweed's ear. 'Could even be an Armalite, like mine.'

'Welcome to my restaurant,' the manager said smiling broadly. 'I am only a temporary manager for a month. I go when the real manager returns from holiday. May I offer you some lunch?'

'Yes, we'd like that,' said Tweed.

He sat down at a table for four and was joined by Burgoyne, Paula and Trudy. Newman hosted a larger table for Serena, Nield, Butler and Marler. They all ordered a light lunch with water instead of wine.

Bancroft was relieved when Trudy sat with her back to him. He couldn't recall the number of meetings when Trudy had sat opposite him. In a hip holster he had a Walther. He briefly considered shooting eight of them – the number of rounds in his automatic – with no bullet left for Serena. He rejected the idea quickly. He'd never make it to the helicopter – people from the restaurant might follow, shouting to the pilot. Attempting to drive off in the Peugeot carried the same risk. Now he wanted a distraction, so he could quietly leave without being noticed.

'I've been wondering about something, Chance,' Paula said to Burgoyne when they had ordered. 'Those Arabs who attacked us,' she began, keeping her voice down. 'They had business suits but they all wore a green headband. Why?'

'Because they were Muslims and in their religion martyrs who die for the cause of Islam go straight to heaven.'

301

'Makes them formidable,' Tweed commented.

At his table Bancroft, from behind his dark glasses, saw Serena gazing straight at him. She turned away, began talking to Newman.

They had finished their meal, had paid the bill, when Butler got up, said he would be back in a minute. He had to fetch something from his car. They were leaving the restaurant when Tweed handed Paula the envelope he had opened earlier. She took out the folded sheet inside and read the brief letter. It was written in copperplate, slanting slightly to the right.

My dear Tweed, I apologize for not meeting you in Annecy. I was delayed. May I suggest instead we meet at Talloires, further down the lake. H. Goslar.

The manager, who had been well tipped for the meals, accompanied them to the door. He gave another of his broad smiles.

'I hope everything was to your satisfaction, sir.'

'An excellent meal,' Tweed replied. 'Do you know anything about a place further down the lake? Talloires?'

'You reach it by driving down the far side – the eastern side – of the lake. I can't recommend it. The resort is still out of season. Everything will be closed. A few locals ski there. But nearly everyone goes instead to Grenoble or Chamonix. It will be dead now.'

'Thank you.' Tweed went outside and Butler had arrived back. He was carrying an outsize tennis racquet container. 'What is it you have there?'

'Machine-pistol,' Marler whispered. 'Harry is obviously expecting trouble.'

'I think we'll explore Annecy a bit before we go. Let's walk to the left along the river front.'

Bancroft waited until they had disappeared from view. He then got up and left the restaurant in a hurry.

The Yellow Man had found his vantage point. He just hoped Tweed and his team would walk along the rue Perrière. Perched high above a road, which he trusted was an extension of the rue Perrière, he gripped an Armalite rifle.

A wooden staircase, enclosed with a wooden partition, but open to the sky, ran up the side of an ancient stone tower, topped by a sloping roof. At the end of the staircase where he crouched, it was rather like being in a pulpit. He had a clear view down into the narrow street below. He waited.

30

'This street is the rue Perrière,' Paula commented. She was feeling fresh after her meal. 'This really is the most beautiful place. Like Paradise.'

'It's a maze of waterways and alleys, with small bridges over the water,' Burgoyne called out behind her. 'It just goes on and on with a new delight every corner you turn round.'

'And I love the ancient lanterns hanging from the walls,' enthused Paula. 'At night it must be mysterious – and marvellous. I really should have brought a camera.'

'This is not a pleasure trip,' Tweed warned, walking slowly.

'Don't be grumpy,' Paula chaffed him.

Burgoyne had dropped back. He was now

accompanying Serena, who was also enchanted. She pointed out various features which attracted her, her chin tilted up. Burgoyne took her hand and she showed no signs of objecting.

Butler, carrying his 'tennis' case, had joined Paula and Tweed. She noticed he had opened the zip. Right-handed, he was now carrying it in his left hand. His shoulders were hunched forward, his eyes looking always upward.

'Don't look so serious, Harry,' Paula teased him. She looked back at Newman, walking with Trudy. 'Isn't all this wonderful. I'd love to explore it at night.'

'Without a map you'd soon get lost,' Burgoyne called out. 'And some of the alleys are very dark.'

'When were you last here, then?' she asked over her shoulder.

'A century ago. When I was on my way to Aix-en-Provence. I told you about that trip earlier.'

'Yes, you did. That weird Arab scribe.'

'That ingenious Arab scribe.'

There was no traffic. At the point they had reached the only sound was the running water of the river. It created a soothing, hypnotic atmosphere. In the river white ducks, soaking up the sun, paddled leisurely along the surface.

'There's nothing modern,' Paula observed. 'It's all as old as the hills. There can't be many places like this left.'

She had seen the ducks when they first crossed the bridge to the restaurant. Now she paused by the railing, dropped pieces of bread into the water. Half a dozen ducks rushed towards the floating pieces of bread she had brought from Les Corbières and bumped against each other in their determination to be first to reach the prize.

'I don't think I've ever felt so serene,' Paula said.

'Funny I should say that – considering we have someone called Serena with us.'

'Under the surface she may not be as serene as you think,' Tweed replied.

'Don't you like her, then?'

'On this expedition it's not a question of liking or disliking anyone.'

'Yet another conundrum. I won't ask you what you mean – I know you won't tell me.'

They resumed their walk along the rue Perrière. They were the only people walking. Paula assumed the heat was keeping people indoors. It must be cool inside all these stone buildings.

'Why do you think Goslar keeps leaving these messages?' she asked.

'To keep us away from somewhere else.'

'And where might that be?'

'I'll know if I get that phone call I've been waiting for. I hope it happens soon. We are losing vital time and can do not a thing about it. Those green headbands Burgoyne explained are significant.'

They had come to a corner where the street turned sharply to the left. They went round the corner and Paula felt a tiny stone inside her shoe. She looked up and saw a great tower with a sloping roof looming over the next stretch of road.

The Yellow Man had her head in his cross-hairs. His rifle was perched on the edge of the pulpit for maximum stability. His finger was curled round the trigger. Her head was motionless as she paused, dead centre in the cross-hairs. He pulled the trigger.

Paula stooped to extract the stone from her shoe. The bullet passed over her head, splashed in the water

305

beyond the railing. Butler dropped the tennis case, whipped up the muzzle of his machine-pistol, fired a hail of bullets which shattered the pulpit. Shards of wood tumbled down the side of the stone wall into the street.

Butler took off. He ran up a twisting steep pathway. Through an arch in the wall and on beyond. He reached the foot of the staircase leading up to where the pulpit had existed less than a minute before, looked up it, machine-pistol aimed. No sign of a body. He swore.

He searched swiftly round the base of the tower. Alleys led off in all directions. He listened for the sound of running feet. Nothing. Only a heavy silence. Sighing, he returned the way he had come.

Tweed had hauled Paula back round the corner, out of sight of the tower. He looked a question at Butler.

'Marksman got away. Must be nippy on his feet. God, that was close.'

'I'm perfectly OK,' said Paula quietly. 'Thank you. I'll buy you a present.'

'Don't want a present. What do we do now?'

'Drive on to Talloires,' Tweed decided. 'Let's explore, see what Talloires has to offer us. Back to the cars. It's a bit of a drive, from what I remember from the map.'

31

The blazing row built up soon after they had left Annecy. Again, Burgoyne, in his car, led the pack. Behind him Marler drove with Butler by his side. Just before leaving, Serena had asked Tweed in her most polite manner if she could travel with him. Trudy had immediately volunteered to give up her place to her, saying she would ride with Nield. So now Newman, behind the wheel of his car, had Paula beside him and in the back Serena sat next to Tweed.

They drove past a park where there was equipment for children to play on, and a stationary helicopter. At that point they were at the head of the lake. Checking his map, Tweed estimated the lake was about ten miles long as it swept south. It was rather like a snake fully extended, curving here and there as the coils moved forward. It was mid-afternoon as they set off for Talloires.

A few yachts cruised the upper part of the lake unenthusiastically. Their sails were limp because there was no wind. Then the water was deserted as they moved further south. The landscape also was almost deserted. Steep hills climbed on their left and only here and there stood an isolated house. Paula had a feeling they were moving into no man's land.

'I told Burgoyne,' Tweed said, 'that we'd better hurry. It will start getting dark soon and we may want to race back to Geneva to get there before dark, if we can. He agreed, saying it was a treacherous route.'

'I think we're wasting our time,' Serena suddenly burst out. 'I can't see that our visit there produced anything.'

'Except I was a target,' Paula called back quietly.

'Well, the bullet missed you by a mile.'

'It came rather closer than that,' Paula responded, still quietly.

'I thought we were looking for Goslar,' Serena snapped. 'Who is Goslar? Where is he? We're no nearer finding anything out than we were back in Geneva. I feel I'm wasting *my* time.'

'In that case,' Tweed enquired, 'why did you come with us?'

'I thought you knew that. For protection. Everyone

else who had anything to do with that fiend has been killed.'

'Is that really the only reason you did come with us?' Tweed asked.

'Why should there be any other bloody reason?' she demanded, raising her voice.

Tweed looked at her. She kept her profile towards him. He detected a dominant streak in her nature she had carefully concealed up to then. She looked beautiful, but her Roman nose was tilted and her lips were pressed close together. Turning her head towards him for a moment, she glared, then turned away.

'Because,' he explained, 'I sense there is another reason.'

'Tweed's famous sixth sense,' she hooted, then laughed gratingly.

'Serena – ' Paula had twisted round in her seat to stare at her – 'I think it's time you cooled it. Your belly-aching could distract our driver.'

'Belly-aching! How vulgar. All right. There was another reason. Goslar – if you'd ever caught him – would be world famous. I'm a photographer. If I'd had pictures of him I could have syndicated them all over the world for a fortune. And I damned well need the money.'

'So where is your camera?' Tweed wanted to know.

'Are you calling me a liar? My camera is in my suitcase, which I brought from Nield's boot and put in ours.' Her voice began to drip sarcasm. 'If you like to stop the car, I'll get it out and show you. It's a Nikon. Newman, stop the car.'

'I take my instructions from Tweed,' Newman replied mildly.

Paula was still twisted round, watching Serena. She was getting the impression Serena was putting on a big act. Why?

'That does it, then,' Serena said, her voice cold. 'When we get back to Annecy I'm hiring my own car. I'll drive myself back to Geneva.'

Tweed again looked at her. Serena turned her head, looked back at him. She was no longer glaring. Her pallid eyes had a weird expression, as though she had withdrawn into herself, into another world.

'The temperature has dropped a lot suddenly,' said Paula. 'And the weather is changing. Oh Lord, look what's ahead of us.'

Tweed had noticed a few minutes earlier. The sun had gone. A low heavy overcast of threatening grey clouds had sealed it from view. In front of them, on their side of the lake, mountains sheered up steeply, mountains covered with deep snow. They were moving into a new climate zone.

'Tweed,' Paula called back, 'could you hand me my fleece? It is folded up in the seat next to you.'

'Here it is.'

Paula wriggled into her fleece, being careful not to jog Newman's arm. She pulled a pair of fur-lined gloves out of the pockets, put them on. She settled back, opened the glove compartment, brought out Newman's binoculars. For some time the road had been curving round the edge of the lake, twenty feet or so below them. She raised the binoculars, altered the focus, stared through the lenses for about a minute before lowering them.

'I think we're approaching Talloires. Gloomy-looking little town. No sign of life anywhere.'

'How far off?' Serena asked in a normal voice.

'About a mile, maybe a bit more. Burgoyne has slowed down quite a bit.'

'Tweed,' Paula commented, 'you did say back in

309

Annecy we would find what Talloires has in store for us. Something like that. Soon we'll know the answer.'

'Welcome to the lively resort of Talloires,' Newman began, singsong fashion. 'The jewel of France. Bunting hanging across the Avenue de Joie, people dancing in the streets, girls at windows with flowers they throw at passers-by. Oh, what a cheerful, lively town is Talloires.'

'Burgoyne is pulling up,' said Paula. 'I suggest you do the same behind Nield. And shut up!'

'The lady doesn't appreciate my musical talents,' Newman replied.

'Well, look at the place.'

They looked. Reluctantly they got out of the car and joined the others. Burgoyne, who seemed impervious to weather, stood in his jacket and slacks, his arms folded. Tweed was scanning their surroundings as he issued the warning.

'Spread out, everyone. We make a mass target here.'

'Isn't it incredibly bleak?' commented Paula, standing with Tweed and Burgoyne.

There was snow in the road. Heavy falls of snow on the slopes of the mountains which rose straight up from close to the road. There was a scattering of houses with steep roofs, some with plaster walls on the ground floor and first floors of dark wood. All their shutters were closed, downstairs, upstairs. Two small hotels had a notice on a board hanging from entrance doors. *Fermé.* Closed.

'I'd say the whole place is *fermé*,' Paula snorted and wandered off to join Serena, hoping she was in a better mood.

Tweed stood alone with Burgoyne under a huge fir tree. There was no sound. A heavy silence. An eerie sensation that no one lived here, that all the inhabitants had fled to the Bahamas. Tweed thought he had never experienced a place where *stillness* was the main element in the oppressive atmosphere. He felt that night would fall at any moment.

'What are you going to do when this is all over?' he asked.

'That's a good question.' Burgoyne's weathered face broke into a rueful smile. 'I suppose I'll go back to my cottage at Rydford, see if my girl friend, Coral Langley, is still interested. She's probably gone off with someone else by now.'

Tweed thought this wasn't the moment to tell Burgoyne that Coral no longer walked the planet.

'Rydford is a small place?' he asked.

'Small?' Burgoyne cupped his hand. 'I could hold it there. The place where nothing ever happens.'

'I can imagine you climbing the tors.'

'Rough Tor is only quite a short drive away. I think I've got too accustomed to roaming the earth. To seeing all the strange sights in this bizarre world of ours.'

He lifted his arms high, began to rotate, wiggling his hips, his stomach. He was nifty on his feet as he slowly swivelled round, gazing at Tweed with his dark eyes, pouching his lips invitingly. It was a professional performance and Tweed heard Paula chuckling as she watched from a distance. Burgoyne stopped, resumed his Stonehengelike stance, arms folded.

'Belly dance in Istanbul,' he explained, although Tweed had understood. 'A bit coarse, I suppose,' he said, eyeing Paula. 'But the world is full of coarseness these days. The whole structure is collapsing before our very eyes. No more honour, no more a man keeping his word once he's shaken your hand. All gone with the wind, as that lady novelist said who wrote about the American Civil War.'

'You've been to America?'

'Me?' Burgoyne threw out both arms, danced in a brief circle. 'I have been everywhere. Always on my own. Which is why I chose to join army intelligence. Then became a spy. Couldn't stand taking stupid orders from stupid buffoons who didn't know the time of day.'

'You'll miss that,' Tweed ruminated.

'Will I? Who says I'm going to settle down, grow old gracefully? I prefer to grow old disgracefully.' He grinned at Paula, who watched him, fascinated. 'Don't ever get mixed up with me, lady. I'd lead you one hell of a dance.'

Ever restless, Burgoyne did a little dance, stopped by the massive trunk of the fir spreading its branches above them. Tweed heard a sound, caught movement out of the corner of his eye. To their right the road turned a corner. An old man appeared.

He was hobbling. Had a stick in his left hand to help support him. His right hand was behind his back. Wrapped round his head was a large white bandage covering the top of his head and part of his forehead. His face was covered with white cream, presumably medicinal.

'Looks as though he's been in the wars,' Burgoyne remarked. 'Maybe it was a car crash. But I can ask him when he reaches us if he has seen anyone else at all in this benighted place.'

The old man kept coming, stick prodding into the road for balance. What happened next was a blur of movement. The stick was dropped. The hand behind the back appeared, holding a machine-pistol. His other hand took a firm hold on it. He was aiming it at where Paula stood with Serena.

A shot rang out, echoing across the mountains. Followed so fast by a second shot only a keen ear could tell two shots had been fired. The man with the bandaged head stood stock-still for a moment, then he sprawled forward full length, hitting the road with a heavy thud. The bandage slipped off his head.

Tweed ran forward, bent down, checked his pulse. He stood up and shook his head. Paula lowered the Browning she had fired twice, came forward. Tweed looked up at her as the others ran to join her.

'That was one of the quickest reactions I've ever seen. What was it that made you suspicious?'

'Look at what he's got wrapped round his head, for Heaven's sake.'

Underneath the white bandage which had slipped off the dead man in the road was a green headband. Paula looked at Burgoyne.

'Remember what you told us about fanatical Muslims wearing green headbands when they went into battle – as they did coming out of the mist on the road from Geneva. That they welcomed being martyrs to the cause. Well, I saw a thin strip of green below the bandage, so I was alerted, had my hand on my Browning when he whipped out the machine-pistol concealed behind his back.'

'You've got even better vision than I have,' Marler commented.

'I could have used you in the Gulf War,' Burgoyne said quietly.

'I want that body removed out of the road, and the weapon,' Tweed ordered.

Burgoyne said he'd oblige. As though it were an everyday job, he picked up the white bandage, stuffed it inside the assassin's jacket. He pulled off the green headband and added it to where he had hidden the bandage. Without its disguise, when Newman twisted it round, the face of the dead man was no longer old. It was the face of a man no older than thirty.

Burgoyne, using both hands, expertly picked up the body and the weapon. Standing upright, it struck Paula that Burgoyne, so recently the comedian, was now every inch the soldier. Carrying his burden in both arms he walked to the edge of the road, looked down, saw there was a sheer drop to the lake. He heaved body and weapon over. There was a brief splash and then the grim silence descended once more.

'Oh, my Lord,' said Serena, one hand clutching her throat, 'it's no wonder you work with Tweed. I hardly saw what happened until after it *had* happened.'

Paula was withdrawing the magazine still in her Browning. She tossed it into the lake, replaced it with a fresh magazine, then slid the gun back inside her shoulder bag.

'I should have been quicker,' Butler said to himself.

'So now sing "Welcome to Tailloires",' Paula chaffed Newman.

'There are times – ' Newman rubbed fingers down the side of his jaw – 'when I wish I'd kept my big mouth shut.'

'Someone else is coming round that corner,' warned Paula, her hand back inside her shoulder bag, gripping her Browning.

The last type of person in the world Tweed expected to see in this wilderness was strolling towards them. Tall and slim, he wore a Savile Row suit, a Hermès tie over a crisp white shirt and handmade shoes. The epitome of the Englishman you might expect to see in the City, he was swinging from his right hand a tightly rolled umbrella.

His other arm was swinging back and forth.

'Caw! I don't believe this,' said Butler.

'Don't,' warned Tweed.

The new arrival halted a few yards from them. He was about Newman's height and stood in the road with the end of his umbrella near his shoe while his arm held the handle at an extended angle. He was clean-shaven, had dark hair so trim it gave the impression he had just visited the hairdresser.

'Good afternoon, everyone,' he called out in a highly cultured voice. 'I must say it is rather a pleasure to meet someone from back home, don't you know? Bit like the outback of Orstralia round here.'

'Posh voice, don't you know,' Paula whispered to Tweed.

'Reminds me very much of the voice which introduces the recordings of Goslar,' Tweed whispered back. 'Very much indeed.'

'I have been asked to pass on a message to a Mr Tweed. Sorry, I really should have introduced myself. I am Peregrine Arbuthnot.'

'May I ask how you got here, Mr Arbuthnot?' asked Tweed. 'And I am Tweed.'

'How very pleasant to make your acquaintance, sir. How did I get here? Drove along the road down the other side of the lake, didn't I. Parked the Jag a bit further back, decided I'd take a bit of a walk the rest of the way. So here I am.'

'The message,' Newman said in a rough voice, walking closer and accompanied by Butler. 'Stop fooling around and give me the message.'

'I would appreciate a little courtesy, sir. Actually, the message is for Mr Tweed who, I gather, is standing over there.'

'So you're not armed, then,' Newman snapped, very close now.

'Armed? I say, you do harbour some rather quaint notions. And I must insist on—'

He never finished his sentence. Butler had slipped round behind him, had rammed the muzzle of a Walther into his back. As Arbuthnot began to splutter protests Newman slipped his hand inside the jacket where it bulged, spoiling the otherwise immaculate outfit. From a

315

shoulder holster he withdrew a Beretta 6.35mm auto-matic. He held it in the palm of his hand. Closer up, Arbuthnot was more heavily built than he had realized.

'Call this a quaint notion?' Newman enquired pleasantly.

'We're rather in the wilds out here. One does need a modicum of protection.'

'And one lied in one's teeth when I asked whether one was armed,' Newman said savagely.

'Does Tweed want the bloody message or not?' Arbuthnot snapped, his upper-crust accent slipping. 'And he doesn't get it unless the thug behind him takes his gun away.'

'Just give me the message,' said Tweed, who had joined them.

'I'd do as he says,' Marler warned, arriving so silently no one had noticed his approach. 'Mr Tweed has the most frightful temper when people try to play games with him.'

'I have attempted to deliver this message in a civi-lized fashion. That being so, I would appreciate some sign of respect.'

'The message,' Tweed repeated grimly.

'If you would kindly ask these morons to keep their distance – the message is for your ears only.'

'Let me take him behind that tree,' Newman pressed. 'I doubt if it would take me long to extract his perishing message.'

'Go ahead,' Tweed agreed, throwing up his hands in disgust.

Newman grasped Arbuthnot by his tie, dragging him behind the tree Tweed had stood under with Bur-goyne. His captive used one hand to try and wrench Newman's grip away but his efforts were futile. With the other hand he kept pointing at his mouth. For a

316

moment Newman eased his grip, realizing Arbuthnot was desperate to speak.

'Tweed! Tweed!' he gasped.

'I'm here,' said Tweed.

'Give you the message . . .'

'Let him talk,' Tweed ordered. 'If it's rubbish give him hell.'

'A moment, please . . . A moment.' Arbuthnot put up a hand to rub his bruised throat gently. 'Give you the message now . . .'

Tweed held out his hand, expecting an envelope with another scrawl inside it. Arbuthnot shook his head. Newman was just about to grab hold of him again when Arbuthnot spoke slowly, painfully.

'Message is verbal. Need my umbrella to show you . . .'

Butler, who had been close to Newman all the time, went back, fetched the umbrella which had been lying in the road. He first examined it carefully – to make sure there was no hidden weapon, that it was not a swordstick. Then he passed it to Arbuthnot.

'Up the mountain.' Arbuthnot walked a few careful paces to where he could see across the road. 'That cabin up there.' He pointed with the umbrella. 'See it?'

Tweed had earlier noticed a very large wooden cabin perched about two hundred yards up the steep snow-covered slope. Along the front, overlooking the lake, ran a long veranda. The shutters over the windows were all closed. No sign of life in the place.

'I see it,' Tweed acknowledged. 'What about it?'

'Dr Goslar is waiting there. To have a meeting with you. Just you. But the members of your team can escort you to the door at the left-hand side.'

'How were you given this message?' Tweed demanded.

'I had to call a number from a phone box in Annecy. He said, "Tell Tweed I will meet him at the cabin on the mountain at Talloires. It has a veranda at the front. We can settle this problem with a quiet talk." That was the message. He ended by telling me not to call the number again, that it was in a rented house. He would not be going back to it. That is all.'

'So how much did he pay you for this service?'

'Twenty thousand Swiss francs.'

'About ten thousand pounds,' Tweed calculated. 'Expensive message. Where did you collect the money?'

'From behind the phone box I was using. Inside a waterproof envelope.'

'Show me.'

'It is *my* money.'

Arbuthnot extracted from his breast pocket a fat white envelope and handed it to Tweed. Glancing inside Tweed saw there was a wad of about twenty thousand-franc notes. Swiss banknotes. £10,000. Goslar was throwing his money about. He handed back the envelope.

'What does Dr Goslar look like?'

'Look like?' Arbuthnot sounded astounded. 'I have never seen him. No one ever sees him . . .'

'It is a him? Or a her?'

'How the devil do I know? I've listened to the screeching voice on the tapes I have to play back. I can't tell whether it's a man or a woman.'

Tweed believed him. He turned again to stare at the isolated cabin. Single storey. Snow piled on its roof. He looked at Newman.

'This is where I take over,' Newman said firmly. He took off his camel-hair coat, stared hard at Arbuthnot. 'Put this on. Don't argue. Do it. You are going to walk up to that cabin to make sure Dr Goslar is waiting inside. Make with the feet.'

'There's snow on the slope,' Arbuthnot protested indignantly. 'I'm not dressed for it.'

'You're not dressed for anywhere within a hundred miles of here. I give you ten seconds to start climbing.'

'Otherwise,' Marler interjected, 'say goodbye to this paradise.'

Lifting his Armalite, Marler shoved the muzzle underneath Arbuthnot's chin. His target retreated, bumped into Newman, who held him still.

'You couldn't shoot down a man in cold blood,' stuttered Arbuthnot.

'Unfortunately,' Marler told him, without a smile, 'I'm the hot-blooded type. Now get moving. And while you're climbing remember I'll have your back in my cross-hairs.'

32

Arbuthnot had begun his climb up the slope through the snow. His feet sank into it up to his ankles, soaking the bottoms of his trousers. At one point he paused, looked back, waved his umbrella to express his rage. Marler raised the barrel of his rifle. Shaking a fist, Arbuthnot continued his climb, still some distance from the cabin.

'I don't like this,' Burgoyne said. 'There could be another bunch of Arabs inside the place. We're very exposed here. They could burst out suddenly and mow us down. I think we ought to hurry up the slope to that big copse of firs.'

'I agree,' said Tweed. 'Take everyone with you. I'll wait here with Paula and Newman. In an emergency we can hide behind the massive trunk of this fir. I'd go now . . .'

Burgoyne gathered the others together. They began climbing, heading for the copse which stood about the same height as the cabin and a hundred yards or so away from it to the right. Burgoyne led the way, holding Serena's arm to help her keep moving. Trudy went up behind them on her own, striding briskly. Behind her Nield and Butler brought up the rear.

Serena glanced back, saw Trudy by herself, tore her arm away from Burgoyne, said something to him, continued up under her own steam. Although they'd started later, they gained height more rapidly than Arbuthnot, who was trudging resentfully at a slower pace. Again he stopped, looked down. Marler again raised the muzzle of his Armalite and Arbuthnot started climbing once more.

'Do you really think Goslar is waiting inside that cabin?' Paula asked.

'No idea,' Tweed replied. 'Goslar is full of tricks. He could be close to us, he could be miles away.'

'I can't feel sorry for Arbuthnot,' she said, watching the solitary figure plodding upward. 'You seemed sure it was his voice which introduced Goslar's screeching recordings. Arbuthnot must have realized some of them would end in murder.'

'He probably closed his mind to that aspect – for the sake of the money.'

Paula switched her gaze to the five people who were disappearing into the copse. She started, grabbed Tweed's arm. He looked at her.

'What is it?'

'That photo you always carry, the one of Goslar disappearing behind the Iron Curtain east of Lübeck all those years ago. The blurred image – the way it swung its arms well clear of its body. I just saw that.'

'Are you sure?'

'Oh!' She let out her breath. 'I was wrong. It was Trudy in her trouser suit. She just reappeared for a moment.'

'Bet Arbuthnot finds that cabin empty,' Newman speculated. 'And another message from bloody Goslar.'

'Could be,' Tweed mused.

'On the other hand,' Pauia suggested, 'Chance could be right. He is a soldier with a lot of experience. If there are Arabs waiting inside that cabin I think we'd better take shelter behind that fir trunk.'

They moved behind the massive trunk, peering round it to watch the solitary figure with its absurd umbrella getting close to the door in the left-hand side. Marler used a convenient short thick branch to perch his rifle on.

Paula was again aware of the haunting silence of the place. Not a sound. No movement – except for the plodding figure approaching the side of the cabin. It was beginning to get on her nerves, to emphasize their isolation from the rest of the world. Clenching her fingers tightly inside her gloves she took in a deep breath, had a presentiment of great danger.

She tried to locate the source of what was bothering her so much. Burgoyne's group had become invisible, hidden deep inside the copse. Then her gaze became fixated on Arbuthnot's movements as he slowed down. He had just passed the end of the long veranda, had stopped close to something at the side of the cabin. The door, she assumed.

The nerve-racking silence was broken by the sound of his distant voice. He was calling out something, but she couldn't catch the words. She guessed he was asking Dr Goslar if he was inside, maybe telling him Tweed had come to meet him. Arbuthnot still paused for a short time. Then he began to move, hand extended, presumably to take hold of the door handle. He began to move inside, to disappear from view. The world blew up.

A booming roar smashed the silence. It coincided with a brilliant flash. The deafening explosion elevated the entire cabin. It broke into pieces in midair, casting beams of wood across the slope, sending shards towards the sky like shrapnel, everything bursting into flames. Tweed pulled Paula behind the tree as debris clattered on to the road. As the clatter ceased she peered round the trunk. A column of black smoke mushroomed above where the cabin had stood, was rapidly dispersed by an icy breeze which sprang up suddenly. The heavy silence again descended on Talloires.

Butler, holding his machine-pistol, was the first to emerge from inside the copse. He cautiously approached what was no more than a pile of ash. Paula realized he was wary of a second explosion. Then he moved close, used the muzzle of his weapon to stir the ash.

Paula ran up the slope, accompanied by Newman. Tweed followed at a more leisurely pace. Trudy appeared out of the copse with Nield on one side, Burgoyne on the other. The last figure to arrive was Serena. Butler looked up as Paula and Newman reached him.

'Nothing left of Arbuthnot. Can't find a trace of him.'

'I'm not surprised,' said Burgoyne. 'We felt the shockwave inside that copse. That was quite a load of explosive.'

'Triggered off when Arbuthnot opened the door,' Paula suggested.

'I guess so,' Burgoyne agreed.

'It would have wiped out the lot of us,' Tweed

322

commented calmly, 'if Bob hadn't had the sense to send Arbuthnot up first. Another typical Goslar trap.'

'I suppose Arbuthnot was an employee of Goslar's,' Serena remarked. She lit a cigarette. 'I don't think we need waste time mourning him.'

Paula glanced at her. Serena's tone of voice had been cold, verging on the indifferent. You, my girl, she thought, are one tough cookie. Far more so than you pretend to be. Tweed thrust his hands into his coat pocket. His tone was decisive.

'I think now we'll drive on to the end of the lake and back along the road on the other side to Annecy. I need to have an urgent word with that estate agent, Periot. So let's try and get back before he goes home.'

'What about?' Paula whispered as they started to descend the slope.

'The Chateau de l'Air. I may just have missed something.'

33

Marler was waiting for them by the roadside. Tweed guessed he had sensibly stayed there in case more trouble arrived while they were exposed on the slope. Within minutes they were travelling along the lakeside road. Paula took one last glance at the place where the cabin had stood. The ashes were still smouldering but she thought that soon it would snow again, burying for ever Arbuthnot's funeral pyre. She heaved a sign of relief as they left Talloires behind.

They passed a number of old houses set back from the road. In all of them the shutters were closed, both downstairs and upstairs. It was like a small town the inhabitants had abandoned, fleeing from the plague.

The dark trees clustered close to the road did nothing to lighten the atmosphere.

Before leaving, at Serena's suggestion, they had changed places in the cars. Now, in the rear car, driven by Newman, Paula still sat next to him. But instead of Serena, Tweed had Trudy seated next to him. He was puzzled by Serena's request – she was now seated next to Nield in the car in the middle of the convoy. Ahead of Nield, Marler drove with Butler and Burgoyne was again in the lead.

'I expect you found that a pretty frightening experience,' Tweed remarked to Trudy.

'A brief shock – the sound of the bomb exploding – but nothing more. After living with Unit Four it takes a lot to upset me.'

'I can understand that. Especially after the death of your husband. What was his name, by the way?'

'Er . . .' Trudy hesitated. Tweed glanced at her. 'It was Walter Baron,' she then said. Another hesitation. 'Third-generation American. We lived for each other. No, that sounds rather like something from a poetic sonnet. How can I put it? We were a good match.'

Paula had heard the hesitations. She twisted round in her seat, looked at Tweed.

'Why do you think Goslar is still trying to kill us? There's something relentless, even desperate about his attempts.'

'Desperate is the word,' Tweed replied. 'I'm convinced he is almost ready to deliver his horrific weapon to the highest bidder. He's getting nearly frantic that in some way I'll thwart him at the last moment.'

'So you think there isn't much time left to stop him?'

'That is my great anxiety. There could be only hours left.'

The conversation ended. They were now moving along the far side of the lake on their way back to

Annecy. Paula was pondering the situation. She sensed in Tweed a grim determination to reach Goslar in time. Then something else occurred to her.

'We haven't seen sight or heard sound of either the Yellow Man or Bancroft. I wonder where they are now?'

'I have no idea, but I can hear a helicopter approaching.'

'And now we're getting close to Annecy I can see a speedboat on the lake.'

After his botched attempt to kill Paula, the Yellow Man had escaped Butler's attempt to kill him by dodging a devious path along the network of alleys inside Annecy. He had then returned to the rue Perrière – in time to see Tweed's cars leaving. Running to his parked car, he had followed them a short distance until he had realized they were heading for the far end of the lake.

Parking his Peugeot near the car-hire firm, he had hurried across the park to a small marina. As he had hoped, he found a jetty where speedboats were for hire. He'd had to wait a while for one to be returned. In the meantime he had used field glasses to follow the progress of the convoy along the lakeside road until it disappeared from view.

'How much longer am I going to have to wait?' he had demanded.

'Until the previous hirer returns. Do not ask me how long that will be,' the owner had replied unhelpfully. 'He said he only needed it for an hour – and that was an hour ago.'

'Can't you call him on a mobile phone?'

'You tell me how. I have one, but he hasn't. Just a moment. I do believe he's coming back now . . .'

In a fever of impatience, which he fought to control, the Yellow Man had watched enviously as an agile man ran towards a helicopter resting in the park. He could have hired that machine to follow Tweed. Then he had an idea.

'I'll be back in a minute,' he said to the speedboat hirer. 'And you will promise to keep that boat coming in for me?'

'How long do you want it for?' the hirer asked off-handedly. 'The charge is one hundred francs an hour.'

'Take this.'

The Yellow Man pulled out of his pocket a wad of French francs. He peeled off six fifty-franc notes, shoved them into the hirer's hand. Confident that such an amount would hold the speedboat for him, he dashed back to his parked car. When he returned he carried a canvas holdall. Inside it were four grenades.

The speedboat was now waiting for him, moored to the wharf. The hirer, with three hundred francs in his pocket, was now most helpful. He handed down the Yellow Man into the craft, offered to show him how the controls worked.

'I've often used powerboats,' the Yellow Man replied and started the engine.

Before he took off he rammed his beret more tightly over his hair. He then headed at a modest speed along the western shore – the shore opposite to the one Tweed's convoy had proceeded down along the road. In this way he would be less likely to be noticed.

Earlier, when Tweed and his team had left the restaurant in Annecy, Les Corbières, Bancroft had also left a short time afterwards. He had decided he could wear his panama hat again and walked into a nearby bar. Tweed and his men had to return for their cars sooner or later.

Impatient by nature, Bancroft had swilled down only half his drink when he decided he had made another mistake. When Tweed and his team returned to pick up their cars, he'd have to wait until they had gone before he dared to walk out of the bar. He was convinced their arrival in Annecy was only a stopover, that as soon as they'd come back from their walk they would drive to the highway leading to Geneva.

He left the bar quickly, went to his car, backed it away from the wall and headed for the highway. He needed somewhere he could park until he saw the convoy leaving the area. Turning onto the highway, he drove a short distance in the Geneva direction, parked his car on a grass verge. He took off his panama hat but kept on his large wraparound glasses. This time he made no attempt to pretend he was fiddling with the engine. He slumped in his seat like a man asleep. Then he waited.

Stirring restlessly in his seat, he went on waiting – and waiting – and waiting. Eventually he could stand the inaction no longer. He drove back to the Old Town. The moment he saw the parking area he was appalled. All the cars belonging to Tweed's team had gone. He parked again by the wall, jumped out of his car and ran across the park to where the helicopter stood, the pilot in his seat, gazing round.

'I've lost track of the terrorists,' he snapped as he climbed up beside the pilot. 'They're in a convoy of four cars . . .'

He described the cars while the pilot listened. The pilot scratched his forehead, nodded.

'Well, have you seen them, for God's sake?' Bancroft rasped.

'Yes. They went east along that road over there. They continued along the road by the lake, heading south towards Talloires.'

'Then let's find them. I'm paying you good money . . .'

The pilot switched on the engine, the two rotors began to whirl – the small one at the rear which stabilized the machine and the large brute which lifted the chopper. The pilot flew out over the lake, climbing all the time. He didn't want any complaints from the locals about the noise it made. He'd experienced that before. The few yachts crawling over the water became like toys and then the pilot headed his machine south.

'Fly closer to the western shore,' Bancroft ordered. 'Then they're less likely to hear us coming.'

He had the communication kit strapped over his head. Headphones were clamped to his ears. At his mouth was a small microphone he could use to speak to the pilot, who had his own communication equipment.

'Why don't you just arrest these terrorists?' the pilot asked.

'We can't – without evidence.' Bancroft's legal mind improvised as a reflex action. 'We need to locate them when they are collecting weapons from one of their arms dumps. I can summon the CRS on my mobile.'

'CRS? They're a tough lot. Just what you need to cope with terrorists.'

'Where does that lakeside road they drove along lead to?'

'Only to Talloires, then it curves round the end of the lake and returns on this side to Annecy. You can't lose them . . .'

The pilot was flying at a moderate speed. Bancroft would have liked to tell him to hurry up, but decided not to put any more pressure on him. He looped the powerful binoculars he always carried round his neck, used them to sweep the road along the eastern shore, saw nothing. He stopped looking.

A short time later he heard a faint distant *boom!* He saw smoke rising a good way off on the eastern shore. When they got closer he raised his binoculars again, made out four cars parked below a snow-covered mountain. People were getting into them and the cars started moving.

'I think that's them,' he told the pilot. 'The cars have started to move off, still heading south.'

'In that case they'll soon be moving up the road by this side of the lake.'

'Then we'd better keep this height and cross the lake – so we'll be flying well away from them. I'd change direction now, if I were you,'

'There's a powerboat ahead of us, hugging this shore. Powerboats don't often get this far south at this time of the year. It will be cold down there . . .'

The Yellow Man, not wishing to get too close to Tweed while he had a large team with him, was staying close to the western side of the lake. He had to launch a surprise attack. He stopped the engine, looked above him. The trouble was that a cliff, about twenty feet up, leaned over the water. He looked at the holdall which contained the four grenades. It was going to be difficult at this point to lob grenades at the cars as they passed him on the road.

He had watched Tweed's team through binoculars at the moment when Arbuthnot was nearing the wooden cabin. He had arrived too late to see Newman drop the Arab's corpse into the lake. Now trees masked his view of what was happening on the snow-bound slope. His first clue that something had happened was when he heard the explosion.

He saw debris soaring into the air, dropping back again. He was mystified, therefore bothered. Later he saw the four cars driving off down the lakeside road. When he had escaped from Butler, after attempting to kill Paula, he had bought a map of the area. He was studying it now, noting that the road led round the base of the lake and returned towards Annecy above him.

He started the engine, glanced up at a helicopter crossing to the far side of the lake, turned the boat round, began chugging back along the smooth surface. He was still close to the shore while looking for a place where the road was exposed to view. Again, he switched off the engine briefly. He could hear the cars coming.

He was bitterly cold and wrapped a cloth round the lower half of his face. Starting up the engine, he moved out towards the middle of the lake, looking ahead for a suitable location to use his grenades. He was now moving at speed, spray bursting over the prow, splashing on his half-covered face.

When he looked back to the shore he saw the four cars racing along and realized it would be almost impossible to throw a grenade and hit the lead car. It was partly this realization – and partly the icy cold – which made him take a fresh decision. He would overtake the cars and reach Annecy ahead of them. He opened the throttle.

The prow lifted itself out of the water. A surging wake tumbled the lake behind him. He looked back at the road. The cars were now some distance behind him. He would be waiting for them when they reached Annecy.

So great was his concentration on Tweed's convoy that he missed seeing another development. The helicopter had also changed course. It also was now heading at great speed for Annecy.

34

It was still daylight and very warm again when they reached Annecy. Their cars pulled up outside the estate agent, and there were lights inside. Tweed jumped out, followed by Paula, and as they walked inside Periot came forward to greet them.

'A surprise to see you again, sir. We were just closing but you are most welcome. Both of you.' He bowed to Paula. 'What can I do for you?'

'I've decided I'm interested in the Château de l'Air,' Tweed explained. 'Would it be possible to borrow the keys? We shall be driving past it.'

'Certainly you may have the keys.' Periot smiled. 'It will be dark when you get there but the electricity is still on. Excuse me for a moment.'

He returned quickly with a bunch of keys. As he handed them over he showed them which was for the front door, the back entrance and the main drawing room. He also gave Tweed a thick addressed envelope.

'To save a long journey you could post them back.'

'Thank you.' Tweed turned to go, then swung round. 'I believe you said you had inspected the place recently. How long ago would that be?'

'Let me see. At least a couple of months. Could be longer. If you are interested in buying we could try to come to some arrangement with Mr Masterson.'

'Oh, you can get in touch with him, then?'

'Yes. Via a poste restante address in Grenoble. A curious method of communication, I thought. But, as I told you, we never saw Mr Masterson. Rather an eccentric character I would imagine.'

'Thank you.'

Burgoyne was waiting for them outside. He lowered his voice so the others across the road could not hear him.

'I think it might be a wise precaution if I drove on ahead by myself. To check the road again. We can't assume Goslar has given up on his murderous attempts to wipe you out.'

'Good idea,' Tweed agreed.

'I'll check the route all the way to Geneva. If I spot anything I don't like the look of I'll call you on my mobile. No news from me is good news.'

'Where can we make contact again, then?'

'At the Richemond, I suggest. It's a very good hotel. See you . . .'

'The tough soldier plays his part,' observed Tweed as they watched Burgoyne drive off.

'I'd like to take another look at Annecy,' Paula said. 'Despite the bullet episode I think the place is enchanting.'

'Give us the excuse to have a drink,' remarked Newman who had joined them. 'Don't you think so, Marler?'

'If you say so.'

Tweed stared at him. He thought he'd detected a note of doubt in the way he had replied. At that moment Serena crossed the road to join them. Her pallid eyes gazed at Tweed.

'Did I hear you say you were going to spend a little time in Annecy?'

'Just a short while. It's such a beautiful town.'

'Then I'll come with you to that old bridge. When we drove off to Talloires I noticed a car-hire place. I'm going to hire a car and drive by myself to Geneva now.'

'Why?'

'Do I damned well have to give a reason? It looks as

though I have to. I don't think you're ever going to find Goslar. And I do have another photographic commission in Geneva. Quite a lucrative one – a fashion thing. By getting there this evening I can contact the director and he'll start setting things up for me. You can always get me at the Richemond.'

'It's up to you,' said Tweed. He looked at Nield who had crossed the road. 'Maybe you could drive Serena to this car-hire place.'

'Not necessary,' Serena said in her most commanding voice. 'If you drop me by the bridge it's only a short walk across that park.'

'As you wish.'

They got into their cars. Nield, on his own, was now following Marler, also on his own. It took no time at all to reach the Pont Perrière, to park their cars by the wall. Serena got out quickly, waved a hand, walked briskly away. Tweed followed her, watched her hurry across the park, saw there were lights in the car-hire establishment. He also noticed the helicopter had landed, that the pilot was seated in his cabin. He walked back as Paula began to cross the bridge.

Butler rushed forward, Walther in his hand. He pushed in front of Paula, raised his automatic, fired a shot at a shadowy figure at the entrance to an alley. The shadow vanished. Customers seated under umbrellas outside Les Corbières with drinks gazed in astonishment.

'What is it?' Tweed asked urgently.

'Man with gun just about to shoot Paula,' Butler said quickly. 'I saw him for a second by a street lamp, his yellow hair. It's the Yellow Man. I'm going after him.'

'Wait,' Tweed ordered.

'Time we cleaned this place out,' said Newman.

'I said wait.' Tweed had a map of Annecy in his hands. Swiftly he drew a cross, dividing Annecy into four quarters. 'Butler, this is your zone – where you saw the gunman. Newman, Marler, this is your section. Nield—'

'I'll go with Nield,' Trudy rapped out.

'Then this is your quarter. Paula will take this quarter with me. Scour the place. Hunt him down. I don't want him leaving Annecy alive. Watch the dark alleys. Go to it.'

Paula thought she had never known Tweed look so grim. Butler had disappeared inside the alley where he had seen the shadow. Trudy and Nield had gone, hurrying along the nearer bank of the river. Paula noticed Trudy had her right hand inside her fleece. She knew she was gripping her automatic. Newman palmed a Walther and ammo inside Tweed's jacket pocket, then moved off with Marler. Tweed and Paula crossed the bridge together. The temporary manager of Les Corbières came out to meet them, addressing Tweed.

'May I ask what the devil is going on?'

'You just did. It's a game we play with schoolboy cap pistols – and the winner makes a lot of money.'

'This is the oddest day I have experienced since I came to Annecy.'

'Livens the place up a bit. One of your customers inside wants his bill . . .'

They began walking along the rue Perrière, the same route they had taken when Paula missed death by inches. As they approached the same corner Tweed held Paula back. With the Walther in one hand and a torch he had brought from the car in the other, he peered round the corner. He turned on the torch. A powerful beam illuminated the wrecked 'pulpit' by the side of the strange tower. No sign of anyone. He nodded for Paula to join him.

'I thought Serena acted very weirdly,' Paula began. 'Her sudden rush to reach Geneva. I can't imagine the director of any fashion house being available by the time she gets there.'

'She did seem in a bit of a hurry.'

'I find her weird altogether. Her eyes.'

'Don't underestimate her extraordinary intelligence. Now, keep *your* eyes open – for any unexpected movement . . .'

The helicopter transporting Bancroft was flying slowly over the northern end of the lake, close to the children's park, when Bancroft gave the pilot a fresh order.

'Keep to your present height. Circle round a bit. I can see the four cars which have stopped outside the Old Town.'

He had the binoculars pressed to his eyes when he saw Tweed and Paula walk out of Periot's office. His tactic now was to check whether they were going to return to Annecy or proceed north towards Geneva. He wasn't going to be caught out again. The moment he saw three of the cars turning along the road to the Old Town he rapped out another instruction.

'Land in that park – where you did before. As fast as you can . . .'

The machine bumped down on the grass. Bancroft threw open his door, dropped to the ground. He waited impatiently for the engine to stop so he could be heard.

'Wait for me again. I may be some time.'

He hurried across the park at a diagonal, crossed the road, looked towards the bridge. He had chosen just the right place. He slipped into the shadow thrown by a closed shop, raised his binoculars. What he witnessed puzzled him. A burly man, close to Paula and Tweed, about to cross the bridge, produced a handgun, fired a single shot. The rest seemed to be confusion, then Tweed and his team departed in different directions.

335

He lowered his glasses. He didn't want to make another mistake. He decided quickly. Walking quickly along the road to the Old Town, he passed the wall where they had parked their cars. Then he went into the same bar he had visited earlier for a short time. Sitting down at a table by himself he ordered a drink.

I've got it right this time, he said to himself. They have to come back here to pick up their cars. Then I can go back to the chopper, follow them from the air.

Paula and Tweed walked slowly along the narrow street, which they had to themselves. Dusk was beginning to fall. The Old Town was illuminated by ancient lanterns, some projecting in iron brackets from the old walls, some perched on top of posts. The glass in the lanterns was amber-coloured and now they were lit they cast an eerie glow at intervals between the shadowed areas.

'This town is Heaven,' she said. She glanced at Tweed. 'You look angry.'

'Anger? No. Anger – like grief – upsets a man's judgement.'

'What are you trying to do here then?'

'Use the same strategy I have adopted ever since we left England. Eliminate all the enemies who might get in the way of our locating Goslar. In Paris I used Lasalle to get rid of the Americans – by getting Newman to plant false documents in Karnow's suite. In Geneva I used the Swiss police chief, Charpentier, to get rid of our pursuers. I certainly didn't intend it to end so brutally in that underground garage. My original idea had been to have Karnow himself – and Bate of the Special Branch, as it turned out – arrested and deported.'

'But you did eliminate them.'

'Yes, I fear I did. Now, here in Annecy, I am sure we

have both Bancroft and the Yellow Man. I need to eliminate both – without too much compunction considering what they are – so we can concentrate finally on Dr Goslar.'

'I think you've been very clever.'

'If you say so . . .'

They turned down another narrow street of amber glow. It led them to a wide stone walk alongside a river. The silence of the previous street had gone. Now Paula listened with delight to the sound of water gushing over a small weir. She pointed with her left hand to flowers draped over an iron bar above the weir. They were a riot of yellows, greens and whites, a massed fantasy of colour.

'That's beautiful. Early flowers out in full bloom. It must be the sun and the warmth they get here in the spring. This place is a galaxy of dreams. Look at those walls opposite, caught in the lamplight.'

She was gazing at ancient houses where their walls fell straight down to the river's edge. Their plaster hadn't been painted for a long time so they were a mosaic of ochre and brown. All the shutters were flung wide open. From inside one of them drifted the strains of violin music.

'I could stay here for ever,' she enthused.

'Just so long as you don't forget why we are here,' he warned.

Tweed's eyes had been everywhere, scanning the street in both directions. He even kept glancing up at the open windows. When he looked at Paula he saw her right hand was inside her shoulder bag and realized he had underestimated her. The hand, gripping her Browning, could appear in a flash.

'We'll next check this way,' he said.

Further along the street, deeper into Annecy, tables were laid outside a bar. As they drew nearer he saw locals sitting outside, enjoying drinks and snacks. The joyful chatter of their voices – people enjoying themselves – was a relief. Paula then spoke, showed her mind was still alert.

'That was the Yellow Man Butler fired at across the bridge, was it?'

'Harry said so and therefore it was him. He also said he'd caught a glimpse of his hair.'

'I don't know how we're ever going to find him in this maze.'

'By trawling it street by street – until we do.'

Trudy and Nield walked side by side as they explored their own district. She found her companion's presence comfortable. He made no attempt to talk just for the sake of talking. It was almost as though they had known each other for years and didn't need to keep up an endless stream of meaningless chatter. They were walking along a paved pedestrian area with a stone wall separating them from a fast-moving stream, part of the network of waterways which sprawls everywhere through old Annecy.

Ahead of them was a footbridge with a tumbling weir just beyond. No one else was about in this part of the town and the light was the haunting mixture of light and dark when dusk falls. They came to the bridge and paused. Nield looked at her.

'Let's cross over.' He checked the map divided into quarters Tweed had handed to him, because it was a complex district. 'We will still be in our area.'

Halfway across the bridge Trudy stopped, leaned on the rail to stare at the weir. It had a hypnotic effect on her. Brushing back her blaze of red hair, she watched the rushing water, the whirlpools which formed beneath it. Nield stood beside her, also leaning on the rail. He kept glancing along both banks of the stream, content to let her drink in her pleasure. She stood up straight.

'I suppose we'd better get on. Sorry to hold you up.'

'After what you've seen today a few minutes' restful contemplation is good for you. On the other side of the bridge where we're going is a dark narrow alley. I'll go ahead with my torch.'

They left the narrow bridge. On the far side, before venturing inside the alley, Nield paused. He wanted to give Trudy a last opportunity to look at the stream which had so caught her fancy. They stood together in the street which ran parallel to the stream along its other bank. Trudy took one last look at the weir.

It happened so quickly they were both taken by surprise. At one moment they were the only people in sight. The Yellow Man, running, appeared on the other side of the footbridge. Trudy was startled by how tall he was. He rushed over the bridge straight at them. Nield was lifting his Walther when the Yellow Man head-butted him in the chest. Nield fell back, knowing there was a hard stone wall behind him. As he fell he jerked his head forward to prevent his skull smashing into the wall. Trudy aimed her automatic but the assassin was gone, running inside the dark alley.

Butler appeared, moving at great speed. He charged over the footbridge like a rampaging bull. He stopped briefly at the entrance to the alley, Walther gripped in both hands. As the assassin passed under a wall lamp he fired. The bullet grazed the Yellow Man's right leg. He stumbled, recovered his balance, ran on as Butler followed.

Nield was at Butler's heels with Trudy just behind him. Yellow Man was zigzagging from one alley to another. Trudy lost all sense of direction, heard running feet behind her. Risking a look back she saw Newman and Marler racing along the same route.

Butler, pounding along, zigzagged, refusing to lose sight of his target. Suddenly Tweed and Paula appeared out of a side alley, joined the marathon pursuit.

Bancroft's impatience had given way. He walked out of the bar, headed across the park to the helicopter. He'd decided to get a better view of where all Tweed's team was from the air. He reached the chopper.

'What happens next?' asked the pilot, after throwing open the passenger door.

'We take off. We fly as low as you dare. Over the Old Town. I want to locate those terrorists fast.'

'There's a regulation as to how low I can fly over a built-up area,' the pilot warned.

Bancroft put on his headset as the pilot did the same. Now they'd be able to communicate above the roar of the engine and Bancroft was in no mood to argue. He pulled out another sheaf of hundred-franc notes, thrust it into the pilot's hands.

'Goddamnit!' he snarled into the mike. 'I want to see down inside every street, every alley. How much more do I have to pay to get you to do what I tell you?'

The pilot started the engine. The rotor blades began to swivel – tail rotor, main rotor. They had their backs to the Old Town so neither of them saw what was happening, what had happened.

The Yellow Man emerged from the Old Town into the children's park. Butler was about two hundred yards behind him. About the same distance behind Butler the others had appeared, running across the park.

Seeing the helicopter, the assassin knew he had found his way to escape his pursuers. He was short of breath now but his powerful legs kept running. He'd threaten the pilot with his Smith & Wesson, force the pilot to take him aboard.

His one fear was Butler. The bastard had clung to him like a leech through the labyrinth of alleys. He looked back to see how close Butler was, kept running at high speed across the soft grass. It was when he looked back that Butler hurled the grenade he'd grabbed out of his pocket. The missile soared through the air, landed close behind its target.

The Yellow Man couldn't stop looking back. For once in his murderous life he was scared stiff. When the grenade detonated it would probably be close enough to reach him. The grenade lay on the ground, didn't detonate. The Yellow Man couldn't believe his luck.

He turned to face the front and opened his mouth to scream. The main rotor blade struck him just below the jaw, sliced off his head. It flew through the air like a melon, a leaking red melon. The Yellow Man's trunk fell forward, brushing against the side of the chopper's fuselage as the machine took off.

35

They were driving north along the N201 in the direction of Geneva. Only three cars made up the convoy this time. The lead vehicle was Marler's, who was driving with Butler. Behind him came Nield, driving alone. In the third and last car Newman was behind the wheel with Paula alongside him. His passengers in the rear seats were Tweed and Trudy.

'No message yet from Chance,' Paula called out.

'Not yet,' Tweed agreed. 'But he'll still be somewhere on the road between here and the city.'

After the 'execution' of the Yellow Man, as Newman

had referred to the event, Tweed had ordered everyone to move straight back to the parked cars. He had urged them to walk without appearing to be in a hurry to get away from the park. There had been no one else about to witness what happened and it was Paula who had made the observation.

'Thank Heaven there were no children left in the park,' she had said.

'All gone home for supper, fortunately,' Tweed had remarked.

They had been driving away from the Old Town when Newman had made a suggestion just before Tweed voiced the idea himself. Newman had parked by a public phone box, looked up the number of the local police station, and spoken through a silk handkerchief when he called it – to report that he had seen a body in the park. He had ended the call when asked for his name. He had also taken the precaution of speaking in French.

It was quite dark now and Paula found herself gazing along the headlight beams as they drove within the speed limit. After a while she turned to look at Trudy, to see how she was feeling. Trudy seemed to read her mind.

'I'm OK,' she responded with a smile. 'How many people had that awful man beheaded? You told me about him when you came to see me in my room at the Richemond.'

'One in London, a reporter called Sam Sneed. Two in Paris – one was a bookseller, the other an innocent landlady. The bookseller was equally innocent. But there were others. He was known as the most professional assassin in Europe.'

'Then how ironic,' Trudy commented, 'that he ended up being beheaded himself in an accident.'

'Which shows that there is some justice in the world,' Newman said.

'Will we ever know who he was?' Trudy wondered.

'We know now,' Tweed told her. He extracted a British passport from his pocket. 'Don't worry – Butler slipped it out of his jacket before anything had tainted it.' He meant blood. 'Have a look.'

'Darcy Stapleton,' she read out aloud. 'Born in Manchester. Aged forty-two. He'd been to the States. There's a Non-Immigrant visa stamped in it by the embassy in London.' She handed it back. 'His photograph is authentic. I caught a good look at him when he rushed over that footbridge and headbutted poor Pete Nield.'

'We can trace where he lived when we get back,' Tweed said. 'I have a friend who is high up in Scotland Yard. That is if the passport is genuine, which I doubt.'

'So that only leaves Bancroft,' Trudy said quietly. 'Apart from Dr Goslar, of course.'

'No news still from Beck?' Paula asked.

'Not a whisper,' Tweed replied. 'And I do need that call by the time we reach Geneva. But first we must explore the Château de l'Air.'

'Expect to find anything there?' enquired Newman sceptically.

'We have to try. Leave no stone unturned, to coin a cliché. At some point Goslar must slip up.'

'He didn't ten years ago,' Newman reminded Tweed.

'Most important, while I remember. When we do get there we won't risk driving up the main entrance – not after that anti-personnel mine Burgoyne spotted. But I did notice another track leading up to the crest near the mansion when we were there this morning. So we must look out for an earlier entrance of some sort. Bob, better warn Marler about that now. The best way is to risk using your mobile . . .'

'At least there's no sign of Bancroft following us,' Paula commented. 'And no more helicopters, thank goodness. Haven't heard one since we left Annecy.'

In this assumption Paula could not have been more wrong.

When their helicopter took off from the children's park neither the pilot nor Bancroft was aware of the violence their machine had committed. They were staring towards the eastern shore of the lake as they gained height. When the chopper changed direction, on Bancroft's orders, he used binoculars and was just in time to see the three cars leaving Annecy.

'The terrorists are heading back towards Geneva,' he reported. 'It will be easy to track them by their headlights. I want you to gain much more height, then move away from the highway so they can't hear our engine.'

'They might see the port and starboard lights. Obligatory when flying at night. I'm not risking losing my licence.'

'Goddamnit! That's why I told you to gain plenty of height. They are not likely to see us from any of the cars. Just do as I tell you. I'm paying you enough. And any minute now it will be dark.'

'There will be a moon.'

'I do not like people who argue with me. Just do as I've told you.'

It was soon dark. The pilot gained height as instructed. He also changed course, flying well away from the highway. Bancroft proved to be right. Through his binoculars he was able to track Tweed's convoy by their headlights. He settled down, assuming his quarry

344

was returning to Geneva. But he still kept the three cars under observation.

'I expect everyone is hungry,' Tweed remarked at one point. 'We will be able to refuel palatially when we reach the Richemond.'

'I can go for hours without food,' Trudy assured him. 'Just so long as I've had a big breakfast, which I did. It's an American habit I brought back with me. I'm going to cure myself of it.'

'Why do that?' Paula asked.

'Because I hate anything American. The US is a land of barbarians.'

They then travelled a long distance in silence. Tweed had relaxed, his back firmly against the seat. He might have been asleep but when Trudy looked at him his eyes were wide open. She kept quiet, sensing that he was sunk deeply in thought. Paula peered out of her side window, stared.

'I can see a winking light high up and a long way off to our right. It couldn't be that helicopter, could it?'

'You're thinking of Bancroft,' Newman told her.

'So am I,' said Trudy. 'I never stop thinking about Bancroft.'

Her tone was grim. Paula decided it would be best not to enter into conversation with her on that subject. They drove further on. The moon had risen, casting a luminous glow over the countryside they were passing through. She lowered her window and an icy blast blew in. She hastily shut it again.

'I thought it was getting much colder,' she remarked.

'That's the Bise wind blowing off Mont Blanc,' Newman explained. 'At times it freezes this part of France. I remember it from long ago. I was down here visiting a girl friend. A shade from the past.'

'And that's what we are pursuing,' Tweed said, his voice very alert. 'A very dark shade from the past. Dr Goslar. The most evil man I have ever fought at arm's length.'

'Let's hope we confront the swine face to face this time,' Newman responded.

'If he hasn't already disappeared again to the East. This time to a different East – the Middle East . . .'

He had just spoken when Newman leaned forward, staring at something ahead of them. As he did so he reduced speed a lot. Paula peered through the windscreen, realized what he had seen. A dense white mist was swirling across the highway. She recalled the encounter with the Arab fanatics on their way from Geneva in the morning.

'At least we've had no warning from Burgoyne of an ambush,' she remarked.

'Unless he ran into them and is no longer in a state to warn us,' Trudy said quietly.

'I don't think Burgoyne is a man who would run into anything,' Tweed said flatly. 'Why have we stopped, Bob?'

'Because Marler has stopped. Nield has stopped. And both of them are here on foot.'

'We'll get out and see what's happening.'

'Tweed,' Paula asked, 'could you hand me my fleece? I bet it's like Siberia outside.'

The mist swirled around them as they alighted. To Paula, for a moment, she thought ghosts were materializing out of the mist. Then she saw they were Marler and Nield. Marler spoke first in his normal way – calm, terse, cooler than the mist floating everywhere.

'I thought we were close to that old suspension bridge. I spotted an old farm gate with a crumbling tarmacadam track behind it. I'm sure this is the back way to the château. Don't be startled – you will hear a grinding engine starting up. Butler found behind the gate a huge excavator with one of those big scoops in front. The machine was padlocked but he said he'd get that open in a tick – and the fuel gauge shows a full tank. There, hear it?'

The question was superfluous. They all heard the grinding noise of heavy machinery starting up. At first it started, stopped, started again. Then it got into its stride and was a steady humming sound, broken at regular intervals by heavy metal thumping the ground.

'May I ask what is happening?' Tweed enquired. 'It's making enough racket to wake the dead. If there is anyone inside the château it will be like a cavalry charge announcing our arrival.'

'Do you really expect to find anyone inside?' Marler asked.

'Well, no. Goslar has gone somewhere else. Always moving on.'

'It was Butler's idea,' Marler explained. 'Have you fogotten that landmine Burgoyne spotted, just in time, at the main entrance? Harry, in his youth, worked for a quarry firm. Used to operate a similar machine. He's testing the ground ahead of us while we drive behind him. Actually, it was an anti-personnel mine Burgoyne detonated. If the scoop he keeps hammering down hits one it will warn us.'

'I don't like that,' Paula said vehemently. 'It could kill Harry.'

'Harry says it wouldn't. It might mess up the scoop but he's sitting well back in the control cab. I suggest we get cracking. I'll drive behind the machine, Nield will drive his own car behind me, then Bob can bring up the rear with Tweed, Paula and Trudy as passengers. All systems go . . .'

347

Paula peered through the windscreen as they moved past the broken-down gate and started bumping over the potholed road. The mist cleared suddenly. She saw the side road curving and climbing up a steep hill with grassy fields on either side. The moon was casting a strong light and now she could see the château, perched by itself on the top of the ridge.

It was a large oblong four-storey building of no great beauty. It had a mansard roof peppered with tiny oval dormer windows, which looked in danger of sliding off at any moment. Paula observed that all the windows had their shutters closed, some of them tilted at an angle. It was an old hulk no one had bothered to preserve for many years. Stone steps led up to a terrace running the full length of the front of the château.

'Not a masterpiece,' she commented.

'I don't think Goslar is interested in fine architecture,' Tweed replied. 'Gargoyle Towers on Dartmoor was an ugly brute. He simply needs space and isolation to perfect his weapon. Now what is Harry doing?'

Butler had driven the machine more than halfway up the drive to the château. He had suddenly turned off the bumpy road, had steered the machine onto the grass. Getting out of the cab, he ran back to Nield's car, which stopped to let him climb into the front passenger seat.

'Harry,' Newman said, 'has decided – correctly, I'm sure – that they didn't lay any mines on this side of the drive. Soon, Tweed, you'll be opening the front door. What's the betting we find nothing inside?'

'I repeat, Goslar has to make a mistake sometime. So we make the most thorough search of this property.'

'I wonder where that helicopter went to,' Paula mused.

*

Leaning forward in the copilot's seat, Bancroft had observed everything from a distance. He was puzzled when he saw the convoy stop as it reached the bank of mist. Then he assumed they were being cautious. When the mist cleared he was even more puzzled – watching the large machine with the scoop rising and falling as it made its way up a drive leading to a château. He decided quickly when he saw the cars following it.

'That machine must be making one hell of a row. It will cover the sound of your engine. See that plateau halfway down the steep slope running from the side of the château? You could land me there, wait for me to come back.'

'Anything you say,' the pilot agreed wearily.

Still some distance from the château, he lost altitude, flying now about a hundred feet above the ground. Smoothly, he settled the chopper on the plateau, switched off his engine.

'Wait a minute,' he warned. 'Don't get out until I tell you. The rotor blades are dangerous.'

Given the word, Bancroft opened the door, dropped to the plateau. Before beginning his steep climb up the rest of the slope he took out his Smith & Wesson from its holster. He was armed with the .22 automatic model, which had a magazine capacity of ten rounds. More than enough to kill all of them.

I'll try and get Tweed last, he said to himself. Ram the muzzle inside his mouth and ask him where Goslar is before I pull the trigger. If Goslar himself is inside this place I'll use the same technique to make him tell me where the weapon is. This is where I win the battle. Then return to Washington. Karnow's dead. I'll be the next chief of Unit Four.

With these triumphant thoughts in his mind Bancroft increased the pace of his difficult climb up the slope. A short while later he reached the top. The side of the château lay before him.

36

By the time the three cars had parked under the terrace and turned off their engines, the pilot of the invisible helicopter below them had also switched off. A weird stillness descended, a silence broken only by their foot-steps as they mounted to the terrace.

Something about the atmosphere disturbed Paula. She looked up at the closed shutters, which did not invite entrance. Tweed was holding the bunch of keys Periot had given him, the largest one projecting, the key to the tall, wide double front doors. He pursed his lips, looked sideways, caught Butler's gaze.

'I don't think so,' he said.

'I can't see any giveaway wiring round them,' Butler replied, the beam of the torch in his left hand sweeping round the entrance's top, sides and bottom. 'But I still don't think this is the place to enter.'

'What do you suggest, then?'

'A window at the side,' Butler said firmly, pointing to his right.

'I see you've brought your tool kit.'

'Won't take me a moment to find a way in. Let's get on with it – if you agree.'

'I agree.'

'So do I,' Paula whispered to Tweed as Butler left them. 'Without my fleece I'd be a statue of ice. Lord, it's cold up here.'

'The mist is coming up behind us. What was that wind you mentioned, Bob?' Tweed asked.

'The Bise. Straight off Mont Blanc.'

'Oh, do stop reminding us,' Paula chided him as they followed Butler, who had disappeared round the side of the mansion. 'Are you warm enough, Trudy?'

'I'm OK,' Trudy assured her with a smile. 'In New York the temperature can drop out of sight in January. In February and March, too. This coat is fur-lined – and so are my boots. And can you tell me what Butler is doing?'

They had walked round the corner at the end of the mansion. A stone ramp led down from the terrace to ground level. Further along Butler was crouched down with Nield helping him. They had the shutters of a window open, pushed back against the wall. Butler was working a long steel bar, bevelled at one end, inserting it under a security lock.

'What is that tool?' Trudy asked.

'I think he calls it a jemmy,' Newman told her. 'It levers a lock open, often without leaving a trace.'

As he spoke Butler took hold of the lower sash, heaved it up until it was wide open. Between his teeth he held a pencil torch. Leaning forward, he peered inside, nodded to himself.

'He was checking for a trip-wire,' Newman explained. 'Or any other extra security device. Looks all clear.'

Butler had wriggled his burly body through the opening, vanished. Holding a Walther, the slimmer Nield followed him with ease. They waited a short time, then the lights came on inside the room. It was as per Tweed's earlier instruction given on the terrace.

'Switch on the lights in every room in the house, one by one.'

Trudy peered inside. She saw Butler, gun in hand, standing to one side of the door inside the large room while Nield stood on the other. They looked out, then Butler disappeared. Nield followed him after thirty seconds. It was an operation which had been practised over and over again at the training mansion in Surrey.

'I'm going in now,' said Trudy.

Paula went in after her, followed by Newman who had been going to enter first. Tweed stood alone for a moment, listening. The mist had now reached the mansion, was swirling everywhere. He had cold droplets on his face. He climbed in, found Paula waiting for him.

'Look at it,' she exclaimed. 'Clean as a whistle. Even the wide window ledges have been washed down.'

'Goslar's trademark,' Tweed said and grunted.

'And this room was . . .' Paula began.

'The dining room, probably. With French windows at the back giving, I suspect, a panoramic view in daylight. You've noticed in that opposite wall one of those old-fashioned serving hatches?'

'Yes, so the kitchen must be behind that wall.'

Tweed turned back to the open window. Leaning out he took hold of a shutter, pulled it to. As soon as he let go it swung open again. He pulled a face.

'So we can't do anything about that.'

'They've switched on more lights. Let's explore.'

She swung round, aiming her Browning as she heard a noise outside the open window. Marler appeared, holding his Armalite in his right hand, his left raised in a salute. He grinned.

'Don't shoot. I'm just delivering the milk. Actually, I was checking all round the house. Quite a walk. All shutters firmly closed. Back door locked.'

'You gave me a shock,' Paula chided him. 'Don't do that again.'

'I don't like leaving that window open, but there's nothing we can do about it,' said Tweed. 'Let's see what the others are up to.'

Marler had already disappeared after Butler and Nield. Gazing cautiously round the open door, as she had been trained to do, Paula saw Butler pressed against a wall, peering upwards. She walked into what she realized was a vast hall with the double entrance doors leading from the terrace in the middle of the far wall. Nield was crouched a few yards beyond Butler, also staring up. She caught up with Trudy, who was gazing up over Butler, who had now dropped into a crouch.

She was looking up a grand curving staircase which split into two at a landing halfway up. No carpets anywhere. Not a single stick of furniture. Not even a film of dust. She whispered to Tweed, 'It's eerie. It's so incredibly clean. No dust even. Like a haunted house.'

'Goslar's trademark,' he repeated. 'I'm willing to bet there's not one single fingerprint in the whole place. As to dust, it's high up, so far from any traffic on the road miles below.'

'And our footsteps don't make the slightest sound. I find that eerie too.'

She was referring to the fact that everyone had rubber soles on their footwear. Even Trudy's boots were rubber-soled. Newman opened a door, reached in, switched on the light. As Paula had guessed, it was the kitchen, a large room without any equipment. Tweed pointed to dents in the wooden floor.

'Things like the fridge and freezer and cooker stood there – and were taken away. Goslar leaves nothing which might give us a clue.'

Tweed walked round, looking down, looking up. Newman shrugged in exasperation.

'Just so long as we don't find another bloody pair of useless gloves.'

They explored a huge drawing room leading off the hall which had a polished woodblock floor. Here there were wall lights – ancient lanterns which threw a soft glow over the room. While they explored more rooms

Marler had taken up station at the bottom of the wide staircase, his eyes never leaving the curving landing high up.

'Ah!' said Tweed as they opened another door, turned on lights. 'I would say this was the library. Obvious remark.'

He was referring to bookcases which lined the walls from ceiling to floor. They had glass-fronted doors and Tweed quickly walked along, peering into all of them with Paula behind him. She sighed audibly.

'They've even carefully washed the shelves behind the bookcase doors. You were hoping for something here, weren't you?'

'Yes – and no. Where have you been, Newman?'

'Enjoying myself – checking the toilets. Old-fashioned but very clean. We'd better look at the upstairs, although it will be a waste of time.'

'Wait in the hall while Pete and I take a shufti,' ordered Butler, using the odd Arabic word.

Trudy, standing with the others in the hall, was fascinated at what happened next. Nield went up first, slowly, his left hand on the banister. Several treads behind him Butler followed, keeping to the wall side, staring up all the time, like Nield. Both men had guns in their hands.

They reached the landing, which had stone pillars at intervals, opened several doors, switched on lights. Then they gestured for the others to follow. Trudy skipped up the many treads like a young fawn. Paula was impressed by her agility, followed her and went inside a huge bedroom. Trudy came out, passing her.

'Not a damned thing. The door in the wall leads to the bathroom. In case you feel like a bath.'

Left to herself, Paula walked slowly, looking at the floor, at the wide window ledges, at the chandelier light which was suspended from the ceiling. She opened the side door, saw the point of Trudy's joke. There was a toilet and an enormous old-fashioned bath with claw legs. She went back into the bedroom, started walking along the edges of the room. Her foot caught something.

Bending down, she saw the floor had dropped slightly from the skirting board, leaving a gap. Slightly protruding, something glittered, the something which her shoe had brushed against. She eased it out, stood up as Tweed entered. She looked at him.

'I've found something. Goslar's first mistake, maybe.'

'What is it?'

'Looks like a large piece of tortoiseshell. Here you are.'

Tweed took it from her, sat down on a window ledge. Placing what she had given him in his lap, he took off his horn-rims, polished them on a clean handkerchief, put the horn-rims back on the bridge of his nose. Then he picked up her discovery, studied it, held it up to the light.

'It doesn't look like normal tortoiseshell. Remember what Cord Dillon told me? Some rumour about Goslar visiting the Galapagos Islands, stealing several giant turtles. This is a very unusual piece. Turtles,' he repeated. 'Then the fisherman with the distinctive sail on his boat who saw them. Later he was found murdered in Guayaquil, the port in Ecuador on the South American mainland.'

'Just rumours I thought Cord Dillon told you.'

Tweed held up the specimen Paula had discovered.

'This isn't a rumour.'

When Bancroft reached the top of the slope he saw, almost opposite him, the open window with the shutters thrown back. He listened carefully before easing his way into the lighted room. His right hand held the Smith & Wesson. He stood still, listened again. He heard creaking boards above him.

Goddamnit! he thought. If they're all upstairs – scattered in different rooms – they're the perfect target . . .

He peered into the vast hall. Empty. Quietly he checked all rooms downstairs. Empty. For the second time he looked up the great staircase leading to the landing. Empty. He began walking up the long curving staircase slowly, his gun by his side. He was two-thirds of the way up when he took the precaution of looking up at the landing again. Trudy appeared from behind a pillar near the top of the staircase, automatic in her hand.

She stared down at Bancroft, her face a frozen mask. Bancroft stared back at her. Normally he'd have raised his weapon at once, but he was in shock. His voice was hoarse and quiet when he spoke.

'Trudy! What the hell are you doing here with these people?'

'Do you remember Walter Jewels Baron?' she asked in a whisper.

'Who?'

'You drove to a small town in Virginia. To two houses on their own just outside the town. On a mission. To kill Walt Baron, accountant to Unit Four. You greeted him amiably. Then you rammed the muzzle of your gun inside his mouth, blew off the back of his head. I was his wife. I am his widow . . .'

Bancroft started to elevate his gun. She fired her first shot. It hit him in his right shoulder. He dropped his own weapon. It clattered down the stairs. His left hand grabbed the banister. She fired again. The bullet entered his stomach. He doubled over in agony, groaning. She fired six more times in rapid succession, emptied the

356

magazine. Both his arms jerked up. Already dead, he toppled backwards down the stairs, slithering down the last few treads. The others had just rushed out on to the landing when his corpse reached the hall floor.

37

Newman drove along the bumpy road from the château, stopped close to the broken-down gate leading to the highway. Paula, who had had a word with Marler before leaving the terrace, sat next to him. In the rear seats Tweed had Trudy beside him. Now they waited for the other two cars to join them.

'What happened to it?' Trudy asked.

'It,' said Tweed quietly, 'is being put in a place where no one will find it for ages. Probably ever.'

By 'it', Paula knew Trudy was referring to Bancroft's body. Marler had told her they had discovered the ideal place – a septic tank in the back garden, the lid half-covered with grass. Butler had prised the lid off and, with Nield's aid, they were dropping the corpse inside the tank before replacing the lid. Paula thought it was a suitable resting place for Bancroft.

'You will never hear a word about him again,' Tweed assured his redheaded companion.

Trudy's hands were shaking. She clasped them together. Her face was ashen. Reaching down between his feet, Tweed unzipped a small canvas bag, produced a flask, a spoon, a carton of sugar. Taking the top off, he carefully poured tea into it, relieved to see it was steaming. The flask had been wrapped in cloths to keep the contents hot – and the weather in Annecy had helped.

He used the spoon to add sugar from a carton to the tea. He stirred it, then turned to Trudy.

'Drink some of this. Sweetened tea is the best thing when you are in shock.'

She grasped the plastic cup with both hands. It wobbled. Tweed placed a hand underneath it to help her from spilling it. At first she sipped, then she began to drink mouthfuls. She emptied the cup and handed it back.

'Thank you so much. That really is much better.'

'You've kept that a secret,' Paula accused him, twisting round in her seat. 'Where did that come from?'

'Just before we left the Richemond I visited the chef in his kitchen. He was most obliging. Even supplied the canvas bag. I kept it for an emergency.'

'I think I rank as an emergency,' Trudy said, turning to him with a hint of a smile. 'Any more for the fake invalid?'

He gave her another cup. This time she was able to cope with it by herself. Paula saw colour beginning to return to her face. Trudy winked at Paula, who was surprised at how swiftly Trudy was returning to her normal self.

'My hair's a mess,' Trudy decided.

She began to ferret in her bag. Paula gave her a comb and a pocket mirror. Trudy looked sideways at Tweed before she started work.

'Do excuse me. I wouldn't normally do this in public.'

'But we're not public,' Tweed replied. 'We're your friends.'

'I do know that – and I do appreciate it . . .'

She used her hand and the comb to bring order back to her blazing red mane. Handing back comb and mirror to Paula, she sighed deeply.

'Thanks. Now I feel half-civilized. And the mist is returning.'

A white fog shrouded the car. A few minutes later they heard the cars from the château crawling down behind them, stopping. Marler jumped out and Tweed lowered his window. Glancing at Trudy, Marler turned away from her so only Tweed could see his movement. He gave the thumbs-up sign. They had disposed of the body. He leaned in.

'So what next?'

At that moment Tweed's mobile started to buzz. He was taking it from his pocket when Newman spoke urgently.

'Burgoyne?'

'Hello,' Tweed said.

'Arthur here,' a familiar voice answered. Beck. 'I am a trifle nervous, knowing the instrument you are using. I'm speaking from a public phone box. How long before you get back here?'

'At a rough guess, one hour.'

'Well, you'll find Harrington, Minister of General Security, waiting for you at the Richemond. He knows you're staying there. I heard him saying at reception that his friend, Tweed, was staying here, and asking for his room number. The trainee receptionist told him. I complained to the manager. No sign of that receptionist now. He's been given his marching orders. The Richemond prides itself on its discretion.'

'"Friend"!' Tweed snorted. 'When did the bastard arrive?'

'On a late-morning flight from London. I shouldn't say it, but I do not like him.'

'He's the man they invented the word *arrogant* for. Thanks for the warning. Anything else?'

'Yes. I should have put this first. I have three different prospects for properties you're interested in. Won't give you them over the phone. Any luck down there?'

'One or two interesting events. Tell you later. Where can I meet you?'

'I'll stay in the lobby at the Richemond until you arrive. Take care.'

Tweed put his phone back in his pocket. Newman turned round to face him.

'Who is the bastard?'

'The Right Honourable Aubrey Courtney Harrington, who has arrived in Geneva and is waiting to see me. That I could do without at this vital stage. I could do without it at any time.'

'I wonder how he knew you were in Geneva?' Paula speculated.

'My guess is that Bate, in that underground garage and before he was killed, phoned His Lordship to report where he was – where I was. My first task when we get back is to get Harrington out of Geneva. To anywhere. Singapore would be a good idea.'

'Anything else?' asked Newman.

'Yes. The important thing. Beck has located three properties, any of which might be occupied by Goslar.'

'So how do you decide which is the right one?'

'Frankly, I have no idea.'

Marler had remained by the open window, listening to every word. He started stamping his feet, clapping his gloved hands together. Then he spoke.

'I don't trust the route back to Geneva. I know we haven't heard from Burgoyne, but he may have walked into something he couldn't handle. So I suggest the same driving sequence. I go in front – with Butler at my side – and in the car behind me Nield drives. You bring up the rear. It's worked so far.'

'Agreed,' said Tweed, 'if that's all right with you, Bob.'

'Marler is right,' Newman agreed. 'They can just ease their cars past me and still stay on the drive. Let's get the show on the road.'

'You don't think we're going to run into trouble again?' Paula queried.

'No guarantees. And Marler's instinct for danger has

so often proved to be right in the past. We're not out of the wood yet.'

When the two cars had driven past on to the highway Newman followed. They had to crawl. The mist was now very dense and their foglamp beams penetrated only a few yards. Paula glanced back. Trudy had fallen fast asleep, her head resting on Tweed's shoulder. Tweed looked back at her, smiled briefly, raised his eyebrows. As much as to say, *what other choice do I have?*

38

They crawled on. Almost at once they reached the old suspension bridge and the mist thinned. Paula stared at the ancient structure, which looked unreal – with coils of mist curling round the cables. She glanced back. Trudy had opened her eyes, had seen where they were. At the place where a solitary Arab had come close to heaving her down into the bottomless valley. Paula could have sworn Trudy gave a little shrug with her elegant shoulders, shut her eyes, fell asleep again. Nerves of steel, Paula said to herself.

Within minutes the mist vanished. The moon shone down, illuminating the deserted highway ahead clearly. The three cars increased speed, drove on and on. All Newman had to do was to follow the red rear lights of Nield's car. He straightened up. His driving was becoming too automatic.

They had travelled some distance, but were still quite a way from Geneva, when it happened.

In Marler's lead car Butler had started to study a map, trying to locate where they were. He took out a glasses case, extracted a pair of horn-rims, perched them on his nose. Marler stared at him, then decided to comment.

'I didn't know you needed glasses.'

'Just for the small print,' replied Butler, embarrassed. 'I got them recently before we left London. I can easily read a novel without them, a newspaper. But it's the small print in the index of a map I find difficult.'

'You were wise to get them then.'

'Didn't like going to the ruddy optician. They make such a song and dance about it. To justify their fat fees, I imagine. The woman who saw me said map indexes are in four-point print. Very small. She told me novels are in ten- or twelve-point print. A bloody big difference.'

'Where are we, then?'

'No idea. That village we passed through didn't seem to have a name.'

'No villages round here. No sign of anyone. You'd think a meteor had wiped everyone off the surface of the planet.'

Marler's remark was apt. They were driving up a gentle hill. On their left hedges lined the highway and beyond them fields stretched away for ever. On their right a steep hill slope climbed. A few feet from the highway black stands of fir trees mounted the hill as though about to sweep down and overwhelm them. The moon illuminated the highway clearly – and the cars moving along it. Marler was driving at a moderate speed, remembering there were sudden sharp bends.

He arrived at one and slowed down further. He was rounding it when some kind of large animal scuttered across in front of him. He slowed almost to a stop. The animal vanished under the hedge to their left. The bullet hit his bonnet, ricocheted off at an angle. If Marler hadn't slowed for the animal Butler would have been killed.

Marler switched off engine and headlights, grabbed his Armalite, was out of the car as Butler left on his own side. Marler called out his order quickly.

'Sniper. In the trees. I'm going straight in from the road.'

'I'll make a wide circuit, try and get up behind him.'

A second bullet whipped past Marler's shoulder just before he had plunged up the hill, into the trees. Behind them Nield realized what was happening, pulled up, switched off his own engine and headlights.

Newman had also stopped, had taken the same precautions. Behind him Trudy woke up, totally alert. She already had her automatic in her hand. Tweed stared at her.

'I heard a bullet hit something metallic, probably Marler's car,' she said. 'I'll give them a hand.'

'You will please stay exactly where you are,' Tweed told her in a kindly tone. 'They can deal with it.'

He was startled for the second time by Trudy's quicksilver reaction. The first time had been when he stood on the landing at the château. Bancroft's body had already hit the hall floor, was tumbled in an untidy heap. Obviously as dead as dead can be. *Trudy, at the top of the staircase, had extracted the empty magazine, inserted a fresh one.* Most professional.

'They were heading up the bank on the right side,' Newman warned. 'We'll get out of the car and shelter behind it, crouched down. Tweed, Paula, don't get out on your side. Wriggle your way over to the left and join us.'

Marler, who had caught a glimpse of a flash from the forest when the first bullet arrived, was slowly advancing up between the tree trunks. He held his Armalite at the high port, ready for a moment when he could shoot very fast. Butler had vanished some way over to his right.

Butler was circling as he climbed. Shafts of moon-light shone on the ground between the trees. He was avoiding stepping on last year's dried leaves – crumbling them could announce his presence. Instead, he trod on cushions of moss, silent as a phantom. He heard the sound of running water to his right, moved towards it.

A narrow stream gushed down, tumbling over rocks, some of them flat, acting as stepping stones. He crossed over to the far side, then continued climbing, following the course of the stream. Its sound would muffle his steady upward approach. He was aiming to reach the top of the hill, his Walther held in his hand.

The nearer he came to the top the more moonlight flooded through. He began to move faster, his head swivelling to his left. He was worried about Marler, who had to be moving up towards a head-on collision with the sniper. It was cold inside the dank forest, but he welcomed the cold – it gave an extra edge to his alertness. He was thankful when the stream's course moved to his left, closer to where the sniper had to be hiding.

He reached the summit unexpectedly. Beyond the forest a great panorama of the French countryside spread away for miles. Still crouching, he began to make his way along the top of the ridge, then he stopped. His eye had caught movement lower down, below him.

Stationed behind a tall tree was a squat shadowy figure. It was holding a rifle loosely, muzzle pointing upwards. Butler now moved very slowly, downwards, treading always on moss. He was close to the squat figure when he became alarmed. Marler was climbing slowly up towards it, obviously couldn't see the squat sniper. Butler did not panic. He kept moving down-wards, watching where he placed his feet. The sniper suddenly came alive, raised his rifle to his shoulder, held it steady. Butler guessed he had Marler in the cross-hairs of his weapon.

He aimed the muzzle of his Walther within a foot of the back of the sniper's head, pressed the trigger. The squat man fell forward, half his head blown away, a cloth dangling from what was left of the head. Butler bent down, took hold of an end of the cloth untainted with blood, pulled it free. It was a green headband.

'Why they're so keen on green I wouldn't know,' Butler remarked.

'You saved me there,' Marler told him. 'I couldn't see him. Now where are you going?'

Butler, still holding the end of the headband, walked across to the stream, dropped it in. He watched it caught up in a swirl of water, washed down way out of sight. Then he straightened up, looked at Marler.

'All in a day's work. Do we have to move the body?'

'No point.' Marler paused. 'You realize he thought he was shooting Tweed when that first bullet hit the bonnet?'

'Why would he think that?'

'He'd have been given a vague description. You sat beside me wearing those horn-rims – so like Tweed's.'

'I'll have to change the frames,' Butler ruminated. 'I just took the nearest ones to get out of the place.'

Newman, by himself, met them as they emerged from the forest. He had a grim expression. He listened while Marler explained in a few words what had taken place.

'I don't think I'll mention to anyone it was an Arab,' he decided. 'Trudy is holding up amazingly well but she's gone through enough already for one day. We'll just say "a sniper", and leave it at that.'

'I think you underestimate her,' said Tweed, who

had appeared behind Newman. 'Now I think we'd better get on back to Geneva. I'll need a stiff drink before I manipulate Harrington.'

'What happened?' asked Trudy as Newman got behind the wheel while Tweed settled in beside her.

'A sniper,' Tweed said. 'Just one. Goslar is artful. This morning we had a massed attack. Didn't work. So this time he uses a solitary sniper. Marler and Butler dealt with him.'

'Was it another Arab, then?' she pressed.

Newman turned round to look at her. Tweed suppressed a smile before answering.

'Yes, it was.'

'It looks to me as though Goslar has already decided that he can get the biggest price for his weapon from that Arab state where the fundamentalists have taken over,' she remarked. 'Hence the ease with which he can get hold of Arabs to attack us.'

'You could be right.'

Inwardly Tweed was admiring the way she had hit the nail on the head. Her supposition exactly fitted in with his own private reading of the situation. Newman had already started driving again, keeping up with Nield, who was pressing his foot down.

'We didn't get any warning from Burgoyne,' Trudy went on.

'Not surprising,' Tweed explained. 'The sniper would have been informed we were in three cars. I think he was after me, probably. You've seen the way Burgoyne drives. The sniper would see one car only coming at speed – I doubt if the mist was about then. Therefore Burgoyne wouldn't have been the sniper's target – assuming in any case that he'd have a cat's chance in hell of hitting him.'

'And I imagine by now Serena will have arrived at the Richemond,' Trudy continued. 'I suppose she and

366

Burgoyne will get there about the same time in their separate cars.'

She does cover the waterfront, thought Paula, approvingly. I'd expect her to be exhausted after what happened inside the château.

'I think Serena will arrive ahead of Burgoyne,' Tweed commented. 'I sensed that when she drives she goes like the wind. In any case, she wouldn't be checking ambush points – which in places would slow Burgoyne down.'

'Would it be a good idea to phone her? I think she wasn't in the best of moods when she left us.'

'Good idea,' agreed Tweed.

He had to dial three times before he got through to the Richemond. Paula glanced back. Trudy had fallen asleep again, her head on Tweed's shoulder. The best medicine for her, Paula thought.

'Am I speaking to reception at the Richemond? Good, I'm staying with you. Tweed speaking. Can you tell me whether another guest, Serena Cavendish, has arrived yet?' He cleared his throat. 'She has. Can I speak to her? What was that? Did you say she has reserved her suite for seven weeks? She has. And now she's left the hotel? Thank you.'

'That,' said Paula slowly, 'that arrangement has strange echoes for me. She can't possibly need that amount of time for taking pics of some fashion do. Yes, it definitely has echoes.'

39

Inside the circular laboratory with its conical roof Dr Goslar wore whites. The third canister, which for many hours had slowly filled with drips from the glass tube suspended above it, was now full. A hand carefully placed an airtight lid over the top.

There was enough of the deadly liquid inside the three canisters to destroy seventy-five million people. Maybe far more. Two hands, wearing surgical gloves, grasped the latest canister, lifted it, placed it alongside two more filled canisters resting on a tiled table top. They were now a distance away from the ancient chimney-like structure elevated thigh-high above the floor. It was necessary for the contents of the third canister to cool a little before being transported. The cooling process would take a while.

The figure's feet were clad in close-fitting slippers made of polystyrene, this material protected with a hygenic covering composed of the same cloth as the surgical gloves. Slippered feet shuffled back to where the third canister had stood, a hand closed a tap at the end of the glass tube where liquid had dripped from it.

The feet then shuffled over to where the Norman-style window in the large turret was let into the stone-work. Goslar stared out into the moonlit night. More snow was falling. Beyond and below the flakes the moon illuminated the steep slope running down to the distant lake. Ice rimming the shore had now spread further out and the lake's surface, at this point, looked like mottled glass.

Goslar walked slowly away from the window, approached the elevated mouth of the chimney which heated the room. Heat rose from the crackling flames burning thirty feet down. Removing the surgical gloves, Goslar bent down to where three small logs perched against the chimney. The logs were lifted, one by one and dropped down inside the opening, which was six feet in diameter. The fire flared up.

Tucking the gloves, which had been held under an armpit, into the pockets of the gown, Goslar left the room, opening a heavy door, stepping carefully down the stone steps of the circular staircase – after closing the heavy door – and reached the living room at the next level down.

Goslar sank back onto a sofa, legs crossed, gazing at the luminous screen of a TV set which was turned on permanently. Soon there would be a weather forecast. The figure checked its watch. The timetable had to be adhered to. One important factor had been built into it. The time taken to drive to the airport with the canisters, carefully packed inside special containers.

40

Tweed and his team arrived back in Geneva without encountering any further hostile action. The street lamps' reflections were glowing in the still waters of the Rhône. The city was quiet, with very little traffic. They arrived outside the Richemond.

'All peace ceases now,' Tweed warned.

He was right. As he walked into the large lobby with Paula and Newman, a slim man, over six feet tall, impeccably dressed in the most expensive suit, stood up from a sofa and strode forward with a smaller man a step behind him. That's right, Tweed thought, keep one step behind your master.

The Rt. Hon. Aubrey Courtney Harrington towered over Tweed, looked down his long nose at him. His grey hair was perfectly coiffeured, his nails were perfectly manicured, his lean hungry face was perfectly shaved. Paula smelt powder on his pugnacious jaw. His long, lean face had a bleak expression.

'In here, Tweed.' He gestured as he might towards a child. 'I have reserved a private room. Only Adrian Diplock, my assistant, will also attend.'

He gestured towards the smaller man behind him, who had ferret eyes. Harrington had totally ignored Paula and Newman. Very erect, he went towards a closed door. Tweed went in another direction, on his way upstairs. Diplock ran, caught him up.

'The Minister wishes to see you *now.*'

'Get lost,' said Newman.

'Where the hell do you think you are going?' demanded Harrington, catching up with them.

'I am going up to my suite,' Tweed began quietly, still walking. 'I am going to have a shower, a drink and a snack before I come down again. It has been quite a day.'

'I have been waiting *hours* while you have been off gallivanting God knows where,' Harrington snapped.

'I don't think you'd have enjoyed what you termed our gallivanting,' Tweed informed him. 'My guess is you'd have been scared witless.'

'The Minister expects you to confer with him at once,' Diplock explained in his soft upper-crust voice. He laid a hand on Tweed's arm. 'I would comply with his wishes if I were you.'

Newman jerked the hand roughly away from Tweed's arm. He was very angry.

'Touch him again and I'll break your arm,' he growled.

370

Diplock took a step back. He was frightened and couldn't think how to handle the situation. And Harrington had seen the fiasco.

'In about an hour,' said Tweed. 'Now, I'm off.'

Beck appeared from nowhere as Tweed was entering his suite. Tweed ushered him inside, indicated to Paula and Newman that they should join him. After consulting everyone he called room service.

'We want scrambled eggs for three people. One double Scotch, two brandies and soda. If you could get the drinks and the food up fairly quickly I would much appreciate it.' He put down the phone. 'Do sit down, Arthur. I'm sorry we have been so long. And thank your lucky stars you have hardly any government in Switzerland.'

'I've already encountered – yes, that's the word – your Minister,' Beck explained from the comfort of a sofa. 'But first things first.' He got up as Paula was about to sit down, hugged her, kissed her on both cheeks. 'Welcome to Geneva.'

'Thank you, Arthur. It's always good to see you.'

Those two always get on well together, thought Tweed. From the moment they first met, which is nice. He looked at Paula.

'How is Trudy? I didn't have time to have a word with her when that bear advanced on me.'

'I did. She's very tired. She said she might just flop into bed. I told her she should. She's in good spirits.'

'I'm relieved.' Tweed looked at Beck. 'Arthur, you have the floor.'

Beck, slimly built, about Newman's height, had grey hair and a trim moustache. His eyes were alert, as always, his manner courteous. He had a high forehead and his personality exuded dynamic energy. The Chief of Federal Police was a man they all felt comfortable with.

'The first thing,' he began in his fluent English, 'will be a shock. There's a strong rumour – which I think is reliable – that Ali, the head of the coup which took over an important Arab state, is paying Goslar three hundred billion pounds for the weapon.'

'Billion?' echoed Paula. 'Sure you don't mean million?'

'*Billion*,' Beck repeated. 'And pounds – not dollars. The price of oil may have dropped but he has oil gushing out of his ears. He can easily afford such a gargantuan sum.'

'So the weapon,' Tweed remarked, 'must be ready for delivery – or almost ready.'

'I think you are right. Time has run out. There's more. I know through confidential sources that one hundred billion has already been deposited in the Zürcher Kredit Bank – to be made available the moment the weapon reaches Ali.'

'Time is running out, then.'

'I'd say time *has* run out.'

'Is that Grumman jet still at Cointrin?' As Tweed asked the question Paula detected a note of anxiety in his voice. 'I mean is it still waiting on the tarmac?'

'It is. Still being attended to with nonstop mainten-ance. And a twenty-four-hour roster of crew ready to take off at any time.'

'Can't you stop it? Fake some regulation?' Tweed pressed.

'Sorry, but, as you know, Switzerland is a neutral country. There is no reason I can think of to have the machine impounded. Heaven knows I've tried.'

'I understand, Arthur. Can we turn to another subject? You told me on the phone you had traced three likely properties Goslar may be occupying.'

'I had to twist the arms of certain estate agents, but I twisted hard.' Beck picked up an executive case he had brought into the suite. He took out three folders, handed one to Tweed. 'There's a brochure of the property inside. It's a big old mansion just outside Montreux. Rented for a year by an American, a Mrs Jefferson.'

'How long has she been there?'

'Eleven months. Her husband is a millionaire banker in New York. I checked that. There is a banker called Jefferson in New York.'

'This doesn't seem at all likely. Montreux is too far from the airport here. And I don't detect Goslar's pattern of behaviour.'

'This one,' Beck said, producing another folder, 'is a palatial villa in Vevey, not too far this side of Montreux, as I'm sure you know. Rented by a Professor Gastermann. Supposedly a successful owner of hypermarkets in the Far East. Couldn't trace much data on him.'

'Rented for how long?'

'Two years. He's been living there for eighteen months.'

'Very doubtful,' said Tweed, scanning the brochure. 'Again, too far from the airport. Again, not Goslar's behaviour pattern. He rents for a long period, then disappears overnight – long before the lease is up.'

'Last one, then. The Château Rance. Built ages ago by an eccentric Swiss banker. A weird place,' he went on, handing the brochure to Tweed, 'looks like a castle – not your idea of one. It's up in the mountains behind Geneva. Rented for two years by a Mr Arnold Aspinall. Lease started two months ago. Very isolated. Behind a village called Le Brassus – at one end of the Lac de Joux.'

'Charterhouse, Gargoyle Towers, Masterson, Château de l'Air, now Aspinall,' Tweed said half to himself.

'Pardon?' queried Beck.

'Just talking to myself. How long to drive from Château Rance to the airport?'

'Roughly three-quarters of an hour. Might be a bit longer just at the moment. There's been yet another heavy fall of snow.'

'I like the look of this, Arthur.' Tweed was examining the brochure carefully. 'Weird-looking, as you say. Has a big turret at one corner. Bizarre architecture. Anyone ever seen our Mr Aspinall?'

'I phoned a friend I have in Le Brassus. He said no one had ever laid eyes on the occupant. But after dark all the lights are on. They are tonight.'

'It's him! I can smell him,' Tweed said with the nearest to excitement Paula had ever witnessed. 'What do you think, Bob?'

'Sounds like our man to me,' Newman agreed. 'Isolated. Chap never seen. Within driving distance of the airport.'

The food and drinks arrived at that moment. The waiter, at Tweed's request, gave each of them separate tables. Tweed gave the waiter a generous tip. They began eating immediately. Within five minutes their plates had been scooped clean.

'What's the drill now?' Newman asked.

'Get rid of Harrington first. Then we'll drive up to Le Brassus. I suppose you couldn't guide us to the area, Arthur?'

'My pleasure. I'll go down and get my car brought round. I'll be waiting when you're ready. Take your time. One thing I haven't mentioned. I've posted a man outside all three properties. At any sign someone is leaving I'll hear on my mobile. So take it easy . . .'

374

'I'm going to have the quickest shower of my life,' Tweed decided. As he spoke he was gathering new clothes from his case. 'Give me seven minutes.'

'I'm doing the same,' said Paula as Tweed vanished into the bathroom.

'Me too,' said Newman, leaving the room.

Paula was about to follow when the phone rang.

As she picked up the phone she could hear Tweed's shower running behind the closed door. She hoped she'd be able to take a message.

'Hello,' she said.

'Urgent call from the United States,' the operator told her. 'From a Mr Cord Dillon.'

'Put him on . . . Hello there, Cord. Paula speaking. Tweed is in the shower. Can I pass on a message?'

'Sounds like you,' the familiar gruff voice said. 'Where were we when you saved my life in London?'

'Albemarle Street. I'd just come out of Brown's . . .'

'OK. Sorry to be so wary. Tweed asked me to vet Trudy Warner. I have done so. Her history equates exactly with what he told me. She was married to a Walter Jewels Baron. Accountant to Unit you-know-what. Her husband was murdered in their house. Out in the sticks in Virginia. Killer never found. She left overnight for New York, got a job with a big security agency. OK so far?'

'It equates.'

'Spoke to the boss of the security outfit. With them two years. The boss praised her ability to the moon. She meets Vance Karnow at a party. He's impressed, hires her as a member of the Unit. She's a big asset there. Oh, going back a bit, to Virginia. She has a sister in San Francisco. I spoke to her. Sister had a plea from Trudy – if anyone enquires about me, say I was there but then went to Seattle. To me she sounds to be quite something. Oh, she's British. Only in the States because she met the guy who became her husband. OK so far?'

'It still equates.'

'Karnow is dead now. Some business about being caught up in an explosion in Geneva, triggered by terrorists. Karnow took a heavy mob with him to Paris. I hope Trudy is OK?'

'She is, Cord. She's sleeping in a room here in the hotel I'm in.'

'On that vetting I'd pass her one hundred per cent. OK? Must get moving now.'

'Thank you so much, Cord.'

Her reply was wasted. In typical American fashion he had suddenly broken the connection. Frowning, Paula put down the phone. What was going on? Why had Tweed vetted Trudy?

41

For two reasons Paula delayed telling Tweed about Dillon's call. The first was that when Tweed rushed out of the bathroom, fully dressed, he said he must call Burgoyne. The second was that when the call was over the others arrived, filing into the suite. Newman, Marler, Butler, Nield and – to her great surprise – Trudy.

'Is that reception?' Tweed asked on the phone. 'Could you put me through to a friend of mine, also staying here, Alan Burgoyne.'

'I'm sorry, sir,' the receptionist replied, 'but Mr Burgoyne went out a while ago. He said he was going to the Old Town on the other side of the Rhône.'

'Thank you.'

Tweed put down the phone, looked round, thanked

everyone for being ready so promptly. He then relayed to them the information about Burgoyne.

'I can guess where he's gone,' Marler said. He phrased his next words carefully, probably because Trudy was in the room. 'He'll have gone to meet my friend, the one who supplies me with extras. My friend recently moved his address.'

Everyone except Trudy knew what he meant. He was referring to the Swiss who dealt in illegal arms – for an extortionate price – under cover of running an antique shop. To her credit, Trudy did not ask what 'extras' Marler was referring to.

'So now we know where he is,' Tweed said briskly. 'Time to go down and confront Lionheart. Lord of All He Surveys. Paula, Bob, I'd like you both to come with me. The rest of you relax. We shall not be long.'

Reaching the ground floor, they found Diplock pacing nervously back and forth in front of the closed door, hands clasped behind his back. He straightened up as they approached, opened the door for Tweed, who paused in the entrance.

Diplock tried to assume an air of authority. He made a mess of it. Tweed noticed he had thick dark eyebrows which didn't match his fair hair. The lad can't be more than twenty-five, he thought.

'I'm afraid you can't go in, miss,' Diplock said to Paula.

He lifted a hand to touch her arm, to restrain her. Then he caught Newman's expression, remembered what had happened when earlier he had touched Tweed's arm. He withdrew his hand as though it had landed on something very hot.

'They are both coming with me,' said Tweed and walked into a large room.

The Minister was seated in a tall hard-backed chair covered with tapestry which would have suited

Elizabeth I. In front of him was a massive antique desk with a single ordinary straight hard-backed and uncomfortable-looking chair, facing him. *Autocratic* was the word which came to Tweed's mind.

Harrington did not stand up. Instead he glared with his dark eyes at Paula and Newman. For a moment he pursed the thin lips on his wide mean mouth. Then he orated, as though at the despatch box in the House of Commons.

'I expected you to come along. You appear to have brought with you a delegation. We have to confer in private.'

Tweed glanced back. Paula and Newman had seated themselves on a long sofa. Close by, Diplock was perched on a more comfortable hard-backed chair – perched so far forward that had he moved no more than an inch he'd have ended up on the carpeted floor.

'Then why is Diplock here?' Tweed demanded, still standing.

'Adrian is my chief and confidential assistant.'

'Newman and Miss Grey are *my* chief and confiden-tial assistants. Either they stay or I'm leaving this room at once. And I do not like this chair.'

Saying which, Tweed removed the offending piece of furniture, replaced it with a comfortable armchair. He then sat upright in it, took off his glasses and proceeded to clean them on his handkerchief.

'Lord!' exclaimed Diplock. 'I forgot to lock the door. So sorry, sir.'

Jumping up, he produced a key from his pocket and locked the door. He was about to slip the key into his pocket when he found Newman beside him.

'I'll take that key, sonny boy.'

He took the key before Diplock could react. Then he returned to the sofa and sat down again.

'We'd better get on with it, whatever it is,' Tweed began. 'I have only five minutes to spare.'

'*Five minutes!*'

The Minister shoved back his chair, stood up to his full height and started walking back and forth behind the desk. He waved his arms high as he spoke, then circled them as though silencing a mob of hecklers.

'Do you realize who you are talking to? Do you not comprehend the rank I hold? As far as I am concerned this meeting may well go on for half the night. We have the most important matters of state to discuss, to explore and to delve deeply into all the possible contingencies which may be involved.'

Having finished his speech, Harrington pushed his chair back to its original position, sat down, stared at Tweed. Then he leaned back, folded his arms.

'I have it from the most confidential source, who shall remain nameless, that a certain state has offered Dr Goslar for his weapon the sum of three hundred billion pounds.'

'That news is gossip in the streets,' Tweed told him.

'So what, if I may be so bold as to ask, are you doing in Geneva – when my informants assure me Dr Goslar is hiding somewhere in the Paris region?'

'The trail to Paris sometimes leads via Geneva.'

Tweed was secretly amused. The opening he had been looking for had been offered to him on a plate, unknown to the Minister. It was at this monent that Harrington noticed Diplock was looking most unhappy. Paula, glancing at the assistant, thought Diplock reminded her of a child who had had his sweets stolen.

'Something wrong, Diplock?' the Minister enquired. 'Some aspect of what I have just said?'

'I'm supposed to be official key-holder,' the assistant complained.

'Well, we've changed roles, haven't we, Didlock,' Newman said amiably.

'Diplock. Adrian Diplock,' the assistant corrected furiously.

Didn't Lock, Paula said to herself. She had trouble keeping her expression neutral.

'Now, Tweed,' the Minister continued at his most pompous, 'you are saying that Dr Goslar has an association with Paris? That it is in the French capital we are most likely to lay our eager hands on him?'

'La Défense. Goslar has a long lease on an address there known to the locals as the Goslar Building. The lease is in the name of a company called Poulenc et Cie, registered in Liechtenstein.'

'Liechtenstein, by God!' Harrington smiled for the first time and Paula thought the smile far more nauseating than the man's normal icy demeanour. 'We appear to be moving towards a consensus. Which is the way all these matters of high state ought to proceed, I am sure you will agree. Liechtenstein – that has the ring of authentic Goslar accounting. Wouldn't you think so, Diplock?'

'Yes, sir. I most certainly would agree,' replied his assistant, leaning forward as though in the presence of a pasha.

'So the hunt is riding well – closing in on the fox. Eh, Tweed?'

'Let us just hope so.'

'Now, let us summarize.' The Minister leaned back, hands clasped behind his neck. 'Goslar has his lair in Paris. Under the noses of French security, which is clever. Why? Because the French security services are not known for their successes. Look at how they botched the Carlos business, let him shoot down their own men sent to arrest him. Carlos then vanishes into the ether – at that time, anyway. Goslar then leases one of those glorious skyscrapers.' His arms shot vertically into the air. 'Like wonderful New York. But no one ever sees him. Why? Because he's probably the doorman. By the by, Tweed, I have a fresh team arriving in Paris.'

Tweed had openly looked at his watch twice. Now, preparatory to flight, he was easing his chair further away from the desk.

'Incidentally,' he said, 'how did you know I was temporarily in this part of the world?'

'Bate phoned me, didn't he? Poor Bate. Probably from that underground garage here before the terrorists killed him.'

'So who will replace Bate?'

'Pardoe.' The Minister's lips curled. 'Honest Caspar Pardoe. Just back from attending some nonsensical security convention in the US of A.' He leaned forward, very stern now. 'So I can expect you to be on a mid-morning flight to Paris tomorrow. I'll be aboard.'

'All things being equal,' Tweed replied, standing up, 'I will be on a flight tomorrow.'

On a flight tomorrow – only Paula noticed the ambiguity of Tweed's phraseology. He had omitted the word 'Paris.'

'Just before you depart,' the Minister spoke, 'I suppose Dr Goslar is a man? The most presumptuous rumours have been circulating in certain quarters I have lent an ear to.'

'Goslar is a man – or a woman,' said Tweed.

42

'What a fool,' Paula said when Diplock had shut the door. 'But I did admire the way you handled him. He started off raving and we left him quietened down. Or, rather, you did.'

'The main thing,' Tweed said as they made their way back to his suite, 'is that I diverted his attention from Geneva and back to Paris.'

'And without telling a single lie. You really did dupe the idiot.'

They entered the suite and found the others listening to Trudy who was telling them about America. She stopped when Paula came to sit next to her, prior to their departure. Tweed had picked up the phone.

'Reception? I have a friend staying here. A Ms Serena Cavendish. Could you put me through to her?'

'I'm afraid she's not in the hotel, sir. I can see her key,' the night receptionist reported.

'Any idea when she might be back? Did she say when she left?'

'I gather your friend was in a hurry, sir.'

'But she has left her bag in her room,' Tweed persisted. 'There is something inside it which she is carrying for me.'

'I understand one bag was taken to her suite. Shortly afterwards, when she had been to her suite, she left, sir. I wouldn't worry. She will be coming back.'

'Thank you.'

'The night receptionist is very discreet,' Tweed commented. Then he relayed to everyone what he had been told. 'Although the receptionist didn't say so I gather she may not be back tonight.'

'You're very interested in her movements,' Paula said, fishing.

'She has been with us for a little while.' Tweed gazed into space as though he saw something. 'Yes, she has been with us. And now we must hit the road.' He looked at Marler, who had the long tennis racquet case by his side. 'I don't have to guess what's in there.'

'The Armalite.' Marler pointed to a large bulging canvas bag. 'Plus a variety of grenades. I've handed some of them out.'

'I've got a few,' Trudy said with a smile. 'In here.' She patted her shoulder bag. 'The Unit Four mob showed me how to handle them in training sessions.'

'You're coming with us?' asked Tweed, startled.

'I've been trying to talk her out of the idea,' Paula said. 'She has had enough for one day. Like talking to a brick wall.'

'And the brick wall *is* coming with you,' Trudy added with another smile.

'Then we'd better move right now,' Tweed decided. 'I must have a word with poor Beck, who has been waiting ages. Paula, come with me. You, too, Bob.'

Leaving the hotel was like walking into a vast refrigerator. Paula zipped her fleece to the collar. Beck was sitting in a Mercedes, studying a map. He was standing on the pavement when they reached him, the map spread out on the roof of his car.

'A thousand apologies, Arthur,' Tweed said. 'A blasted Minister kept us while he mouthed platitudes.'

'He does that,' Beck agreed. 'He tried to get information out of me about you. Ended up by calling me as close-mouthed as an unopened sardine can. I told him I didn't like sardines. Now, before I lead the way, I think the three of you should look at this map.'

'Where is this Château Rance?' Paula asked.

'There. Marked with a cross. We drive out of Geneva

383

and up a road into the mountains. We arrive at a point where we are on the far side of a high ridge and then descend into the Vallée de Joux. We reach a small town, Le Brassus, where I have a friend I want to call on. He knows the area well, owns a small hotel. From there we drive on to a beautiful little lake – little by Swiss standards – Lac de Joux. The Château Rance is perched high up by itself on a mountain overlooking the lake below. Arriving in the Vallée we have entered a secret world – invisible to anywhere else.'

'Promising,' Tweed commented. 'Sounds like Dr Goslar.'

'To reach the château,' Beck continued, 'without being seen we avoid the main drive up to the property. Instead we drive up a very steep road, sunk between high banks on either side, until we turn at the summit along a similar road. There is a natural layby where you can park your cars. At this point, where I will leave you, I fear it's a matter of hoofing it down the side of the mountain, but then you are immediately above the château. Some way below you, that is. I see you have boots. Good. What about the rest of your team – including that red-haired beauty?'

'All with boots,' Paula told him. She chuckled. 'Including that red-haired beauty. You always did have an eye for the ladies.'

'As a policeman I have to be observant,' Beck responded with a quizzical smile. 'Also I advise everyone to tuck their trouser tops inside their boots. There's been another heavy fall of snow up there. You don't want to be wet through when you reach your objective.'

'You could show us the entrance to this mountain road,' Tweed suggested, 'then we could drive up by ourselves. We are putting you to a lot of trouble.'

'Not at all. And if, by some twist of fate, you locate

Goslar, then you are serving the interests of Switzerland. Also I wish to consult my friend in Le Brassus, Gilbert Berger. He may have seen Goslar – if this Aspinall is Goslar.'

'I doubt that very much,' Tweed told him. 'No one has ever seen him, or her, so far.'

'I said I would show you the natural layby and leave you. Unfortunately I have no official reason to come with you to the château. And in this country it is a serious crime to invade private property. So have a care. Let us start now.'

Following Beck's Mercedes, they drove in the same sequence as before. Marler was in the lead car, close to Beck. Behind him Nield drove with Butler at his side. Newman gripped the wheel of the last car with Paula next to him while Trudy and Tweed occupied the rear seats.

After they had left the city behind and started climbing a steep road into the mountains Paula had a mixture of emotions. She was excited, her adrenalin was flowing, but she was apprehensive. They had come so far, experienced so much – so what if this expedition turned out to be a flop?

She turned round to look at the passengers behind her. Tweed was leaning back against his seat, his eyes closed, apparently asleep. Trudy, on the other hand, her trouser tops shoved inside her boots, gazed out of the window and was humming to herself. Trudy, you really are a cool customer, Paula thought.

They drove as quickly as they dared. Looking ahead, as the narrow road turned yet again, Paula saw the moonlight reflecting off a sheet of ice on the road. At least we have four first-rate drivers, she comforted herself. They drove higher and higher and now the snow on the banks on either side was deeper. What would it be like near Le Brassus?

Suddenly they reached the top. Through a gap in the bank on her side Paula caught a glimpse of faraway Lake Geneva, glowing in the moonlight, more like a sheet of glass. Then it was gone. They were moving *down* a steep incline. She began to look for Lac de Joux, then remembered Beck had said it was beyond Le Brassus – and damnit!, wake up. She had seen its location for herself on the map.

'We're going down into the Vallée,' Tweed called out.

'You're a fake,' she said, looking back, 'I thought you were fast asleep.'

'I felt the change of direction.'

'And now you're alert,' Trudy said sternly to Tweed, 'you'd better tuck your trousers inside your boots.'

'I always do as I'm told,' Tweed replied in a tone of resignation. He bent down and did what she had suggested. 'There. Satisfied?'

'Not really.' She reached a hand out and fitted inside his left boot a fold of trouser still exposed. 'I'll just have to keep an eye on you.'

In front Paula was having trouble suppressing a giggle. She had never known Tweed accept instructions so meekly.

The steep descent, twisting and turning, continued. They were going round a bend when the car started to skid. Paula gripped the door handle. Newman went with the skid, resumed control just before he went slap into the left-hand bank.

'That was skilful,' Paula said, laying a reassuring hand on his arm.

'That was stupid,' he replied. 'I realized some way back I should watch out for a light covering of snow masking ice beneath it. I must keep my mind on what

I'm doing. I was thinking about Burgoyne, how he would have driven this route. Like a bat out of hell, I suspect. And got away with it.'

'That reminds me,' Paula said, turning her head. 'Just before we left, Tweed, you dashed back inside the hotel. What was all that about?'

'I left a note for Burgoyne, giving him our route. So when he gets back, laden with goodies, he'll be able to follow us.'

'Bet he catches us up.'

The road had now levelled out and they were driving along the Vallée. To their right the mountain slope they had just negotiated reared up, with here and there an army of tall firs dusted with snow. The Vallée had a closed-in sensation, a secret world, and Paula tensed with anticipation. Trudy's reaction was rather different.

'What an oasis of peace,' she called out.

'Your peace may be shattered when we reach the Château Rance,' Tweed warned.

'Jonah!'

Leaning forward, Paula was just able to make out the lettering on the snow-covered sign. *Le Brassus.* Prosperous-looking houses appeared on either side of the road, houses with steep roofs to shed snow, with green shutters on the first floors, some still thrown back open. She guessed the windows had to be double-glazed, or with one closed window behind the other. They parked in a small square and she saw the sign on the side of a large attractive building. Hôtel Blanc. Lights blazed in all the windows and the other buildings surrounding the open area had shops, now closed, on their ground floors.

Beck was talking to a man outside the hotel as Paula alighted. The man came running forward, treading carefully in his boots. He held out a hand.

'I am Gilbery Berger. Do be careful. There is a lot of

ice and we have not yet salted it.' All this in English. 'Welcome to Le Brassus, Miss Grey.'

Berger was of medium height, well-built, in his forties and had a warm smile. He shook her hand.

'Now you come into my hotel. Have something warm to eat. Maybe a drink or two?' he suggested with a twinkle in his shrewd eyes. 'So this is Mr Tweed,' he went on as Beck arrived and introduced everybody. 'I hear great things about you from Arthur, Mr Tweed.'

'Wildly exaggerated, I am sure. And thank you for your most kind invitation, but we must hurry on to the château.'

'OK. Perhaps when you come back. I take you to see the Château Rance at Arthur's suggestion. This strange person who lives there. Aspinall. We never see this person. Do not even know if it is a man or a woman.'

'Aspinall must need supplies from here, surely? Groceries – all the things you need to keep you going?'

'You would think so.' Berger threw back his large head, laughed. 'No good for business, Aspinall. Refrigerated truck arrive from Geneva. Driver never see him. Goods delivered into cold store in great cellar. Paid for by cash – yes, cash! – sent to Geneva store by motorcyclist service. Most mysterious. You wish to go now? I am ready. I lead way in my big Volvo . . .'

Paula was sorry to leave Le Brassus so quickly. She would have liked to talk longer to Berger, who was so cheerful. And she liked the look of the small town. Solid-looking houses, some of wood, some with plaster walls, stood fairly close but still had ample space between them. As they drove off she saw more impressive houses perched on the mountain slope with a road leading up to them from Le Brassus. Then the town was behind them.

'I liked the look of the place,' said Trudy. 'One day I wouldn't mind coming back to it.'

'Me too,' Paula agreed.

With Le Brassus only a memory they were driving through a wilderness. The mountain slopes rose steeply, punctuated by isolated fir trees here and there. The moon shone down on the narrow Vallée, cold and remote, the warmth of the town's lights forgotten. When she least expected, Paula saw Lac de Joux come into view, a wider lake than she had imagined, ice sheets projecting from the shoreline. A few minutes later the cars stopped, Berger hurried back, warning Paula and Trudy that the road was slippery and they could fall so easily.

Paula walked a few paces. Her boots had deep perforations in the soles and they gripped the surface firmly. She thanked Berger for his concern, assured him she would be all right.

'I think you will,' he said with his broad smile. 'I watch you both walk and you have confidence. Now, I have parked near the gates to the drive, out of sight. Come with me and I will show you the Château Rance. Mr Tweed does stride like an atthelete.'

Tweed had gone ahead past parked cars to join Marler, Butler, Nield and Newman. They were standing at a point where the high snow bank blocking a view dipped. Beck, who had a pair of binoculars pressed to his eyes, handed them to Tweed.

'There it is. Those field glasses are the latest advance – from Zeiss in Germany. Excellent for night vision.'

Tweed altered the focus slightly. He scanned not only the château but also the surroundings. Noted that way below the mountain's summit, probably a couple of hundred yards above the château, a huge limestone crag projected out over the slope. Underneath it was a large dark hole. The château itself was quite a distance up the mountain slope and a curving drive, marked by large stones, led up to it, presumably from some entrance further along the road. He handed the binoculars to Paula.

'I see it clearly without field-glasses,' said Trudy, who had joined them. 'It's really weird. One huge turret with a window at the right-hand corner. Nothing to balance it on the left. A Gothic-like edifice – pseudo-Gothic.' She looked at Berger. 'I hope I'm not being rude.'

'Not at all.' He laughed. 'I listened to how you describe. It is a perfect picture you paint. I can say that?'

'Very idiomatic English,' Trudy assured him. 'I think it's creepy.'

'So do I,' Paula agreed as she lowered the glasses.

'You noticed all the lights are on,' Beck said to Paula. 'I can even see a glimmer behind the closed shutters. At all levels – which is strange if only one person is living there. But someone is there.'

'Where is the main entrance door?' Nield enquired.

'Immediately below that ugly balcony on the first floor,' Berger told him. 'I don't know what you are going to do.'

'Neither do I, until we get there and approach it from behind,' Newman admitted.

'The mountain road Beck tells me you take will muffle the sound of your engines,' Berger commented. 'It passes between very high steep banks.'

'There's a giant crag behind the château,' Tweed observed. 'Is that a cave underneath it?'

'Yes,' Berger told him. 'A very deep one I have heard. Round here the villagers call it the Cave of the Devil. I have no idea why.'

'One thing I don't like,' Beck said after scanning the mountain again, 'and something you should consider before we drive up that mountain road: so much snow has fallen recently – out of season, too – that there is an avalanche danger. I have a device in my car which registers the temperature outside it. I noticed that the temperature has started to rise. Which increases the danger.'

'Look behind us,' Paula remarked. 'I hadn't realized the lake is immediately beyond the other side of this road. The ice sheet looks very thick.'

'I wouldn't skate on it,' Beck half-joked. 'Not after observing my car's thermometer. You skate on it, the ice breaks, you go under, the ice sheet instantly re-forms above you.'

'Then I won't skate tonight,' Trudy joked back.

'That château,' said Newman, who had lowered his glasses, 'is one of the most sinister so-called castles I've ever seen. There is a peculiar atmosphere about it.'

'Haunting – like something out of a horror film,' Paula remarked.

'Before you all scare yourselves silly,' Tweed told them, 'I think we should start up the mountain road at once.' He turned to Berger, held out his hand. 'I want to say how very grateful we are to you for bringing us out here.'

'It is nothing.' Berger waved his hands dismissively. 'You can thank me later, if you have the time, by returning to my hotel. I should not say, but I am an excellent chef. You come back for a meal as my guests. No matter how late.'

'Thank you again.' Tweed looked at Marler, Nield and Butler who stood in a group. 'Are you ready?'

'We have the picture,' said Marler.

43

At Beck's invitation, Paula travelled seated next to him in his car as they drove back a short distance the way they had come – and then swung left up the mountain road. Beck had turned his headlights on full beam and Paula soon realized why.

The mountain road was just wide enough for the Mercedes to drive up it. On either side the banks, very heavy with snow, were the highest she had encountered on the whole trip so far. The road was more like a rabbit warren inclined at an angle of over thirty degrees. No moonlight penetrated it.

'A bit tricky if we meet anyone coming down,' she remarked.

'Do not worry. At this hour no traffic. Also it is the long way round to the small town of Le Pont at the other end of the lake. Any traffic would drive along the lakeside road.'

'You drive well, if I may say so. Is there ice under the snow?'

'The higher we go the more ice there will be. Which is why I am not driving as though I am at Le Mans.' He glanced again in his rear-view mirror. 'I am glad to see Marler is being most sensible. A formidable man. Says little, does much.'

'Totally reliable. With these banks being so high I can't see the château.'

'And whoever is in the château cannot see us – or hear us. I sense that Tweed has the bit between his teeth – is that correct?'

'It is. And you are right. There comes a moment when Tweed is unstoppable. We have reached that moment.'

Beck said nothing for a few minutes as the gradient increased. At times Paula thought it was a miracle the car did not topple over backwards. Beck wore motoring gloves and she noticed his grip on the wheel was light. She felt no tension emanating from him. The tension was inside herself. Always the same for a while during the approach to danger.

'I hope Tweed realizes that if he finds it is not Goslar inside he may find himself in a very difficult situation. The owner could bring criminal charges against him. The Swiss law is very strict.'

'Tweed has talked himself out of more difficult situations. The worry is that we find it is *not* Goslar inside. Then we have played our last card.'

'Then let us hope it is a grand slam.'

They were still climbing the incredible burrow-like road. Paula kept glancing to her left, hoping for a glimpse of the château.

She was disappointed. They were hedged in totally by the height of the banks. She had the impression the snow was getting deeper. Beck must have read her mind.

'I'm very worried,' he said. 'Can I ask you a favour?'

'Of course.'

'I know you have great influence with Tweed. The snowfall which came recently is far worse than I had thought. Could you try to persuade Tweed to abandon this attempt? To get him to return to the Hôtel Blanc in Le Brassus.'

'Might as well argue with the Statue of Liberty. I've never known you suggest we retreat.'

'That is now my strong advice. We could put up at the Hôtel Blanc for the night. Conditions may be more favourable in the morning.'

'You're forgetting that private jet waiting at Cointrin. By the morning it could easily have flown off with its diabolical cargo. You said yourself that it would be a service to Switzerland if we located Goslar in time.'

'Oh, dear.' Beck chuckled. 'You are worse than Tweed. I can see why he relies on you so much. On we go, into the unknown . . .'

A few minutes later the road swung round a bend to the left and its surface levelled out. They were still submerged below high banks but the road was wider. Beck let out a sigh, looked at Paula.

'We made it. We are now travelling along the crest of the mountain. And the rest of your team is close behind us. So what do we shout?'

'Hallelujah! I'll remember this drive for a long time.'

'Unless you have other events to come to remember.'

'You don't give up, do you? I'm not saying anything to Tweed.'

A short distance further along the road widened considerably for a brief stretch. It curved to the right and when Beck drove into it and stopped at the end Paula knew they had reached the layby.

'All change,' said Beck, giving her an encouraging smile.

She got out, treading carefully. The other cars arrived and the occupants were beside her in no time. Butler was carrying his tool kit in his left hand, his Walther jammed behind a belt round his coat. He had the look on his face of a man prepared to collar three murderers. Nield was his normal self, his expression almost off-hand. Tweed put on a Russian-style fur hat he had borrowed from the Richemond's receptionist. Paula thought he looked like a commanding President of Russia.

'Thank you, Arthur,' Tweed said. 'Where do we meet up after this business is over?'

394

'I will be waiting in my car on the lakeside road – a distance from the entrance gates. You have your mobile? Good. I have mine. You run into trouble – find the wrong owner – you call me at once. I have worked out a cover story. I have heard that the terrorists who blew up that underground garage have hidden themselves in this château. It's the best I can think of.'

'I don't think that's going to be necessary. But thank you again. Now how do we get into the grounds of the château?'

'Follow me.'

He strode further down the road beyond the layby. He stopped and when they caught up with him he pointed to an old farm gate closing off an opening in the bank. The gate was a bizarre sight. Its framework was covered with solid ice. It looked more like a prop from a film of a Grimms' fairytale.

Butler took a tool from his kit, began to insert it inside an ice-coated padlock. The padlock crumbled, fell to the ground. He reached out a gloved hand, gripped the top of the gate. The whole gate gave way, toppled away from him, created a grid shape in the snow, sank almost out of sight.

'Beware,' warned Beck, 'the snow is softer than I'd realized.'

Tweed took a giant stride, just cleared the half-submerged gate. As the others followed he stood quite still. The château lay far below, the large corner turret now on the left-hand side, seen from the rear. It had no window looking up at the mountain. The massive stone building was masked with snow and above the shutters of each closed window rows of icicles dangled like a palisade of daggers. Viewed from the summit of the mountain, illuminated by moonlight, it looked as though it were constructed of crystal.

'Let's get on with it,' said Tweed, leading the way.

He was glad Beck had warned them to tuck their trouser tops inside their boots. His feet sank into the snow at least a foot deep. Paula, by his side, seemed to manage better, plodding ahead of him, probably because she was lighter in weight.

There was not a breath of wind, something else for which Tweed was thankful, since at this altitude a Siberian wind would have scarred their exposed faces. He looked to his left, then to his right. His team was well spread out, which meant they posed a more difficult target. Tweed paused to glance back up the slope. He saw Beck standing in the road, waving a hand, then vanishing. Soon he must have started driving back down the rabbit burrow, but there was no sound of his engine. They had made a silent approach.

'Paula,' he said quietly, 'I want to take a look at this crag for a moment.'

They had made surprisingly quick progress when Paula stopped below the huge limestone overhang. Tweed joined her, stared up.

'Looks as though it has survived since the beginning of time,' he commented.

'The cave looks enormous – and the snow hasn't penetrated it. Have we a moment? I'd like to go inside.'

'I'll come with you.'

They were joined by Newman and Trudy, who peered up at the great width and length of the projecting crag. Tweed switched on his torch, shone it on the ground, saw the rock floor was smooth, so easy to walk on. They walked several yards before he swivelled the beam upwards. The cavern was enormous, the roof a good thirty feet above them.

'You could hide an army in here,' Trudy said in a tone of wonderment. 'And there's no sign of where it ends.'

'I've seen what I want to,' Tweed announced. 'We must get on to the château . . .'

His knee-length boots, similar to those worn by the others, kept him dry as he plunged closer to the stone building below. He noticed that Butler was now in the lead, pushing on at speed, leaning forward. He looks like a hunter, thought Tweed – but then I suppose that's what we all are. He was about to warn everyone to hug the walls of the massive hulk when they reached it, but they were already doing so. The shuttered ground-floor windows were well above head height and now he could clearly see rims of light between the sections of each shutter.

'Silent as the grave,' Trudy whispered.

'We can do without similes like that, thank you,' Paula replied.

'Look up,' said Tweed. 'This place was designed by a mad architect.'

The gazed up, saw what he was referring to. At regular intervals, high up, gargoyles projected in the shape of venomous eagles ready to swoop on their prey. They wore coats of ice.

'Must have been the same chap who designed King Ludwig's castle in Bavaria,' Trudy observed.

'Be careful how you tread,' Tweed warned. 'Make as little noise as possible.'

The problem was that to stay unseen they had to hug the wall, but the ground below it was crusted snow which crackled as they trod on it. They came to a corner. Tweed emphasized the need for quiet by putting a finger across his lips, then pointed upwards. For the first time, Paula, concentrating on her footwork, realized they were immediately below the large turret which bulged out way above them. She pulled a face, moved a short distance away from the wall, trod instead in soft snow. Tweed and Trudy followed her.

397

As they rounded the corner, frequently staring up, they saw at the far end of the side wall Butler, Newman and Marler. Butler beckoned to them to join him. Looking up, instead of down at the ground, Paula caught her breath. The scenic view way below the château was hypnotic.

Beyond the bottom of a long steep slope, across the road leading to Le Brassus, the lake spread out, stretched away to the east out of sight. It was like looking down on a great mirror, broken at the edges where the ice sheet projected. In the moonlight the water was absolutely still, had a solid appearance. I wish I had a camera, Paula thought briefly, then dismissed the thought, remembering where they were, what might face them in only a short time.

Arriving at the corner, they looked round it, saw an impressive flight of steps leading up to the main entrance. Butler stood at the top, staring at a huge iron-studded door. Tweed joined him, took from his pocket the tool kit Butler had given him. He selected the largest. Butler put out a hand, held him back.

'I was going to wait until you've checked,' Tweed told him.

'Good job you were.'

'More explosives?'

'I don't think so, but there's an alarm system. I'll need a bit of help to neutralize it. Bob,' he said to Newman, 'you are taller than I am. Watch me first.'

Butler had in his right hand a large tube, not unlike a toothpaste tube. He looked up, moving his head slowly, scanning all the edges of the huge door.

'There's a grey wire, almost the colour of the stone, running round the side edges of the door and also along the top,' Trudy whispered.

'Lady, you have good eyesight,' Butler told her. 'I

have now to break – neutralize – the electric circuits. Bob, you watch me closely.'

He held the tube close to one of the hinges low down, pointed with his other hand to a join in the wire. Squeezing the tube, he ejected a brown paste over the join without letting the tube touch it. He repeated the process with the centre hinge, then turned his attention to a further join alongside the large new metal lock. He capped the tube and handed it to Newman.

'You want me to deal with the top hinge and the join in the middle of the wire running along the top of the door,' Newman suggested.

'Right, mate. But don't let the tube touch a circuit. We must all pray now,' he joked with a dry smile.

'I've seen you do this before, remember?' Newman snapped.

'Just don't get overconfident,' Butler replied.

No one spoke as Newman dealt with the remaining circuits. He then handed the tube back to Butler.

'Any complaints, Harry?'

'Not bad for a beginner.'

'I can try the key now, then?' Tweed asked.

'While we all pray again,' Butler said with a dry smile.

'Before I unlock the door I want to make something quite clear,' Tweed told them. 'I will go in first and everyone will stand outside on either side of the doorway.'

So if someone is waiting inside with a gun you will get shot down first, Paula thought grimly. Great to be the leader.

He inserted the large key with great care, keeping it straight, sensitive to any obstacle, to holding it at the wrong angle. It reminded Newman of how he had once watched an officer of the Bomb Squad dismantling a suspect object. He hoped the simile wasn't relevant.

Tweed used the same care when it came to turning the key. He felt to make sure the tines were engaging in the correct place. The lock opened with a quiet *plop* which, to Paula, sounded like a detonation.

Now Tweed was grasping the ring handle, turning it also slowly. He paused. Then, gently, he began to push the heavy wooden slab away from him. At any moment he anticipated there would be a sound – everyone waited for the night-splitting creak of the ancient door. It swung open gradually, under his control. He realized the hinges had been well oiled. He pushed further and light flooded into his face. The château was open to them.

'I'm off,' Butler whispered.

'Where to?' Paula whispered back.

'To check all round the outside of Bleak House.'

44

'It's like the Château de l'Air,' Paula said in a hushed voice.

But it wasn't. The vast empty hall which stretched before them was much larger and there were no wood-block floors. Here the hall, illuminated by wall lights, was paved with great slabs of raw stone. More like a prison, Tweed thought.

They had disobeyed his recent order. The moment the door was open Newman and Nield, by prearrangement, darted in ahead of Tweed, each taking up a position against the stone wall on either side of the interior beyond the door, each holding a handgun. Trudy and Paula also moved in ahead of Tweed, each holding a weapon.

'Goslar's had it cleaned out again,' Paula observed. 'Ready to leave.'

'Unless he has left already,' Tweed warned.

Marler entered the hall, his Armalite ready for instant action. He took in the situation at a glance. The doors to all the rooms leading off the hall were wide open, the lights on in every room. Marler darted across the hall, his rubber-soled boots making no sound on the stone slabs. He peered inside each of the rooms, moving swiftly from one to another, then returned to where Tweed waited.

'Not a thing. No one. Whole place cleaned out.'

Tweed, holding a Walther, walked swiftly across to a corner of darkness, a corner where the lights did not penetrate. He looked up a spiral staircase of stone steps which led to the upper floors. No grand staircase here. He began to mount the steps, right hand holding the Walther, left hand passing over a stone banister. The others followed, anxious because they hadn't seen this way up, that Tweed was leading the way.

The first floor had a narrow curving landing. Doors to rooms were again open, again with the lights on. He stood listening. Then he climbed the second curving flight of the spiral. Paula had tried to get in front, but his body was in the way and there was no room to pass him.

It was the same story at the second level. More open doors, more lights on inside bare rooms. Tweed stood for a moment, listening. He didn't bother to check the rooms. Nield, coming up behind, did check every room, to guard against an attack from the rear.

Tweed realized before Paula – before anyone – that he was climbing up to the huge turret situated at one corner. Arriving at the third level, he paused. Paula tugged gently at his fur-lined overcoat. He took no notice. She tugged again, spoke to him in a whisper.

'Where are we going? Only Nield is checking the rooms.'

'He'll find nothing but emptiness. We are climbing up to the turret. Shh!'

'Someone has been here. It is so warm. The heating has to be on.'

'Pleasant, isn't it?'

At the fourth level he stood still, beckoned to Newman to join him. He put his mouth close to Newman's ear.

'I'm ordering you to stay here. To prevent anyone going further up this staircase until I ascend to the fifth level. I repeat, that is an order.'

Despite the heat Paula felt chilled. Tweed's grim tone made her sense that they were close to a terrifying climax to all their wanderings. There were three doors open – fewer than on the lower levels. Tweed walked into the first room. Paula, following him, suppressed a gasp of surprise.

This room, large and spacious, was comfortably furnished: a wall-to-wall carpet on the floor, sofas and armchairs scattered about. A large antique desk stood against one wall, all its drawers pulled out and empty. An expensive leather swivel chair stood in front of it. The walls were decorated with gilt frames – the pictures had been removed.

What particularly caught her eye was an enormous stove, standing in the middle of the room and at least eight feet in diameter. An extension of the huge round stove continued upwards, vanished inside a hole in the ceiling. The mad architect had been clever, she thought. There had to be an extension of the stove inside the room above them. The architect had created an immensely tall stove which heated the rooms on more than one level. Even at this distance from it she could feel the ferocious heat inside it. A TV set, turned low,

402

was on. Sniffing, she frowned. A smell of petrol. Then she saw a row of cans lined up behind a sofa a long way from the stove.

Tweed had walked out. She found him in the next room, furnished as a bedroom. A huge four-poster stood against one wall. Lying on the floor was a mess of crumpled sheets and duvets. The bed had been stripped bare.

Tweed was opening the drawers of a small bedside table. From one he took out a small leather-bound notebook. He riffled the pages slowly. At the top of each page there was a heading – Stage One, Stage Two, etc. Below were groups of formulae, written in slanting copperplate. He handed it to Paula.

'What do you make of that?'

'Nothing,' she said, after perusing it and handing the notebook back to him.

'The writing is Goslar's.'

'You've seen the petrol?'

'Yes. So Goslar is still here. Upstairs.'

On a coffee table Paula noticed a small bullet-shaped object. It looked like a lipstick. Tweed had walked out, entered the third room, so she followed quickly. Newman still stood on guard at the foot of the next section of the staircase. He was holding up his hand – gathered below him were Trudy, Nield and Marler. She walked into the third room. It housed a massive bath of marble with gold taps. Behind an open shower curtain in a corner was a shower and behind a clear glass door a toilet. She hurried back on to the landing to join Tweed.

He was already on the staircase, slowly mounting the stone steps to the level above – the fifth level. The Walther was in his right hand while his left hand passed over the stone banister, steadying him on the curving climb. Newman stood aside to let her follow Tweed.

Trudy came up behind her, then the others. Tweed stopped in front of a heavy door.

The studded door had a large round handle. Tweed gripped it with infinite care, turned it inch by inch. He hoped the hinges were as well oiled as those on the main door leading into the entrance hall. Paula glanced over the edge, almost had an attack of vertigo. She could see down the centre of the spiral all the way to the hall floor. She jerked her head upright.

Tweed felt the turning handle stop. He pushed gently. No creak. He opened the door wide, then, as he had anticipated, walked into the turret room. The others followed, very close together. A figure in whites had its back to them. The figure turned round swiftly and Tweed stared into its face.

45

The face of Alan 'Chance' Burgoyne stared back at Tweed.

His expression was different from any expression Tweed had seen Burgoyne adopt before. The eyelids were narrowed, the eyes hard as bullets. In his right hand he held a Magnum revolver aimed at Paula and Trudy. His voice was different when he spoke, a soft, menacing voice with a trace of some foreign accent. His mouth was different – twisted, evil, brutal. Tweed remembered an old film he had once seen on TV – Dr Jekyll and Mr Hyde. The transformation in Burgoyne was almost as startling.

'No one moves a muscle. You have two seconds to drop your guns. Then I shoot the women first before I blast the rest of you. Foolish to come in so close together.'

Tweed dropped his Walther instantly. He heard other weapons hit the stone floor, then a clatter which he knew was Marler's Armalite. He took two tentative paces forward, further into the room.

'Far enough,' Burgoyne ordered in the same soft voice, quite different from the British military-style way of speaking he had always adopted before. 'Anyone tries anything clever and the women go down first.'

'I see you will soon be ready to leave for the airport,' Tweed remarked.

He was looking at a table some distance behind Burgoyne, who was standing about six feet away from the thigh-high stove. On the table was a latticework crate, not unlike those milkmen use to carry milk bottles on their electric wagons. Inside, the crate was divided into sections. A canister with a lid stood inside three of the sections. A slightly larger polystyrene container stood next to the crate. Tweed assumed this would provide protection when the first crate was placed inside it.

'The airport next,' Burgoyne rasped harshly.

'Where you have a long-distance Grumman Gulf-stream jet waiting for instant departure. It's a long way to the capital of Ali's Fundamentalist state.'

'I always thought you were my most dangerous opponent, Tweed.'

'Which is why you brilliantly attached yourself to my team in the role of a British officer. I wondered about you from the very beginning, but couldn't be sure.'

'All of you!' Burgoyne snarled. 'Immediately place your hands on the top of your heads. Two seconds.'

Tweed clasped his hands over the top of his head. Everyone else followed his example. Paula stared stead-ily, eye to eye, at Burgoyne. Apprehensive, but fasci-nated, she sensed the power which exuded from this

405

evil man. She marvelled at his capacity for meticulous scheming, for his flair in planning ahead for every possible contingency. How is it that I never suspected him? she asked herself.

'You said you wondered about me from the beginning,' Burgoyne said to Tweed, whose remark had intrigued him. 'So why did you wonder?'

'*Toujours l'audacité*,' replied Tweed, 'your favourite maxim. When I mentioned it to you at Park Crescent you paused, then correctly attributed it to Napoleon. The pause, Burgoyne – I had a flicker of doubt deep down. Because of the pause. Then there was the incident at La Défense – when you warned about the wire round the entrance door to the building. You spoke out about the wire a second before Butler also warned us of its presence. But I couldn't see it – and I was standing beside you. Butler has very exceptional eyesight. But you *knew* it was there. It was part of your confidence-building exercise – so we would trust you completely. Again, I wondered, but could not be certain.'

'So, Mr Tweed, can you list any more so-called mistakes that I made?'

Paula was now casually glancing all round the laboratory. She followed the network of glass tubes and bulbous containers below the ceiling, guessed that this was how Burgoyne had produced the deadly liquid now stored in those three canisters. She knew she was right when she saw the system ending where a vertical tube with a closed glass tap was suspended no more than a foot above the table where the crated canisters stood. And she became aware that Tweed was keeping Burgoyne talking, playing for time. Why?

She glanced round the circular stone walls and suddenly gazed at something. Hastily she averted her gaze before Burgoyne saw her. She had seen another heavy door let into a wall almost behind Burgoyne. What had gripped her was seeing the handle of that door slowly turning from the outside. Why another door in the wall?

Then she remembered. Their approach movement round the outside of the château had been so tense she had registered something only for seconds, then had forgotten about it. The metal-treaded fire-escape staircase winding its way up towards the turret.

'Yes, there were other incidents which aroused my suspicions,' Tweed explained, holding Burgoyne's gaze. Paula realized that Tweed also had seen the slowly turning handle. 'You drove on ahead of us, saying you'd warn us of ambushes. But when a mob of Arabs broke through the mist your warning came at the same moment. Doubtless, you hoped you'd be too late. But superb planner that you are, you covered yourself in case we survived. There were other mistakes, too.'

Paula dug her fingernails into her hand to ease the tension building up inside her. She had risked another glance towards the door, had seen it was now being pushed open very slowly. *Don't creak!* she prayed.

'Another move I found suspicious,' Tweed went on, 'was when you urged members of my team at Talloires to take cover inside the copse of firs. That was so you could protect yourself. You *knew* the cabin Arbuthnot was approaching would blow up into a thousand pieces. Again, I wondered. Then there was something else.'

'You were dangerous when we duelled in the Cold War. Certainly, you have not lost your touch. A pity you will not survive tonight. You say there was something else. What was that? I am learning from you, Mr Tweed. In some ways I think maybe you should have won, but . . .'

Burgoyne never finished his sentence. The door was now half open. Butler slipped through the gap, summed up the situation. Later he thought that it was his remembering how in Annecy, when he was pursuing the

Yellow Man across the bridge, he saw how he had dealt with Pete Nield, head-butting him.

Burgoyne had caught movement out of the corner of his eye. He was swivelling round, ready to aim the Magnum, when Butler hit him. Crouching, Butler had charged like a shell from a cannon. His round head slammed into Burgoyne's chest with great force, sending him backwards. Burgoyne lost his balance, dropped the Magnum, toppled with his back and buttocks on to the wide edge of the chimney. His arms flailed, the lower part of his body sank inside the opening. His strong hands desperately grabbed at the edge, then he was hanging in space, most of his body out of sight in the chimney. He was suspended, held there only by his hands holding the edge, his head in full view.

'Help me!' he yelled.

Tweed strode quickly forward. He picked up off the table a green leather folder, glanced inside, saw sheets covered with formulae. He waved it as he looked down into Burgoyne's horrified face.

'Before we even consider saving you I have questions. You will answer them truthfully – and I will know if it is the truth – or *you* will go down. Into the fires of hell.'

'Three hundred billion pounds. Yes, *billion*. That is what Ali is paying for the weapon. We could share—'

'Kindly shut up.'

Paula noticed that Burgoyne's hands were beginning to blister. The chimney edge he was clutching must be very hot. How long could he hold on?

'This green folder,' Tweed said, 'contains formulae. What are they?'

'Shows you how to make the weapon. We could share . . .'

'Where are the photocopies?'

'*No* photocopies,' Burgoyne screeched. 'Only that . . .'

'What about the turtle? Part of what you needed to produce the liquid?'

'Yes. Key ingredient. Fed sedatives to kill it. Used syringe to extract vital element. Galapagos . . .'

'I know where it comes from. You stole two at least. What about the others?'

'Mess up first one, throw it in here. Only two.'

For the first time Paula saw what Tweed was referring to. Inside an enormous plastic container on a lower table rested the remains of a turtle which must have been four and a half feet long. Part of its shell had been cut away, exposing its insides.

'Where are the other canisters containing the weapon?'

'Only three. In plastic crate. Kill seventy-five million. Ali pays three hundred . . .'

'Billion pounds,' snapped Tweed. 'We've been through that. What else is needed to produce the weapon?'

Paula put her mouth very close to Tweed's ear. Her tone was urgent.

'I don't think he can hold on much longer.'

'You have everything,' Burgoyne pleaded. 'We share. My legs are burning. Get me out! Please! Quick! Qui—'

Burgoyne never completed the last word. Both hands lost his grip on the edge. He plunged down out of sight. There was a terrible scream. Fear. Agony. It cut off suddenly. Tweed peered over the rim of the edge, saw only an inferno of flames, like red hands reaching up for him. He straightened up.

'He's gone. Nothing left, I imagine. There are people in the world who should be eliminated. What's that noise?'

He rushed over to the window, opened it, leaned out, came back and shook his head, smiling.

'Can't hear a thing. Must have been my imagination. Or, more likely, the fire rumbling down below. Now, we have work to do. No one in the world – including Britain – is going to get their greedy hands on this diabolical weapon. So what do we do? We destroy it.'

46

'You've left that window wide open,' Paula complained.

'Deliberately,' Tweed told her. 'The air coming in will help to cool this place down. It's almost like an inferno up here.' He looked at her, Trudy, then at the others. 'If I were you I'd take off your coats. You'll need them when we eventually leave here.'

Tweed began work at once. He picked up the green folder and, without hesitation, cast it down the chimney, followed by the notebook from his pocket. Paula had an amusing thought, chuckled.

'Harrington would go mad if he could witness this.'

'Harrington can go jump off a cliff. I'm happy to show him the way to Beachy Head. Now for the turtle. It's quite dead. I think I'll need a hand to throw the container and what's inside it into the fire.'

He was bending down over the low table when Newman gently pulled him back. He guessed the turtle alone would be very heavy. Nield joined him. Each took hold of the container at one end and lifted. It weighed a ton. They hoisted it up, perched it on the edge of the chimney, then both gave a hard shove. The container and its contents dropped out of view. Tweed was giving orders.

'Marler, I want you to guard the door to the staircase we came up. Perch on the top landing so you get a bird's-eye view.'

'A bird wouldn't like that view,' Paula commented, recalling her own glance down into the spiralling chasm.

'Harry,' Tweed ordered Butler, 'you guard that door to the fire escape. I'm sure Burgoyne was on his own, but let's be very wary.'

Tweed now walked over to the crate containing the canisters of the deadly liquid. He picked up a pair of surgical gloves off a shelf, found they were a size too large, but put them on anyway.

He looked round at everyone inside the turret. Then he looked at the canisters again. He shrugged, a rare gesture Paula recognized. He only did that at times when he was faced with a highly dangerous situation. He turned, faced all the members of his team.

'I want all of you out on the top landing – with the door shut. I think this should work, but I'm not absolutely certain.'

'You think what should work?' demanded Paula.

'I'm about to throw the canisters, one by one, down inside the chimney. I think extreme heat will destroy their contents – that the weapon only works when dropped into water. As it did at Appledore, which seems a million miles away. But as I'm not sure I want you all out of here.'

'Nothing doing,' said Trudy.

'You can issue orders until you're blue in the face but we're staying,' Paula snapped.

'I second the motion,' said Newman.

'Hear, hear!' called out Nield.

They stood staring at him and Tweed realized he was completely out-voted. Looking at their expressions he saw nothing could shift them. Marler, who had heard from outside the open door, walked in, holding his Armalite.

'Don't hold your breath, then,' said Tweed. 'On second thoughts maybe that's exactly what you should do.'

He pulled his gloves further over his hands, flexed his fingers to test his grip. He looked at his team once more. They stared back, stone-faced. This is the first time I've had a mutiny on my hands, he thought.

Very carefully, he eased both hands down inside the crate, keeping well clear of the lid of the first canister. Grasping the side of the canister, he was able to insert one hand under its base, which gave him more control. He lifted it out slowly and carried it to the chimney. He happened to glance at Paula and saw she was smiling, holding up one hand with her fingers crossed. He managed to smile back. Then he held the canister as far over the chimney as he could, released it.

He thought he heard a brief sizzle a long way down. Wasting no time, he dealt with the two remaining canisters in the same way. Everyone was still alive but he thought he caught a sigh of relief from somebody. He peeled off each glove carefully, consigned both to the flames.

It was then that he heard a distant growling rumble through the open window. It was not his imagination this time. He reacted instantly.

'Avalanche coming. Everyone outside this horror of a building. Down the fire-escape would be quickest . . .'

'No it *wouldn't* be!' Butler shouted. 'There's ice on the metal treads. I had one hellava job getting up without slipping.'

'Then down the staircase we came up,' ordered Tweed. 'Quickly as you can, but don't run down. I don't want any broken legs.'

He waited until everyone had preceded him, pushing Butler to make him go first. Despite the fact that he was the last one to leave, Tweed, breaking his own rule, hurried after them and, reaching the hall, pushed past everyone and walked out of the front door first.

He turned in the direction of the turret, waving to the others to follow. Passing under the turret he couldn't resist looking up, saw that the first section had been pulled down – like the safety device often used on fire escapes in America. God knew how Butler had hauled it down to the ground. Reaching the rear of the building he paused, waiting for the others to catch him up. He was staring at a frightening phenomenon.

About two hundred yards away to the east the avalanche was on the move, sweeping down like a great wave. He didn't think that would be the full extent of it by any means.

'Make for the cave under that huge crag,' he shouted.

He began plodding up through the snow. Then he felt a hand wrap itself rouhd his left arm, another one round his other arm. He had Trudy on his left, Paula on his right.

'Look after yourselves,' he snapped. 'We may have only a minute to get there in time.'

He jerked himself free, was surprised at how quickly he could move uphill, which was much harder work than when they had come down the slope. With a tremendous effort he kept level with both women. The looming crag seemed a mile above him. Marler, Butler and Nield were spread out on either side of the three climbers. Tweed was sure they were moving more slowly than they needed to – in case their help was needed. He resisted the temptation to check the progress of the wave sliding down to the east, refused to check the situation on the mountain behind the crag. Just concentrated on getting there. One ... two ... three paces. Then he counted again and again.

'We're nearly there,' shouted Trudy.

'We are?'

Tweed looked up, saw the overhang of the crag yards away. Saw also that the mountain behind it was crumbling. He'd thought the banked-up snow on the level stretch of road had concealed hedges. It hadn't. It was all snow, all now in motion like another giant wave.

Then they were all under the crag, inside the vast cave. Tweed, almost breathless, sank down in a sitting position thirty feet or so inside the cave. Trudy sank down on one side of him as Paula sat heavily down on his other side. Newman was close and so was Marler. Butler and Nield were deeper inside the cave. They waited, watched.

The first indication Tweed had that it was a double avalanche, a mix of countless tons of snow and a rock slide, was when a huge boulder thumped on the top of the crag, then shot down the slope beyond at incredible speed. A Niagara of snow poured down over the lip of the crag, blotting out any view for a short time. Marler had his night glasses against his eyes.

'It's going to submerge that château,' he called out.

The dense curtain of snow cleared, was replaced by the thunder of great boulders hurtling down the slope at frightening speed. Tweed watched in astonishment as the now immense snow wave, the army of boulders larger than houses, crashed into the château. He saw the turret wobble, break off, fall in pieces, be swept down the lower slope. The snow wave obscured sight of the building for a short time. When it passed on there was no château.

It had been literally ripped from of its foundations, smashed to pieces, carried down the slope. The crag above them shuddered under a fresh onslaught and Tweed glanced up anxiously. Would it hold? The second, even larger wave of snow carrying tumbling boulders thundered down and the crag remained intact.

'I would say Burgoyne's gone for ever,' Marler called

out. 'I saw a large piece of the chimney caught up in the snow, riding on the wave's crest.'

The finale was dramatic – even more than what had come before. The snow – and rock – wave, carrying the relics of the château, crossed the road and swept over the ice at the edge of the lake. Tweed could have sworn he caught sight of half the turret sinking below the water. The lake surface churned. There was a sudden silence, shocking in its unexpectedness. The mountain was still.

Epilogue

'It's over,' said Paula, sinking into the seat behind her desk in Tweed's office at Park Crescent.

'No, it's not over yet,' Tweed warned from behind his own desk.

When they had emerged from inside the cave, below the crag, they had plodded wearily up the slope, wondering whether their cars still existed. It had been a rough climb, over snow which was freezing again, over snow littered with rocks. Reaching the top they had found the road was still there – and so were their cars in the layby.

Their next anxiety had been whether Beck had survived. They had found him standing by his car at the entrance to the mountain road. Tweed had travelled back to Le Brassus with Beck in his car. He had explained what they had experienced.

'So Goslar – or Burgoyne – is a dead letter.'

'He's a dead man. And, as I've explained, his weapon has been totally destroyed. My story about that – to Howard and, later, to the PM – will be that Butler came in through the fire-escape door and shot Goslar. Before he could kill all of us. Then we had to run for our lives to escape the avalanche. After Goslar had told us he was about to fly the weapon to the Middle East.'

'Simple, therefore neat,' Beck had commented.

They had then eaten a splendid meal at the Hôtel

416

Blanc before driving back to Geneva. After spending what remained of the rest of the night catching up on some sleep at the Richemond, they had flown back to London.

'What was the last mistake Burgoyne, I mean Goslar, made?' Paula asked. 'You never had the time to tell him.'

'The biggest one of all. Burgoyne had retired from the army.' He looked round at everyone else in his office – Marler, Newman, Butler, Nield, and Trudy. 'Before we left for Paris I phoned my friend in the MoD again, asked him which bank Burgoyne's pension was paid into. After a lot of persuasion he gave me the name of the bank, promised to have a word with the bank manager and call me back. Oh, we shall be having a visitor shortly.'

'What about Burgoyne's bank account?' Paula prodded.

'He'd called at the bank at regular intervals after retirement, had drawn the monthly amount of his pension. Then he'd stopped doing that. For a longish period he had not called again and quite an amount – I don't know how much, of course – had piled up. He'd never appeared again. I thought that very strange.'

'Yet you let the fake Burgoyne join us,' Paula commented.

'Because I still couldn't be sure. But *toujours l'audacité*, so I thought if this is Goslar, keeping an eye on us at close quarters, I'd play the same game – keeping my eye on him.'

'So how on earth did Goslar come to choose Burgoyne as the man he would impersonate?'

'I can only guess. Knowing Goslar's incredible thoroughness, I'd imagine he searched Europe to find a likely candidate. Don't forget Burgoyne had a brief, unwanted, moment of notoriety during the Gulf War. I also imagine that when Goslar obtained a photo of

Burgoyne – heaven knows how – he realized that he, Goslar, looked rather like him. Marler, tell them what you told me on the flight back when I asked you to recall a detailed description of what happened when you visited Burgoyne's home at Rydford on Dartmoor.'

'I told most of you how when I arrived at Burgoyne's cottage near Hangman's Tor I met his girl friend, Coral Langley. How she was shot dead by a man on the tor, a man I killed with my Armalite. How I found his body almost buried under a rock fall. Running back to the cottage, I tripped between the tor and the cottage – sprawled full length on an oblong arrangement of rocks. Later it struck me that they were a long way from the tor.'

'And,' Tweed said, taking over, 'the oblong of rocks was shaped like a grave, Marler told me on the plane. I phoned Roy Buchanan at the Yard. He's called the local police and they're digging up under those rocks. I think I know what they'll find.'

'The real Burgoyne's body,' Paula said in a hushed tone.

'I'm confident that is what they will discover. And Goslar, posing as Burgoyne, made another slip. At one stage I asked him if he climbed tors. He said he did, that he went to Rough Tor, which is miles away from Rydford. Why do that – when Hanging Tor was on his doorstep? It was an accumulation of small slips which made me more and more suspicious.'

The phone rang. Monica, who had been listening avidly, answered it.

'Serena Cavendish is downstairs.'

'The visitor I was expecting. Ask George to bring her up.' Tweed looked at Paula. 'We don't want any loose ends, do we?'

*

418

Serena walked in very erect, smartly dressed in a white trouser suit and a Hermès scarf tucked under her dominant chin. She smiled at the men, ignored Paula and Trudy, accepted Tweed's invitation and sat down, her shapely legs crossed. Paula knew she was aware that the men had noticed them.

'Sorry,' Tweed began, 'to drag you here. I tracked you down to your photographic studio at the other end of Bond Street.'

'Business is good. Really good. Soon I'll be able to buy myself a small mansion.' She used a hand to push back her glossy black hair. 'Preferably something designed by Lutyens.'

'Congratulations, Davina.'

'Thank you.'

She half-lifted a hand to her mouth. Then she dropped it back into her lap.

'You mean Serena.'

'No, I meant Davina. Chief Inspector Roy Buchanan of the Yard is reopening the case of the car crash which killed your twin sister, Davina. You were the first one to arrive at the scene – I was told it was in the middle of the night. Buchanan is getting an order to have the body exhumed.'

'Oh God! No! That would be sacrilege. Horrible. Quite horrible.'

'Then tell me the truth about what happened that night, Davina.'

'Can I have a glass?' She hesitated. 'I carry a small flask of gin. There are times when I need it – the pressure of work.'

Monica brought her a clean glass. She produced a small flask from her shoulder bag, poured a strong tot. Tweed waited while she drank it in two gulps. Then he continued.

'I need to know exactly what happened. Precisely, please.'

'I couldn't sleep. I thought I'd go for a walk – to maybe meet . . .'

'Don't stop now,' Tweed said quietly.

'To meet Serena. She was very late back. That wasn't unusual – she loved parties. I sat on a gate by the side of the road. She came round a bend like a rocket. At that moment a juggernaut came from the other direction, also driving at too great a speed. She skidded, the juggernaut rammed her, reversed, drove on. I was so shaken I didn't even get his registration number and there was no firm's name on its side. Serena was dead, badly smashed up. Her face . . . It was awful.'

'So what happened next?' asked Tweed, doodling on a pad.

'I was desperate to disappear. In fear of my life. I suddenly realized that I could change places with her, become Serena. I gritted my teeth, took her things out of her shoulder bag – passport, driving licence, other papers. Then I put my own stuff – from *my* shoulder bag – into hers.' She tossed her head. 'She was dead, so I thought, what difference does it make?'

Cold-blooded little madam, Paula thought.

'And of course you were frightened,' Tweed went on amiably, 'because you had helped Dr Goslar in some way. Right, Davina?'

'You're clever. You always worried me. Yes. Because I'm known as an outstanding biochemist Goslar had certain problems he wanted solved quickly. He phoned me in his screechy voice, told me what he needed, promised me a lot of money. This was some time before Serena was killed by the juggernaut. I worked out the solution, left it in an envelope in a Mayfair phone box at the time he'd specified. Two days later, again after dark, a huge man delivered the money – pushed an envelope through my letterbox.'

'So you helped Goslar build the weapon,' Tweed said casually.

'That's not true!' Davina protested vehemently. 'The problem he gave me to solve could only have been one per cent of the whole project. I have no idea of what else is involved. I swear it.'

'I find it hard to swallow the word of a woman who impersonated her dead sister. How much did he pay you? They could start that exhumation within the next two days – unless I stop it.'

'Ten thousand pounds . . .'

'Then I expect you to deliver ten thousand pounds in cash to this building by ten o'clock tomorrow morning. You may go now.'

He was dismissing her as some might get rid of a servant. Flushing, she stood up, walked quickly to the door. On the point of leaving she turned round.

'How did you guess I wasn't Serena?'

'The wording on the gravestone at Steeple Hampton. It was so curt and the normal wording was missing. Tomorrow morning at ten – at the latest.'

She nodded and left, closing the door behind her.

'What will you do with the money?' Paula asked.

'Burn it. No reason why she should profit from what she did. She is not a nice woman. She was also a damned nuisance. There were times when I thought she could be Goslar.' He smiled. 'Now all of you need sleep so I suggest you go home. I'd appreciate it if Paula and Trudy would stay for a few minutes longer.'

He was alone with them – except for Monica, now busy at work. He looked at Trudy.

421

'I was most impressed with the performance you put up. With your toughness, your resourcefulness, the cool way you reacted to grim situations. Would you be interested in becoming a member of my outfit? Subject to vetting, of course.'

Trudy's face lit up, she glowed. She had trouble finding words to reply. Then she smiled. Paula also was smiling with pleasure. She then realized she'd forgotten to give Tweed Cord Dillon's message over the phone – when Tweed was in the shower at the Richemond. He'd had Trudy vetted in the States.

'I'm lost for words,' Trudy eventually said. 'I'd love to join you. Subject to vetting.' She lifted a hand to check her blaze of red hair, then dropped it quickly. Not the done thing. 'I'll do my best to justify your confidence in me. That is, if it's all right with Paula.'

'Great idea,' Paula assured her.

'It was a sinister tide,' Tweed reflected.

'You mean at Appledore – when the wave carried in the dead fisherman, the dead seal, the dead fish.'

'That, yes. But even more the sinister tide of Muslim Fundamentalists who, armed with Goslar's weapon, would have flooded over the West.'